SUMNER LOCKE ELLIOTT was born in Sydney on 17 October 1917. His mother was the writer Helena Sumner Locke. She died of eclampsia the day after his birth, and the boy was raised by his aunts.

Elliott wrote his first play when he was twelve, and while he was still at school joined Sydney's Independent Theatre. In 1942 he was drafted and served out much of the war as a typist in remote parts of Australia. But he was besotted with the theatre. He found success after the war with plays including *Rusty Bugles* and *Invisible Circus*.

Elliott went to the United States in 1948. Three years later his play *Buy Me Blue Ribbons* premiered on Broadway. He launched a prominent career writing plays for the television networks, and based himself in New York. He became an American citizen in 1955 and did not visit Australia again until 1974.

Careful, He Might Hear You was Elliott's debut novel. It won the Miles Franklin Award in 1963, was translated into a number of languages and became an international bestseller. In 1983 it was made into an outstanding film directed by Carl Schultz, starring Wendy Hughes, Robyn Nevin and Nicholas Gledhill.

Elliott wrote ten novels in all. He won the Patrick White Award in 1977. After a lifetime of concealing his homosexuality, he spent his final years living with his partner, Whitfield Cook. Sumner Locke Elliott died in New York City in 1991.

ROBYN NEVIN AM has been a leading Australian actress for over fifty years and has directed for more than twenty-five years, directing for all state theatre companies. Robyn held the position of Associate Director with the Sydney and Melbourne theatre companies before being appointed Artistic Director of the Queensland Theatre Company.

Robyn was Artistic Director and CEO of the Sydney Theatre Company from 1999 to 2007.

Robyn played Shasta in the TV mini-series based on Sumner Locke Elliott's novel *Water Under the Bridge* and Lila in the film adaptation of *Careful, He Might Hear You*.

ALSO BY SUMNER LOCKE ELLIOTT

Some Doves and Pythons
Edens Lost
The Man Who Got Away
Going
Water Under the Bridge
Rusty Bugles
Signs of Life
About Tilly Beamis
Waiting for Childhood
Fairyland

Careful, He Might Hear You
Sumner Locke Elliott

Text Publishing Melbourne Australia

Copyright Agency
Cultural Fund   Proudly supported by Copyright Agency's Cultural Fund.

textclassics.com.au
textpublishing.com.au

The Text Publishing Company
Swann House
22 William Street
Melbourne Victoria 3000
Australia

First published by Victor Gollancz Limited 1963
This edition published by The Text Publishing Company 2012

Cover design by WH Chong
Page design by WH Chong & Susan Miller
Typeset by Midland Typesetters

Printed in Australia by Griffin Press, an Accredited ISO AS/NZS 14001:2004
Environmental Management System printer

Primary print ISBN: 9781921922244
Ebook ISBN: 9781921921841
Author: Elliott, Sumner Locke, 1917-1991
Title: Careful, he might hear you / by Sumner Locke Elliott;
introduction by Robyn Nevin.
Series: Text classics.
Subjects: Parenting—Fiction. Families—Attitudes—Fiction. Aunts—Fiction.
Other Authors/Contributors: Nevin, Robyn.
Dewey Number: A823.3

CONTENTS

Between Two Aunts
by Robyn Nevin

NOT long ago I saw a small boy walking in the city with a couple I imagined were his grandparents. He seemed absorbed in his thoughts; he was gazing at the river under the bridge he was crossing. His grandparents called and without looking at them he dutifully, solemnly caught up. I wondered what he was thinking about.

The central character in Sumner Locke Elliott's great Australian novel of childhood, *Careful, He Might Hear You*, is a six-year-old boy named PS. And the difference between him and my boy on the bridge is that we can eavesdrop on PS's thoughts: we are privy to his interpretations of adult conversations, the misunderstandings that lead to doubt and disbelief, the way his imagination creates exotic meanings out of the mundane. As his two aunts, sisters to the dead mother he never knew, struggle to take control of his life, we witness his increasing confusion and fear. We worry for him as his certainties are irrevocably fractured. Vanessa, his rich aunt, woos him with gifts and privilege and dinner at eight o'clock at Point Piper, but he longs for the comfort and predictability of 'tea' at six in his suburban home with Aunt Lila and Uncle George. We want for him what he wants for himself; and we know what he wants because we are inside his head.

Sumner Locke Elliott left Sydney for New York in 1948 and published *Careful, He Might Hear You* fifteen years later. It was his first novel after many years of writing for theatre, radio and television. He had long lamented Australia's rejection of its own writers. Indeed it was the lack of opportunities for this young, prolific and gifted writer that persuaded him to try America. It was a familiar story: so many of our talented writers and actors believed an overseas career might launch them in their own backyard; they sought opportunities abroad to achieve acceptance at home. Sumner Locke Elliott was one of those who never came back. I recall Patrick White's words of advice to me to stay and 'paint one's own landscape'. Perhaps Sumner needed the geographical and emotional distance. He wrote with clarity about the painful struggles of PS because PS is based on his own experiences in childhood after his mother died giving birth to him.

The story of *Careful, He Might Hear You* is a simple one. PS's mother, Sinden, a successful writer, has before the novel opens met and married Logan, a charismatic dreamer, all in one gloriously hazy week of love and romance. He goes off to war, leaving her pregnant. She dies giving life to PS. The boy is burdened forever by his name, which suggests—as Sinden declared—that he is a postscript to her 'ridiculous' life. And he must carry her legacy of fame. In Lila's care he comes to know the community of writers who peopled his mother's world. These wonderfully drawn eccentrics—failed, drunk, deluded, political and passionate souls—sentimentalise her and expect PS to prove worthy of her weighty legacy.

Before her labour Sin wrote separately to Lila and Vanessa, suggesting that both of them were capable of caring for her child should 'anything happen' to her. PS has been raised by Lila, but now Vanessa returns from London to claim him. Long ago Vanessa too was in love with Logan. In her loneliness she reaches out to the small boy seeking the love she longed for from his father, and employs increasingly manipulative strategies to secure him for herself.

The crunch comes when Vanessa takes Lila to court for custody of PS. In a tense and moving scene the judge interviews him in his chambers. Lila has insisted to PS that he tell the truth. In responding honestly to a question that is too nuanced for him to interpret, the boy makes a 'wrong' answer and in turn the judge makes a 'wrong' decision. Our hearts begin to crack…and so the story reaches a dramatic and satisfying climax.

Careful, He Might Hear You had immediate commercial success in Europe and America. It sold less well in Australia but earned the praise of Patrick White and Christina Stead, and won the Miles Franklin Award in 1963. By 1974 the worldwide sales of the book were around ten million copies. The movie rights were sold to Hollywood's Joshua Logan (Vivien Leigh was considered for Vanessa) but nothing happened. Twenty years after the book was published—by which time Sumner had written a number of novels, the most successful of them set in Australia—Jill Robb (who had already, with John McRae, co-produced the TV mini-series based on *Water Under the Bridge*) acquired the rights and made the film that Sumner loved and which put his novel on the Australian map.

I had met Sumner Locke Elliott during the filming of *Water Under the Bridge*. I loved that novel and carried it around with me on the set. I played Shasta, a vaudeville actress who adopts a small boy after his mother's death, a character whom Sumner had modelled on his adored Aunt Blanche. Shasta remains one of my favourite roles. Sumner loved my performance and I responded immediately to his warmth and wit.

In the film of *Careful, He Might Hear You* I played Lila, and Wendy Hughes played Vanessa. Again

I carried the novel that had inspired the film around with me while we worked, and, after playing two of his favourite aunts, I began to feel very familiar with Sumner's personal world.

The film was released in Australia in September 1983, and did very well, going on to win eight AFI awards. Just before it was to open in New York City in mid-1984 I was due to appear in David Williamson's play *The Perfectionist* at the Spoleto Festival in Charleston. I agreed to go to New York before the premiere and to do some publicity. Agreed? I was thrilled to be invited. Imagine! What a way to visit New York for the first time, as an actress with a leading role in a movie! And I was looking forward to seeing Sumner again, in the city he had made his own.

At Kennedy Airport I was met by a car and driver, a good beginning. My schedule had been organised by Sumner's agent and friend, a memorable character named Gloria Safire. She was short, square, loud and lovely. I instantly warmed to her, and felt blessed to be introduced to New York by her. I stayed in a modest room at the great Plaza Hotel (shabby chic before shabby became chic), across the road from the Paris Theater where the film was to screen.

To my relief Sumner loved the film and my performance. He was affectionate to me, and openly expressed his emotions. I am sure that seeing his childhood on screen was an overwhelming experience for him. It is always a privilege for me, as an actress, to portray a life; I felt this keenly in relation to Sumner's aunts, and returned his affection, with great respect.

We did an interview together at the Algonquin Hotel, a haunt of Sumner's that had been immortalised by Dorothy Parker's and Robert Benchley's Round Table luncheons. It was during this interview that I began to understand the extent of his fame in America as one of the fabled Golden Seven who wrote weekly live television dramas. Virtually unknown in Australia, he was a writer with a major reputation in New York.

We attended the first screening at the Paris Theater, and afterwards did a Q&A session. The film was very well received and I relished the sight, in the following days, as did Sumner, of long queues outside the Paris where it had an impressive run of thirteen weeks.

What do we make of *Careful, He Might Hear You* almost fifty years after Sumner Locke Elliott wrote it? He created a cast of marvellous characters who inhabit the various worlds through which PS moves: adorable Aunt Vere, for example, with her bright, impoverished life in her bohemian bedsit in Kings Cross; or Winnie from next door, a plain bossy little know-it-all who enjoys breaking the news to PS that his life is about to change: 'She chanted in a sing-song voice, "PS is going awa-ay. PS is going awa-ay".' There's the new school, attended by the children of the rich and snooty, where Vanessa sends PS, or the frightful mourning picnic turned on by the 'scribes and daubers'. Sumner had perfect recall of the Australian suburban speech of the period, between the wars.

There was a tap at the door and Vere's friend, Opal, came in. Opal was the most beautiful girl in the world and wore soft, shining dresses; always a new one every time he saw her, always pretty shoes to match, always great big hats piled with roses.

Opal said, 'And who is this handsome man?' bending to kiss him and smelling of honey-suckle.

Vere said, 'Girl, how are you?'

Opal said, 'Girl, I'm thwarted.'

She pronounced it to rhyme with 'carted'.

Vere said, 'We're all thwarted.' It was always a 'thwart', never a 'thwort'. 'Thworted' meant having warts.

Vere said, 'I thought you were going to the races with Archie.'

'His wife's in town.'

'Wouldn't that thwart you!'

'It's the supreme thwart. So is she. He's lashed to the mast for days now.'

'How sick-making, girl.'

'Girl, it's gall and wormwood. I am undone.

'Has he told her about you yet?'

'Says he can't until she's in a less thwarting mood.'

'Which means never.'

'Girl, you are probably right about him. I always pick the ones with no guts. The whole thing undoes me to the point of stupor, but I am lashed to him, as to a mast. I must have a drink, pront.'

And there is the sensory experience *Careful, He Might Hear You* offers of a Sydney summer; the heat and humidity; sultry days broken by electrical storms in the late afternoon; the sights, sounds, colours and smells of trees, flowers, birds, sky, water and the Harbour.

I grew up a voracious reader of English fiction and, like Sumner Locke Elliott, I watched American films from an early age. What a surprise, a delight, to recognise my own world, the vivid textures and sounds of my own country, in his novels. It took an expatriate—a man forced from his own landscape to earn a living as a writer, to be published and performed as a writer, and ultimately to become famous as a writer—to bring that period of Australia to life for me. This beautiful story, told with wit, warmth and irony, is one of the most moving and evocative books about childhood I know. *Careful, He Might Hear You* remains, in my view, among the greatest of our Australian novels.

Careful, He Might Hear You

For H. S. L.

'P S,' THEY SAID.

And 'Vanessa'.

Or sometimes 'Ness'.

PS. PS. PS. PS. Ness. Ness. Ness.

It sounded through his half sleep like surreptitious mice foraging through tissue paper. It was as mysterious as the lateness of the hour—after nine o'clock—and only as far away as the kitchen door, ajar so as to hear him if he should call to them or have a nightmare.

He turned in bed, listening to the whispering undertones, as steady and continuous as a tap left running and broken only by a cough or sometimes a chair scraping back on the linoleum; then a dish being taken from a cupboard and now and then a voice would catch on fire and break adrift from the murmuring, but always with the same word, Vanessa, said sharply like hitting a brass gong at dead of night and then someone would say, 'Shhh, was that him? Did he call out?' and tiptoeing would startle the old floorboards while a shadow grew larger and larger on his wall; bent to hear if he was stirring and so, annoyed with their secrets, he would feign sleep until whoever it was retreated to the kitchen and the whispering hissed up again like damp green eucalyptus logs burning.

They were talking secrets to Mrs Grindel from next door. He had heard the front gate squeak and her loud voice quickly shushed; then something about scones. His Aunt Lila had whispered, 'Not *scones* in January!'

After that had come the familiar summer night sounds of the opening and closing of the ice chest and the fizzing of ginger beer bottles being opened by his uncle, George. He had been about to call out that the pillow was hot and perhaps be given a tin mug of cool ginger beer when the Vanessas had started. It was a brand-new word and it must be a terrible one because when they said it in front of him they often looked down quickly to see if he had heard, then warningly at each other; winked and shook their heads just a little, which meant 'not in front of you-know-who' and then began the spelling out of simple words. Vanessa had something to do with the Letter. They were always talking now about the Letter and taking it out of the dresser drawer with its pages and pages of pale-blue paper and very thin, stiff writing. It seemed to him a long time since 'Postie' had brought the Letter. They had heard the whistle one scorching morning just before Christmas and Lila, looking as damp as one of her own wet mops, had appeared out of a cloud of steam from the laundry and said, 'Go and see what Postie has brought, PS,' so he had run down the cracked path through the dandelions and shivery grass to the front gate and held up his hand for the Letter. He had followed Lila back into the white steam cloud while she wiped her misty glasses and opened the envelope. She had read a few lines and then, it had seemed to him, had grown smaller, sagged, leaned on the hot copper tub, burned her elbow, said 'Ouch', then sat down heavily, leaving the washing and wooden pole to sink in the suds while she read the Letter very slowly, turning the pages over shakily and working her mouth the way she did when she added up the grocery bill. Then she had gone into the house to telephone to his Aunt Vere, all the way across the harbour in Kings' Cross.

'Vanessa,' she had said, 'is coming.'

Right then, talking to Vere, the spelling-out had begun and by the time George came home from work at the Trades Hall, Lila had begun the purring sounds in her chest and was breathing through her atomiser, which meant that the house was full of trouble.

George had read the Letter while unlacing his boots, had kicked one of his boots right across the kitchen floor, then had laughed and said that the Assyrian was coming down on the fold. 'Who?' he had asked George.

But Lila was cross and said it was no joke. 'Don't joke,' Lila told George, pointing to lines on the Letter and spelling them out and breathing in all the time through her atomiser, and George finally said, 'Now and then won't hurt.' Then seeing his upturned face over the edge of the kitchen table they looked down at him with put-on, birthday-treat smiles and said, over-lapping each other to be the first to tell him:

7

'Oh, aren't you lucky, PS.'

'Goodness, what a lucky boy.'

'What a *treat*!'

'Your Aunt Vanessa is coming.'

Vanessa was coming all the way from England back to Australia and she was coming on a piano boat.

'Why is she coming on a piano?' he asked, and they laughed, rocked back and forth on their chairs, forgetting to be worried, and said:

'No, darling. No, pet—not a piano. P and O. That's the kind of ship it is—a P and O ship.'

But he couldn't get out of his mind a picture of Vanessa lashed with ropes to a grand piano that was breasting its way through giant green waves and foam. It was not unlike a picture in a book called *The Little Castaways*, in which the evil captain who had set the children adrift came to a bad end by drowning. Perhaps Vanessa would drown too. Like that little boy at Balmoral Beach when they had hurried him away saying, 'Quick, quick, run after the ice-cream man and get a big sixpenny cone.' He had asked Lila if Vanessa would drown on the way from England, but she had put down his porridge plate and said in a cross voice, 'Of course not. What a terrible thing to say, PS.' Then she had explained that it was one of the great big boats they often saw going up the harbour and out the Heads to sea.

Now, turning again in bed, he wished that Mrs Grindel would go home; that the whispering would stop. He thought of calling out that the mattress was lumpy and that he was hot and thirsty, but now they were speaking the other bad word—'Logan'.

Lila said, 'Shhh, was that him?' and they listened for a moment, inclining their heads towards the hallway, hearing only the slight breeze that came from the open front door.

She wished now that she had not left it open. The house was no cooler and the light, streaming from the hall, had only served to attract Mrs Grindel, who nightly wrapped stale scones in a serviette and fluttered up and down their street like a huge moth seeking lamps and company.

Lila sat down again at the kitchen table, took a mouthful of dry scone and said, 'Mmmmmm, nice.'

Mrs Grindel said, 'You look terrible, Mrs Baines. You look dead, dear. You ought to be in bed with that asthma of yours.'

Lila said, 'No,' and thought, Yes, I am bone tired. I feel every one of my forty-one years and I wish you'd go home. But I asked you to stay and have another piece of fruitcake because I want to talk. Talking helps and in spite of the fact that you eat cake rudely with your mouth open and you are what my mother would have described as 'not our class', you are a mother yourself and a hard-working good woman. George is tired too and I'm selfish keeping him up. But then George has been tired for years. Tired and quiet from disappointment.

'Have another piece of fruitcake,' she said. 'It will only go stale.'

Mrs Grindel said, 'Well, good-oh, dear, if it will save you throwing it out.'

Lila cut another slab of cake. For a moment she could not remember what the new trouble was. Then it clicked back into her mind like a pitiless white electric light.

'Vanessa,' she said, picking up the theme, 'was born without the long Scott chin and so she was the beauty of the family. We used to say, "Vanessa got the looks. Sinden got the talent. Vere got the voice. Agnes got religion and Lila got George." '

She smiled at her husband. I love you, she said silently, but he merely looked surprised. She thought, I mustn't slide back down the years or we'll be here all night.

'After Pater died—'

'Who was Peter, dear?'

'Not Peter. *Pater*. My father. After my father died, my mother's rich cousin, Ettie Bult, came and saw what a state we were in and said to my mother, "I'll take one of the girls off your hands." We all knew it would be Vanessa. We said, "It'll be Ness, you watch," and it was. It was as though she'd been getting ready for it for years. She used to wear little white cotton gloves even to go to the greengrocer. She said it was the mark of a lady, and she had some calling cards printed "Vanessa Scott", which made us all laugh very much, seeing that she never went anywhere; we were much too poor to go anywhere except to visit old sick people in my father's parish. But Ness didn't care. She kept the cards in a little ivory box with her white gloves. She wanted to be ready, she told us, and she was. So Vanessa went to England as companion to Cousin Ettie Bult and they had a big house in London with maids galore and a chauffeur and travelled all over the place to Paris and Rome and so on—'

'Catch me,' said Mrs Grindel.

'What?' asked Lila, not wanting an interruption.

'You wouldn't catch *me*! Me, I like my own backyard. I'm a real dinky-dye Aussie. You wouldn't catch me deserting my own country.'

'We used to *get*' Lila went on, laughing a little, but raising her voice a fraction to silence any further irrelevancy, 'gifts from her wherever she went. Once we got a box of dates and figs from *Egypt*! And when Mater—when my *mother* was having her last long illness, Vanessa sent two silk nightgowns from Paris. What we needed was sheets! Sheets, pillowcases, towels—the *rent*. Mater was living with us by then and George was out of work at the time.'

George said, 'All right, *all right*, you don't like her,' and Lila waited respectfully, holding open the door of the conversation for him to enter, but, as usual, he let her go on alone. (And to think that once you never could shut him up.)

'Oh, I *do* like Ness. But we were never close, even as girls; I never understood her. It's not the same thing. And believe me, *believe* me, I've never resented her having the opportunities—although I would have liked to see Paris just once.'

'Not *me*!' Mrs Grindel shovelled a fat piece of cake into her hippopotamus mouth. Wouldn't catch *me*, dear.'

'It's only that it all came so easily to Vanessa. She's never had to struggle for anything. Fancy never having to worry about money your whole life and getting paid every week for not having to worry about it. What I'm saying is Ness has had a great deal so why does she want PS?'

'Part time,' said George, unlacing his boots. 'Part time is—'

'Is what?' asked Lila, having waited long enough.

'All she wants.'

Lila said, 'His home is with us. A child doesn't need two homes. Do you mean you approve?'

George looked beyond her, one boot in hand, beyond the situation, out of the window and was gone again.

'*I'm* his legal guardian. He doesn't need two guardians and if Sinden knew it was going to be Vanessa she'd die.' Lila gave a little laugh, thinking of Sinden already dead.

'She would,' agreed Mrs Grindel, 'poor little dear. I remember when she was stopping with you here. Nothing stuck-up about Sinden. She'd come over the fence and into my kitchen and sit there in those little-boy's togs of hers like it was Government House. "Oh, Mrs Grindel," she'd say, "you and your lovely scones. Can I have another?" "Eat all you want, love," I'd say. "You're eating for two now, remember." "Three or four, judging by my size," she'd say, and laugh. Oh, she'd cheer you up no matter how lousy she felt herself and I often caught her lookin' sad and I'd say, "Haven't you heard from *him*, love? No letter yet?" Next minute she'd be on a chair doin' an imitation of Queen Mary with my tea cosy on her head. She'd talk about her writin' and all that stuff, just as if I understood all about it, nothing put-on or posh about *her*. "I'll put you in a book one day, Mrs Grindel," she said, and I said, "Ta, love." She'd come over while I was feeding Winnie and ask me, "Is it wonderful to feed a baby? How do you do it?" "You've got this far, love," I'd say, "nature will provide the rest, don't you worry." I can't see her doin' cartwheels over some foreigner gettin' her paws on PS.'

'Oh, Vanessa's not a foreigner.'

'She's not *here*, is she?' Mrs Grindel swept crumbs from the tablecloth with her chipped-beef hands. 'What's the lawyer got to say, dear?'

'He's looking over the deed of disposal.'

'What's *that*?'

Lila's tired mind went reeling back to the interview with Sam Hamilton a week ago in that hot, stuffy office; the endless confusion of legal jargon—deeds of guardianship of 'said infant', deeds of disposal, of rights and privileges so difficult to understand (and not keep Sam too long; after all, we're not paying him)—when the head and heart are beating with unidentifiable fear and the feet are throbbing in tight cheap shoes.

Lila passed her hand over her face, brushing away invisible microscopic spiders that were creeping into her hair. She looked at George, almost asleep.

'I don't know,' she said. 'Vanessa is the one with the legal mind. Logan made the deed of appointment when Sinden died.'

'*Logan*!'

'Shhhh. Was that him? Did he call out?'

'Logan!'

'Shhh, yes.'

'Why didn't he take PS himself?'

'He couldn't. No job, no proper home—'

'Drunk as a tick.'

'Well, but—'

'Bastard, if you ask me.'

'Well, *she* loved him,' said Lila, hearing Sinden say that day at the Carlton Hotel, 'How could you *not* marry a man like that?'

'Logan shouldn't *have* a say. I don't care what the court says or any bloody lawyer in the land.'

'A father—'

'Only in one way, if you ask me.' Mrs Grindel licked her finger and picked up cake crumbs.

(Why did I bring this up? She's never going home; she's eyeing the cake again.)

So Lila said, to wind it up, get George to bed, 'Well, anyway, it looks as if we'll have to give in. Logan's given Vanessa permission to have PS part time.'

'He's in with her then.'

'They knew each other slightly years ago, before he married Sinden.'

'Where's he now?'

'The last word we had was a postcard about two years ago from some wild mining place up north. All it said was, "Good luck".' Lila picked up her atomiser and squeezed.

Mrs Grindel said, 'I'd good-luck *him* in the well-known you-know-what. How can he do this, eh?'

(No, I'm not going into it all now. I'd have to explain all about Ernest Huxley and she'll never go all night.)

Lila said, rising with dishes, 'Logan is PS's father—'

The kitchen clock whirred, announced some muffled hour. She looked at George, asleep now; at Mrs Grindel, a huge rag doll in that awful print dress with a design of watermelons. (No earthly use going over and over it. But my mind is reeling and I won't sleep for hours yet. Why not? Why not explain all about Ernest Huxley and what happened? What's a couple of hours?)

She heard herself say:

'Why not just finish up the cake?'

'Well, all right, dear, if it will save you throwing it out.'

Hearing George's slow, regular breathing in the dark, hardly any different in sleep from when he was awake and walking around, she eased herself gently out of the bed and felt under it for the cardboard hatbox. ('Saw this in the Rue de la Paix, Lila, and thought it might amuse you. Love, Vanessa.') She carried the hatbox into the kitchen, snapped on the cold white light, and reaching for her glasses, untied the worn green ribbon.

The box was filled with letters, all in the same uneven handwriting, mostly in pencil. She searched for the one she wanted and read, inhaling the letter like oxygen, hearing Sinden's quick, bright voice underlining the date three times. 'October 28th, but do I have the right year? Wasn't my child due in 1927?'

16

And beneath that, the address, 'Bedrock, otherwise known as The Laurels Private Hospital, Neutral Bay. Lila, you dear. Glad you didn't try to come today as I'll sleep early tonight. *Nothing* doing, old kid, but sunshine and blue butterflies outside and the big white screen inside. Doctor just looked in and said, "Hey, you, when are the pains going to start?" I suggested TNT. The amount of oil they're giving me, you'd think I was a piece of machinery! The artillery is still rumbling, but the INFANTRY is very silent. Vere came yesterday (out of visiting hours and Matron was rather hostile), brought me a box of razberry tarts and borrowed a pound! I dare not let myself think of the depleted bank account—though what depresses me more is that I shall have to drop the new book for a while and hack or take a job (if my reluctant babe will ever let me get back to work). Oh, Lila, if only *Marmon* had *sold* instead of getting good reviews. The critics won't pay my bills. Logan writes from someplace called Jacob's Ladder, full of dreams and love and assurances that they will strike gold any day now and that there will be a mansion for me and the babe that will make Vanessa jade green with envy. What a husband he would be if only he could make it *pay*! I could go to Pony Wardrop for a while when I get out of here, but her chaos of living would flatten me. I think yearningly of your little haven and Mrs Grindel's scones.'

Lila turned a page and here the voice seemed to grow suddenly confidential:

'Lila, don't tell Vere or Agnes, *please*, but this damn kidney thing worries me. I'm scared and admit it to you. If anything should go wrong, will you and George take the babe? Logan will be lost in the blue and except for Ernest, you are the only ones I could trust to look after my "PS", for that's what he'll be— a postscript to my ridiculous life. Sinden.'

Lila folded the letter and the night silence returned thick around her. She replaced it carefully in the hatbox and retied the ribbon.

She snapped off the kitchen light and crossed the hallway to the small bedroom, wincing at the squeak made by the door. Greyish light was beginning to lap at the windows. She looked down at the small bed; saw him stretched diagonally across it, one foot thrust angrily from under the sheet in a corresponding line with his left arm struck out urgently towards the window, already reaching out for tomorrow.

She replaced the foot under the sheet, tucking in and around, then lifted him, turning the pillow to the cool other side, and laid him down, protesting her intrusion and turning immediately from her and back to the nestling secret of whatever dreaming held him between night and morning.

Lila smoothed the sheet, lightly as air touching it.

'Don't *worry*, PS,' she said, reassuring herself.

* * *

18

Vere said, 'Now watch, PS, while we do a funny thing.' And he giggled because everything Vere did was funny; she always did a funny thing the first moment she saw him, even if they were on the street; no matter where they were or how many people were looking, she would do a pretend game of not seeing him or screaming and rushing away from him, swearing that he was a wild, dangerous tiger let loose from the zoo. He knew that Vere would, if he wanted it, throw herself in front of a tram to make him laugh.

Now she took a pot from the popping gas ring on her little marble-top washstand and filled the wash-basin with hot water. Then she danced across the room and picked up a dusty, scratched gramophone record from where a whole stack of them stood, falling sideways.

She said, 'Now watch what we do with Paul Whiteman.'

She dropped Paul Whiteman into the hot water. It was very funny, one of her best funnies in a long while, so he laughed very much, but was curious also and said, still gurgling, 'Vere, why are you washing the gramophone records?'

'Wait and see,' she said. 'In a minute it will go all soft.'

'Why do you want it to go all soft?'

'Because then we can bend it into any shape we want. This one is going to be a vase.'

19

'A vase!'

'Yes, a lovely vase to put flowers in; once it's hardened we'll paint it gorgeous bright colours.'

Vases out of gramophone records. Oh, Vere was marvellous, really marvellous. Lila never thought of doing funnies like this; Lila was so very, very usual, but Vere was full of surprises (she called them 's'prizes', but he didn't correct her). Now he edged forward and stood on tiptoe looking down at the submerged record.

'Vere?'

'What, treasure?'

'What'll you do about the little hole in the middle?'

'Oh, you bright-as-a-button *thing*,' she screamed, hugging him. 'We'll cover it with a little dab of red sealing wax. Where's my cigarette? Oh, there on the clock. Reach for it, sweetness, thank you. Now look, we can make anything we want, little hairpin trays, ashtrays, bottles and soap dishes.'

'All out of gramophone records?'

'Yes, now watch.'

She plucked the record out of the water and sure enough it was as limp as a wet straw hat.

Working quickly with her hands, dropping cigarette ash down her front, Vere twisted the limp record into twirls and curves and stood it up. Lo and behold, it was a vase for little flowers like pansies.

20

'There, pet. Now we let it harden.'

'When they're all finished, can we give them away as surprises?'

'No, these are not for s'prizes, dearest thing.'

'Why not?'

'Because Vere sells them to Mr Jacoby at the little shop on the corner and he gives me five bob for each.'

A fortune. 'Each?'

'Yes, the rat.'

'But why do you want to sell them, Vere?'

'Because that's what Vere is doing at the moment, pet. Making vases out of gramophone records!'

She whirled on him, picking him up and swinging him around and saying, 'I've got gorgeous milk and a piece of chocolate cake for you, but first I think I'll eat you up, eatyouup, eatyouup!'

She made ravenous noises, kissing him all over his face and neck until he wriggled, trying delightedly to escape.

They had had a wonderful day. Lila had brought him into the city on the ferry. He loved the ferryboats with their tall black funnels, their squat red railings, the clatter of their little gang-planks on the suburban jetties and their wonderful names all beginning with K—the *Kuttabul*, the *Kiandra*, the *Kookaburra*. Lila and he had got off at Circular Quay and there beyond the turnstiles in a bright blue hat and her red hair curling out around her face was Vere, waving her patched gloves and swinging her long strings of beads and right away she had done a funny thing; she had screwed up her eyes as though she could not make out who or what in the world he was and then she had let out a wild shriek so that lots of people turned around to see whether someone's bag had been snatched, and she had reared up very tall and afraid and cried out, 'Lila, who's *that* you've got? That's not PS, that's a *dangerous* leopard,' then appearing to recognise him by his cap, rushed to gobble him with kisses and said, 'Oh, no, it's my child, my *child*!' and Lila said, 'Vere, everyone's looking,' ashamed of such carryings-on because what would people *think*?

Then there had been one of those moments of tall whispering and nudging far above him and he had seen Lila take a postcard out of her bag and give it to Vere, saying, 'Vanessa from Colombo—only a few weeks now.' Lila had waved and said she would pick him up at five o'clock and gone off, moving her sore feet gently on the hot pavement where the tar was melting in soft puddles, and he and Vere had climbed on a tram (Vere being very funny with the conductor and pretending she had lost her bag) and they had gone to the cheap seats at the pictures, feeling their way in the sudden dark of the Regent Theatre, nearly empty at that time of the morning, but with the giant grey faces on the screen that he loved so much. Vere said that the picture was *The Gold Diggers of 1933* and that the girl wearing nothing but a big gold coin was Ginger Rogers. When the picture was over, a man came up out of nowhere playing the big Wurlitzer organ in a bright pink light and then sank out of sight again; they sat through the newsreel and a cartoon and Coming Attractions and through *The Gold Diggers* again until after Ginger had sung 'We're in the Money', which is where they had come in, and groped their way out, blinking into the hot sunlight to find it was afternoon already. While they were sitting in Sargent's having a meat pie each, he had asked Vere was it a good thing to be a gold digger and she had laughed and said, 'Oh, yes—my God, yes, pet; get anything you can in this damn life; you'll be a long time dead.' He thought this was a bit strange because *Logan* was a gold digger; he'd heard them say so. Yet Logan was one of the things you didn't mention out loud.

Now they were back in Vere's room at Kings' Cross, which was best of all because it was so full of Things. Vere collected things from everybody and her little narrow room was crammed with them. Whenever anybody was about to throw something away, Vere would snatch it from them saying, 'Oh, I know a poor woman who'd love to have that,' only the things were all for her and she herself never threw out anything so that there was hardly room to sit down, let alone move, and every time she opened her wardrobe door out would fall cardboard boxes, handbags with broken clasps, shoes that were not her size, musty old furs, galoshes, umbrellas, newspapers and old magazines. The wardrobe was so packed tight with other people's dresses and coats that Vere often had to tug and pull for minutes to get at the one she wanted. There were mountains of dusty letters lying around everywhere; Vere never tore up a letter and he'd heard them joke about her even keeping notes from the milkman saying, 'Sorry, no cream today.' Stuck on the pink walls with pins were hundreds of pictures and he liked to stand on a chair and look at them and pick out the people he knew like Lila and George being married in front of a waterfall (George sitting down in a wicker chair and Lila in a white lace dress standing with her hand on George's shoulder as if to stop him from getting up) and Vere all dressed up in costume when she was on the stage in *The Student Prince*, and old Mater Scott all buttoned up to the neck in black and looking not pleased at all with anyone and Pater Scott with his white beard, and another one of them all together, the five girls all grouped around Mater and Pater with Lila and Agnes standing at the back, Dear One (as he was told to call his mother) all by herself at the side as if she didn't quite belong to them, and two little girls with long curls and in fluffy white dresses, sitting in front.

'Me,' said Vere today, pointing to herself.

And the other?

'That's Vanessa,' said Vere, and he leaned forward to see Vanessa long ago. She was a very pretty little girl with hair ribbons and a misty face, and she leaned her little arm along Pater Scott's knee and rested her head against his waistcoat, curled against him like a white kitten. Now, today, they all stared at him curiously as much as to say, 'Well, for goodness' sake, who are you? Which one of us had *you* for a little boy?' but Vanessa, curled against her father, seemed to stare harder than all the others.

What was she coming back for? What was this little girl in a white dress with a big silk sash going to do to him? He was just about to ask Vere when there was a tap at the door and Vere's friend, Opal, came in. Opal was the most beautiful girl in the world and wore soft, shining dresses; always a new one every time he saw her, always pretty shoes to match, always great big hats piled with roses.

Opal said, 'And who is this handsome man?' bending to kiss him and smelling of honeysuckle.

Vere said, 'Girl, how are you?'

Opal said, 'Girl, I'm thwarted.'

She pronounced it to rhyme with 'carted'.

Vere said, 'We're all thwarted.' It was always a 'thwart', never a 'thwort'. 'Thworted' meant having warts.

Vere said, 'I thought you were going to the races with Archie.'

'His wife's in town.'

'Wouldn't that thwart you!'

'It's the supreme thwart. So is she. He's lashed to the mast for days now.'

'How sick-making, girl.'

'Girl, it's gall and wormwood. I am undone.'

'Has he told her about you yet?'

'Says he can't until she's in a less thwarting mood.'

'Which means never.'

'Girl, you are probably right about him. I always pick the ones with no guts. The whole thing undoes me to the point of stupor, but I am lashed to him, as to a mast. I must have a drink, pront.'

Vere fished a tall, cold bottle out of the shopping bag that Opal had brought with her, along with a black lace nightgown. When Vere saw the nightgown, she gave one of her shrieks. 'Oh, girl, what's *this*?'

Opal said, 'Girl, I'm hurling it at you because it's so full of evil memories of my other great mistake. Now wear it, don't just put it away. You put everything away in that evil wardrobe.'

Opal had taken off her dress and shoes and was sitting on the bed in a yellow slip and lighting a cigarette. Vere poured the golden-coloured bubbles into two peanut butter glasses and handed one to Opal. They immediately forgot him and began talking about their friends who were all in a mess, thwarted, broke, maddened or suicidal, my dear. They had wonderful names like Dodo, Ukulele, Widget and Gussy. When they came to visit Vere they brought her old shoe buckles, brooches, half-used pots of cold cream, combs and long, cool bottles because they were always dying of thirst, just dying of thirst, my dear, and their voices would grow brighter as the daylight faded, would fly around the small room like birds let out of cages telling about gay-sounding things, about parties and dancing, full of mysterious words that had to be spelled out in Lila's house and which made his heart jump for the time when he would understand and be a part of the things they told about with such laughter.

He heard Vere say, 'I didn't tell you about our thwart.'

'Which is?'

'Ness is coming back.'

'My dear! What will they do without her at Hampton Court?'

'They will be undone.'

'Is Cousin Ettie coming too?'

'But of course. They are lashed to each other, she and Ness.'

'Is Cousin Ettie still in the money, Vere?'

'Rolling.'

'I thought no one was any more.'

'Oh, girl, Ettie's evil husband bought shares in everything in the year one—things like Broken Hill

Mining and Dalgetty's and wool and shipping and little unimportant stock like Woolworth's!'

'My dear! I suppose one day Ness will cop the lot.'

'The *lot*! That's why she has stayed lashed to Ettie all these years.'

'Of course. She is Crafty Alice in the Fairy Palace. Well, we must get out our ostrich feather fans and practise our court curtseys.' Opal reached for a cigarette. 'But, girl, why is it a thw*a*rt?'

'Because Vanessa wants the c-h-i-l-d.'

'Jesus, *no*!'

'Shhh. Yes. She has been up to some evilness with Ernest in London.'

'Sinden's Ernest?'

'Yes, and it seems he's relinquished his guardian-ship to *her*.'

'But wouldn't L-o-g-a-n have had to agree?'

'Apparently he did. By letter.'

'Where is he?'

'Over the hills and far away, gold digging.'

'Mad, of course.'

'Crazy as a cut snake, always was, but it's *most* undoing.'

'Does it mean Lila will have to give up *le petit enfant*?'

'*Qui*. Part time, anyway.'

'Is she thw*a*rted?'

'Thwarted to an absolute faretheewell, asthma and the *lot*, and poor sleepy George waked up out of his seven-year trance. PS? Where are you, darling?'

He said, 'Under the bed.'

'What are you doing there, dearest thing?'

'Looking for Hester.'

'Don't let her scratch you, blessed angel.'

He had found comforting old Hester and dragged her, miaowing, from the shadows of luggage and strange things under Vere's bed; hugged her to him, spitting and protesting and curling the feather of her tail around his face.

He listened to the conversation rumbling on above him, all about him and Vanessa and Logan and 'custardy'; about who was going to have the 'custardy' of him. But what had desserts to do with Vanessa? He felt cold and funny inside and he wished Vere and Opal would stop.

Fortunately, Gussy knocked on the door, bringing a cool bottle and some old gramophone records for Vere to make into vases.

Vere shrieked, 'PS, come and say hello to Gussy.'

He loved Gussy, who did funny things and right now was pretending to faint with surprise at the sight of him, fell back into a chair, closed his eyes, recovered, sprang up and seized two saucepan lids, clashed them together like cymbals, screaming, 'PS is here. Slaves, bring grapes and dancing girls.' Then he did a slave dance while Vere poured more golden stuff into peanut butter glasses and said, 'Sing a song, PS', so he sang 'Painting the Clouds with Sunshine', remembering all the words so that they clapped for him very hard. Then Dodo, very fat and funny, came rolling up the stairs, screaming to them that she was dying of thirst, my dear, and behind her came Ruby, bending to get in the door because he was so tall, and once in the room he seemed to be everywhere, like a tree that had sprouted up suddenly through the carpet, but mostly all around Vere with his long arms until she shrieked, 'Stop it, you evil thing.' They were all having a good time now because it was getting on towards evening when they did all sorts of delightful things and forgot that they were broke, maddened, thwarted and suicidal, my dear.

By the time Lila came to pick him up, the room was so smoky and noisy that only he noticed her at the door in her prune-coloured hat and her blue dress wet all around the middle with being so hot and having to walk so far from the tram down Vere's long street.

Lila shook hands with Vere's friends and gave them the look she sometimes gave the butcher when he tried to cheat her; then she hurried him into his coat with her mouth working because she had seen the long, cold bottles.

'*Really*, Vere!'

'Oh, God, Lila, it's only beer, for heaven's sake.'

'What did the l-a-w-y-e-r say?'

'Sam said it's perfectly legal. Nothing we can do.'

Opal said, over the noise of the others, 'Lila, Vere's just told me about Vanessa. My dear, what a black thwart!'

Lila drew herself up, showing that she did not like Opal, saying in her very polite visitors' voice, 'It will be very nice to see her after all these years. Come along, PS, or we'll miss the half past five boat.'

He went around kissing them all goodbye, sorry the lovely day was over. Vere gobbled him all over the face, saying, 'Oh, I could eat you up. I could *eat you up*!' gave him a piece of chocolate cake in a greasy bag and Lila marched him out and down the stairs, past the nasty landlady's door. In the street, a wild drunken man called out something to them twice which made Lila's hot face even redder, made her say, pulling him along like the Red Queen, 'Faster, PS, we'll miss the boat.' Sure enough, as they rushed from the tram to the turnstiles, they saw the half past five boat chugging away from the wharf, leaving them with half an hour to wait.

'I *knew* we'd miss it,' Lila said, and seemed pleased that she had turned out to be right.

The sign on the gate read: THE TEMPLE OF EVERLASTING LOVE. NO TRESPASSING.

31

Lila pushed open the gate and went in. Tiers of cracked concrete rose in a Greek amphitheatre, led down to ionic columns, standing high above the darkening bay and dwarfing the figure of Agnes, holding a broom and shielding her eyes against the dying sun to see who it was.

Lila called to her sister, 'It's only me,' and waving little assurances that she was not an intruder, started down the steep steps between the tiers. Dotted here and there were metal plates bearing the names of the hundred or so disciples of Dr Pollack who would gather here to witness the Day of Judgement and presumably to watch the sea yield up its dead (which here in Balmoral Bay, thought Lila, couldn't amount to more than half a dozen souls, considering the vigilance of the beach lifesaving clubs).

Some of the name plates had become rusted and loose; their owners, weary of waiting for the millennium through several false alarms, had gone ahead on their own steam.

The Temple, built in a clumsy approximation to the Acropolis, had a run-down appearance and Lila, stepping on cracks that had burst between lantana weeds, heard Sinden laugh and say, 'Agnes, I *know* what it says in the Bible, but why would He return through the Sydney Harbour Heads?'

Poor Agnes. Poor Agnes, they always said, laughing and shaking their heads as Lila found herself doing now and regretting it when she saw the disappointment on Agnes' horse-like face. (Poor thing. She thought I might be a new disciple.)

'I was near by—' Lila said, reaching the bottom and sitting down on a concrete slab marked THOMPSON to get her breath, offering this feeble excuse for the whim that had brought her half a mile out of her way to the tram and up the steep hill to the Temple. 'News,' she added, fumbling in her worn handbag for Vanessa's letter.

Agnes said unexpectedly, 'Oh, those seagulls!' darted forward with the broom to sweep seagull droppings off the seat next to THOMPSON. Brushing away, Agnes said, 'How did you know I would be here today?'

'I don't know. I just thought you might.'

Agnes, under her tricorn hat and looking more than ever like Lord Nelson, gave Lila a swift, triumphant glance.

'But I'm never usually here on Tuesdays, Lila. Something *brought* you!'

'Yes,' said Lila. 'News from Ness.'

'No,' said Agnes. 'It's a Sign,' and Lila nodded, accepting the strange fact of her being here; reminded that when it came to signs and portents she and Agnes were alike; had searched through girlhood for secret clues in order to sustain their faltering hopes that in the end all would be well, money would be theirs, the sick would recover, lovers would return. ('I dreamed of So-and-So last night, Agnes, and today I ran into her on the street, isn't that *funny*?' 'Lila, I *knew* the doorbell was going to ring, isn't that *funny*?') Heads together, they had peered out through the windows of the dark, cramped manse in Waverly, looking for the silver lining; straining their eyes to see the first light of their brilliant futures.

The only difference, Lila was thinking, is that Agnes took it up professionally; and she saw, for an instant, Mater Scott rising black-bodiced and stern, saying to Agnes, 'Necromancy! I will not have necromancy in this Church of England house, so you must choose between your father and the devil'; watched again while Agnes packed a cardboard suitcase, went down the front path to board a ship for Seattle and the glorious teachings of a Mr Norman B. Pringle.

Poor Agnes.

What had she found? A life of handing out pamphlets to scoffers who heckled her on street corners, and of trying to raise money to help sustain a temple going to rack and ruin with the financial uncertainty of Eternity when she could not even afford a new hat; trudged around in that old tricorn which she had worn proudly back from America.

Now, wearing her hat like a vow of poverty, she was often subjected to the cruel little singsong chant of 'Where did you get-that-hat?' when she spoke in

Sydney Domain along with the Communists, Pacifists, Prohibitionists and the other soapbox orators screaming for attention from the listless Sunday strollers under the giant fig trees.

Lila watched her now, sitting down on UPDIKE FAMILY, searching for her imitation tortoise-shell glasses, the little navy-blue ribbon on the back of her hat fluttering like a tiny, brave pennant on a sinking ship, and jumped when Agnes said, before unfolding the letter:

'Is Ness coming home?'

'Yes. How did you know?'

Agnes smiled. 'I knew.'

What? A good guess? Even the most bogus prophets can hit the mark now and then.

Agnes said, 'I had a revelation about it a few weeks ago.'

Lila said, 'You might have warned me,' and laughed, wondering at the same time about Agnes' gift for signs, remembering that years ago Agnes had said, apropos of nothing in particular, 'Sinden won't live to be very old.' Nonsense, nonsense, they had all said, all of them secretly loving Sinden the best, angry and frightened that Agnes might be right and hushing her instantly in case Sin might have been in the pantry and overheard.

Nonsense, Agnes! They were incensed that she should have said this about Sinden, who was the only one of them who ever stuck up for Agnes against Mater and had done so right from the very first time when Mater had found Agnes' notebook of 'Conversations and Disagreements with St John the Divine' and had read aloud from it amid whoops of laughter from everybody except Sinden who, seeing the red-faced young girl motionless as death watching Mater from the hallway, snatched the book from Mater's hand and said, 'Mother, don't. Let her have God any way she wants Him.' They all had expected an explosion but instead, Mater had handed the notebook to Sinden and gone rather red in the face herself.

Once Sinden had said, 'You should only listen to every nineteenth thing Agnes says, but *then* you should listen very carefully.' Over the years they had stopped laughing occasionally and listened intently to Agnes in case she might be saying the nineteenth thing and Lila knew that this was why she was here today; this was why she had turned suddenly from the tram and toiled up the hot, treeless hill to the Temple.

She watched the sad Lord Nelson face bent impassively over Vanessa's small handwriting and waited until Agnes had read the last page.

'Well, what do you think of that?'

Agnes turned her head and stared away through the columns across the bay towards the open sea, narrowed her eyes as though she could already see someone coming—but not by ship.

Agnes said, 'You better not oppose her, Lila.'

'Why not?'

'She'll make trouble if you try.'

(Oh, Agnes, tell me something I *don't* know.)

'I *know* that, Agnes. Even Sam Hamilton says we'd have to apply for adoption, which means finding Logan and—'

'You must let Ness have PS.'

'But don't you think it's a piece of cheek?'

'There's a reason, Lila.'

'What reason, if you don't mind my asking?'

'A reason.' Agnes closed her eyes. 'If you go against the current, you'll be *wrong*!'

'George and I should just let her walk all over us?'

'*I* am speaking metaphysically.' Agnes grew terse. 'There are reasons for everything and we must abide by them. If you go against the reason there will be a terrible overturning.' She handed back the letter and said calmly, 'It won't make much difference, anyway—the time is growing short.'

(Oh, here we go again. Might as well have saved myself this walk.)

Agnes said dreamily, 'Dr Pollack has worked it out now to the very month, almost the day. The day when we will all be received into the joy of understanding will be in October.'

(October! How *funny*!)

'Well, Agnes, I thought you'd like to know—'

'What?'

'That Ness is coming.'

Agnes stood up and walked away to the rotunda which they called the Circle of Revelation and Joy, saying what sounded for a second, on the still, evening air, like a nineteenth thing.

'PS has to learn something.'

A lion roared near by and Lila jumped up, not startled so much by the lion as by what it might be that PS had to learn.

'The zoo,' said Agnes.

'What?'

'The zoo is within earshot. Often when I'm here alone on moonlight nights I hear them crying out for Africa.'

'What does PS have to learn?'

But Agnes had gone away now quietly on an expedition of her own so they stood together silently, looking down at the bay where, in the deepening blue, the currents ran dangerously against each other, secretly fighting so that the bay shuddered blackly and moved as a sleeper to toss and turn on the beach. Across at the Heads, a Manly ferry passed and the Watson's Bay Lighthouse began its little winking in the first awareness of the twilight.

The timelessness of it swept over Lila and she felt that they might stand here until they took root in the concrete and that in all that time she would never understand about anything, but that perhaps Agnes would.

Then Agnes gave a little cry and said, 'Oh, *look*,' and pointed down to where a dead bird lay at their feet.

A dead rainbird. And how they hated rainbirds, always the childhood announcers of trouble.

Ridiculous. Of course, it didn't *mean* anything . . .

Just the same—how *funny*!

Now they were going to Dear One's Garden and he liked this, even though this Saturday morning he had had plans of his own to get married to Winnie Grindel in her pepper tree because it was his turn to be bride, but Lila said no, said don't go through the fence in your good blazer because we're going to Dear One's Garden as soon as I've cut the sandwiches.

'Why are we going *today*?'

'Because it's her birthday.'

He laughed. How funny they were. How could you have a birthday when you weren't there? Would they have a cake with candles and ice cream? Birthdays were Treats, like going to the beach or the zoo or the pictures with Vere. He never quite thought of going to Dear One's Garden as a Treat because really it was rather dull, although the trip there was a Treat. You took the ferryboat across the harbour to Circular Quay and then the tram to Central Station and then the electric train, which you stayed on a long time, stopping at a great many stations, passing through tunnels and stone cuttings and best of all you crossed over a high iron bridge across a river and if you stuck your nose right against the train window and looked down you could see the green river thick with yellow jellyfish. If you happened to fall from the train through the girders into the river the jellyfish would sting you to death in a minute; so Winnie Grindel had told him when she had once come along with them for a Treat. From the train window the jellyfish had looked about as big as upturned saucers, but Winnie said they were really bigger than breadboards and they had feelers as long as your arm. She knew of a little boy his age who had fallen out of a rowing boat and when they'd fished him out of the river he'd already turned black all over with stings. It had been in the paper, Winnie said, and told him to be very careful because that railway bridge was very old and ready to give way any minute; probably *today*!

He was thinking about this now and about the little boy stung black to death. They were rattling across the old unsafe bridge and he had his nose squashed to the window, looking down at the great jellyfish trailing their feelers in the water, when Lila put her face to the glass next to his and said:

'Look over there.'

'Where?'

'Over there, see? Right down the river. Quick, watch where I'm pointing, see? A great big white house with verandas running all around it and a red roof with towers? See it?'

Where? Oh. He saw it just as it disappeared.

Lila said, 'That's the hotel where Dear One spent her—where she went away to stay with your father.'

They *stayed* together?

But that meant she stayed with Logan! Stayed with a gold digger in that big house which looked so lonely and damp in the middle of all those sad-looking trees bending over the river and the river so dark green and awful and too dangerous even to put your toe in the water.

How strange it all was and embarrassing too for Lila to mention Logan, which she never did if she could help it, and right out loud like that in the train where anyone could hear. And surely it was wrong of Dear One to go off like that and stay away with Logan. Dear One never did a wrong thing in her life. They were always telling him that. She was a saint and an angel and too good to live and so God had called her away.

He wanted to ask why she had gone away with Logan, but Lila had already hidden behind a newspaper and George was asleep.

Why?

The train stopped at Sutherland Station and they got out (George forgetting his Good Raincoat and having to run back for it) and walked up the steps and across a bridge with a lot of other people who were all carrying flowers, then down a dusty white road and through tall iron gates.

Just inside the gates a fat lady sat on a canvas stool beside tin buckets holding flowers, and they stopped while Lila spoke to the fat lady and asked how much were the carnations, how much were the asters? How much were the pink hydrangeas? To each reply from the fat lady, Lila said, 'Tch, tch, that's much too *dear*. Don't you have anything for about one and sixpence or two shillings a bunch?' and finally she bought daisies which had brown spots on them and two bunches of violets and said, 'Put some fairy fern with them and some gum leaves and a sprig of forget-me-not,' and George paid the fat lady and they went on down the road under the gum trees and everywhere there were people putting flowers in vases on the little gardens.

Dear One's Garden was just off the road a short distance, and as Lila always said, 'so handy to the tap, thank goodness', because her feet hurt.

The little garden was raised slightly from the dry red earth by a stone step. It had a white marble cross, taller than he, which had lettering on it and read, according to Lila:

SINDEN.

BELOVED DAUGHTER OF WILLIAM AND ANNIE SCOTT.

'TO THE PURE IN HEART, ALL THINGS ARE PURE.'

at the top, and at the bottom (but not unless you cut away the grass and weeds):

BELOVED WIFE OF LOGAN.

Once there, things always got busy. George would spread last Sunday's paper on the garden so as not to dirty his trousers, and unwrap the garden shears; then he would take off his jacket and fold it neatly on the stone step. One time he had asked George why he didn't hang his coat on the cross, which would be a good coat hanger, but they had said, 'Oh no, oh no, darling, you mustn't hang anything on that, *ever*; it's not supposed to be for that.'

What was the use of it then?

While George cut the dry long grass and complained that the shears were so blunt they wouldn't cut hot blood, he and Lila would gather up the glass jam jars and vases from around the bottom of the cross, pouring out the muddy rainwater and the dead flowers. Then they would go to the tap and fill the jars with fresh water and arrange the new flowers nicely in them. There wasn't much talking while all this went on and he was always glad when it was over and they could all sit down on the stone step and open the nice, damp packets of sandwiches and uncork the thermos of tea. There would be butterfly cakes, plums and little green pears, and they would sit, enjoying the nice picnic, while the locusts squawked in the trees and little bright insects buzzed around them and no one said much more than 'More tea?' or 'How about another ham sandwich?' or perhaps how pretty the poplar trees were over there around the new crematorium. After lunch they would all turn and stare for quite a long while at the garden in silence until Lila would say to him, 'Say goodbye to Dear One.' It was silly really to say goodbye to no one, but he always obeyed politely, feeling foolish.

Dear One wasn't there. She was in an aeroplane in the sky. He'd found out that much, anyway. He'd been under the table in the kitchen when his Aunt Agnes had come for tea, and heard her say, 'Lila, why do you take him there?'

'For his mother's sake, Agnes.'

'Sinden isn't *there*. She's on the Seventh Plane of Understanding.'

'Well, maybe, but it's all we've got of her.'

Agnes had laughed at Lila. 'You and your old theology. You're as bad as Pater.'

'Well, all right, but I think Sinden would like it.'

'She doesn't have any memory of this Plane.'

'It wouldn't hurt *you* to put a flower there sometimes.'

'I will have nothing to do with old-fashioned death and burial.'

'Do you mean you want to be *cremated*?' Lila had sounded shocked.

'There will be no *need*, Lila.'

Since that time he had watched the sky whenever he heard the drone of an aeroplane coming across the house from Mascot, where they took off. But how to tell the seventh plane from all the others?

When he had asked Lila, she had laughed and said, 'Oh, pet, *never* listen to what Agnes says.'

Suddenly today, as they were doing the first things, he heard Lila say in one of her quiet voices, 'George, someone's been here.'

George stopped cutting the grass.

Lila said, 'Look, someone's put some blue irises in this jar and it looks to me as if they've only been here a few days.'

George said, 'Vere.'

'Oh, no. I asked her if she wanted to come with us today and she said she didn't even have the train fare at the moment.'

George said that perhaps it could be one of Sin's pals from the Pen and Ink Club. Pony whatsername.

'I doubt that they'd remember her birthday now. They remember the other date, but not the birthday. And these look—oh, I don't know, perhaps it's silly, but—it's not the way a woman puts flowers in a vase, all bunched up like this. More like a man.'

They looked at each other for a minute in silence and he looked at them and then George said:

'Well, whoever he was, I wish he'd cut the bloody grass for us.

'George. Don't swear here.'

'These shears wouldn't cut hot blood.'

Lila said, 'But I don't like the idea of some stranger poking around.'

After a minute, George said, 'It might not be a stranger to *her*,' and he went on cutting.

Lila moved the intruding irises away from the cross and placed her own squat jug of daisies in front of it. She felt suddenly hotter and not from the sun; from an old resentment.

Strangers.

Yes, how peculiar it was. Always strangers, Lila thought, coming again out of a shop years ago and finding Sinden deep in conversation with someone on the street corner. ('Who was that?' '*I* don't know, but a most *interesting* chap.') How many times had they waited, sick with worry, when Sinden was so late coming home from high school that it was almost evening; peering anxiously from the front windows expecting the police with terrible news and then her casual, 'Oh, I met a boy and don't worry, his *sister* was there too.' Mater scolding to no avail, talking to a brick wall, and Lila, in her role of eldest sister, dropping hints like hairpins behind the closed bedroom door only to get an amused, 'Oh, Lila, tell me something I don't know.'

Total strangers knew Sinden infinitely better than her family and traces of them appeared everywhere. 'Oh, what a pretty jade brooch, Sin. Who gave you that?' 'Oh, someone I know.' Sorry they asked.

Then after Mater died and Lila assumed responsibility, the periods when she went off into limbo, came back without a word, disappeared again. ('Where's Sin?' 'Oh, we never know. Off somewhere writing, no doubt.') Getting 'copy', more likely, for that was what she called it. After a long while they had learned the uselessness of asking questions. ('But it sounds awful. How could you write in a place like that?' 'You can write sitting on the edge of a bath if you *want* to write.')

All those peculiar people, really *peculiar* people in her book *Marmon*, supposedly drawn from life.

And then—and *then*—

A telephone rang suddenly in Lila's mind:

'Hello.'

'Lila?'

'Sinden! Where *are* you? I've been trying for days to—'

'I'm in a telephone box at the Carlton Hotel. I've just got married.'

'Why haven't you rung me up? I've been—*What did you say?*'

'I just got married to Logan Marriott. Lila?'

'Yes?'

'Come on in at once and bring George. We've got champagne and Vere's just arrived. I'm in heaven, dearest, absolutely in the blue sky and, Lila, I made a wedding dress out of that lace you gave me and some creamy silk Ness sent from Paris—'

'Sinden, who is Logan Marriott?'

It still hurt.

Bending over the grave, arranging fern around her wretched-looking daisies, it hurt still and she said to George:

'If it hadn't been for a stranger we wouldn't be here today, bringing flowers to her.'

George said, 'If it weren't for strangers *none* of us would be here.'

'Don't talk that way in front of you-know.'

PS was looking curiously at her and so Lila rearranged her face into a false smile and said, 'There now, isn't that nice? Haven't we made Dear One's Garden look neat and pretty for her?'

'Yes, but can we have lunch now?'

Now it was all over, the lunch scraps carefully wrapped and put in the wire basket, the shears in a paper bag, and they were walking back down the red dust road towards the gates and hurrying a little because the sun had gone suddenly behind black clouds, shaped like whales, that were storming towards them, wrapping everything in grey light, and Lila was saying, 'I knew the day would spoil. I heard the rainbirds this morning. We'll be caught in that before we get to the train, you watch!' and was waving her umbrella, pleased that she was right.

But he was watching a group of people standing around one of the gardens. There was a big gaping hole in the ground and some men were lowering a box into the hole with ropes while the others stood around watching. The men all had their hats off and two of them were holding on to a lady all dressed in black with a veil covering her face and holding white flowers. Lila was jabbing him, saying, 'Oh, look over there, pet, the other way—I think I see a bunny rabbit,' but at that moment the lady in black gave a scream, pulling away from the two men, and rushed towards the hole as though she was going to throw herself into it, but the others reached out for her and held her back while she went on and on screaming so that people at other gardens turned to see and Lila said, 'Quickly now, PS, or we'll miss the train,' and started to run, pulling him by the hand away from the screaming.

'What's the matter with that lady?'

'Nothing.'

'Then why is she calling out?'

'She's sad.'

'Because they're taking that box away from her?'

'Perhaps. Oh, look at that *funny* dog!'

'What's *in* the box?'

'Just some old things she doesn't want any more like we give to the ragman.'

'Then why is she upset?'

'*Oooh*. I felt a raindrop. Run now.'

The rain came down. Lila's umbrella stuck and wouldn't open.

They ran for the train and got on, drenched.

Lila was still wiping and dabbing at them all as the train rattled across the bridge over the river with the jellyfish, but this time he closed his eyes. He didn't want to look at that sad hotel, all damp and lonely by the river with the darkness coming on.

What was in the *box*? Boxes like that had something to do with that hotel. This he knew without being told. And that sad hotel had something to do with him.

He said to Winnie Grindel, 'You know what?'

'What?'

'Tomorrow morning we're going down to see the piano boat.'

'What's a pianner boat?'

'It's the biggest boat in the world.'

'It is not.'

'It is. It's bigger than your house.'

'You're a fibber.'

'Am not.'

They were sitting in Winnie's pepper tree. She was Tarzan and he was Jane, because he was smaller.

It was funny about Winnie; he didn't like her much and yet he did. She was ugly and freckled and had long stringy hair tied up in rags to try to make it curl and she was bossy. But she knew a lot of things. Like where babies come from. They came, Winnie had told him in a whisper, out of your mother's navel. He had found it unwise to correct Winnie because then she had a habit of twisting his arm and making him say, 'Hell and spit,' but he knew she was wrong about babies. Babies were made at hospitals like bread at the baker's. Dear One had bought him at a hospital (Lila had pointed it out to him once, saying, 'That's The Laurels, where Dear One got you').

Even so, Winnie knew a lot of things. She had shown him a picture of God. God had a black beard and a moustache and his name was Mr Marx. Winnie's father was always saying that if people listened to Mr Marx there would be no depression or the dole. He had asked Lila about Mr Marx and she had laughed and said, 'No, pet. What Winnie means is that Mr Marx is *a* god to some people.' Winnie didn't have to go to Sunday school and she had brought a note to school saying that she didn't have to sing 'Rule Britannia' on Empire Day and salute the flag.

Winnie was looking at him and her small eyes

seemed to have crept closer to each other the way they did when she was afraid he might know something she didn't. She had caught a fat locust and was holding it in her hand, opening her hand every now and then so that the locust wriggled and waved its legs frantically in the air. Just when it thought it could escape, Winnie closed her fist on it.

She said, 'Why is it called a pianner boat?'

He said, 'I don't know. That's what they call it.'

'Why are you going to see it?'

'Because Vanessa's coming on it.'

'Who's Vanessa?'

'My aunt,' he said. 'She's coming all the way from England.'

'Is she a Pommy?'

He wasn't allowed to use that word. Lila always said, 'Don't say Pommy, PS, say Englishman.'

He said, 'No, I think she's Assyrian.'

'What was she doing in England?'

'I don't know,' he said.

'That's where the King is.'

'*I* know.'

Winnie said darkly, 'But they're going to kill him soon.'

'Why?'

'Because he's got dimonds and jewles and rides around all day in a carriage.'

'A *baby* carriage?'

'No, stupid. A gold carriage, and he lives in a palace while the poor people have to sleep in the park and they don't even have bread to eat so they're going to shoot him and give all the dimonds and jewles to the poor people.'

'Who said?'

'It was in the paper.' It was always in the paper, according to Winnie.

She shook her fist in the air to make the locust squawk and making her eyes into narrow little slits she said in an important voice:

'I know a secret.'

'What?'

'What'll you give me for it?'

Greedy Gertie. She was always snatching things from him, eating half his play lunch in exchange for secrets, and most of the time the secrets turned out to be dull things that didn't interest him like 'Lorna Palmer's going to have a baby sister.' She said, 'Gimme your rainbow ball, you haven't sucked much of it.' A rainbow ball cost a penny and if you didn't suck too fast you could make it last more than an hour while it changed colours all the way down to the end.

He said, 'But I haven't got down to the orange bit yet.'

'Come on! I'll give it back when I get to the licorice.'

He knew he was caught, like the locust, so he

handed over the rainbow ball, sticky and fluffy from his pocket.

'What's the secret?'

Winnie sucked on the rainbow ball, wriggled her feet, shook up the locust and kept him waiting.

Then, her mouth full, she said, 'Bor oing umwhere ess a iv.'

'What?'

She took the ball out of her mouth and said, 'You're going somewhere else to live.'

He stared at her and heard a funny buzzing sound in his head, felt a bit shivery as if a cold drop of rain had fallen on him.

'Am not.'

'Yes, you are.'

'Who said?'

'Your aunty told my mum.'

'She did not.'

'She did.'

'Did not.'

'Did. They're comin' in a big car to take you away for good.'

'They are not. Who's they?'

'Whoever they are, they're *awful*. Your aunty *said*.'

'Fibber. Fibber.'

Winnie popped the rainbow ball back in her mouth, pulled a face at him, jumped down from the tree and started kicking up the dry dust of the yard with her bare feet while she chanted in a singsong voice:

'PS is going aw-ay-ay. PS is going aw-ay-ay.'

Seeing a flash of something that looked like blue fire, he flew from the tree, found himself twice as tall with rage and fright, hit Winnie hard in the face with his fist. Right in her silly mouth.

She dropped like a stone in the dust and set up a wail.

'Mumma. PS *hit* me.'

He ran, ran wildly for the hole in the paling fence, scrambled through it, feeling no legs under him, feeling the way it was the minute before being sick, ran across his own yard while close behind, reaching out long arms for him, were Vanessa and Logan; burst into the kitchen to find Lila bending over the sink.

'I'm not going away.'

'PS, what—'

'I'm not. I'm not.'

Flung himself on her, holding tight to her waist, filling up and spilling over into tears and sobs while she gathered him up to her and safe on to her lap.

'What is it? What's the matter?' But her voice sounded as though she already knew.

He gasped it all out. That Winnie said her mum said *you* said someone was coming in a car to take him away to live somewhere else. But he would not go, ever. He would take a gun and kill them if they tried.

He would hide where they would never find him for a million years—

Lila said, her chest going up and down too fast, her heart beating as wildly as his, next to his face, 'Now, nonsense. Nobody said such a thing and Winnie has got it all wrong. She was teasing you,' and Lila gave an imitation of laughing and said, 'Oh, what a silly joke and I'm surprised at a big boy of *six* being such a baby.'

He said angrily, 'Are you trying to escape?'

Lila was shocked, he could tell, that he remembered. One evening, about a year ago, he had wakened up and called to them, called and called until he knew he was in an empty house and they were gone. They had come back and found him screaming. Heavens above, they'd only gone up the street, they said, only a few doors up the street to take some jelly to Miss Gulf's sick sister. He said, 'I thought you escaped,' and Lila said, 'Now, you know George and I would *never* escape.' 'We can't escape, dear old boy,' George said, and kissed him.

Now Lila was rocking him the same as she had that night and she was saying that Winnie was teasing, only teasing. Nobody was coming in a car and it was silly, just as silly as when he'd been scared by the funny man in the circus. 'But you were a baby then. Remember how we told you the funny man was just dressed up and wearing a rubber nose and that really he was just like George and went home in the tram to have his tea with his wife and children, just like us?'

Yes, he remembered but—

'Well, it's just as silly being scared about this, PS.'

'I won't go anywhere with Vanessa,' he said, and Lila was quiet as if she was thinking about this, so he said, 'And I won't go anywhere near that *hotel*.'

'What hotel? What are you *talking* about?'

'You know,' he said, warning her that he would make no end of trouble for them all, scream the world down, fight and spit and kick everything to pieces. Stamp on Dear One's picture, which would be the wickedest thing in the world.

Lila, nestling him, said, 'Now I'm going to tell you about a gorgeous surprise.'

He didn't want it. 'I don't want it.'

'You will when you hear it.'

'No, I won't.'

'All right then, I won't tell you.'

'What is it?'

'Well, you know about holidays.'

'What sort of holidays?'

'Well, for instance, like the holidays you're having now from school . . .'

She was saying it very carefully, thinking out the words. 'Well, now, if you're good, if you're very, very good, you might go for a *little* holiday.'

'With you and George?'

'Noooooo, not exactly. Although we'll take you there and bring you home after.'

'But *where*?'

'Across the harbour.'

'Near here?'

'So near, so very near that you could look out the window and we could look out *our* window and wave to each other and say, "Goodnight, PS. Are you having a nice holiday?"'

'Who'd I be with?'

'Er—Cousin Ettie, and—'

Who's *she*?'

'Goodness, gracious me, Cousin Ettie's the most lovely, laughing, kind lady in the whole world. Oh, and the lovely presents she gives, you just won't believe it. Why, she's so nice, she's *almost* as nice as your Aunt Vanessa.'

'I won't go anywhere with *her*.'

'Now, PS.'

'I'll *kill* her.'

'PS, stop that. Now stop it. Do you want to hurt poor Vanessa's feelings when she's come all this way on the piano boat just to see you and bring you surprises and when she's written such lovely letters saying, "Please, Lila, couldn't I borrow PS just for a *little*—"'

'I don't belong to her.'

'I said *borrow*, PS.'

'I belong to you and George.'

'Yes, of course, and that's why Vanessa had to write and ask us. Like George has to ask Mr Grindel if he can borrow Mr Grindel's lawnmower. Now, did you ever hear the lawnmower cry and say it wouldn't come?'

That was a joke so he laughed a little at it, at the thought of the lawnmower crying, and Lila said:

'Remember once when George and I had to go to Wollongong on the train and you went to stay the night with Vere?'

He nodded into Lila's chest.

'Remember what fun that was? Packing your suitcase with your 'jamas and toothbrush and Mrs Tiggywinkle to read in bed? Well, it will be just like that, only you'll be going to spend the night with Vanessa.'

'But I don't *know* her.'

'But you will, silly. You're going to meet her tomorrow and oh, you are probably going to like her so much that when you go to visit her you won't want to come home.'

Then, smelling the rabbit burning in the oven, Lila jumped up, rushed to the stove and snatching the first thing that came to hand, found she was trying to spoon gravy over the sizzling rabbit with the dish mop. They burst out laughing at this, forgot Vanessa and any trouble there was in the world, roared and held their sides. In fact, Lila laughed so hard that tears were

running down her cheeks and she had to run into her
bedroom and shut the door.

They got up very early. Even though it was midsummer, the sun was not even up when George came
into his bedroom, tickled him and said, 'Come on now,
PS. Rise and shine now, because the piano boat gets in
very early.' He had never before washed and dressed by
the electric light and after George had helped him with
buttons, combed his hair on the wrong side and let him
correct it himself with a jagged parting, when they had
gone into the kitchen it was still barely light outside
and Mrs Grindel's rooster was only then beginning to
crow at the day.

It was even stranger having breakfast with the
kitchen light on and Lila serving them all fried eggs
which none of them wanted. When breakfast was over
and the dishes washed and put away, they still had an
hour to wait before the seven o'clock ferryboat. Of
course Lila had got them up too early. Much too early,
George said, yawning and complaining that she was
always too early for everything and reminding her that
she'd even got to their wedding before *he* had. But Lila
said, well, you never know, the boats don't run as often
on Saturdays and suppose the tram broke down or we
got to the wrong pier? Something would be bound to go
wrong, it always did, and wouldn't it be awful if Vanessa
and Cousin Ettie found no one waiting for them?

Lila wandered around wearing her Sunday hat, finding things to do, dusting and tidying drawers and looking into the linen closet until (with a scream) she remembered that the kitchen clock was slow and of course now they were late and flying around the house locking windows and doors, colliding with each other, remembering they had not gone to the bathroom; rushed out of the house as though it were on fire and then had to run all the way to the tram.

On the ferry, which they had practically to themselves, George read the *Labor Daily* and Lila talked through it to him. She said, 'I can remember when they sailed for England, that Mater couldn't come to see them off because she was already beginning to have the b-l-a-d-d-e-r trouble and Sinden was so late that they were already taking the gangplank away when she came running on to the pier. She'd brought a little farewell gift for Ness; it was a little rose-coloured silk bag to keep bottles of lotion and things in and she was so funny because she was determined the ship mustn't sail without it and Vanessa was calling out, "Post it to me!" and there was a sailor looking out of a porthole and he called out to Sinden that he'd take it and one of the wharf labourers lifted her up so she could reach the sailor's hand. I had to close my eyes, I was sure she'd fall in and be crushed between the ship and the wharf, but she didn't and when she finally managed to reach the sailor's hand, everyone on the pier cheered.'

Lila went on and on. She seemed to be wound up, seemed excited and gay as if they were all going to a picnic. She kept taking out her purse mirror and looking at her face in a surprised way as though she had never seen it before; kept tugging at her hat, pushing pieces of hair this and that way, asking George, 'Am I all right? Is my hat on straight?'

'You are gorgeous,' said George without looking.

She was still talking when the Wooloomooloo tram turned a corner into a street of piers and George said, 'Look, there she is,' and turning their heads they saw the tops of two huge black-and-yellow funnels.

Now it would happen. In a very few minutes he would see Vanessa and he began to feel a little bit sick, felt creepycrawlies in his stomach and the same feeling as when, waking in the pitch dark of night, there are sounds of ghosts.

At the entrance to the wharf he hung back a moment, pretending his shoelace was undone, but Lila tugged him forward, saying, 'Faster, PS,' and they went into the cool shadow of a huge tin shed and out into the sunlight to gaze up at a silent, grey ship which sailors were painting and Lila said, 'That's not *it*.'

George said, 'All right, don't get so excited.'

'But they may get off before we get on.'

They hurried back across the dark shed, he and Lila running ahead almost as if they *wanted* to meet Vanessa, and George said, 'It won't fly away, you know.'

Then, blinking the sunlight away, they stood and looked up at the piano boat, rising up into the sky, black and as tall as the tower on the General Post Office. Every inch of its white railings was crowded with people only as big as dots and some of them were waving to people down on the wharf while others just stared down silently. Green water gushed out of holes in the side of the ship and he asked why. 'Why is all that water coming out, Lila?'

'I don't know, pet. Now look up and see if you can find Vanessa and Cousin Ettie.'

'But I don't *know* them.' Why was she so stupid?

A woman near them jumped up and down and screamed, 'There she is. There's Jean. Coo-ee, Jean.' Another woman held up a baby and one of the dots waved and blew kisses to it. Someone said, 'Would youse mind not standing on my bloody foot?'

They picked their way along the wharf with Lila saying, 'George, don't lose us now,' and suddenly there was his Aunt Agnes wearing her funny pointed hat and carrying a grass fan shaped like a meat axe.

Agnes said, 'Well, PS, I don't often see *you*, do I?' She kissed him. Her face was as perspiry as blancmange and she held some carnations. 'Smell,' she said.

Lila said, 'Have you seen them?'

Agnes said, 'They won't let us on yet.'

'But have you caught sight of them?'

'Ettie was up there just for a minute, a little while ago.'

'Where?' Lila was peering up, working her mouth.

'Up there, next to that woman in the red hat on the lower deck.'

'Seen Ness?'

'No.'

They stood together, hands across their eyes, while the heat, rising, shimmered around them and the big ship seemed to shake in the brightness of so much white paint and glaring sun. Pieces of brass caught fire and dazzled their eyes. They would all be blind before they could see Vanessa.

George said, 'How about this, old chap? Ever see a boat as big as this?'

Agnes said, 'Big boats are nothing new to me. I have sailed on a big boat, PS. I sailed to San Francisco on the *Sierra Leone*.' There was a sharp scream behind them and they all turned to see Vere scrambling through the crowd, pushing people right and left, not caring whom she stepped on. She was wearing a yellow dress of Opal's, a huge green straw hat too big for her, and had a red bag with a silver *K* on it and she came prancing towards them like the Pied Piper and right off did a funny thing—frowning at George and saying, 'Where's PS? Why didn't you bring PS?' so that he giggled and ran to her.

'Vere, I'm here.'

'Is that you? Is that my *child*?' Screams and kisses.

'Vere, not in *front* of everyone.'

'Oh, Lila, don't be such a thw*a*rt. Hello, Agnes. Phew, what a scorcher. Aren't you dying in that wool dress?'

'We are *all* dying in a sense, Vere.'

'Oh, don't start that, dear. It's too early.'

'It is later than we think.'

'*There*'s a nice sailor. Hell*o*.'

'Vere, don't wave. He might think you're serious.'

'Girl, I am.'

Then Vere, dancing ahead of them, pointed and shrieked, 'Look, there's Ettie.'

'Where? Where?'

They pushed forward in a knot, all staring up.

'There by that lifeboat. She's seen us.'

A dot in a big black hat was waving a handkerchief.

'Coo-ee,' they cried, waving back. 'Coo-*ee*, Ettie. Wave to Cousin Ettie, PS. George, lift him up so she can see him. Ettie, this is PS!'

The dot blew kisses.

Lila said, 'Where's Vanessa?'

He thought he could see Vanessa then. A black shadow half hidden behind the lifeboat so that she could spy on him without being seen. Yes, there she was, ugly as sin, gaunt and bony; little beady red eyes staring out from under a witch hat, wisps of hair,

65

snaggle teeth, a broomstick and cackling now, licking her thin lips. 'Aha, wait till I get my claws on *you*!'

But Lila said, 'She's not there. Isn't that *funny*? Wouldn't you think she'd be looking out for us?'

Vere cupped her hands and yelled up, '*Where's Ness*?' and the dot that was Cousin Ettie waved again.

'She can't hear you, Vere.'

But where could Vanessa be, they asked. Why was Ettie up there alone?

He suddenly felt hopeful. Maybe Vanessa had drowned. She had leaned too far over that high railing and fallen into the sea and now he would never have to meet her, never have to go on a holiday with her.

'Vanessa fell off,' he said, but no one heard him because someone had yelled that the gangway was up and they were being pushed and shoved along in a stream of people going up the steps and up on to the deck.

Vere said, 'I feel like a salmon going upstream to breed.' Lila said that she hoped that gangway was safe. He was enclosed now by the crowd, sealed into an envelope of hot people, his nose pressed into the fat lady in front who kept saying, 'Don't shove, sonny,' and packed together, they pushed and were pushed forward, tripping, stumbling and gasping for air, breaking through the bottleneck until suddenly they broke into the open and were going up the gangway in twos, up and up with the dirty water far below, a terrifying dizzy drop down the side of the ship and then over a high brass step on to the deck and he was lifted up by George into the arms of a little, chubby, silver-haired lady in black. A tiny, glittering heart swung from her neck on a golden chain and when she reached out her little hands to him he saw flashes of sparkling lights. She folded him to her. She smelled fresh as early morning and just a little bit of violets.

'I knew your mother,' she said. 'I knew your dear little mother.'

A warm tear dropped on him and so he stepped out of the way of it, looking up at her, and saw that she was giving him that sorry, sad look they all did and which he hated. Her face was pink and all withered up like an apple left too long uneaten but shining with tears which she brushed away with her little hands that glistened and burned in the sunlight from her rings. So many jewels that if Winnie's father heard about it, he would want to shoot Cousin Ettie like they were going to do the King. Cousin Ettie kissed Lila and Vere, then Agnes and George, dabbing at her eyes and laughing now and saying, 'Oh, you poor dears, standing all that time in the hot sun. Oh, you poor mites, you must be so hot and thirsty.'

Everyone talked at once. No, nobody was tired or hot or thirsty. They were all just delighted to see Cousin Ettie looking so well and not a day older. No, they meant it. No, they were not just flattering her.

Had she enjoyed the trip? Had the sea been calm and where on earth was Vanessa?

Now he expected Cousin Ettie to tell them that due to some carelessness, Vanessa had been allowed to fall overboard and that no one had noticed until it was much too late to go back and pick her up. But instead, she said that Ness was in the cabin. 'Seeing to the luggage. You know how particular she is about hatboxes and, my dears, we've brought the earth with us, including most of the furniture.'

'Where, Ettie? Cabin Twenty-six on A deck?' Lila, as usual, was arranging them all, telling George and the others to stay there with Ettie and not to get lost while she took him to find Vanessa; pulled him firmly forward when he held back, asking to see the funnels first (to see anything, anything but Vanessa). They pushed down a stairway against people coming up and then on down endless white iron corridors that smelled of fishy oil and engines, peering into empty cabins while Lila asked the way, saying in her best-manners voice, 'Steward, could you direct us to Cabin Twenty-six?' as up and down they went, hoping never to find it, but knowing the moment was coming nearer every second, and he saw that Lila's face was pale and that she was as shaky as he by the time they finally stopped outside a closed door and knocked.

A low voice said, 'Come in.'

Lila opened the door and they went in. He felt very small and as light as paper.

Someone, bending over suitcases, straightened up and turned towards them, jangling keys. For a moment she was just a thin shadow against the glary porthole, standing in blue smoke from a cigarette.

The low voice said, 'Hello, Lila,' sounding calm and unsurprised as if they had just parted the day before, and Vanessa moved, came forward to kiss Lila lightly on the cheek, then turned slowly and as gracefully as water swirling to look at him and he felt the breath go out of him with surprise and sudden joy, not able to believe, for a minute or so, that this could be Vanessa or even a member of the family. Not like any of them, except for her dark-red hair; not aunt-like at all but tall and beautiful, made out of the best china, so special and delicate that he half expected Lila to cry out, 'Don't touch, darling, she'll break.'

Vanessa? Or were they playing a joke on him and was this someone else, just a stranger they knew slightly? But then he heard Lila say, 'Ness, you haven't changed.'

Vanessa was looking at him with her strange green-coloured eyes that he knew saw right through him, right down to the very bottom of everything he had ever thought about her so wrongly. He wanted to say something. To explain something to her. But what?

So he stood there, lost in the moment of looking and being looked at until Vanessa smiled so that her eyes flicked on suddenly with light and she came forward to him, her soft grey dress moving around her like haze and her hands making little musical sounds of silver bracelets.

Then she said in that low English-sounding voice: 'Are you PS by any chance?'

She did a strange thing. Instead of gushing over him like a baby as they all did, she held out a spotless white-gloved hand as if he were quite grown up. They shook hands politely.

Lila said, 'Give Aunt Vanessa a nice kiss.'

Vanessa said, 'Just "Vanessa" will do. I imagine you have enough aunts already.'

She bent a little closer and lifting his chin with her glove, she kissed him on his mouth. Then she said:

'Well, well, PS. At *last*.'

But before he could say anything, there was a little choking explosion behind them and turning, both at once, they saw that Lila's face was as green as lettuce.

'Ness, where's the bathroom? I'm going to be sick.'

Lila said to herself, almost pleased, that wouldn't you know something would have to go wrong?

To be frightfully sick all over the bathroom floor, stewards having to be called and Vanessa, always unruffled, calmly getting bismuth tablets and eau de cologne, attending to it all in the most matter-of-fact way.

('Something you ate, no doubt.' 'No, no, I'm always like this on a ship.')

She had gone on and on about how she could be sick even on a ship that was in dry dock; all about her nightmare honeymoon trip by sea to Tasmania twenty years ago, while Vanessa had listened with that irritating, pitying smile.

It was simply galling to have been put at a disadvantage at the very moment of meeting; getting the whole thing off to a bad start before they'd even disembarked. Surely this was a bad sign, Lila said to herself; and nodded, knowing that it was.

And now the Carlton Hotel!

She said to Vere in a low voice, 'Why the Carlton?'

They were standing in the frayed elegance of the hotel lobby while a perspiring manager fussed and cooed over Ettie and Vanessa counted bags.

They had driven up from the pier in a hired limousine and when it had pulled up in front of the Carlton, Lila had thought, Oh, *not* the Carlton, *please*. It's too much on an emotional day.

'The Carlton,' she went on, wheezing slightly. 'It's so peculiar.'

Vere said, fussing with beads, 'Why? You know Ettie doesn't like the Metropole or the Australia.'

71

'But don't you think it's *funny*?'

'Why?'

'Vere! The *Carlton*.'

'Oh, for God's sake, Lila, don't be morbid. I often come here for drinks with people. I never think of *that*.'

Lila said, 'Well, I'm not as cold-blooded as you.'

She glanced around the marble lobby with its brocade-and-pink-shaded lamps and sought out the maple-panelled telephone box.

('Sinden, where are you?' 'At the Carlton. I just got married to Logan Marriott.')

'So peculiar,' she said. 'All of us here together again. As though Vanessa did it on purpose. All right for *her*. She was far away in London then.' Lila shook herself, feeling ghosts. 'I don't like being here. This is where everything started to go wrong and now here we all are again.'

Vere said, laughing, 'Why don't you look around and see if you can find "mene, mene" written on something?'

Lila said sharply, 'PS, don't *wander*. Stay with *me*.'

She saw that he was watching Vanessa raptly as she came up with a train of bellboys and said:

'Sorry about this delay, but they don't seem awfully efficient here. *Ghastly* accents. I'd forgotten. Well, *en avant*! We're going up now.'

72

Vere gave a scream. 'Where's my *child*? PS, come here, dearest thing. We're all going up now in a *lift*.'

Vanessa said, 'Vere, pianissimo, please.'

They rose in a sedate lift and entered a large suite.

Vanessa looked around it appraisingly, said, 'Oh, well, it's not the Ritz but I suppose it will do. What do you think, Ettie?'

'Oh, my love. Whatever you say.' Ettie was fumbling for banknotes in her bag and, Lila thought, overtipping shockingly. 'But *do* order something cool to drink. Order some iced champagne for the poor dears.'

'What for PS?'

'Orangeade, Ness.'

'Oh, no,' said Lila, bristling, 'Lemonade.'

Vere said, 'Well, he always has orangeade with *me*.'

'I think—ha ha—that *I* should know what he likes, Vere.'

Vanessa said in her low voice, 'Why don't you both let *him* decide?'

PS, looking up at Vanessa, said, 'Can I have a ginger beer?'

'You *may* have a ginger beer.'

Vanessa gave orders in a tone that clearly said, 'And don't fail me in one iota,' and Lila, watching her, thought, How good she is at all this, but then she always was assured and she's been running a big house in England and used to being obeyed by underpaid and probably non-union servants. She'll find it harder here; no class systems here, thank goodness, and with good people like George working at the Trades Hall for better arbitration. She'll be out of her depth here. Poor Ness. Poor Ness, nothing! Look at her. Just the same. With her swank clothes and la-di-da manners. Must say she looks marvellous though. Doesn't look thirty-six. A few lines here and there and her chin always *was* a little too pointed. Wonder if she dyes her hair. Still that pretty auburn, like Pater's. All the rest of us were carrot. I've got this horrid mole in my eyebrow. Not Ness. Oh, no. *Her* little mole is like a beauty spot. God saw to *her*, all right. Not like any of us. Remote. Always was. Never could get close to her, even when we were girls. And woe betide you if you got on the wrong side of her. Like the time I made the mistake of locking the door to Pater's room—the look in her eyes. Murder. Frightened me to death. But then she's *always* frightened me a bit and I don't know why.

'Feeling better now, Lila?'

'Oh, yes, Ness. Much, much better, thanks. I *am* sorry to have been a nuisance.'

She *seems* friendly. Should I bring it up now? Seize this chance while the others are talking? Now, while she's all sunny smiles, might be a good time to say very calmly and in a most friendly way, 'Why exactly have you come back, Ness? Just what do you have in mind, dear?'

74

Lila smiled and patted the sofa next to her invitingly, but Vanessa had already turned away and was saying that she thought they'd ruined the harbour by putting up that monstrous bridge, just ruined it. Was it an American design? It looked American. 'Not that I have any prejudice against Americans, Agnes. Some that we've met on the Continent have been jolly nice and well behaved.'

Agnes rose to the defence of Seattle and the conversations overlapped, crossed and looped, knitting the divided years together. Knit the year Mater died, purl the year George campaigned for the Labour party in the state election, cast off the year Agnes returned from Seattle, the year Sinden's book was published, purl the summer Vere nearly married Gilbert whatwashisname, knit PS and cast off Ness.

Hats and shoes were off now and they lolled on sofas and little hard gilt chairs and opened their presents. French gloves and Italian scarves for Lila and Agnes. ('Oh, *thank* you, Ness, just what I needed.') A Florentine wallet for George (and not a pound note to put in it, poor love). For Vere, a vain bottle of perfume from Coty in a turquoise bottle (and while only Lila was watching, two hand towels and an ashtray from the Carlton Hotel). For PS, a little French sailor's cap with a red pompon ('Oh, how lovely, pet') and *Winnie-the-Pooh*.

Vanessa sat down by him as he turned the pages.

She said, 'By the way, I hope you *like* books.'

Lila, trying on her gloves and finding them (wouldn't you know) a size too small, said, 'Oh, yes, he loves books, Ness, and he loved the Beatrix Potters you sent him.'

Vanessa said quietly, 'I was asking *him*, Lila.'

She put an arm around him, lightly.

'Never had Pooh and Piglet? Glad I thought of it. Like Peter Pan?'

'Who's Peter Pan?'

'The boy who never grew up. One day you shall go to London and see his statue in Kensington Gardens, but meanwhile I'll get you the book and we'll read it together. Would you like that?'

'Yes.'

Lila said, 'Say yes, *thank* you. Ha ha, we're a bit s-h-y.'

'Well,' said Vanessa to him, 'that makes two of us.'

He smiled downward.

'We have to get to know each other, don't we, PS?'

Nod.

'What kind of games do you like?'

Long pause. 'Make-up games.'

'So do I. Look here, would you care to come and stay with Cousin Ettie and me sometime?'

Nod. Nod. Nod. So eagerly that Lila felt a little spasm of jealousy heat her already overheated face.

Vanessa kissed him lightly on the forehead; got up to admit the waiter, smiling and saying, 'About time. What did you have to do—trample the grapes?'

Her cool, unfamiliar voice rode through Vere's sharp chatter and Ettie's giggling. 'Shall I order luncheon, Ettie? Cold lobster all right for everyone? Some chicken? Do you have any *foie gras*? Chopped *liver*! Is that what one calls it here? Makes it sound so disagreeable. George, would you mind pouring? Well, I know you *don't*, but today's sort of an occasion, isn't it? Will they run you out of the Temperance League if you have one glass of champagne? Well, cheers, everybody.'

Cheers, they all said. Welcome home, Ettie. Welcome home, Ness. But instead of conviviality the champagne brought an ugly constraint to settle on them. They fell back on forced compliments, withdrew behind screens of politeness. Because, Lila decided, being all together again has reminded us that someone is missing.

What a difference if she were here. They wouldn't be just sitting around, meekly allowing Vanessa to rule the roost and show off. Not a bit of it. If Sin came bursting in the door now, why, they'd be roaring at some ridiculous thing she would say and Vanessa's solemn importance would be punctured in five minutes.

Lila sipped her warmish champagne and stared down at the carpet, seeing through the pattern of roses and ferns to another room below them; to the pink-lit room with its frescoes of fat plaster cupids: 'Mrs Marriott's party is in the small annex, madam.' *Mrs* Marriott's party? Was she having to pay for it herself then? But George said, 'Don't ask, Lila, don't spoil today for her. It isn't our business.' *My* sister is not our business?' A pianist thumping out 'Avalon' and the hot little hatbox of a room full of Sinden's strangers multiplied by the tarnished mirrors into a crowd from which she came flying, arms outstretched.

'Lila, you good thing. George!'

Some nonsense of flowers and lace on her hair; the blue silk dress made that morning and the quickly basted hem already coming down at the back. Tiny blue shoes.

Dim faces and introductions to people looking as if they had all dressed at a jumble sale. Vere screeching in the background. A jolting arm spilling beer all over Lila's dress and then (wasn't it then, at the moment when she was concerned only with her dress?) someone detaching himself from the crowd and coming towards them, tall and unhurried.

'Him,' Sinden said.

Well, no wonder.

That smile. No wonder.

Even Lila's resentment faltered at that smile. It could take anyone by surprise. Had taken Sinden.

'Hello, Lila.'

The same amused casualness as Sinden, but with the gift of listening with total absorption, so that his sudden glances said, gratefully, Thank you for your rare intelligence. Said, Be my friend. Then, squashed into a group of strangers at a brass-topped table, they drank cool shandies while Sinden and Logan explained (but explained nothing), seeming to re-discover every few minutes that they were together and married so that they laughed and fell into little silences, letting the rest of the talk rush by them while they gazed transfixed at the miracle; withdrawing from the present moment, they embraced secretly without touching; returned slowly and reluctantly to what was being said around them. Pardon? What? Lila, locked out, felt unmarried by comparison and drab as a mouse in the glare that seemed to come from them. She could hear nothing and could only watch the dumb show of their hands moving, for they were alike in gestures, constantly building structures in the air.

Occasional words filtered through.

'Then my lovely Logan said—'

'So my impulsive girl here said.'

'Oh, but you left out the marvellous part about—'

'But *you* said that.'

'No, wasn't it *you*?'

'We both nearly fell out of the cab when—'

We. We. Marvellous, hilarious us. Something about

lost shoes and going off in a hansom cab to Tom Ugly's Point in the dead of night for oysters.

Even George was laughing, but Lila couldn't get the point and sat mopping at her beer-stained dress until that curious little Pony Wardrop (and hadn't Sinden introduced her as *Miss* Wardrop? Then how could she look so suspiciously pregnant?) stood up and screamed that everyone must drink to the fifth anniversary.

'Of what?' asked Lila, finding her voice.

'Our meeting.'

What, weeks? 'Weeks?' she asked.

It sent them into fits of laughter.

'Days,' the two of them said automatically, and seeing the consternation on her face, put arms around her and drew her towards them, saying, 'Five days that shook the world, Lila,' but as though this were the most natural thing in life, as though any other arrangement would be unthinkably pedestrian, and Lila, marvelling at the identical look of pleased innocence on their faces, thought, They're as alike as two peas.

Against her will, she found that moment by moment she was thawing, melting unwillingly into smiles, so that once when Logan pressed her arm and winked at her, she turned completely liquid, washing over him with assurances that she was glad, so glad for them and sure, absolutely positive that he would look after their little Sin.

He seemed surprised that she felt it necessary to bring this up, merely nodding as though she had made a remark about the weather and the next moment they were all talking about curry. 'Lila's marvellous curry,' Sinden was saying, 'for which I yearn.' Logan too. Already one of the family, Logan was longing for one of Lila's good home-cooked dinners and Lila, all protests gone, said, pink with pleasure, 'I put in a little ginger and sometimes little white seedless grapes.'

But they were already on another tangent, on to this and that subject which led always back to one shining thing: themselves. Only once, rousing herself from the lethargy of being in the presence of this enormous happiness, did Lila voice one question, quickly and aside, under the safety of babbling voices.

'Sin, what about Ernest? Does he know?'

'Oh, yes.'

'Well, I mean—is he terribly wounded?'

'Oh, Lila, Ernest and I *love* each other.'

That was all.

Useless, as Mater used to say, ever to question Sin, senseless to pry, so save your breath to cool your porridge and anyway they were darting up now, tipping over chairs, saying it was time to go, time to go, darling, and thank you, thank you.

'We'll be in touch,' they said.

Kissed everyone in the room twice and together, like children leaving a party, then off down the marble stairs with Vere's arm hooked through Logan's so that Conchita Ewers, that huge vulgar woman, asked in her booming voice, 'Is Vere going *with* them?' Then out into the street, everyone shrieking at once because of course Sinden had forgotten her suitcase, someone running back for it, a wretched suitcase for a bride— with the handle broken, bursting at the seams with all the things she possessed in the world. Now where was Logan? Disappeared. 'Left you already, Sin,' the friends roared, crowding to the curb and throwing confetti over her, standing there with her terrible suitcase and with her hem coming down at the back and while Lila was searching in her handbag for pins, another cheer broke out and looking up, they saw Logan arriving in a decrepit hansom cab and leaning out to help Sinden get in, and Sinden was saying quickly to Lila, 'You see? How could you *not* marry a man like that?' But why a hansom? Why not a sensible taxi? Why, that thing would break down long before they got to wherever they were going. But that's the *joke*, George was saying, and why didn't Lila listen? They'd explained all about it being *their* hansom and how they'd hired it to go to Tom Ugly's Point the night they met. But you never *listen*, George said. So she shut up and watched them wobbling away down Castlereagh Street and holding up all the traffic so that angry motorists leaned out and yelled to 'get that bloody thing off the road!' Disgraceful, really. What on earth would people think? George said, 'He's got a good head on his shoulders. He's going to *be* something.'

Lila said, watching the ancient hansom totter around the corner out of sight, 'Just the same, I'd love to know who paid for that party.'

She was still staring down the street when someone asked her something about her stomach.

'What?'

'I said, is your stomach up to lobster?'

Vanessa was holding out a plate to her.

Oh, yes. 'Oh, thank you, Ness. Dreaming. Sorry. Oh, *lobster*. What a treat for us. What a jolly party. Isn't this a jolly party, PS?'

Everything that Vanessa did, she did slowly. Like lighting her cigarette, drawing in the smoke and holding the match until the little flame almost reached her fingers, then blowing it out in a blue puff. When she laughed, it was slow too. Not like Vere's sudden screeches, but beginning low inside of her and coming up gradually to the top and breaking like soda water bubbles in a silvery way that was pleasing and which brightened her face so that her funny green eyes flicked on and off with light.

She talked slowly too, using wonderful-sounding words that he didn't understand. Things were 'obtuse' and 'oblique', she said, and somebody was 'artificial'. When she sat, it was graceful, one long leg crossing over the other, one foot moving up and down in the air like the end of a cat's tail while all the time she ran her fingers through the strings of bright beads around her neck or touched the big dark-red bun of hair as though to make sure it was still there.

But she seemed to have forgotten all about him, simply talking in her low voice to all the others, over his head and around him so that he made excuses to be near her, to make her look at him, but she took no notice and said nothing to him except once, rather sharply, 'Careful of my *cigarette*! Don't want to burn you.'

She asked them all questions, except him. 'George, what is it exactly that you do at the Trades Hall? Oh, I see. But I don't see how you can have much arbitration when there isn't any employment.' 'Agnes, how's *your* work going? Oh, really? Well, but I'm an unbeliever and anyway I *never* read pamphlets. Oh, *you* wrote it, jolly good! Arresting title, isn't it?' 'But, Vere, how on earth do you *survive*?'

They all seemed to want to please her, especially Lila, who laughed at everything Vanessa said, whether it was funny or not, but with the laugh she used only when she wasn't amused at all really and which always ended in her saying, 'Well I *never*.' Once Vanessa said, 'But, Lila, I'm *serious* about that,' and Lila said quickly, 'Oh, goodness, I *know* you are, Ness. Heavens, I didn't mean it *that* way.'

Then suddenly Vere screamed that, my *God*, it was after four o'clock and she had to meet a beastly man for drinks at Usher's. Oh, hell, it was a thw*a*rt, my dear, but a free *meal*. They all got up and found coats and hats and he heard Lila say:

'But, Ness, when are we going to talk?'

Vanessa said, watching the flame on her match, 'Oh, I don't know. There's no hurry and we're going to be jolly busy looking for a house.'

'Do you have our phone number?'

'Aren't you in the book? Yes; well, I'll ring up then. Goodbye, Lila. Goodbye, George. Nice to see you looking so jolly fit. *Au 'voir*, Vere, and pianissimo going *out*, please. Cheerio, Agnes.' Cousin Ettie leaned down and kissed him wetly and they all moved in a bundle to the door, still talking while Vanessa leaned on the door, nodding to them and looking now as if she was bored, very bored with the whole thing, glad they were going.

But wasn't she going to say *one* thing to him?

Halfway out the door with Lila pulling him ahead, he stopped and held out his hand politely so that Vanessa looked down, trying to remember who he was.

'Oh, goodbye—PS,' Vanessa said.

She shook his hand.

'Ta-ta,' he said, and the door closed behind them and as they were going down the hall to the lift, Lila said to George:

'Not a *men*tion. Not even a hint. Isn't she *strange*?'

He said, looking up to Lila, tugging at her to get her attention:

'Vanessa didn't say when I could go to stay.'

'She *will*,' Lila said, and shut her mouth in a hard line.

Vanessa closed the door and said, 'Thank God *that*'s over!'

She crossed the room and seeing that Ettie was sitting down and was ready for a nice gossip about them all, went deliberately past her and into the bedroom.

She took off her shoes and lay down on the bed. In a minute she heard Ettie's telltale little humming, just loud enough to let it be known that she was unconcerned and would wait for an opinion on things.

Tum-tee-tum-tee-tum. The humming went on, accompanied by creaks to and fro across the floor and the sounds of tissue paper. Take your time, this meant.

But Ettie was rudderless without another's opinion to guide her, and impatient now to be set on a course, wound up and set off in the right direction, and Vanessa heard the humming grow a little desperate, the creaks grow nearer until there she was, dangling uncertainly in the doorway, her diamond heart glittering and her baby hands making little useless movements in the air; smiling like a sheep.

'Are you lying down, dear?'

'No, I'm attached to the chandelier by a cord.'

'Oh, Ness—are you tired? Upset?'

Vanessa threw one arm across her eyes to blot out Ettie, sighed and let her wait.

'Ness?'

'What?'

'They're dears, aren't they?' Waiting to find out if they were.

So Vanessa removed the arm for a moment, waited and said:

'Ettie, do you see now? Do you *finally* see now how important it was for me to come back to that child?'

'Yes, Ness.'

'I'm glad you do, dear.'

She got off the bed and went to the dressing table. Pulling hairpins out, she let down her hair and sat at the mirror, starting to brush with long, hard strokes. She saw Ettie's reflection behind her, waiting patiently, and stopped brushing and said what was in her mind.

'He's like Logan.'

After two weeks of silence, Lila went to the phone in order to get relief from her asthma.

'Carlton Hotel.'

'Mrs Bult, please.'

'Bult? Hold on.' Clicks and then a nervous child's voice. 'Yes?'

'Ettie? It's Lila.'

'Ahhh, you *dear*. Ah, how sweet of you to ring up in all this heat. How are you, dear?'

'We're all right.'

'How's the dear little lamb?'

'He's fine. Is Vanessa there?'

'Yes, dear. Just one moment, dear. Ness? Ness? Are you out of the bath? It's Lila on the telephone. Can you come?'

Mumblings, whispers. Then the low, disciplined voice.

'Hello there.'

'Ness?'

'Yes. How are you keeping alive in this heat? Is January always so rugged? I'd forgotten.'

'It's been worse, I think. This summer. So few busters.'

'So few what?'

'Busters. Southerly busters, you remember. The nice cool wind that comes in the evenings—'

'Oh, yes. Southerly buster. Sounds like a cocktail.'

'It's so funny because last summer we had one almost every hot night and this year I simply can't remember when we had the last. Good one, I mean. Just before Christmas—'

'Look, I haven't *terribly* long, Lila.'

'Oh, yes, yes; well, Ness, I was wondering, well, I thought I'd have heard from you by now. I thought for sure you would have rung me by now and I said to George last night—'

'Yes, I'm sorry, Lila. But you see—Just a minute; trying to light a cigarette with one hand. There. Well, you see, we've been house hunting like mad, couldn't find a thing we'd even *consider* and I must *say*, Australian *incompetence*! Well, I don't want to be chauvinistic but at *home*, I mean in England, agents are co-operative, if you know what I mean. Lila, this dreadful *lackadaisical* attitude here drives me mad! However, I think we've found one at last. A nice large house in Point Piper. We can get it on a long lease because the people are going to England for two years, lucky dogs. Hel*lo*?'

'Yes.'

'Oh, thought we'd been cut off, you were so long interrupting me.'

'Ness, I was wondering—it's not too long now before PS has to go back to school and—'

'What do you mean, school?'

'Well, kindergarten, really. He doesn't start *real* school till next year.'

'I see.'

'Ness, don't we have things to *talk* about?'

'We can talk without the child.'

'But don't you want to *see* him?'

'Oh, yes. Give him my love.'

'When can you come? Or shall I come to the hotel?'

'Oh, no, I'd like to come and see your house.'

'Tomorrow?'

'Tomorrow? Well, just a minute till I get my book. Ettie, would you hand me my little red book. No, not that one, the little red morocco—that's the one. Sorry, Lila. Now let's see . . . Oh, no, tomorrow I can't. Have to sign the lease.'

'Thursday?'

'Thursday seems all right. We've got something in the evening, some old friends of Ettie's, but I think Thursday during the day would be convenient.'

'Thursday then. Come to dinner.'

'No, I said *during* the *day*. I'd have to be back here by five.'

'Ha ha. We call the midday meal dinner.'

'Do you? What do you call dinner then?'

'Tea.'

'Tea! How confusing. Tea in London means four thirty and it's *always* dinner at night unless it's Sunday, when it's supper. One *dines* midweek. One *sups* on Sundays. I shall come to you for *luncheon*.'

'Lunch, yes. Now let me tell you how you get to us. You take the Neutral Bay ferry from Circular Quay and then the tram to—'

'Oh, I couldn't cope with ferries and things, Lila. I'll take a car.

'Oh. That'll be quite expensive all the way from town, but—'

'Lila, do you have a cold or something?'

'No, no, just a touch of my asthma.'

'Oh, do you *still* get that?'

'Not very often.'

'Poor thing. Agony. I remember.'

Vanessa, before dressing for dinner that evening, unlocked her black attaché case and drew out a folder of letters, searching to find the one she wanted.

'The Laurels (I call it Bedrock), Oct. 25th, '27. Ness, you love. The dear baby smock and bonnet from Harrods came yesterday and lifted me from a blue mood. Even PS seemed to be pleased, as he kicked hard! I didn't like opening the box, it seemed so neat, like you. But *where are my children*? PS seems excited at the idea of living at *all* but keeps well out of sight. They have given me so much oil that my babe will slide into this vale of tears on his little bottom. I get low at times, wondering what will become of the three of us. Ness, if Logan strikes gold (he says he will daily), we shall all come from the colonies to throw ourselves upon you and Ettie in that gigantic house you describe, SO BEWARE. I yearn sometimes for your profound sense of ORGANISATION. Ness, you could run the Tower of Babel. One day when I'm rich, I shall pluck you from Ettie and you shall run my house and *discipline* my outrageous brats while I'm writing the Great Australian Novel. I've always said, "I'll *have* the children and

Ness will *manage* them." My book is selling like very cold cakes and the till is low but I try not to worry or attract trouble if it's not actually knocking at the door. Lila is the only one allowed to do that, as she OWNS the door! I will cable you the Glad News the moment they wheel me out of the delivery room. Logan, my five-minute husband, is up north and DYING that he can't get down to me because his foreman *had* to go and have an accident, so he is in charge. I *wish*' (something crossed out here) 'PS just kicked to say "hello" to his favourite aunt and Cousin Ettie in faraway London. Your Sinden.'

Lila and Vanessa sat on the back veranda in the shade, dulled by the heat and a heavy lunch of Lila's special cottage pie and a green gooseberry tart with custard.

Above them in the white haze of sky, the rainbirds cried and mourned.

Lila said, 'Hear the rainbirds?'

Vanessa said, 'Yes, I hate them. Mournful things.'

'So do I. They've always seemed to me to be—an omen of something.'

'Rain.'

'Well, rain, yes, but—Sinden used to say they were the town criers of the damned. She was always very superstitious of them.'

Lila leaned forward and tapped Vanessa's knee.

'On that last day at The Laurels, she heard them cry outside the window.'

Lila felt that she had brought the point up rather neatly.

But Vanessa was staring into the distance as though she had detected something incorrect about the horizon.

Lila went on, 'All through the pains she heard the rainbirds, poor little darling. She said to me, "Lila, will you tell those damned birds that I'm not holding a *wake*, I'm having a *baby*!" I said, "Darling, it only means later on we'll have a lovely cool rain." She said, "If Logan were only here, I wouldn't care if they perched on the end of the bed and sang 'Waltzing Matilda.' " Then they took her away and, Ness, everything was all right. The baby came at seven o'clock and the doctor told us everything was fine, he said the boy was fine and she was resting comfortably and no need for us to stay any longer that night. I remember we sent a cable to you and one to Agnes on the way home. Well, later a tremendous thunderstorm broke and I thought of the rainbirds and, Ness—I knew, I don't know how but I just *knew* something had gone wrong. I said to George, "I've just got to ring the hospital." We didn't have the phone on then and, my dear, I was just going up the street to Miss Gulf's house to ask if I could use her telephone and there *she* was running to meet me with a message from the hospital for us to come at once.

When we got there the doctor said, "Mrs Marriott is dying." She didn't know us, Ness. She held on to my hand and kept saying, "Where is he?" and I didn't know if she meant the baby or Logan so I said, "He's coming, dearest," but she slipped away—just slipped away.'

Lila got up and poured tea.

'More tea, Ness?'

'No, thank you.'

Lila sat down, stirring her tea.

She said, 'You know, don't you, that he never came back for the funeral. He's never even been to see the Little Garden.'

'What little garden?'

'The grave. We call it Dear One's Little Garden.'

Vanessa crossed her legs, regarded her shoes for a minute.

She said, 'I don't think *she* would have liked *that* very much.'

Lila said, 'We think it's nicer for PS. To make it a glad place with pretty flowers and not a sorrowful thing. He doesn't really understand, you see.'

'No, of course not. And he never knew her, so why should it be sorrowful for him in any case?' Vanessa laughed suddenly. 'Really, Lila. "Dear One's Little Garden." It sounds like something out of Ella Wheeler Wilcox. Besides, if you don't mind my saying so, I think it's wrong to feed him all this Mary Pickford fantasy about his mother.'

94

Lila, corrected, pursed her mouth. Annoyance lent her courage. 'Vanessa,' she said in her formal voice, used only for weddings, funerals and the Lord's Prayer. 'Vanessa, I was very surprised at your letter and so was George.'

Vanessa looked directly at her and the green eyes seemed to flicker with the dim amusement of someone dealing with an obstreperous child. Lila, seeing herself reflected clearly in Vanessa's pupils, thought:

No, you aren't going to bamboozle *me* with your big innocent eyes, my dear, and we're going to have this out *now*!

She drew up her chair, declaring the meeting open, and said, 'Furthermore, I'm shocked that Ernest Huxley, Sinden's greatest friend, should let her down.'

'Let her *down*?'

'Yes, I think it's trampling on her memory to pass his guardianship over to you. It was Sinden's wish that Ernest and I should be co-guardians but that the child should live with George and me. And I don't think the arrangement should have been interfered with by you or anyone.'

Vanessa sighed, looked at her nails, and Lila said, 'It took a great deal of trouble and correspondence to draw up the dead of guardianship so that it would be exactly what Sin would have wanted, and Ernest *agreed*.'

There was a short pause while both of them

95

listened to squawking locusts and then Vanessa said, 'Would you hand me my bag?'

Lila reached for the black crocodile bag and said, 'Now if Ernest had no intention of sticking to a bargain he should not have agreed to it in the first place—'

'Just *one* moment, Lila.'

Vanessa reached into the bag and drawing out a letter, scanned it while Lila waited. Then, with startling suddenness, she thrust the letter into Lila's hands with a dazzling smile.

'What's this?'

Ernest's aristocratic handwriting:

'My dear Vanessa. You have asked me to put my feelings into writing and that is, I find, difficult to do. Many of them are untranslatable even to myself. However, since talking to you last night and learning of your proposed return to Australia, I am more than ever convinced that you are the only right and proper person to take over my part of the guardianship and also to relieve Lila and George of some of the burden they have been carrying alone for six years. You have the means to do a lot of good for the little boy whereas I can do nothing. The arrangement was totally unworkable from the beginning as Sinden knew of my plans to settle permanently in the United States. I should never have agreed to be one of the guardians but her letter to me came a month after the news of her death and therefore was a posthumous appeal to me. How could I refuse her? However, my consent was based upon certain emotions I felt at that time. Now it is the future that matters. If Logan Marriott can be located in Australia, then I think that a deed of disposal of my guardianship to you should be drawn up without delay, if possible while I am still here in London. I leave it to your superior and more eclectic knowledge of the situation to persuade Mr Marriott and also Lila that this rearrangement would be beneficial to all concerned and especially to the child. My kind regards to Ettie Bult and, as always, I remain yours most sincerely, Ernest.'

Lila, looking up from the letter, saw Ernest momentarily smoking his pipe under the pear tree and Sinden, in khaki shorts and a man's shirt, climbing through the hole in Mrs Grindel's fence and running through the shimmering heat, shouting to him and being lifted up like a child, laughing and protesting as he carried her towards the house and vanishing as Vanessa said:

'I think it's a very honest letter.'

'Dry as dust,' Lila said. 'Just like Ernest. He doesn't even say how he felt about Sinden or even if he'd forgiven her.'

'I think that's implicit in the letter.'

'Do you!'

'Would you have preferred that it were written in verse?'

'Sinden worshipped Ernest.'

'Yes,' said Vanessa. 'She probably did.'

97

'She loved him. She loved everybody.'

'Yes, that was her trouble.'

Lila said, going up an octave, 'There'll never be anyone like her again.'

'Actually, Lila, there are millions of people just like her and just as emotionally untidy.'

'I must ask you not to speak of her that way in my house.'

'Lila, you're *wheezing* again. Be calm now. I adored her too. You know that. But you must also admit she led a wildly impractical life hunting for bluebirds and impossibilities.'

'Well, and she achieved something too and all on her *own*. She became a famous writer, didn't she?'

'Well known, I think, would be more accurate, but I'm not talking about that. I'm talking about how she *had* to get close to people and snuggle up.'

Yes, thought Lila, that's true, but I'm not going to agree with *you* about it.

'In a curious way,' Vanessa went on, lighting a cigarette and watching the match burn down to her fingers, 'Sinden never considered what other people were thinking. The fact that she loved them was enough for her. She didn't want to be aware of their shortcomings so she put on blinders and led a very happy and inaccurate life. Ettie does the same thing. She never looks at faces and so everyone is a "dear". Everyone has to have *their* method of getting through life, Lila.

Vere *borrows* her life from other people. Agnes can't stand hers so she's decided to put an end to *everyone's* with the help of God and Dr Whateverhisnameis. Sinden simply put her own emotions into other people and convinced herself that that was how *they* felt.'

'Have you finished?'

'Yes.'

'Thank you.'

'Is that a waratah bush over there?'

'Yes, but it hasn't produced any waratahs for a long while.'

'Probably something in the soil.'

'We brought it from the old house; I don't think it liked being transplanted.'

'Lila, let me ask you this. Why do you think Sinden wrote and asked Ernest to be a guardian?'

'Well, because, for one thing, she had great ideas about having a book published in America and—'

'Aha.'

'Wait, let me finish, please. You see, she already had it plotted out and she had an idea of going to New York and taking PS.'

Vanessa pinned Lila with a look.

'Was she going to leave Logan?'

'Oh, no, but I think she'd already realised that she'd always have to be the breadwinner. I never knew really what was going on in her mind those last weeks. Except America. That was in her mind a lot. She had me buy a map and pin it on the wall by her bed and she made out routes. She wanted to go to a place in Arizona—Gravestone? No, Tombstone. She liked the sound of it, she said. She said, "I'll hitch my way to Tombstone with PS on my back like a papoose." I felt at the time it was a terrible sort of omen. That name, Tombstone . . .'

'Lila, don't wander.'

'You asked me something, Ness, and I'm telling you.' This time she let Vanessa wait, dangling, then went on. 'Anyway, she wanted to get to New York, where of course Ernest would be able to help her sell her book and—Why is that funny?'

'I'm laughing because it's so typical of her.'

'I don't see that at all.'

'To expect Ernest to turn the other cheek and open doors to her in New York.'

'He's *in* the publishing business.'

'Certainly.'

'And he did all that work on *Marmon*, pushing it with his publisher and—'

'What has it all got to do with PS?'

'Well, *I* personally think she found out about the BD.'

'What's that?'

'The Bright's Disease.'

'You don't have to whisper, there's no one around.'

'I think at the end she *knew* she'd never get to America, poor little pet, but if she couldn't, then perhaps PS would, when he was older, and in the meantime Ernest would act with me in an advisory capacity.'

'Now you've got to admit that that is all nonsense and as foolish as anything she ever did in her life. Even Sinden couldn't be so mad as to think that Ernest would want to look after Logan Marriott's child.'

Lila said, 'Just the same, it's what she *wanted*.'

'Her blinders again.'

'It's what she wanted, Vanessa, and we had to do what she wanted.'

'What did Logan think of this ridiculous arrangement?'

'Oh, *Logan*!' Lila lifted her hands, warding off visions. 'Logan came to Sydney for one day—*one* day. He came with George and me to Sam Hamilton's office and said, "What do I sign?" He didn't even read it through. The whole thing took ten minutes and he was gone to catch a train. All we've had from him for two years was a postcard saying "Good luck". How did you ever find him anyway?'

'Wrote to his sister in Bacchus Marsh.'

'Oh, *Alice*,' said Lila. 'Well, I'm surprised she didn't write and tell me that you'd been trying to get in touch with Logan.'

'Is she in the habit of writing to you?'

'No, but it's peculiar. But then I've always thought the Marriotts were a very peculiar family. Even though they do live in another state, they've never shown the slightest interest in PS.'

'Let's be grateful for small favours,' said Vanessa.

'And do you mean that Logan simply signed the papers you sent?'

'Yes, and returned them with insufficient postage.'

They both laughed at this, laughed in unison, saying, 'My dear', and 'Typical', until Lila, catching herself in a truce, said sternly:

'It was very wrong of him to agree right off without even consulting me.'

'Perhaps,' said Vanessa, smiling, 'he was in a hurry to catch a train.'

A rubber ball hit the wicker table, upsetting a cup, and they both turned to see a barefoot PS darting through the paspalum grass, pursued by a very grubby Winnie Grindel, wearing only underpants.

'PS!' Lila rose in the role of guardian. 'PS, you nearly hit Aunt Vanessa. Come here and say you're sorry. Now don't do that, pet. Don't roll in the grass. Winnie, don't do that. Don't twist his arm, he's smaller than you.'

'He pulled my hair.'

'She's a fibber.'

'Now, children.' Lila clapped her hands. 'That's enough. Where are your panamas? You know better than to run around in this sun without your hats.'

They came towards the veranda, kicking up storms of dust and giggling.

'Now who wants a piece of cake? Don't grab! Winnie, this is Miss Scott.'

'How'd you do, Winnie.'

'Fine.'

Lila cut and handed them each a piece of fruit-cake.

'What do you say?'

'Ta,' said Winnie.

'Ta,' said PS.

Vanessa said quietly, 'Not "ta". "Thank you".'

A gate slammed and Mrs Grindel materialised around the side of the house in her watermelon dress and bearing scones.

'Hello, love. Thought you might like some scones.'

'Oh, thank you.' Lila gritted her teeth, seeing Vanessa's sharp recoil from Mrs Grindel's outstretched hand, covered in flour.

'This is my sister, Miss Scott.'

'Pleased to meet you, dear.'

'How'd you do.'

'Hot enough for you?'

'Yes, I'm a little unused to it.'

'I'll bet. Cold in the old country, isn't it?'

'We do *have* summers.'

'That so?'

'But it was midwinter when we left.'

'They have winter while we have summer,' Lila explained.

'Tch, tch!' Mrs Grindel was laughing at the whims of foreigners, trying to close the safety pin in her brassiere. 'Well, I suppose you get used to it, but give me a nice hot Christmas so you can take the kiddies to the beach. Well, are you glad to be home?'

Vanessa said that she supposed so and became absorbed in her shoes.

'Oh, there's no place like home, is there?'

'Well . . .' Vanessa shrugged politely, smoothed her flawless skirt.

'I've never been out of my state,' said Mrs Grindel, 'and I'm proud of it.'

Lila said quickly, 'I'll make some fresh tea.'

Vanessa glanced at her watch and Lila thought, She mustn't go yet, we've talked about nothing. I've got to have some hint of what's up her sleeve or I'll never sleep tonight. 'Ness, have one of Mrs Grindel's nice homemade scones?'

'Just out of the oven, love.'

'No, thanks. We've just had tea.'

'This early?'

'Vanessa means *afternoon* tea, Mrs Grindel.'

'Oh. Your sister used to love my scones, didn't she, Mrs Baines?'

'Oh, yes. Well, I *think*—'

'Dear One, I mean. When she was stopping here with Mr and Mrs Baines, every time I seen her in the backyard I'd sing out, "The scones are on, little mother." She loved me calling her that. She'd hop over the fence like a kangaroo, even in her condition, and come and sit in my kitchen and gab away by the hour. Make you laugh, cheer you up no matter how blue she was feeling herself. Oh, there never was no one like her, was there? She was a real larrikin.'

'A what?'

'Tomboy,' Lila translated. 'Take a piece of cake *home* with you, Mrs Grindel.'

'Ta. If it'll save you throwing it out.' Mrs Grindel stuffed cake into her mouth, said indistinctly, 'Oh, we knew Dear One, Miss Scott. Every morning I'd hear her going hell for leather on that typewriter. Then in the arvo she'd sit out here and make hats, didn't she, love? Oh, she loved making hats. Give her any old bit of stuff and she'd make a hat out of it. Everybody loved her. Didn't they? The whole street went into mourning when she went over. You shoulda seen the big mob that turned out for the funeral. Have you been up to see the Little Garden yet?'

'No, I haven't been to the *grave*.'

'Yes, well, you know *we* call it—'

'Yes, yes, she knows,' Lila said. And thought, Oh, go, just go!

'Oh, it's lovely. They got a lovely cross. My hubby knows someone in the business and got them a nice reduction. I woulda liked an angel but Mrs Baines reckoned a cross would be nicer and last longer and you want something that'll last on a grave. I said you get something nice for *her* because she was a *saint*. That's why God took her so young. Shut up, you bastards.' Mrs Grindel addressed the last remark to the rain-birds and smiled at Vanessa. 'Excuse my French, dear.' She poked Vanessa on the knee with a fat red sausage of a finger.

'Whaddyer think of *him*?' She winked an eye towards PS. 'How's he for a bottle baby? Big for six, isn't he?'

Vanessa looked just to the left of Mrs Grindel, into nothing.

'I'll tell you one thing, Miss Scott. He's got a wonderful home here and a bosker mum and dad to boot; he's been treated like he was their own. In fact he started to call them Mumma and Dadda until Mrs Baines says, "No, love. Dear One's your mum but she's away in heaven and your dad's away too." But Mr Baines has been a dad to him; he'd take the food out of his own mouth if he had to and give it to the kiddie—'

Vanessa's eyes had begun to flick and Lila said, 'Oh, look over there. Rain's coming. The birds were right.'

Vanessa stood up and said, 'I must think about running along.'

Mrs Grindel said, 'Come on, Winnie. PS can come over and play with you after tea.' Heaved herself up. 'That your car outside, Miss Scott? When I seen it coming up the street, I sang out to Mrs Andrews next door, "Look; Mrs Baines must be havin' dinner with an undertaker," I says, "or else she's havin' a bit of hanky-panky with the Duke o' York behind George's back." Oh, well, if you didn't have a bit of a laugh now and then you might as well cut your bloody throat, eh? Pleased to have met you. Ta-ta.'

'Goodbye.'

Lila followed Vanessa into the house.

'I'm sorry, Ness. Nuisance her coming in like that. Well, I mean, they're just ordinary working people but she *was* kind to Sin.'

'Uhuh.'

'And the little girl brings him home from school to save me going—'

'I see.'

PS had wandered into the bedroom behind them. He sat down on the double bed and watched Vanessa while she put on lipstick.

Lila said, 'When are we going to talk again?'

'After Ettie and I get settled in the house.'

'When will that be?'

'I expect by the end of the month.'

'Ness, I'd like to have *some* idea of what you have in mind.'

'Well, I hadn't really thought, to be honest.'

'You must have *some* idea.'

'I'll be in touch with you.'

'Vanessa, George and I would like to know *now* just *how* you propose we're to share the—arrangement. School starts a week from Tuesday.'

Vanessa turned from the mirror, putting on her hat, and said quietly:

'PS, would you go out of the room for a moment?'

'Why?'

'Because I'm asking you to, very nicely.'

'We're talking about the lovely *surprise*, pet.'

He got up, resentfully, unused to being asked to leave rooms, trailed out and hung about in the hall until Vanessa crossed the room and closed the door.

Lila said quickly, 'Oh, don't. We never close a door on him. He got frightened once and thought he'd been abandoned and ever since then—'

'It's only for a moment, Lila. Don't baby him.'

And, thought Lila, don't give me orders in my own house, you and your Pommy accent and looking down your nose at us and snubbing the neighbours.

She took a step to the door but Vanessa blocked the way and suddenly Lila felt that she was back in the dark, stuffy hall in Waverly. ('Give me the *key*, Lila!')

108

Vanessa said, 'I don't know why on earth you should treat all this so dramatically. I haven't come back to change anything. He's still going to live with you and George. I wouldn't dream of changing the rhythm of that. But I think that at first—until we see how things go—he might come to me, let's say every second weekend and part of the school holidays if that's agreeable to you and George.'

'Yes,' said Lila. 'That would be agreeable.'

'And I hope you wouldn't be offended if I want to help out a little financially.'

'Oh, George and I wouldn't *think* of taking money from Cousin Ettie.'

The wrong thing to say, for Vanessa's mouth tightened.

'I have my own allowance, Lila, and also I have income from stock that Ettie settled on me years ago, so I'm not hard up and I can't imagine why you'd want to be priggish and deny me the right to buy some of his clothes occasionally. I'm certain Sinden wouldn't have denied me.'

'No.' Lila felt squashed, felt the room growing smaller and shabbier by the minute.

'Well, then,' said Vanessa in her low voice, gently chiding the housemaid, 'I don't know what you're worrying about. I'm not out to usurp your authority. But it's quite evident that you and George have had a struggle to maintain PS alone, without a sou from Logan, which of course is disgraceful of him.'

Lila said, 'Well, George has a good job now with the unions and we're not exactly on the dole, Vanessa. Of course the house is small and so on, but the landlord's promised to paint—'

'Lila, don't apologise.'

The door opened and George, home from work, said, 'What's going on? Why is he shut out in the hall?'

PS's insulted face peered at them around George's leg.

'We were talking,' said Vanessa, and picked up her red silk umbrella, tightly rolled, never to be unrolled even in rain.

'We don't ever shut him out,' said George and, 'It's all right, old chap,' to PS.

'Just going,' said Vanessa, and passing George, touched him lightly on the arm. 'How are you, George? Lila gave me a jolly nice luncheon. Thank you so much for waiting, PS.' A pat on his head and an imitation kiss on Lila's cheek. 'Cheerio, Lila, and don't be a worrier.'

The three of them watched her go down the little path and, leaving the gate open, she allowed the chauffeur to help her into the car. A wave from a white glove and she was gone.

'Pomp and circumstance,' said George, closing the gate.

'She didn't *take* me,' said PS, sounding offended.

Lila said, 'She will, darling.' And not just for a weekend either! For all time, if she can possibly get her way, which so help me God, she won't, so help me God!

She said aloud, 'Crumpets for tea.'

As they pushed open the iron gate and stood in a circular red-gravel driveway, looking up at the house, Lila thought that in an extraordinary way it looked like Vanessa. It had her look! Remote and withdrawn, it sat on a rise of ground, admiring itself, rearing up with sharp tiled roofs and tall chimneys, in dark-red brick; the windows, hooded by canvas blinds, expressing nothing but mild surprise at the gall of this woman and child daring to come up the drive; defying them to come a step farther. So they went on bravely up the path, looking at the wide lawns and the shivering yellow poplar trees in silence.

A house in which everyone had died suddenly and quietly by gas. So quiet that as they stood uncertainly on the stone porch outside the half-open front door, the steady tick of a grandfather clock could be heard in the dark hall beyond. Lila rang the bell and they waited, she, smiling falsely at him, keeping up the desperate pretence of this 'treat' and he, smiling up at her, nervous but pleased at this outrageous adventure.

Then, nothing happening, Lila began to worry that perhaps the bell was out of order and what should they do? Blunder into the house? Would that start things off badly and annoy Ness? Or would their waiting outside to be found distress her even more? What was the protocol? They were so used to banging through kitchen doors shouting, 'Coo-ee. Anyone home? Here we are.'

She rang again, her mouth working nervously now and the prepared feeling of calm deserting her, thickening her legs, turning her hands to wriggling crabs that fumbled with her bag, nearly let go his little suitcase.

At last footsteps sounded far away in the depths of the house and quickened until a breathless, red-faced girl appeared on very large feet, wearing her white cap a little askew on rat-coloured hair.

PS put out his hand politely, but Lila laughed and said, 'No, pet. She's the maid,' and smiled at the red-faced girl to apologise for imposing this undemocratic formality.

'I'm Mrs Baines,' said Lila, adding unnecessarily, 'I've brought my nephew.'

'Yes; good-oh,' the girl said in a heavy Australian accent, and led them inside. She seemed to be as inexperienced at the whole procedure as they; clumsily took Lila's umbrella and PS's suitcase, smiling and revealing artificial teeth embedded in bright pink gutta-percha. She tiptoed across the wide parquet hall to the foot of a staircase and, clearing her throat, called:

112

'Miss*cot*. Visitors!'

They heard a door open upstairs, the sound of quick high heels, and then Vanessa was coming downstairs, fastening her beige silk dress with a dazzling clip, no more dazzling than the smile which preceded her down the stairs, beamed at them from the landing, lighting up the dim hall.

'Hello, hello, hello! Welcome. Aren't you a bit early or am I late? Never mind.' Creak, creak. Now at the bottom and her tan-and-white shoes flashing across rugs, straightening them as she came, so that even her walk created a function.

'Diana, put the umbrella in the rack for which it was created and take Master Marriott's suitcase up to his room. Tell Mrs Bult that Mrs Baines is here.'

'Yes; good-oh.'

'Yes, Miss *Scott*.'

'Yes, Miss*cot*.'

Diana flew upstairs and Vanessa led the way into the drawing room, saying:

'I don't know how long *she's* going to last. She's bristling with inefficiency and can you imagine naming a lump of a girl like that "Diana"? "'Di' for short," she says, but *that* makes me shudder. I'm used to maids having proper, sensible-shoe names like Annie or Maude. But she's eager, poor thing. Well, here we are. Things are still in rather a mess. We had to wait until they got *their* furniture out (awful, by the way) before we could get *ours* in.'

Lila said, 'Oh, it's *lovely*, Ness.'

'Yes, I *like* a huge drawing room. I crave space and I rather like what they've done with those vines outside; keeps the room so cool in summer.'

Thick wisteria vines clung to the columned side porch and gave the drawing room an eerie, marine light which touched the walls and ceiling with a greenish tinge and, moving in the breeze, created rippling pools of shadows where light and shade moved like seaweed over the carpet, glimmering and darkening so that the room could have been underwater and they divers, exploring a sunken liner.

'But won't it be very dark in winter?' asked Lila.

'Ah, but in winter the nicest time of the day is shutting it out. In London we always drew the blinds at four o'clock and turned on the lamps in time for tea.'

As she spoke, Vanessa turned towards the high fireplace and touched a switch. Light sprang on beneath a gilt frame and Sinden looked suddenly down at them.

'Well, goodness me. It's the portrait that Walter Hatfield did of her.'

'But it was lost. Even Walter didn't know what had become of it. How did you find it, Ness?'

'Ernest had it.'

'All this time?'

'Yes, he gave it to me in London and I had it framed.'

'Mmmm. She never liked it. Something about the mouth is wrong.'

'*I* don't think so.'

'She said it made her look as if she'd just had bad news.'

'I *like* it.'

'Look, pet, it's Dear One.'

'It's your *mother*,' Vanessa corrected.

He looked at it a moment, glanced away, dis-interested, and Vanessa switched off the light.

She led the way to the large, sedate dining room with its towering sideboard and long mahogany table around which were grouped, in perfect symmetry, eight stiff Regency chairs, awaiting a conference of foreign ministers, and then through a door to the old-fashioned butler's pantry (and Lila said gaily, 'Look, PS, as big as our whole kitchen'), then into the kitchen itself, as big and white as a small hospital ward and twice as clean, where Diana, flustered at their sudden entrance, rattled cups and the axe-faced cook nodded at them when Vanessa said, 'Tea right away, Ellen. Mrs Baines has to get back.' 'Yes, Miss Scott.' Through a green-baize door into a sombre book-lined study, choking with leather chairs and an upright piano and then back into the hall where they collided with Ettie, who embraced them with little fluttering cries of delight and declarations of her gratitude to them for coming in all this heat, pronouncing them lambs and dears, and finally back to the underwater drawing room for tea, pale-green cucumber sandwiches and thin slices of a very white cake. Vanessa seemed tired by her tour. She retired into silence and twice looked at her watch, leaving Lila and Ettie to flounder through a languid discussion of roses.

In the hall, pulling on her gloves and seeing that his face had grown long, Lila bent and whispered:

'Remember, darling, it's only till Sunday night. Then George will come and get you and bring you home. Now don't forget what I told you, that if you feel a teeny bit lonely, all you have to do is look out the window across the harbour and there we'll be, waving to you.'

'Which way?'

'Why, over there.'

'But I only see trees and things.'

'Well, we're over there anyway and don't you worry. We're not going to *escape* while you're gone:

She kissed his folded face.

'But I don't like this house.'

'Shhh. Shhh. It's a *gorgeous* house. Oh, what a time you're going to have.' Lila kissed him again as Vanessa came up.

'Thank you for bringing him, Lila.'

116

'Well, I thought the first time it would be better for you not to send a car. It might f-r-i-g-h-t—'

'Yes. Sure we can't get you a taxi?'

'Oh, it's no distance to the tram. Goodbye, Ness. His pyjamas and everything are in the suitcase and—'

'Yes, thanks.'

'Bye-bye, PS.'

Lila quickly descended the front steps and walked down the drive, trying to ignore the sudden feeling of wrenching loneliness that had swept over her at leaving him for the first time in her life. At the bend in the drive she looked back. He was standing on the steps so she waved and blew kisses but he didn't respond, simply stood there without moving, a great distance away from her, until Vanessa appeared and guided him into the house, closing the door.

Now, it seemed, he must learn to sit up very straight in one of the tall hard dining room chairs, exactly at the centre of the table, while Vanessa sat at quite a long distance at one end and Cousin Ettie far away at the other. He must learn to serve himself from the dishes that Diana brought to him, being careful not to spill peas or potato on the snowy-white tablecloth and not to begin to eat until both Cousin Ettie and Vanessa had been served, which seemed foolish because the food became cold. Although it was still bright daylight, someone had lit candles in the tall silver candlesticks. Vanessa explained things to him in her quiet, low voice, beginning with his serviette, which as usual he tucked into his shirt collar.

'No, that goes on your lap.'

'But I always put my serviette here.'

'It isn't a serviette. It's a table napkin and table napkins go on laps. Only tradespeople tuck their napkins in their shirt collars.'

What were tradespeople? Was George tradespeople? He always tucked his serviette into his collar and why was it suddenly called a napkin? A napkin was something they put on babies with a safety pin.

Cousin Ettie seemed to understand how he felt because she smiled and nodded at him, her diamond heart twinkling in the candlelight. But when she started asking him about his school and what games he liked, Vanessa said rather sharply, 'Ettie, let him eat his dinner, please.' It wasn't like home at all, where Lila and George chatted and included him. Most of the time it was silent, except when Vanessa said quietly, 'Diana, wrong spoon,' or 'Diana, you may take the vegetables away.' In between the courses, Vanessa rang a little glass bell and then Diana would come running from the kitchen and the serving would go on all over again.

After dinner was over, Vanessa said:

'Now then, how about a nice coolish bath and then you may have a story in bed.'

He said, 'But it isn't nighttime yet.'

'It's bedtime though.'

'No, it isn't. I always stay up after tea.'

'It isn't tea, it's dinner. What time does Lila put you to bed?'

'When it's dark.'

'Ah, but it gets dark so late in midsummer, doesn't it?'

'No, it doesn't.' He was pouting a little. 'Not at *home*.'

Vanessa gave a little laugh. 'Oh, I see. Well, PS, while you're here, *this* is home. Now say goodnight to Cousin Ettie.' Cousin Ettie, laying cards on a table, leaned down, folded him in a lavender embrace and said, 'Nighty night, lambkin. Do I get a kiss? Oh, what a lovely kiss.'

Then he and Vanessa climbed the stairs to the second floor, where bedrooms seemed to open up from everywhere. 'That big one down the hall is Cousin Ettie's, this one is mine and this is yours,' Vanessa said, opening a door, and he saw his room, blue carpet, blue curtains, big white bed with the mosquito netting over it, shelves filled with shiny new books. The only thing that looked real in it was his old school suitcase sitting on a stool. Vanessa said, 'Now look.' She opened a blue wardrobe and he saw rows of suits and blazers hanging up. 'All yours.' How could they all be his? Even George only had two suits, one for work and one for Sunday best. There were new sandals and shoes standing in

119

a neat row on white paper and a pair of strange high boots. 'For riding,' said Vanessa. She pulled open the drawers of a dresser and showed him shirts, under-shirts, underpanties, handkerchiefs and little gloves. All *his*? How could he possibly wear all these things in two days? Or was he going to be allowed to take them home with him on Sunday?

Vanessa said, 'Now look under the bed.'

He flopped down and saw a bright-red cart, big enough for him to sit in and be pulled around by Winnie. Oh, that was lovely. But how would he get *that* home on the tram?

'What do you say?' asked Vanessa, high above him.

'It's a beaut,' he said.

'Beauty.'

She did her little trick with the match, then, 'Pleased?'

'Oh, yes.'

'Like your room?'

'Oh, yes.' Then, remembering his manners, 'Thank you.'

'I'm glad you're pleased.' She kneeled down to his level. 'Would you like to give me a kiss then?'

Oh, they always wanted that.

He kissed her quickly on the cheek and she looked at him with her wide green eyes, seemed to be thinking about something, seemed disappointed because she rose quickly and clicked down the hall to the bathroom and turned on taps; came back and helped him to undress. He didn't like to tell her that he was quite able to do this for himself, all except ties and shoelaces.

'Who gave you this tie?'

'Vere. It's a Mickey Mouse tie.'

'Yes, that's evident.'

She took the tie from him, holding it from the end like a snake, undid his shirt and panties. He felt funny with no clothes on in front of her, which he never did with Lila. She put him in a little blue bathrobe and led him to the big green bathroom, turned off the taps and lifted the toilet seat.

'Can you manage that by yourself?'

'Oh, yes.' Goodness, he'd been doing that by himself for ages, but not with people standing by and watching.

So he said, 'I don't want to now.'

'After your bath then. Now here's some Morny soap from London.' She helped him into the bath, took a glass jar from the cupboard and poured a few little pink stones into the water. 'To make you smell nice.'

The tub felt smooth under his bottom, nicer than the old tin one at home. But he had forgotten to bring his boat.

'I don't have my boat.'

'Sorry. Couldn't think of *everything*. I'll get one for next time.'

Next time?

She soaped his back for him, was particular about his ears and eyes, using a big sponge instead of a washrag. A very strange sponge which swelled up giant in the water, brown and full of holes, reminding him of jellyfish.

She dried him rapidly in a huge towel, big enough to cover two children, then poured powder all over him and watched while he brushed his teeth with the very hard new toothbrush, put on his robe again and said, 'Now, do the other thing.' Went out while he did.

Back in his bedroom, pale-blue pyjamas lay on the bed.

He said, 'I brought my own pyjamas; they're in the suitcase.'

She frowned at this, crossed the room and snapped open his suitcase. 'Flannel!' She laughed and said, 'I think mine will be cooler, PS.'

When he was settled into bed, she sat down in a chair beside him and opened a book.

'Now,' she said. 'We'll have the first chapter of *Peter Pan*.'

She read very well, better than Lila and certainly better than George, who stumbled over words sometimes, and she stopped now and then to explain things. Like English nannies. They were not goats, no, they were women who looked after little boys and girls who came from 'good' families.

The daylight had gone now and he could scarcely see her face when she bent over to kiss him goodnight.

'I haven't said "Gentle Jesus".'

'Oh. Well, you can say that to yourself, PS. Goodnight.'

'Don't shut the door.'

'Now, PS, you're too old for that. There's nothing whatever to be afraid of in the dark.'

'But I always have—'

'No, you may not. Go to sleep now.'

She went out, closing the door, shutting the room into darkness. He waited until he heard her footsteps going away downstairs, then climbed out of bed and tried to open the door, but the slippery glass handle would not turn. He stood listening to the unfamiliar sounds: leaves against the windowpanes and the *swoosh swoosh* of distant cars, a big dog barking somewhere in the shadows. He knocked on the door a few times but the only reply was the low chime of a clock in the hall outside. He said, 'I want Lila. I want to go home,' to nobody and whimpering a little, crept across the room, found his suitcase in the dark and felt for his own pyjamas. He tried to take off the new ones, but Vanessa had tied the knot too hard, so after struggling for a few minutes with the cord, he put on his own pyjamas over the new ones.

He climbed on to the wide window sill and looked out the window. He saw through the moving treetops the harbour in the distance, the lights of the big Harbour Bridge, the twinkling of moving ferryboats and beyond, the paler glistening of faraway houses. But which was his? Which was his kitchen window and were Lila and George looking out as they promised and waving? He waved a couple of times in case they were and felt a strange lump in his throat as though he had swallowed a rainbow ball whole. He said, 'I'm going home on Sunday,' and watched the distant lights moisten and run together into hot tears, and slowly, gradually, into nothing but mixed-up dreams in which he was running from something which reached for him with long rubber arms and it caught him, lifted him in the air and across darkness into bed, where the arms were all around him at once, and fighting them, he awoke for an instant and saw Vanessa's face.

'Shhhh,' she said, or something about sheep, seeming to ask him a question, but he was already safely asleep.

He awoke, surprised not to find himself in his own bed, not to hear Lila rattling cups in the kitchen, but in this strange, much too blue room with the sun coming in on the wrong side. The house was silent. He saw that the door was now ajar so it must have been Vanessa who came in in the night. He slipped out of bed and peeped out. The hall was silent and deserted, all doors closed. Had Vanessa and Cousin Ettie escaped during

124

the night? The stairs beyond beckoned invitingly to come down and escape too before anyone changed her mind and came back.

He tugged at his pyjama-cord knot but it would not come undone. Oh, well, he'd put his clothes on over his pyjamas. But where were they? Everything had been put away in that wardrobe and he couldn't reach the handle. Then he'd go home in his pyjamas like Wee Willie Winkie. It was a thw*a*rt, as Vere would say, but he wouldn't care if people stared at him on the tram as long as he was going home and what fun to walk into the kitchen and surprise Lila and George who would jump for joy.

He looked in his suitcase but there was nothing in it but his school ruler and his pocket money (sixpence and two pennies). Thank goodness he still had that. That would be enough money to take the tram to the Quay and once in Neutral Bay he could walk. He snapped his suitcase shut, and putting on the new slippers, went into the hall. He had just taken one step down the creaky stairs when a door opened suddenly behind him.

'Good morning, PS.'

She hadn't escaped after all. She was wearing a pink, trailing coat and her dark-red hair was hanging over her shoulder in a long pigtail.

'It's only seven o'clock,' she said. 'Did you sleep well?'

'Yes.'

She smiled. 'Going shopping?' she asked, looking at his suitcase, and he laughed. She was really very nice and funny too. He suddenly couldn't think why he'd wanted to run away; began liking her again.

She said, 'Look here, I don't think it's an *awfully* good idea to sleep on window sills, do you? Suppose one rolled out? Quite a drop unless one has wings like Peter Pan.'

While she dressed him in a new sand-coloured suit and hard new sandals, she said, 'Who cuts your hair?' The barber, he told her. 'Does he use a knife and fork?' she asked, and he laughed again. She said, 'Now go downstairs to the dining room and Diana will give you your breakfast.'

He had breakfast alone, sitting plumb in the middle of the long table while Diana set the things in front of him and stuck his serviette in his collar where it ought to be. There was a grapefruit instead of the usual porridge and a brown boiled egg, very gooey, not nice and almost hard the way Lila knew he liked eggs, but lots of toast and orange marmalade and milk. Diana, wearing a starchy blue uniform, chatted away to him. They would be chums, she said. Told him she was from the country. 'Way up in Bunderberg where she used to milk twenty cows a day and cook for a dozen farm hands. But her dadda had fallen off a dray and hurt his back so they'd come down to the city to

126

get jobs, only there weren't any and she'd had to go out and char and do laundry work when she could get it and then her dadda got put in the hospital and was still very crook so wasn't it lucky she'd got this nice job as housemaid in this posh house and the money was bosker and one night off a week into the bargain and old Mrs Bult was lovely to her and so was his aunty, although you had to mind your *p*'s and *q*'s with *her*!

Ellen, the cook, came bursting in to say that Miss Scott's bell had been ringing and that Diana had better get upstairs with the tray on the double and Diana rushed off on her huge feet.

After breakfast, Diana helped him carry the shiny red cart downstairs and into the garden. He trundled it up and down the drive for a while but it wasn't much fun without someone to pull him around in it. He wandered across the wide lawns and stared at the roses and hibiscus bushes, looked into the quiet grape arbour and peered through the door of the glasshouse at the rows and rows of pots and hanging maidenhair fern; worked his way slowly around the side of the big house past the wisteria vines where a window in the drawing room shot up and Diana waved a dust rag at him.

'Having a nice play, lovey?'

He nodded and picking up some little stones, threw them at the fence to show her he was enjoying himself. Then he wandered on, found a lattice gate and stood on tiptoe to look through. Beyond lay a vegetable garden where a man in a grey shirt was digging around the tomato plants. He waved and the man came over and opened the lattice gate.

'Hello, nipper,' said the man. 'What's your name?'

'PS.'

'Pee Ess, eh? That's a funny kind of name. What's that short for?'

'I forget,' he said, not wishing to bring up Dear One and all that stuff in case the man got the look they always got on their faces; sad and sorry.

'Mine's Jocko,' said the man, leaning on the gate and rolling a cigarette. He was very perspiry; his chest was like a door mat.

'You live here?'

'No, in Neutral Bay.'

'Whatcha doin' here then?'

'I'm having a holiday.'

'Yeah?'

'I'm going home tomorrow though.'

'Yeah? Whatcha been doin'?'

'Nothing.'

'Nothing, eh? That's no good on a bonza day like this. That's not much of a bloody holiday, is it? Can't you find no kids to play with?'

'I don't know anyone.'

The man said, 'Oh, there's lots of kids around here. Don't you know the Lawson kids?'

'No.'

'Big white house over there.' Jocko pointed a dirty black finger.

'I work for them on Mondays. They got a crokay lawn and a coupla nice dogs. Why don't you walk over there and interduce yourself?'

'I don't *know* them.'

'You *are* a shy coot, aren't you? All dressed up and nowhere to go, eh? That's no flamin' good, *is* it? I tell you what. You slip outa that swank suit and I'll hose you down like you was on the beach. Good-oh?'

'Good-oh,' he said, and smiled at Jocko.

But Ellen came suddenly out of the kitchen door and called out:

'Jocko, Miss Scott says would you kindly get on with your work and not talk to the little boy.'

Jocko spat. 'Tell her I'm havin' me smoko.'

'Tell her yourself. It's *your* job.'

Ellen turned towards him then and said:

'She says you're to play in the *front* garden, Master Marriott,' and made shooing signs. 'Go on now, lovey, don't make trouble for us.'

Jocko winked at him.

'Got our orders, eh, nipper? Ta-ta then. See you later.'

Jocko closed the gate, and picking up his spade, went back to the tomatoes.

The morning dragged on endlessly. He wandered down the driveway again, found a fat green locust, turned it on its back and watched it wave its legs in the air helplessly. Bored with this, he walked down to the big front gate and stuck his head through. The long street stretched away in the shimmering heat, quivering in time to the locusts, the gum trees standing very still and sad and no leaves moving anywhere, no cats, no children on bikes or scooters; just an empty street where everything had come to a full stop.

How long till Sunday now?

Suddenly someone was banging a gong and he heard Diana call:

'Lunch. Lunch!'

Vanessa, in a black dress and wearing a black hat with a gold ball on it, was sitting at her end of the dining room table.

'Well, how'd you do?' she said brightly as though they had never met before. 'Have a jolly morning?'

'Oh, yes.'

'Yes, *thank* you, Vanessa,' she said, her head to one side and her eyes flicking on and off. He repeated it, remembered where to put the napkin. She patted his hand. 'We're having luncheon earlier today because we're going for a drive.'

'Where?'

'You'll see.' She seemed to like being mysterious. '*Bread*, Diana.'

After 'luncheon', he and Vanessa walked down to the gate where a big black car was waiting and Vanessa said to the tall man in the uniform with silver buttons, 'Good afternoon, Galbraith,' and he saluted her and they got in and drove into the city. In Pitt Street, Vanessa got out and bought red roses and they went on, out of the city and through suburbs that seemed faintly familiar until crossing a bridge, he saw a river crowded with yellow jellyfish and he said:

'Oh, I know. We're going to Dear One's Little Garden.'

But Vanessa only frowned, crossed her long legs and looked for a long time at her narrow black shoes.

When they drove through the big iron gates he said:

'I'll show you where it is.'

It was nice to know something Vanessa did not, and when they got out of the car, he led the way through the other gardens, pointing and saying, 'Over here,' 'Now around here,' and Vanessa followed him.

'Here,' he said, proud of *their* garden.

She stood there, holding the roses, and seemed to be reading the words on the cross. He picked up one of the glass jars and threw out the withered flowers that Lila had brought the last time.

'I'll get the water for you,' he said, and skipped off towards the tap.

* * *

131

Vanessa read: 'Beloved wife of Logan.'

'Tell!'

'What?'

'You were about to Tell Something and stopped.'

She was sitting in front of a mirror, wearing a white muslin slip, and Sinden was brushing her hair for her. They were in the box of a bedroom they shared in the old Waverly house and doubling up on a forbidden cigarette, keeping their voices low because of the thin pinewood walls.

'Sin, did you ever meet Alice Marriott?'

'No.'

'She used to do sewing for Cousin Ettie Bult. Nice, stocky country girl from Bacchus Marsh in Victoria. Well, while I was in Melbourne last month, Ettie wanted some sewing done and Alice couldn't come up to town so we went down to the Marsh for a few days. *Quite* a good little hotel considering it's only a dairy town but pretty, very moist and green the way I've always pictured England—'

'Ness, don't wander.'

'Don't hog the cigarette; let me have a puff. Thanks. Well, Alice Marriott took me to a dance with her brother.'

'Nice?'

'Oh, just a barnyard hop with the local yokels.'

'I mean the *brother*, idiot.'

'Yes, very.'

'Good-looking?'

'Mmmmmm, y-e-s, I suppose in a way; marvellous teeth and a sort of mocking smile.'

'Mocking. Lovely. That's so provocative and aphrodisiacal.'

'Your turn for the cigarette.'

'Go *on*, Ness.'

'Well, he was quite the most marvellous dancer, most attentive all the time and with charming manners for a country boy. A quick mind too. Unexpected bursts of wit.'

'My *dear*! Witty *and* good-looking. Any money?'

'Not a sou.'

'Of *course* not. I wouldn't care, but knowing *you*—'

'Will you let me tell?'

'Sorry.'

'So Logan took me out in—'

'Logan? Nice name.'

'Yes, isn't it? Took me out in an old rattletrap car and showed me the countryside, took me to the local picture show and so forth and—well, it was sort of wonderful for a minute or two.'

'Why just a minute or two?'

'All the time we had.'

'You can do a lot in a minute or two.'

'One marvellous night we drove out and parked in a big dark field and talked for hours.'

'*Talked!*'

'Shhhh, you'll wake Agnes and Vere.'

'But you just *talked*?'

'Yes. Anything strange about that?'

'You mean nothing happened?'

'Oh, well, we agreed there wasn't any use getting in too deeply. We'd probably never see each other again.'

'All the more reason.'

'No. We discussed it, of course.'

'But that's *fatal*! You must never talk about it *first*.'

'Sinden, please. You think everything has to be *that*. Well, let me tell you there can be far, far more. We were *completely* happy. He told me all about himself. Everything. He wants to find gold. Dreams of it all the time. Holds your hand and talks dreams.'

'Ness, you fell in love.'

'A minute or two, I said.'

'And you didn't—'

'Oh, stop it. I'm sorry I told you now.'

'But why?'

'For *one* thing, his father's a *baker*.'

'God, you're a snob.'

'Can you see me as the baker's son's wife?'

'Who said anything about marriage? Did he?'

'No, but—'

'Well, then? What could you lose? Out in a lovely dark paddock and—'

'Give me the brush. I'll do my own hair.'

'Yes, you better. It's standing right on end with frustration.'

'I should know better than to confide in you.'

'But, Ness, you're so pretty and I'd like to know who you're saving it for? I wouldn't have cared if Logan was the garbage man—'

'*Were* the garbage man.'

'. . . if I was in love with him.'

'I don't want it to happen all of a sudden like that.'

'Why not? That's the loveliest way.'

'You are dropping ash *all* over the floor.'

'But, Ness, Ness, don't you want—are you *scared* of it?'

'Can't you ever be tidy?'

'*Are* you? Don't you *want* to have—'

'What I *want* is my own bedroom! And clean sheets every single day. I want to spend hours in the bath without you or Vere knocking on the door. I don't ever want to wash a cup or a dish as long as I live or stand up in a hot, crowded tram to get home. I want silver brushes with my initials on them and hundreds of pairs of shoes that never have to be resoled. I want kid gloves. I want to see Paris. I want—want—*want*—!'

'Ness, you're crying. You do want those things.'

'Put the flowers in this.'

What flowers?

She jumped; said, 'Please don't creep up on me like that.' Her neck was covered with funny red blotches. She said, 'I'm sorry, PS, forgive me.'

Gave him a nice smile and the roses. He put them in the jar for her and placed them near the cross while all the time she stood not coming any nearer.

'Well,' she said, 'that looks jolly nice, PS.'

'This is the cross,' he said, and she nodded again, not looking at it. 'George always cuts the grass when we come.'

'Does he? That's nice.'

'Why didn't you bring Jocko to cut the grass?'

'Who's Jocko?'

'The man in your garden.'

'Oh, the gardener. Oh, don't sit there, PS.'

'But we always sit on the garden to have our *lunch*.'

'Well, we've had our luncheon and graves are not for sitting on.'

What were graves? He looked up at her.

'This is a grave,' she said. 'Your mother is buried here.'

'*Buried?*'

'Yes. Where did you think she was?'

He said, 'Agnes says she's on the seventh plane.'

'Oh, dear. Haven't they told you never to listen to what *Agnes* says?'

'Lila says she went to heaven.'

'People die, PS. She just died. You see, your mother was a *little* girl.'

'A little *girl*? Like Winnie?'

'I don't mean a child. I mean she was little. She only came up to about—here, and she wasn't very strong. Having a baby was jolly difficult for her and you were late.'

Late? How could that be *his* fault?

'Late?'

'Late being born. It made her very tired and she died.'

So that was it. His fault.

'No, it wasn't your fault,' Vanessa said, knowing. 'Being born is very difficult. For everyone. It was very difficult for *my* mother with me, or so she used to say whenever she had the chance, which was often.'

She seemed to be talking to herself now, her face frozen up with annoyance, waving a bee away angrily.

This was marvellous. Much more fun than when he came with Lila, talking this way, and now he was full of questions.

'Did they put Dear One in a box?'

'Darling, don't say "Dear One", it's not what she would have liked. Say "Mother".'

'Did they put—is she in a box?'

'Yes.'

'And it's down there?'

'Yes.'

'*Still?*'

Vanessa cleared her throat. After a while she said, 'After years—after a long time, nothing much is left.'

Rainbirds tore across the sky.

Vanessa said, 'But *you* are left. You are what is left of her.'

That evening he stood in the drawing room and looked up at the picture of his mother over the fireplace and she looked back at him, rather crossly, annoyed with him for being late. But where could he have been and why had he forgotten all about it? She didn't seem to have anything to do with him whatever so why must people look sad and sorry for him, sorry for her too as Cousin Ettie was doing right this minute, twinkling into the room with buckles on her shoes that shone in the pink lights and with the sparkles of her rings flashing as she moved her little hands towards him, saying:

'Ah, lamb, that's your little mother.'

'*I* know.'

'She was like a lovely little fairy, always laughing, laughing. I wish you'd known her, petkin. Oh, how we all loved her.' Of course she wanted to comfort him now and he found himself lifted on to her lap and caressed, folded into her, most uncomfortably, because he was too big now for laps, especially Ettie's, where there was only about enough room for a puppy.

'Do you like this house, dearest lamb?'

'Oh, yes,' he said politely, wishing it would all end now and be Sunday in a minute. In a flash of pink smoke.

'Do you like your room?'

'Oh, yes.'

'And the big garden to play in?'

'Mmmmmm.'

'Cousin Ettie wants to get you something nice. What would you like best in the whole world?'

'I'd like to go home.'

She held him away to look at his face, very startled, and said:

'Are you homesick, lambkin?'

He nodded and she squeezed his hand, saying, 'Aha,' in a squeaky voice. 'Aha! Now I'll tell you a secret. Ettie's homesick too. For her lovely house in London and all her dear sweet friends. But we must be brave together, sweet lamb. Your sweet Aunt Vanessa gave up *everything* to come back here and look after you and *she* isn't complaining and so *we* mustn't. Years ago she gave up everything to look after poor old Ettie and now she's given up everything again to look after *you* so now we must *share* her and be good to her and try never to upset her or make her cross, so don't let her see you're homesick, lamb, not when we've had to come thirteen thousand—'

Hearing quick footsteps, she whispered:

'Don't say anything about Cousin Ettie being homesick, promise?'

She pinched his arm rather hard as Vanessa came in and, finding them huddled together, said, 'Secrets?'

Cousin Ettie laughed. 'Know what we were saying? We were saying how much we both loved our Vanessa.'

'Really?' said Vanessa. 'I *am* touched. PS, chairs are for sitting on, not laps.'

He got up, glad to be free of Ettie's clutching, and Ettie said:

'A bit s-a-d. I don't think you should have taken him to the g-r-a-v-e.'

Vanessa seemed not to hear; she sat down and looked for a long time at her fingernails. Then she said, 'Let us have just *one* cook for this broth, shall we?' Smiled as she said it.

Ettie sang a little tune, 'Tum-tee-tum-tee,' and looked a long while at Vanessa, then at him quickly, then back at Vanessa, pursed her mouth into a pout and said:

'I think perhaps *I'll* have a tiny sherry before dinner.'

Vanessa said in a charming voice, 'The bell is there and this is your house. You are at liberty to turn cartwheels through it if the impulse occurs to you.'

'Oh, Ness, are you cross?'

'I'm not in the least cross. I just don't awfully care for the implication in your voice that I am Simon Legree.'

'Ness—I never suggested that—'

'The only thing I *do* ask is *try* to keep it to *one*, just while *le petit* is here. I don't want stories taken back to L and G.'

She went out of the room and Ettie's face went down into the great soft folds of skin around her neck until she resembled a sad turtle. 'Ooooo,' she said. 'Ness is cross. Oh, not with *you*, lamb. Oh, gracious me, how she loves you. *You* are the favourite. I believe,' she said, laughing, pressing a bell in the wall, 'she even loves you more than she loves me! What fun we're all going to have together.'

When?

From the bottom of his sleep, dreaming he had found a puppy, he was being dragged upward, hearing sounds like the big guns firing on Empire Day. Perhaps it *was* Empire Day because fireworks were bursting in the black dark sky and someone was shaking him and saying something in his ear so he opened his eyes and saw Vanessa lit by the bed lamp. Her hair was hanging over the shoulder of her nightgown and her face without any lipstick was as white as clouds.

He resisted, turning back to the warm pillow, going down again into sleep, but Vanessa wouldn't allow it, fought him, pulling him up by both arms and stripping the sheets off him, forcing his feet into slippers, his arms into his dressing gown and all the time saying something in sharp whispers which he couldn't understand because although her lips kept moving all the time, no sound seemed to come from them over the noise from outside. Not guns, thunder. Right on top of them, falling on the house while outside the window the night lit up for a second, bright as noon, and the house shook from top to bottom and Vanessa jumped away from him, covered her mouth and stood there shaking all over, then reached quickly for him and lifting him, carried him from the bed and out the door into the dimly lit midnight hall.

He moaned, 'Where are we going?'

'Downstairs,' she whispered, 'where it's safe.'

'Why?'

She didn't answer, carried him down the stairs to the landing, where she put him down, and sitting beside him, embraced him tightly.

'Now you're safe,' she whispered.

He could feel her shaking beside him and her heart was beating quickly next to his ear.

'Once upon a time,' she was saying, 'there were three little pigs . . .' Was she going to tell that old story now in the middle of the night with the house shaking all around them and the rain now tearing at the skylight up above them, trying to break it in? But she stopped almost at once and looked at him, holding him away a second, and she was so different that he hardly knew her with her white mouth and her eyes so wide open that at any minute they might fall right out like green marbles. Then she pulled him to her as the thunder came again, and held him, and they lay together on the hard landing floor, arms around each other, and she whispered:

'Don't be frightened. I'm holding you.'

Yet it seemed to him, somehow, as though he was holding *her*. And much later, hours later it seemed, falling to sleep numbed and chilly with the storm ebbing, rumbling away across the harbour towards the sea and with Vanessa very heavy on top of him, he thought she said:

'Hold me, hold me,' but she must have been asleep and talking in her sleep said the wrong name. 'Hold me, Logan,' she said.

He was surprised in the morning, waking later than usual to the bright day, when Diana came in to help him wash and dress. She opened the window and said, 'Good-oh, the rain's made it cooler, love.'

Vanessa was sitting at the dining room table, smoking a cigarette over her coffee and reading the morning paper. She was as neat as ever. She had pinned a little black velvet bow in her bun of hair. Her lips were red again and her eyes said nothing.

She smiled. '*Good* morning, PS. What a jolly nice day. The rain has broken the heat wave.'

She seemed to have forgotten what had happened in the night. Perhaps it hadn't happened. He had dreamed it. Vanessa would not change into a wild woman in the night just because of a little thunder.

He ate his egg and watched her as she sipped her coffee and turned the pages of the Sunday paper neatly. She seemed not to notice when he spilled egg on the tablecloth and even smiled at Diana when she came to take away the dishes.

After Diana had cleared away and he was waiting to be told what was next, Vanessa laid down the newspaper, folding it so neatly that it looked as though it had never been read, got up and looked at herself a long while in the sideboard mirror. She seemed delighted with her reflection and nodded a little, congratulating it. Then she turned and said:

'Look here, I'd rather you didn't mention about last night to anyone. All right?'

So it did happen. She was that wild thing with no lips.

'All right,' he said.

'Yes, Vanessa.'

'Yes, Vanessa.'

'Especially to Lila and George. Promise?'

He'd never kept anything back from Lila and George. Even what the little boy across the street had

144

done once. But Vanessa was waiting. She leaned across the table and kissed him on the forehead. 'Promise,' she said in her low voice.

'OK,' he said.

'Just remember,' she said, 'that lightning can be very dangerous and can kill you. Especially if you are near a window, under a tree or near steel. And don't say OK—it's American.'

He said nothing.

Vanessa said, 'A promise between friends is a very serious thing, PS. It's sacred.'

'Yes,' he said.

'We are friends,' she said, reminding him. 'Now would you like to play a game?'

They sat in the little den and played ludo. Vanessa seemed to be very bad at it for he won all the time, which, after a while, was very dull.

Sunday stretched on and on and Vanessa followed him wherever he went, in and out of the garden, strolling close behind him, sitting near him while he looked through picture books.

Once he said, 'What's the time?'

'Why?' she asked. 'Are you bored?'

'No,' he said.

'Had a good time?'

'Oh, yes.'

'Thank you, Vanessa.'

Repeated it.

She seemed to be waiting for him to say something or perhaps do something which would please her but he could think of nothing except that at five o'clock George would be coming. Perhaps Lila would be wrong about the time and send him too early.

At five o'clock he stood looking out the window and down the drive; began to worry. Suppose it was all a big fib and George wasn't coming at all. Suppose he had to spend the night again, spend all the long tomorrow and the next day and—

'What are you thinking about?' asked Vanessa, right behind him.

'Nothing,' he said.

But there was George! Plodding up the drive in his blue suit. He ran from the room, out the front door and hurtled down the driveway, throwing himself into George's waist and hugging him, hard, hard, around the legs.

'Well, well,' said George, 'a grizzly bear's got me. Oh, oh, I don't often get a good hug like that.' Gave him a wet and bristly kiss.

Vanessa was watching them from the front door. She nodded to George and they said a few words to each other, both smiling and agreeing but not meaning it with their eyes. When Diana came with his suitcase, Vanessa bent to kiss him goodbye and whispered, 'Don't forget your promise to me. If you break your promise, I shall *know*.'

He nodded, not caring about anything but going, went off down the driveway, holding George's hand, happier at every step and beginning to skip.

When they got to the bend in the driveway he turned around. Vanessa was standing on the front steps so he waved to her and called out, 'Bye.' She lifted her hand. She seemed now as small as he and even with the great, long garden between them he could tell that she was looking sad. He wanted to call out something nice but she was already going back up the steps and into the shadowy house.

PART TWO

'Beresford.'

'Present, Miss Pile.'

'Boynton-Jones.'

'Present, Miss Pile.'

'Lawson.'

'Present, Miss Pile.'

'Put away your Yo-yo, Cynthia. We don't play with our Yo-yo's in class. MacArthur-Bode.'

'Present, Miss Pile.'

'Marriott.'

Pause.

'*Marriott?*'

Shuffling, giggling, turning of heads.

'Little new boy. What is your name, dear?'

'PS.'

Smothered laughter now and twenty-four eyes looking at him.

Miss Pile rapping on the desk for silence.

'What is your name?'

'PS.'

'Is that the only name you have?'

'In *my* school—'

'*This* is your school now, and in this school we answer the roll to our surnames. Is your surname Marriott?'

'Yes.'

'Yes, Miss Pile.'

'Yesmisspile.'

'When your name is called you must stand up straight, look directly at the blackboard and call out in a loud clear voice, "Present, Miss Pile." Now then. *Marriott.*'

'Presentmisspile.'

'Rutherford.'

'Present, Miss Pile.'

So on down to W for Wiggham, while he stared down at his brand-new pencil box.

'All right, boys and girls, now "God Save". Quickly now, we're late this morning.'

> *'God save our gracious King.*
> *Long live our noble King.*
> *God save the King.*
>
> *Send him victorious,*
> *Happy and glorious,*
> *Long to reign ov-er us.*
> *Go-od save the King.'*

'. . . the King.' He was behind the others.

'All right, children, now that's enough giggling at Marriott. He's new and you must make him feel at home. Whose turn is it to be prefect?'

'Mine, Miss Pile.'

'All right, Cynthia. Blow the whistle then. Class, be seated.'

He sat still, while Miss Pile gave the older boys and girls sums and the younger ones copying games. Then she moved towards him, a large lady in a brown velvet dress and with a moustache like George. When she smiled she had very yellow teeth like his pictures of Brer Fox.

'Now then, Marriott. Have you started copying yet?'

'Yes.'

'Yes, Miss *Pile*.'

'Yes, Misspile.'

'How many letters do you know?'

'I know up to—um—up to haitch.'

'Aitch. Not haitch. Aitch.'

'My teacher calls it haitch.'

'Did he? I can't imagine where *he* learned the King's English. What school did you go to, Marriott?'

'Neutral Bay.'

'I see. A *state* school. Well, now you're at a nice private school where we pronounce things the right way and take care to keep our vowels nice and open. Say "a piece of cake".'

'Piece of cake.'

'A peeece of keek. Ai would laike a naice peeece of keeek.'

'I would like a nice piece of cake.'

'Ai would laike a naice peeeece of keeeek on a naice plate.'

'I would like—'

'Not *loike*. Laike. Laike. Watch my lips and my tongue. Laike, caike, peeeece. See how I open my lips and my tongue is lying *rah*ther flat. Do you see my tongue? Now watch. Peece of caike. See it? Good. Now say, "Did you see the bee in the green tree."'

This is what Winnie and Mrs Grindel would have called 'talking with a bloody prune in your mouth' but he went on playing the game with Miss Pile until she grew tired of it and wrote out some lines of a's and b's for him to copy. He leaned over the exercise book, his tongue working inside his cheek to help him round out the letters, his head burrowing into the new exercise book, which was the only place to hide.

Cynthia blew the whistle for play time and they all ran out into the bright autumn sea morning on to the lawn beside the harbour wall beyond which moored launches and yachts pulled and worried at their buoys. The children grouped around him while he stared at the boats. There was a good deal of whispering and then one of the older boys came up and said:

'What's a boat do when it comes into port?'

He said he didn't know.

'Ties up and anchors *down*.'

At this the boy flipped up his tie and stamped heavily on his foot. He gave a little cry of surprise and pain and the children rocked with glee.

154

Cynthia said, 'What's your name?'

'PS.'

'What's that stand for?'

'I don't know.'

'*I* know.'

He said, 'You don't.'

She said, 'I do and don't be cheeky with me because I'm prefect. I know what PS stands for. Pretty Silly.' Cynthia was a tremendous success. Three of the children rolled on the lawn, holding their sides and repeating, 'Pretty Silly. Pretty Silly,' until the rest of them took up the chant. PS is pretty silly. PS is pretty sil-ly.'

Cynthia, swollen by now with importance, turned on the others and said in her prefect-for-the-week voice:

'Shut up. You heard what Miss Pile said. He's new and we have to be nice to him.'

She smiled at PS.

'What's your mother call you?'

(Oh, why do they always bring *her* up?)

'Nothing,' he said.

'*Nothing!*' More giggles.

The freckled boy who was Cynthia's young brother said:

'Oh, hello, Nothing. How are *you*, Nothing? Come here, Nothing.'

Cynthia said, 'Shut up, Ian. I'm asking the questions.

Come on,' she said to PS. 'Don't be frightened of *him*. What's your mother call you?'

He said, 'I don't have a mother.'

Cynthia toyed with her whistle. 'Who was the lady who brought you to school this morning?'

'Vanessa.'

'Who's she then?'

'My aunt.'

'Do you live with your aunt?'

'No, I live with Lila and George.'

'Who are *they*?'

'My aunt and uncle.'

'Where do they live?'

'Neutral Bay.'

'Why are you coming to our school then?'

'Because.'

He wasn't going to start explaining all *that* to Cynthia. She was nosy, he could see that, and he wasn't going to explain why he was now living all week with Vanessa and only going home on Fridays for the weekend. He didn't understand it himself. There had been that funny day at his own school, when sitting with his class under the gum tree, he had looked up and seen Vanessa standing in the distance watching them and then speaking to the teacher but never to him, and then going away with the teacher while he felt suddenly sick because he knew something strange was going to happen, and then all the whispering in the kitchen that night and Lila having trouble with her breath all next day and talking to Mr Hamilton, the lawyer, on the telephone. Then a week later, suddenly, he wasn't to go to his own school any more and Lila saying, 'Oh, you lucky boy, you're going to a nice new school, won't that be fun?' He had said that he would not go, they would have to get a policeman to make him go, but in the end Lila had taken him in the ferry-boat on a Sunday evening to the Big House and left him with Vanessa for the whole week so there didn't seem to be anything to do but come down here to something called the Point Piper Yacht Club where Miss Pile had classes in the morning for girls and boys who had English nannies like in Peter Pan and were little ladies and gentlemen, but Lila had said, 'It won't be for very long, darling, but be good just to please me and don't make Vanessa angry, *please*.'

Cynthia was smiling at him and so he smiled back.

'All right,' said Cynthia. 'Do you want to join our secret club?'

Ian said, 'If you don't join you can't play with us and no one talks to you ever.'

'You better join,' said Cynthia quietly.

'Everyone else belongs,' said Ian.

'I'm the president,' said Cynthia. 'And if you don't join you don't get asked to our house when there's a party. Do you want to join the club?'

He supposed he should. 'All right.'

Cynthia held out her hand. 'Give me your pocket money then.'

He felt in his pocket. Vanessa never gave him pocket money but he had ninepence from Lila. He kept it tied in his hanky in case he should ever have to escape by tram. He handed it over reluctantly.

'Is that all?' Cynthia looked at the shiny sixpence and threepenny bit. 'How much does your father give you a week?'

He said, 'I haven't got a father.'

'Is he dead?'

'No.'

'Where is he then?'

'*I* don't know. He's a gold digger.'

'What's that?'

'I don't know but that's what he does. He's away.'

'Where?'

'I don't know.'

Cynthia's eyes were very wide with inner knowledge. 'Haven't you ever seen him?' she asked in a very kind voice.

'No,' he said.

Cynthia turned and whispered to Ian. 'Pass it on,' she said. Ian turned to another boy and whispered. 'Pass it on,' he said, and went into fits of sniggering laughter.

Each one in turn passed it on and the information seemed to grow in importance and hilarity until it reached a small knot of four heads together. The four leaped with joy and excitement.

They had to let it out. 'PS is a bastard,' they screamed.

Everyone except Cynthia took up the chant.

'PS is a bas-tard. PS is a bas-tard.'

How could he be a bastard? Vere had said that Mr Jacoby, for whom she made the vases, was a bastard. But then so was the saucepan on her stove because once she had said to it, 'Boil, you bastard.'

Well, anyway, he had pleased them about *something*. He smiled and accepted the praise.

Cynthia said, 'Now listen. If you don't join the club we'll tell everyone you're a *bar*stard.' She pronounced it in a very Pommy accent as though she had been listening behind doors to Vanessa. 'Come on,' she said, and took his hand. 'You have to be initiated.'

She tugged him forward and the others followed, laughing and shouting, prodding him from behind.

Scrambling and pushing, they dived into the low, dark space between the cement pylons supporting the building. It was littered with empty beer bottles and dead crabs. It smelled of stale seaweed.

'Now where's the stick?' asked Cynthia.

One of them reached behind a butter box and brought out a long switch cut from a rosebush. It had several fairly long thorns.

Cynthia made a swishing noise with the switch and said:

'Now take down your trousers.'

In front of all these little girls?

'No,' he said.

'All right then, you can't join the club and we'll tell everyone.'

'You're custard,' said Ian.

'I'm not.'

'PS is cowardy custard. PS is—'

'All right,' he said. He turned around and let down his short new grey trousers.

'And your underpanties,' said Cynthia.

After he had done so, she said, 'Now bend over. And listen, don't call out. If you cry or call out, I'll do it again tomorrow and the next day and the next until you don't.' She hit him hard across his bare bottom and it was like pepper or fire or both. He wanted to scream out, but he bit his lip hard and smothered it to a gasp. The second and third times were not so bad but the fourth time made his ears sing. His eyes smart and now his whole body seemed to be roasting over a gas jet and at the sixth time he moaned and whispered, 'Stop.'

The whipping stopped, but Cynthia said, 'Stay there.'

He remained bent over while they clustered around him and Ian said, 'He's scratched all right.'

160

Cynthia said, 'Now turn around and say, "I promise on my sacred oath to tell no one."'

He mumbled the oath. It was hurting so much that he didn't even care about them all staring at him without his trousers.

'And I promise to keep all the secrets of the club.'

He repeated it.

Cynthia said, 'All right. Now you can be my friend and belong to my club.'

Somewhere a bell was ringing, but it was real, not in his head like the singing and buzzing. The children scrambled out into the sunshine and he heard Miss Pile calling to them.

He pulled on his trousers and followed them out. Miss Pile, smiling and putting them through the door, turned to him.

'Now, Marriott,' she said. 'When you hear the bell—playtime is *over*.'

Vanessa was sitting in the den with a strange lady dressed like a Scotsman all in tartan and wearing a little tartan cap. Her hair was cut very short like a boy's.

'Here you are!' said Vanessa. 'How'd it go?'

'All right.'

'First day's always a bit frightening, isn't it? Were the children nice to you?'

'Oh, yes.' Feeling the soreness, hating them.

'This is Miss Colden,' said Vanessa. 'Say, "How do you do, Miss Colden."'

'Do, Miss Colden.'

'What a nice, nice boy,' said Miss Colden. She never took her eyes off Vanessa.

'Sing something for Miss Colden,' said Vanessa unexpectedly.

'What?'

'Anything. Don't be shy. Don't you know a song? Lila says you sing a song for people. What is it?'

'Don't look at the Hole in the Doughnut.'

'All right.'

He didn't want to sing anything. He wanted to run upstairs and lie on his bed and cry. He wanted to escape, find a tram to Circular Quay, but Cynthia had taken all his pocket money. He stared at the carpet.

'We're waiting,' said Vanessa.

He cleared his throat and began uncertainly.

'When skies don't seem so blue—'

'Louder, PS. Miss Colden wants to *hear*.'

'There's one thing you can always do,
Find a rainbow smiling thru'

'So, don't look for the hole in the doughnut.
Don't count all the raindrops that fall.

> *Don't cry at the fly in the ointment.*
> *Tomorrow a bluebird will call.'*

'That's very nice,' said Miss Colden to Vanessa. 'He has *pitch*.'

She seemed delighted as though she were about to dance a Highland fling.

Vanessa said, 'Miss Colden's going to give you piano lessons. She's going to come every Monday afternoon.'

'We'll have great fun,' said Miss Colden, laughing. 'We'll play games with scales and we'll do ever such amusing things with arpeggios. My children have a ripping time, Miss Scott. Ripping. Cynthia and Ian Lawson are up to little duets—oh, and they're lovely children. Such *manners*.'

'Did you meet the Lawson children?' Vanessa asked him.

'Yes.'

'Oh, they're such nice, nice children,' said Miss Colden, eagerly handing an ashtray to Vanessa, who was burning a match down and watching PS.

'But then,' Miss Colden went on, 'one would expect them to be. Their mother was a MacArthur and their father's president of the English, Scottish and Australian Bank.'

Vanessa nodded. Put out the match.

'Do you play piano, Miss Scott?' She pronounced it piarno.

'No,' said Vanessa. 'I have no talent for *anything*. It was my sister who was talented.'

'Well, I was noticing your hands,' said Miss Colden. 'If I *may* say so, a pianist's hands. Strong and *very* beautiful.' Miss Colden was staring at Vanessa's hands as though they were the first she had ever seen.

'Darling,' said Vanessa, 'you look a bit peaky. Go up and have a little rest before luncheon.'

'We'll have ripping fun, PS,' said Miss Colden, staring at Vanessa, not looking at him.

As he went out into the hall, Miss Colden was saying:

'It's like a breath of England, meeting you.'

At the top of the stairs he paused. Cousin Ettie's door was open and she was standing with her back to him, holding something up to her mouth. After a little while she turned, and seeing him, gave a gasp. He saw that she was holding a little glass with something the colour of honey in it. She put the glass down quickly and fluttered to the door, her diamond heart glistening.

'Little lamb,' she said. Her eyes were very red and she was sniffing. 'Give Ettie a hug,' she said.

He put his arms around her and smelled lavender and something sweet.

'Blessed angel,' she said. 'Hug poor Ettie tight, oh, tighter than that, lamb. Poor Ettie's sad today. Oh, Ettie's terribly sad today and what she needs most of

164

all in the whole world is for her little lamb to hug her and hold her tight.'

He was almost smothering.

Then she laughed, drew back and said, 'Have a peppermint.'

In her little hand she held two white peppermints. He took one and thanked her.

'Blessed angel,' she said, and bent to kiss him. 'Don't tell,' she said. 'Don't say a *word*, precious angel.'

Undressing him for his bath that evening, Vanessa said:

'Turn around. How on earth did you get those scratches?'

He said, 'I don't know.'

'Of course you know. How did it happen?'

He was remembering his sacred oath. He said, 'I had to go in the bushes.'

'PS!'

'I had to.'

'Why didn't you ask Miss Pile where the bathroom is?'

'I—didn't know where *she* was.'

'Then you should have asked one of the children. That's very naughty.' She bathed him gently, put talcum powder on his behind. 'Better?' she asked.

'Yes.'

'Yes, thank you.'

'Yes, thank you.'

'Do you like the school, PS?'

'I like my own school better.'

'Why?'

'Because.'

'Because what?'

'Because.'

'PS.'

'I like my own school. Winnie goes there.'

'That little girl from next door?'

'Yes.'

'She's *common*.'

Into bed. 'Here's a surprise. Doctor Dolittle. Nice?'

'Hmmmmm.'

'Shall we read a little bit of it?'

'Yes.'

'Please, Vanessa.'

'Please, Vanessa.'

'May I have a kiss then?'

Kiss. Kiss. Kiss. That's all they ever want. That, and secrets.

'Call *that* a kiss? Oh, well.' She sighed, looking deeply into his eyes a long while. 'PS—'

'Yes?'

'Never mind. Look, this is the Pushmi-Pullyu. He has a head at both ends. Amuse you?'

Lila sat in Vere's room, wheezing slightly in the blue vapour of cigarette smoke. The room smelled of stale cooking fat, orange-blossom face powder and cat.

She said, 'Vere, could we have the window open just a crack?'

'Lila, it's chilly-bean outside today.'

'Terribly stuffy in here.'

'But I feel the *cold*, girl.'

'That's because you've got no flesh on your body. If you'd smoke less and eat something *nourishing*—'

'OK, *Mater*!'

Vere scrambled over the clutter and opened the window.

From the back street below came the melancholy sound of a cornet playing 'Songs My Mother Taught Me'.

Vere snatched two dusty pennies from a saucer, flung them into the street and screamed, 'Go away. There's someone very ill here. Go away!'

'Vere, the poor man . . .'

'Can't stand cornets at twilight; they give me the heeby-jeebies and things are bad enough anyway. Do you know that bastard Jacoby I was making the vases and dishes for skipped without paying me? I'm stony.'

'Oh, Vere. After all that work.'

Vere said, '*Do* have a vase.'

'I think I've got a bob I can spare.'

'Oh, Lila, I didn't mean *that*. Take it as a gift.

I want to get rid of the bloody things. Oh, well, thanks. I can buy a packet of cigs with that.'

Vere slipped the shilling Lila gave her into the pocket of the big man's woollen dressing gown she was wearing. It was several sizes too large and gave her the appearance of an inmate in a woman's house of detention. She handed Lila a chipped cup stamped with the legend KOOKABURRA KAFETERIA and sat down beside her on the littered bed, dislodging an annoyed sleepy Hester on to the floor.

'Now show me Pony's letter,' she said.

Lila searched in her imitation-leather handbag and brought out several sheets of hysterical violet-ink handwriting on cheap ruled paper.

'May 20th. Dear Lilah Baines. Where are the snows of yesteryear? Do you even remember Pony Wardrop who loved your gay little sister with all my battered heart? Well, my dear, none of her pals can ever forget Sinden. A light went out in the world when she laid down her sharp-witted pen and was called to the Great Editor.'

'Great *Editor*,' said Vere. 'Holy Je—'

'Go on, Vere.'

Vere read on. 'The reason I'm writing (excuse this awful notepaper, my dear) is that two weeks from Saturday some of us from the Pen and Ink Club are organising a picnic at Fairyland (boats leave Circular Quay from the Lane Cove River Wharf at eleven, twelve and one). Proceeds are to help destitute writers and artists who are given no assistance from the government and many of whom are on relief. Among the writers who will be honoured with in memoriams composed in their honour will be our own Sinden and we would so love to have any or all of her sisters there (is it true that Vanessa is back from Mother England?) But most of all we would love to have her little boy. He is, as Sin put it herself, her "PS" left to all of us. We want him to know he is one of us who all adored his gutsy little mum. There will be games and refreshments and Queenie Waters is putting on some choric dances with her eurythmic group. Give the little boy our love (can it be almost *seven* years?) and I remain, ever your constant friend, Pony Wardrop. PS. *My* own love child is now seven and has won a prize for a story. Perhaps someday the two lads will meet and exchange notes, but of the dreams and troubled wayfaring of their mothers that went into the making of them, how much will they ever know? PW.'

Vere said, 'God! No wonder Pony went off the track with so many men; she can't even stick with a sentence.'

Lila said, 'I'm rather touched with it.'

'Where exactly?'

'Vere, I never approved of Pony—having that child and all the publicity about free love—but she

169

was one of Sin's great friends and I think I should take PS to the picnic.'

'But you've always said they were a lot of pseudo-Bohemian hangers-on, has-beens and never-weres.'

'Ah, but they *were* her friends.' Lila wheezed slightly, looked at Sinden's fly-spotted face on the wall. 'Besides, I'm not going to be bossed around by Vanessa.'

'Aha. So that's it!'

'We've had a go-in over it. She doesn't want PS to go.'

'She loathes Pony. You *know* that.'

'Just the same, she is not going to give me orders! It's getting to the point where I have to ask her permission about everything. We had a really terrible stand-up fight about it in front of PS. Oh, I shouldn't ever have brought it up but I thought maybe *she* would like to go. I should have just taken PS and said nothing about it to her. He's *mine* at weekends anyway but I was trying to be *fair*, Vere. Well, she drew herself up in that way she has and she said, "He's not to go. Those are my instructions!" Instructions! As if I were the maid or something. I said, "Ness, kindly don't speak to me that way in front of the child," and *she* said, "If he goes to that picnic, you'll be sorry, Lila, because I'll take some very strong action," and then she went upstairs and banged her door. PS was standing there listening to it all and poor Ettie shaking and trembling all over. By the way, Vere, have you noticed a change in Ettie lately?'

'No. I haven't seen them. I hate that big morgue of a house. Don't wander off the point, Lila.'

'Well, anyway, it was dreadful. I was ill all night. Poor George with no sleep, giving me inhalations, and—'

'Lila, why declare war over some footling picnic?'

'Because it's the principle. It's the principle of the thing. Now you know that George and I had to give in over the school business. We just couldn't fight it any longer. Not when she said, "Do you want to go to court over it?" I went to Sam Hamilton about it and you know we don't pay him a sou. You know he only gives me advice because he was fond of Sin, but even he advised against fighting it. He said Ness might even try to get full custody. We couldn't *risk* it. But at least I thought—and George thought too—that now she's won her victory over that, she'd be satisfied and we'd have some peace, but now I'm going to be interfered with over *my* weekends and that I'm going to put a stop to, Vere. I'm not going to be told what to do on Saturdays and Sundays, Vere. I'll put my foot down. If I give in over the picnic, I'll have to give in over everything.'

Vere said, 'I know it's very thwarting.'

'Don't you think I'm right?'

'I suppose so, Lila. I think in a way Ness is right too. I wouldn't want to go. Sin's dead so why turn over the sods? My God, isn't life undoing enough as it is without people forcing us to remember *her* all the time?'

Vere suddenly and surprisingly burst into tears and Lila bit her lip, thinking, I shouldn't have brought it up. The pain's still there, how funny. You never can tell with Vere.

Vere's sleepy voice coming through the phone to Lila standing, half falling, in the neighbour's house that dawn.

'Hello? Who's this?'

'Vere, we've been trying to get you since eleven o'clock last night.'

'Lila? I've been at a party.'

'Vere—'

'What's the matter with you?'

'There's terrible news.'

'What?'

'Dear, she's gone.'

'What?'

'Don't you understand? She's gone. She went very suddenly about eleven o'clock last night.'

Tick tick of a clock through the phone.

'Vere?'

'Yes.'

'I'm so sorry, dear.'

172

'Lila. You told me—you said it was all right to go out.'

'I know, dear, we didn't know ourselves—'

'You said it was all right to go *out*.'

'Oh, Vere, I'm sorry—'

'Oh, my God!'

'Vere, there's a little boy. The little boy is here. Did you hear me?'

'Oh, my God. I was at a *party*!'

Clouds of orange-scented face powder and Vere a clown face peering in the cracked mirror, putting on a deep-red lipstick. Lila finding specks of powder in her tea and thinking, she hasn't forgiven me. She thinks she has but I know better!

Vere got up from her three-legged dressing table, slopped tea into her cup and said:

'Lila, I've always kept out of it, but you and Ness between you are doing a first-class job of making him hate Sin.'

'Vere!' Lila, all sympathy vanishing, felt the hot tea spill on her knee. 'Why, I never heard such an unfair—'

'Forcing him to worship—'

'Never. I have never forced him to—'

'Pushing her down his throat. Wait and see what happens.'

'I have never—'

'If he'd been left to *me*—' But Vere trailed off, seemed to be staring at the dusty piles of kept letters and perhaps of one that she never received ('Dearest Vere, If anything should happen to me, I want *you* to . . .').

And they *were* close, thought Lila. Closer than *I* was to Sin. Vere, the first at the wedding, collapsing at the grave. Now with what? Leftovers. From the kind of life she always lived with Sinden, but now trying to live it alone without the guiding spirit of fun that motivated it when Sin was alive, but trying to keep it going just the same.

Poor Vere. Trying to keep an old jig going and meanwhile letting chances go by, always hoping for something more promising the next evening, and so letting rich Gilbert slip through her fingers. At least I have George. *And* PS.

Lila said, 'Well, to get back to the picnic—'

'Must we?'

'I was only going to say that I'm taking PS, no matter what Vanessa says. But I'm putting you on your honour not to tell her.'

'Got more to worry about than *that*, my dear. Three weeks behind with the rent.'

'Oh, Vere.'

'Mind if I have a spot? *Very* undone today.'

Agnes led the way up the concrete tiers of the Temple of Everlasting Love and Vanessa followed, looking around at the weeds, the splitting concrete and the

174

lantana vines creeping over it, thought, 'What a wreck. She too. Two wrecks.'

Agnes said, 'Now, Ness, if you were a bird and you flew on a direct line where I'm pointing you would come to Jerusalem.'

'If I were a bird,' said Vanessa, 'you wouldn't catch me flying to Jerusalem.'

She reached in her bag for a cigarette, but Agnes said sharply:

'Oh, not *here*, please!'

'Sorry. Forgot we were in church.'

'Doesn't it give you a feeling of presence?'

A lion roared nearby.

'Very definitely,' said Vanessa, and smiled.

'I thought it would,' Agnes said. 'That's why I was so anxious for you to come and see it. These seats with the name plaques entitle you to what we call the Joy of Identification when the night comes.'

Vanessa sat down and Agnes added in a low voice, 'The night will be towards the end of October. Very likely the thirtieth.'

Vanessa said politely, 'Really? As soon as that?'

'*Ab*solutely.'

Agnes launched into a recital of the Temple's history but she could not be sure (remembering other times and other dim occasions) whether or not Vanessa was listening. The green eyes had a shuttered look, the beautifully shaped face unreceptive as stone, against which Agnes' words splintered into glass fragments. As Sinden once put it, 'When Ness doesn't want to hear something, it's no use even trying to tell her that her dress has caught fire.'

Vanessa had indeed touched an inner switch and turned off the sound track; was watching a silent film of Agnes preaching; listening only to her own commentary: Oh, that tricorn hat. And that navy blue serge suit. Give her a horse and she could pass for Paul Revere. She's mad, of course. Not Ophelia or Rochester's wife, not straws-in-the-hair mad, just everyday carefully built-in mad. She's made herself believe all this nonsense. But why? What has made her wander down crazy paths to become this ludicrous figure ranting about God and the end of the world? Isn't hell fire awfully dated anyway? As dated as her hat. What is it? What? Something I remember.

Thunder and lightning. The old wooden house at Waverly, shaking and rattling in the wind that night and Mater as disapproving as Queen Victoria, saying, 'Now, *Vanessa*, once and for all you are going to get over this ridiculous fear of lightning.'

'Please, *please*—I want Lila to come and sleep with me.'

'Lila is not coming. Now stop that screaming; you'll wake up the others.'

Mater closing the midnight door on her. Alone now, and muffling the shrieks in her pillow as the dreadful doom broke over the roof again and again. Now the door opening softly and Agnes' rag-doll face peeping in.

'What's the matter?'

Sobbing about Mater, hateful mean Mater.

Agnes snuggling up to her, the smell of her pink flannel nightie, thin little-girl arms holding her now.

'Don't be frightened, Ness. 'I'll sleep with you.'

'Ag.'

'What?'

'She says you can't get hurt but you can. You *can*!'

'Shhh. She'll hear you.'

'I don't care. I hate her.'

'*Ness.*'

'I don't care, it's true. I saw a picture of a little girl struck by lightning and she was all burned up and black all over and all her clothes burned off her. I *saw* it.'

Crack. Rumble. Crack. Roll. Rattle.

'Hold me, Ag.'

'I am, silly.'

'Tighter.'

'Gee whiz, I don't know why you're scared. I love it.'

Agnes darting out of bed, raising the blind an inch.

'*Don't!*'

'But it's lovely, Ness. It's like the end of the world.'

'Don't want the end of the world.'

'Why not? It's lovely after the storm when Jesus comes and they all come up out of the sea.'

'Who does?'

'All the drowned people singing and all the people out of their graves—'

'Stop it.'

'But it's not frightening. It's lovely and peaceful and there's a gorgeous pink light shining—'

'How do you know?'

'I saw it once in a dream. Everyone was so happy and—'

Crack.

'Ag! Come back into bed!'

Now with their heads under the blanket.

'Hold me tight.'

'I'm holding you, Ness and—Mr Pringle.'

Mr who?

'Pringle,' Agnes was saying, and wiping away seagull droppings. 'Norman B. Pringle of Seattle, who broke away from the Theosophists and discovered the Seven Planes of Understanding . . .'

Vanessa looked away from the radiant rabbit face under the tricorn hat. The cement felt cold under her and she stood up.

Agnes said coolly, 'You might at least listen to me.'

Vanessa smiled, admired her pigskin gloves a moment and said unexpectedly:

'How do you like being back?'

'Back?' Agnes, interrupted, pulled down from the Seventh Plane, looked blank.

'Here. Home. If one can call it that.'

Agnes said, after a moment, 'One cannot always choose where one would most like to be.'

'Do you miss America?'

'Sometimes. I missed it terribly at first. I thought all the accents here were so strange and I missed the enthusiasm of Americans and people saying "You're welcome." In Seattle I lectured to crowded halls. I was treated with *respect*! One of my pamphlets was *quoted* once in a Portland, Oregon, newspaper!' Agnes looked up at the sky for quite a long while. 'But I've been back so long it doesn't matter any more.' She smiled. 'Nothing will matter very much longer.'

Kookaburras perched in the dusty gum trees burst into raucous laughter at her.

Vanessa said, 'I hate kookaburras. I hate the rain-birds and people's accents.' Said very quietly, 'I loathe being back.'

'Then why did you come back, Ness?'

Vanessa stared away at the sad oldness of the bay, heard traffic in Trafalgar Square, remembered the hope she nourished and said:

'PS.'

'You didn't have to bother with him.'

'Yes, I did.'

'But why?'

'I want him.'

Agnes looked at her very squarely for a moment, seemed to be peering into her as into a dark closet with a flashlight and finding the most extraordinary things.

Vanessa, slamming the door of the closet in Agnes' face, turned away and started walking down the steps, signifying with the dignity of her back and the precision of her high heels on the concrete that the conversation was over.

Behind her, Agnes was saying, 'Fancy that. I never wanted children. I never wanted a husband. I never could stand men. If any man had ever tried to touch me, I should have been sick on the spot. How did Mater stand it all those years? Seven children, counting the two she lost.' Agnes shook herself, said, 'But *why* do you want PS?'

Vanessa said, 'I was alarmed by what was going on here, what I'd heard about the way things were going and that Ernest was not able to lend a hand. . . .' She went on with her prescribed speech until she saw that Agnes was again peering into her; flushed when Agnes said:

'You are two people, Ness, and one of you is not telling the truth.'

Vanessa looked down at her shoes, then again at her sister. The crackpot in a dreary, dated, navy blue serge suit cut all wrong. Crackpot! And yet—she could see into you, more than all the others.

Agnes continued looking at her unblinkingly and in the silence that fell between them, suddenly a ferry tooted warningly and as if in reply, Agnes said:

'Oh, Ness, be *careful*!'

And Vanessa felt suddenly cold, heard distantly a bell of warning. But not for the end of the world. For something much nearer.

Lila heard it too, squinting into the early-morning sky and listening for rainbirds, wondering nervously should they take umbrellas, raincoats? Should they go to the picnic at all? How foolish to arrange it so late in May when the weather was always uncertain and could turn cold and wet. Wasn't it just like Pony and those writers to mismanage such an affair? But now, staring up at the could-be-treacherous blue sky, she felt something else—a quickening of the heart. One of her premonitions that disaster would sweep them all. She stood a moment, calming herself, remembering her vowed intentions. She would not be ruled over by Vanessa. Besides, she had made a box of sausage rolls.

'We'll go,' she announced to the sky, and repeated it to sleepy George in the kitchen. 'We'll go,' she said to PS, tying the serviette around his neck.

He pulled it away and laid it on his lap.

'Put your serviette around your neck, darling.'

'It's a *napkin*.'

'All right.'

Really! It happened over so many things now. Being corrected by PS as though Vanessa was prodding him with an invisible finger.

She said to George, pouring the tea, 'Won't you come, love?'

'No, thanks.'

'Sure?'

'I said no, didn't I?'

'I thought you'd be interested. There's going to be a little speech about Dear One and—'

'Saturday with that bunch of ratbags!'

'George!'

'Going to do some digging and listen to the races.'

'Whatever you say. PS, eat your egg, don't just play with it.'

'I don't want to go, Lila.'

'What? Not go to a lovely picnic at Fairyland?'

'I'm not allowed.'

'You *are* allowed. I said so.'

'Vanessa said—'

'I *told* you it's all right. I'm the one who says, dear. Not Vanessa. I am.'

'Lila, don't confuse him.'

'Well, I'm not going to have him think that *she's* the only one with authority. My goodness—'

'I'm not allowed,' said PS.

'You *are*. How many times do I have to tell you?'

'But Vanessa said—'

'I don't care *what* Vanessa said. You are going to the picnic to meet Dear One's friends.'

'I don't want to go.'

'Of course you want to go. There'll be swings and slippery slides and all kinds of things. Ice cream too.'

'What'll I say if she asks me?'

Lila hesitated a moment and George looked at her over the top of the *Labor Daily*.

'What will he say?' asked George.

Lila said, 'PS, there isn't going to *be* any row. And even if there is, no one is going to say anything to *you* about it. It is Lila who will take the blame.' She flung dishes into the sink and turned on the tap. She said to George with her back arched, 'I know you think I'm wrong but that can't be helped. I know what is right to do. I know what his mother would have wanted and that's enough for me.'

Tin letters slipping sideways over the jetty said: FAIRYLAND.

Beyond the jetty lay a discouraging picnic area, worn bald of grass in patches of grey dirt. Trellised summer houses leaned and sagged under the ancient gum trees. A kiosk, unpainted for many years, bore

183

a sign: HOT WATER. SAVELOYS SARGENT'S MEAT PIES. Tables and benches were scattered throughout the area between the trees. There were seesaws and a row of weary swings dropping into pools of dust. A wooden stage had been erected near the kiosk, and strings of flags and coloured electric lights had been looped between the trees in an amateurish attempt to lend an air of festivity to the weedy, drab tobacco-coloured landscape. A pall of sadness hung over the place. It was a playground of dead picnics, stale as old sandwiches, wallowing in its own litter of rusted tin cans, schnapper and whiting bones, brown beer bottles, IXL jam jars and old rubber bathing caps. Staler than the news on the yellow newspapers that blew in the breeze and wrapped themselves around legs of tables. But sadder than the rain of dead gum leaves and dried berries was the sense of mortified fun, the smell of old joy. Where now were the lovers, the dancers, the mandolin players, the children skipping rope, the ring-aring-a-roses, the beery, elated, aroused moonlight-seekers in the row boats? The dancers were gone, the lovers had choked to death in the spiky lantana vines and blackberry bushes; the skipping children were skeletons flung away into the shrubbery; the secret whispers in row boats had sunk into the green sludge at the bottom of the river.

What has happened to Fairyland? thought Lila as the ferry blundered towards the rotting jetty. And then, Something happened here. What? Murder? Food poisoning? The razor gang?

She saw a dead dog floating in the water and quickly directed the attention of PS to the tattered flags.

'Quick, quick—see how pretty they are?'

(What had happened here?)

They went up the narrow wooden gangplank with a handful of dispirited-looking people as the sun went behind clouds, casting a bilious tarnished light on the rotting summer houses and heightening the illusion that this fairground was a once lavish stage setting left out on a city dump to be burned.

(We shouldn't have come! . . . Too late now!)

Lila smiled at an emaciated woman wearing a bright dirndl who was handing out tickets behind a table from which hung a banner declaring: WELCOME SCRIBES AND DAUBERS 1934.

'Five bob. Children half price,' said the woman.

Lila said in her best-manners voice, 'I'm Mrs Baines—I'm Sinden Scott's sister.'

The woman stared at her, unmoved as a fish, and Lila flushed slightly, added, 'This is her little boy. We're guests.'

'I don't know anything about that,' said the woman.

Lila, flattened, expecting a fanfare, said, 'Well, we were invited—I'm Sinden *Scott's* sister. Pony Wardrop—'

'Oh, just a minute then.' The woman went on selling tickets and giving chits for billy cans, hot water and tea.

Lila found Pony's letter in her bag and thrust it towards the woman. 'This letter will explain who we are—Sinden Scott's relatives—Sinden Scott, the late novelist.'

'They're all writers here,' said the woman.

Really! This was dreadfully insulting. How like them to have some fool of a woman at the gate who was so common and ignorant and terrible-looking into the bargain. And not to know who they were! Poor little Sin. Could they have forgotten her so soon?

'Stand over to the side,' said the woman. 'You're blocking the line.'

They stood to the side. Like poor relatives, Lila thought. Five shillings! Her heart sank. And another two and sixpence for PS! She felt in her purse. Seven and sixpence could have been George's new hat. And they had defied Vanessa just to be stood aside at the gate like this.

'Now,' said the woman, 'I wasn't told anything about free passes. This affair is for charity. For writers.'

'My late sister—' Lila began, in a voice suitable for laying a foundation stone, but the woman had turned away and was yelling, 'Digger! Digger, come here a minute.'

A young man in dirty white trousers and a sweater disentangled himself from a group of boys and beer bottles and came towards them at a run. He had thinning sandy hair and every few seconds his left eye twitched.

'Digger, see if you can find Pony for me.'

Lila said. 'Digger *Ewers*!'

The young man turned, twitched and stared.

'Mrs Baines,' said Lila. 'I'm Lila Baines, dear. I'm Sinden Scott's sister.'

'Oh, yeah. How are you?'

He took Lila's patched-glove hand and shook it limply.

'My goodness me, Digger. You were just a little boy when I saw you last. Is your mother here, dear?'

'Yes, she's over under that pine tree.'

'Really? Fancy her being able to come with her bad leg—'

The woman at the table interrupted. 'Digger, find Pony and tell her *I* don't know anything about free passes.'

Digger twitched and said, 'It's all right, Daisy. Mrs Baines was invited.'

The woman said sourly, 'Listen, lovey, this is for destitute writers and we won't make a bloody brass razoo if every Tom, Dick and Harry's going to be let in free.'

Lila said quickly, 'But we're *not* any Tom, Dick or Harry, thank you very much.'

She took hold of Digger's thin arm and they went up the dusty incline to the fairground. Digger said, 'I'll take you over to Mum and then I'll see if I can find Pony. She was telling fortunes over in the tent.'

Lila peered around, hoping to see elated faces, outstretched hands, to hear glad cries of welcome, but saw only listless knots of shabby people around a chocolate wheel, some men playing two-up and an apathetic audience clustered beneath the wooden stage where a woman was singing 'On the Road to Gundagai' too close to the mike.

Digger led the way to a group seated under a pine tree. As they came up, several men made halfhearted attempts to rise, holding enamel mugs of hot tea.

Conchita Ewers sat on, or rather overlapped, a deck chair to one side. Spilling in all directions, she was a great ox in grey silk, her hoofs bulging out of grey suède shoes, her horns pushed up under a mammoth grey felt hat on to which a grey and venomous falcon had alighted, her massive flanks bursting through the seams of her dress at both sides, and she clutched in one puffy hand a thick alpenstock and in the other an obscene cream puff. (Who was it who had said that Conchita was really William Randolph Hearst in drag? Sinden had laughed for days but Lila had never quite got the point.)

Digger said, 'Mum, here's Lila Baines.'

Conchita uttered a groan, dropped her cream puff into the dust and extended behemoth arms. Lila bent, tipped forward, nosed into the quivering jelly, righted herself and her hat, said:

'Conchita, dear, well my goodness, fancy you here!'

'Lila.' Conchita spoke in a deep tragedy-queen voice. 'Dear Lila Baines. Little Sin's sister—'

'Digger rescued us from that woman at the gate—we came in on the boat just now—'

'Little little Sin!' It seemed Conchita was about to call for two minutes' silence. 'Sinden Scott,' she added to the others, and a white-haired man wearing shorts said, 'Ah, yes, *Marmon*, a good book. Met her once at Packy's Club.' The others nodded perfunctorily.

'Get Lila some tea,' said Conchita to Digger, and turned towards PS, half hidden behind Lila. 'And is this—'

Lila brought him out proudly. 'This is PS,' she said.

Conchita studied him through a broken lorgnette. 'There *is* no PS,' she said.

Lila made a quick movement.

'I know that's what she called him,' growled Conchita, brushing pastry crumbs into the fissure between her giant breasts. 'But there is *no* postscript to her. When she went, everything died with her.'

The obedient group nodded and Lila gave a

nervous laugh, sat on the edge of a bench and pulled up PS's drooping pants.

'There can be no appendix to a work of art such as she,' continued Conchita, and she beckoned PS forward.

'I shall call you "Boy",' she announced, and the group murmured approval. Conchita nodded graciously. 'Boy's little mother was the greatest of us all.'

'Not greater than you, Conchita,' said the old man in shorts, rubbing cold, white knees.

Conchita said, 'I have not been recognised in my lifetime. I have been overlooked and bypassed for those others who write commercial rubbish, but I shall be recognised posthumously.' Conchita's massive works included a trilogy on the Coptic wars; *Bonaparte, an Inside Study*; and *Joan Heard Voices*, a verse drama in four acts with forty-eight characters and twenty-three sets.

'Since my accident,' she said, 'I have written no more.'

Conchita had fallen between a ferry and a wharf and after being fished out by a grappling hook, had announced her retirement to the one and only news reporter she had ever met.

Since then, she had lived on in the crumbling large house by the river, musing on her failures, accepting compliments on her out-of-print books by anyone who remembered them and gathering around her a carefully selected group who sat at her feet while she handed out the sour grapes.

'In this country,' said Conchita, accepting one of Lila's squashed sausage rolls, 'a cricketer is a national hero but an artist is nothing!'

Her group sucked this in like oxygen; began reviving.

'Did Sin leave any money?' asked Conchita.

Lila said, 'Oh, goodness, no,' and began an inventory of hospital and funeral expenses, but Conchita cut her short.

'There you *are*,' she said. 'The greatest one of all of us died without a farthing.' She made a dramatic gesture and the group brightened perceptibly.

'Queers!' yelled an excitable younger man with bitten fingernails. 'If you're an artist, they think you're queer. Too right. They think you're a poofter!'

Conchita turned an oblique gaze on him. 'Oscar Wilde was *branded* as a poofter, Harry,' she said, as though this were fresh news. 'You must learn to live with that. They pilloried poor Oscar; they did the same thing to our own Gus Trencherman, who took a gun and blew out his brilliant brain. Boy's mother used the episode in *Marmon*, probably the most beautiful chapter ever written about ambivalent love; the affair between the two cane cutters, Dave and John—so aptly named—Biblical in its application, don't you agree, Lila?'

191

Lila glanced quickly at PS, but he was absorbed with a grasshopper.

'It's a lovely book.' Lila gasped and wheezed. (What is Conchita babbling about? *I've* read *Marmon*. *I* never saw anything like that between the two cane cutters. Surely Sinden didn't mean to imply—I must read it again.)

'Was that a rainbird?' she asked, searching the sky for help.

'Boy's mother,' said Conchita, 'had more spunk and talent than all of us put together. She lived among us, drank us all up and then hammered us into characters on her little anvil, sending sparks up into the night. She had her little room in my house, and on and on into the dawn, the typewriter spat, spat, spat—'

'Oh, she never worked at night,' said Lila, and Conchita turned a withering look on her and someone said, 'Shhhh!' 'On and on into the dawn,' continued Conchita relentlessly, 'knowing that she had only a little time to get her brilliant timely message down on paper. Well, that message fell on the deaf ears of *atheletes*! Yes, cricketers are immortal—she is dust.'

'Wasn't there another book?' asked the old man with the marble knees.

'Unfinished,' said Conchita.

Unfinished! This pleased the group enormously. They chuffed with pleasurable sighs, feigned sadness.

'Her *best*.' Conchita handed them the cherry and turned her great white face towards PS.

'Boy,' she said, 'would you like to come here and sit on my knee?'

She reached out and grabbed him, lifted him, squirming, on to her paddock of a lap.

'Boy,' she said, 'someday you will finish your mother's book for her. Will you do that?'

He drew back, alarmed, pushed at her breast with both hands.

'S-h-y,' said Lila to the group.

'Will you do that for your little mother?'

He struck out with one fist, dislodging himself, as the deck chair teetered sideways and Conchita sagged towards the dusty ground. Two members of the group rushed to rescue their dethroned queen. 'That wasn't very nice,' said someone. Lila said, angrily, 'He's too young to understand,' pushed a sausage roll into his protesting mouth, jumped around as a shot rang out.

'What was that? Oh, the ladies' sack race. Look, pet, see the funny ladies?'

Conchita said, not without pride, 'Boy's mother once threw an ashtray at me, but I forgave her. I forgave her everything. Even what she did to Ernest Huxley.'

(Oh, goodness, will she never stop? Are we going to be marooned with her all the afternoon? Where is Pony? Here comes Digger with our tea. That twitch! No wonder. He'll never get away from *her* and she'll never die. PS, I'll never hang on to you when you're grown and want to go.)

'Oh, tea. How nice of you, Digger. And a lemonade for PS. Aren't we having a lovely time, pet?'

'Pony's over in the tent telling fortunes. She won't be long.'

'Oh.'

'Where are you going, Digger-boy?'

'I thought I'd go for a swim, Mum.'

'It's not warm enough.'

'Oh, the water won't be cold, Mum.'

'Not warm enough for *you*! Digger-boy has a heart murmur.'

'Ahhhh.'

'Alf and Rexie are going in.'

'Alf and Rexie are big strong men. Now come and sit down; you've been racing around all over the place. And pick up my stick for me, dear. I was telling them about Boy's mother . . .'

It began all over again. The sky darkened, brightened, darkened again. They sipped bitter tea. The loudspeaker hummed and said, 'Attention, please! Elsie Chaffey will now recite "My Heritage".'

Then a nasal child's voice:

> '*My land is girt with ocean,*
> *My land is wide and free.*
> *No other land more golden,*
> *A precious Eden, she . . .*'

194

'That's Sid Chaffey's little girl.'

'Kids reciting! Bloody boring picnic, if you ask me.'

'Rotten turnout.'

'Where's all the old gang?'

'All dead. Or got the sense not to come.'

'Wish I'd had. Want to see if we can get a beer?'

'I'll give it a go.'

A scream of 'Coo-ee' broke through the monotonous talk and Lila, turning, saw a little girl in a red print dress running towards them, but growing middle-aged as she rushed up and threw her small arms around Lila's neck.

'Lila,' said Pony Wardrop. 'Hooray! I've been looking all over the bloody joint for you.'

'Pony—well, my goodness, you haven't changed a bit.'

Pig's arse I haven't!' Pony's puckish, withered little face gathered itself into a smirk. 'Excuse my French, love.'

She kissed Lila again, turned to look at PS.

'*My* God, is this him?'

She squinted at him a moment, then drew him towards her.

'Oh, my God. He's the spitting image of her.'

Easy tears ran down her small lined face. She kissed him tenderly, then drew back, laughing suddenly.

'PS,' she said. 'The blue-sky gentleman.'

Lila felt a sudden pang. She had forgotten—*almost*

forgotten Sinden's joke: 'What are you working on now, Sin?' 'My blue-sky gentleman.'

'Guess what, pet. Pony knew Dear One.'

His face said, Another one!

Pony said, 'You're not supposed to be here. You're supposed to be with my party.'

'Yes, well, there was a mix-up at the gate and then we found Digger Ewers and Conchita—'

'Come on,' said Pony. She took both their hands and skipped along between them in her little-girl sandals. 'We got some beer going over in a summer-house and some of the old mad peasants are there. Charlie Seay and the Howard girls—you remember them, don't you?' She sped them away across the dusty picnic ground, waving to people as she went. 'I didn't know you'd got stuck with Conchita. What kills me is Sin gone and that old fake Conchita's still poisoning the air. What a fraud. Her and her lousy books and her gab gab gab about "my beloved Sinden" when all the time she was piss green with jealousy. Oh, it was all right when Sin was just battling along without recognition, but once *Marmon* won that prize, whacko the diddle-o, old lady hemlock couldn't *stand* it. Had to go and fall off a ferryboat to get some attention.'

Lila said, 'Oh, but poor thing—she might have drowned.'

'Not her.' Pony went into gusts of laughter. 'Di'n't you ever hear the lovely story? Someone said to Walter

Hatfield, "Conchita fell off a ferry," and Walter said, "Some boy we know?"'

'Ah,' said Lila.

'Ferry—fairy. See?'

'Oh, yes, very funny.'

(Really! All this in front of PS. What *had* Sinden seen in Pony? She really was rather common and raffish and why did she have to dress as a little girl of ten?)

'You remember Walter Hatfield, don't you?'

'Yes, Pony, oh, yes. He did a picture of Sinden once. Vanessa has it in her house.'

Pony said, 'He's the father of my love child.'

Lila said, 'Is your little boy here?'

'Oh, no, love. My new boy friend doesn't like kids around, so he's living up in the country with my cousin. He's mad as a cut snake, my kid. Going to *be* something, I think. Here we are.'

Lila drew back at the entrance of the tottering summerhouse. It was filled with an odd collection of people, all drinking beer and talking loudly. Arguments were flashing around the wooden table and a woman wearing a leopard-skin dress, and a bunch of false grapes in her hennaed hair, was kissing a man in the corner.

Lila said, 'I don't think there's room—'

Pony said, 'Move over, Dot. Here's Lila Baines and PS. Listen, everyone, here's PS.'

Flushed faces looked up and there were greetings. Two men rose unsteadily and offered a seat to Lila.

'Give Lila a beer.'

'Oh, no, thank you. I never touch it.'

'Oh, go on, love. You'll be a long time dead. Have a shandy then. It's a bosker thirst-quencher. Musette, give Lila a shandy, darling. Lila, you remember Musette Munson, don't you? Otherwise known as the Constant Nymph.'

Musette, a horse-faced woman wearing a playsuit, extended a blue cold arm.

'Hello. Didn't I meet you when you and Sin were living in that madhouse at the Cross?'

'That was my sister Vere.'

Pony said, 'How's the mad Vere? How's that crazy Agnes? Where's Vanessa? Are they coming?'

Lila began a family history but no one was listening. Someone pushed a glass in front of her. She said, 'What's in this?'

'Just a shandy, love. Lemonade and stuff.'

'Get the blue-sky gentleman some lemonade.'

'Holy cow, is this *Sin's* kid?'

'Of course, you idiot.'

'How are you, kid? Shake hands.' A man pushed a large red hand out as PS drew back.

'S-h-y,' said Lila. She had begun to wheeze. The man laughed.

198

'He'll be fine,' said the man. 'That kid's going to be fine.'

Lila gave a nervous laugh and said, 'I wonder how often the boats run back? Do you know, Pony?'

'Now, Lila, what are you worrying about the boats for?'

'We can't stay too long. George hasn't been too well and—'

'Oh, you can't go for ages yet. They're going to give PS a boomerang later.'

'A boomerang?'

'For Sin. Bloody silly if you ask me, but old Champion, on the awards committee, likes to make speeches, and this year they're giving boomerangs out. *Memento morti* or whatever the hell you call it. He's written a poem to Sin. Oh, he'd go crackers if you weren't here. I said you were coming. Drink up, love.'

Lila sipped her shandy.

(Well, it certainly is a pleasant drink and I suppose they mean well. Can't offend them.)

They were talking now about Sinden. Good old Sin, poor little Sin, angelic, crazy, gutsy, delightful, bad-tempered Sinden Scott. Each claimed to have known her better than the others. It seemed to Lila that the anecdotes served mostly to point up their own virtues and wit. '*I* said to her –' '*My* point was—' 'Yes, but she told *me* in deepest confidence—' Beer slopped and Sinden arose from the grave and went through a series of unlikely episodes, flickered in and out of an old, badly patched film that they were projecting while Pony commented loudly, 'Bull. You're all ding-bats. Bosh and balls, she never *did*.'

Someone touched Lila's arm and she turned to look at a man with a lined handsome face.

'She'd have a good laugh if she were here, don't you reckon?'

'Oh, *yes*.' Lila was glad to agree with someone.

'You don't remember me.'

'I know the face but—'

'Charlie Seay.'

'Oh, Mr Seay, of course. She had so many friends—'

'Mind if I ask you something?' He lowered his voice, seemed anxious. 'Did she ever mention me to you?'

'I'm sure she must have,' Lila's social voice said.

'I mean, when she was ill—towards the end. Did she ever ask where Charlie was?'

'Not to my knowledge.'

Now he seemed crestfallen, the handsome eyes insulted.

'I was away,' he said. 'I read about it in the papers.'

'It was so sudden.'

'But I was away.' He jerked his head towards the storytellers.

'Did any of *them* come to see her?'

'Only Pony,' said Lila.

'Yes, Pony's true blue,' said Charlie Seay. 'The others wouldn't bother. Left her all alone. *Now* listen to them. Or rather, don't.'

He gave her a strained bitter look and said, 'I should have been with her.'

(Why should you have?)

'I wonder if you can tell me something.' His voice so low now that she had to lean across the table to hear him above the noise. 'Was there a big bunch of blue irises? Did it come?'

'Do you mean at the hospital?'

'No, after. No card. Just blue irises.' It seemed as though his life depended on it.

'I really don't remember now. We were all so upset.' Lila gave a sudden wheeze. 'But it's funny you should ask that, because the last time we were up at—at the Little Garden, someone had left some blue—'

He nodded. 'I go up whenever I can.'

'Oh! Well—it's very thoughtful—'

'We once had a little beach house together, down at Narrabeen. Just the one time. It had irises growing in the yard.'

(Oh, and now I remember; they used to come to the house sometimes in a box from Searl's Florists. 'Oh, Sin, how pretty. Did Ernest send those?' And Sinden's laugh, almost rude. 'Oh, Lila! Ernest send *flowers*?' 'Who, then?' 'Oh, someone I know.')

Lila said stiffly, 'Well, it's nice of you. She'd be pleased to think that one of her friends took the trouble.'

'Trouble,' said Charlie Seay, 'doesn't enter into it. Nor does friendship.'

He looked out over the picnic ground and seemed to be seeing something a great distance away.

Lila said, 'Did you know her long?' and had to repeat it over the noise.

'No, not long,' he said.

(A beach house together. One of those times she slipped away and no one knew where. No explanations. Just like her. One of those shades she pulled down.)

'I just wondered if she'd ever asked for me.'

'It's over six years ago. She may have and I've forgotten.'

(No. Only for Logan those last days. Always for Logan. And you know it. I can tell by the look on your face. But why are you so hurt? What did she do to you?)

'I'm sorry,' she said, but said it now for her sister.

'It's all right,' he said.

Lila, suddenly uncorked with nervousness, began a swift recital of the last days—the hospital, what the doctor said. All right to go home, he said; young, and inexperienced—everyone had said so—but then who could tell with Bright's Disease—

202

He stood up and said, 'Well, cheerio. I have to go now.'

'Oh, do you? Well, look—you must just say hello to her little boy—'

He said, 'Look, I hope you don't mind my saying this. I think all this is putrid.' He indicated the rowdy group in the summerhouse, and the people milling around outside. 'I think it's the most God-awful vulgar thing I ever saw and if I were you I'd take him home on the next boat.'

He walked out of the summerhouse and across the picnic ground towards the gate.

Lila grabbed at Pony, who was sitting across the table with PS on her lap and engaged in some violent disagreement with the woman in the leopard-skin dress.

'Pony, can you come here—I can't shout.'

'What, love?'

Pony edged into the space next to Lila and hugged PS to her.

He looked at Lila mournfully. 'Are we going home soon?'

'Yes, pet. Yes, we're going soon. Oh, look, is that the ice cream man? Go and get a sixpenny cone. Don't *drop* it, darling. Pony, who was that man?'

'What man, love?'

'Charlie Seay.'

'Oh, don't you remember Charlie? You must have

met Charlie. Didn't you ever come to one of the poetry readings we used to give at the Blue Tea Room?'

'He seems to have known Sin very well.'

'Oh, my dear. He had a big thing about her. Poor old Charlie—bit of a no-hoper. Always was. Well, he used to moan around after Sin, mournful as a mopoke.'

'When? When was this?'

'Oh, God, I don't know. About the time she was engaged to Ernest.'

'At the *same* time?'

'Well—yes. We all thought it was a hell of a whoop.'

'But he said they had a weekend cottage together.'

Pony went into a high-pitched little-girl giggle.

'Yes. Sin called it "Wild Oats by the Sea".'

Lila coughed. 'Did it—did it go on for long?'

'No! She never took Charlie seriously. *He* was serious, of course. *Sin*cere Charlie, we called him, but he never saw the joke. That's Charlie's trouble, dear, always the bloody death's head at the feast.'

'He seems sad.'

'Oh, *he'd* be sad if you gave him Government House and everything in it. He's a professional mourner. When he asked her to marry him, she said—'

'He asked her to *marry*—'

'Oh, yes. She said to me, "Pony, he's got beautiful hands and beautiful manners but for sheer

unadulterated fun I'd sooner be married to the Arch-
bishop of Canterbury." We roared!'

(But irises all these years! What was it Vanessa had
said about Sinden putting on blinders?)

Lila wheezed heavily.

'What's up, love?'

'It's my asthma. The wind must have changed.'

'Have another shandy. That'll buck you up. Musey,
pour another shandy for Lila, dear.'

'No, I don't want—'

'Oh, come on. Do you good.'

'You're sure there's nothing in it?'

'Nothing but lemonade and a drop of beer. Couldn't
get a baby drunk.'

'Well, it *is* refreshing. Oh, dear. That poor sad
man.'

'Oh, don't worry about Charlie, ducks.'

'So funny that she never mentioned him; introduced him once in the street, just like a stranger.'

(Confide in *you*—oh, *yes*. Probably to Vere, but
never to me.)

'But, Lila, Charlie wasn't anything to her. Just one
of those times she was pinching herself to see if she was
still alive.'

'What do you mean?'

'That's what she called it when she was on the outs
with Ernest or he was neglecting her—'

'Ernest never neglected her!'

'Oh, Lila. Half the *time*! Mr Bloody Put Everything Off! That was Ernest Huxley. Every time she wanted to get married there was some piddling excuse. He'd have to go to Melbourne or New Zealand or he was editing a book or wouldn't it be better to wait until the hot weather was over? She'd come up to my flat and cry her heart out. "What am I going to do, Pony?" Poor little wretch. "What am I going to do about Ernest? I'm going to be forty by the time he makes up his mind. When am I going to have my *child*?" But he'd go on making excuses and letting the months go by until it was another year. I knew in my pores something was going to happen. She was bubbling inside like a kettle whistling to be taken off the stove and used. Well, of course it happened.'

'Yes,' said Lila. 'It happened all right.'

'Just like I knew it would. Funny that it had to be through Charlie Seay. Slightly ironic.'

'How? What?'

'Charlie Seay introduced her to Logan.'

'I thought—we always thought she met Logan at a party.'

'Did. Charlie brought him.'

'Were they friends?'

'No. They'd only met that evening. In a pub.'

'Pony!'

'Too right. Having a beer in the Carlton.'

'The *Carlton*!'

'Yes. Belting down a beer.'

'But the Carlton—how *peculiar*.'

'Why? Charlie used to hang out there all the time. Charlie walked in one evening and there's L. Marriott attached by an umbilical cord to the bar and telling stories in his own ineffable way and the boys there glued to every word as though he was the Oracle at Delphi; and when the joint closes at six o'clock, they go on up to Charlie's place at the Cross and swap more stories until late in the evening and then apparently Charlie says he has to go to this fancy-dress party at Packy's Club where a lot of cuckoo writers and artists hang out and says it'll be a mad do and why don't you come along and Logan says why not, anything for a free drink, and that's how darkies are born.'

'Did Sin tell you all this?'

'Darling, I was *there*. I remember because I went as Jackie Coogan or something—a boy anyway. Ernest and Sin came as King Cophetua and the beggar maid. She didn't have a brass razoo to her name at the time, so she tore an old blue chiffon dress into rags and came barefoot and with her hair down; and Ernest pinned up in an old red velvet curtain with white bunny fur she'd sewn around the neck and wearing a golden paper crown. God, how it comes back to me with a couple of beers and seeing you today—Ernest in that red velvet curtain with his sensible brogues on and sucking on that frightful pipe and she looking about sixteen! Anyway, the party's beginning to get a bit rough and about midnight, *in* the door comes Charlie Seay and Logan, both a bit blotto. Oh, I thought, *there*'s a handsome devil! Wouldn't say no to *him* on a wet cold night. Well, *you* know, Lila, how Logan could walk in a room and make every other man look like cold porridge. And he's looking around the room and smiling with a faintly superior look—you know, my dear—the earl watching the peasants have fun.'

'Oh, yes—yes. I know *just*—'

'Well, he's been in the room one minute and he sees Sin and he says to Charlie, "Who's that?" and poor bloody Charlie takes him over and says, "Sinden, this is Logan Marriott." She cocks her head on one side—you know the way she used to—and says, "Have you struck gold yet?" And Charlie says, "How would you know he's been on the gold fields?" and Sin says, "There's only one Logan Marriott in the world and he comes from Bacchus Marsh and he once met my sister Vanessa." Logan never says a word, not a word, just keeps looking at her, and she says, "Well, Logan, have you found your gold?" And he looks at her and looks at her and then he says, "I have *now*."'

A clash of cymbals.

Lila jumped; turned to see six heavy girls in white mosquito netting dance clumsily on to the wooden platform while the loudspeaker ground out the 'Dance of the Seven Veils'. She said, 'If only—'

208

'If. If. If,' said Pony, rolling a cigarette in her little tobacco-stained fingers. 'They had to meet. Kismet. Cosmos. Appointment in Samarra.'

'Do you believe in that?'

'Listen, Lila, *she* knew it and *he* knew it too, and it was all settled that minute. Charlie knew it too. We all did.'

Pony giggled, struck a match. 'I remember about two in the morning, Ernest wandering around in his red velvet asking everyone where was she? Had anyone seen Sinden? Then someone said, "Oh, she went off with the tall, good-looking bloke," and Ernest said, "But she doesn't have any shoes!" Typical Ernest remark, my dear. The sky falling in on him and all he can think of is that she's gone off in her blue rags and bare feet. We screamed! Then he said, "But where could they go at this hour of the night?" and I thought, Over the moon, my boy, and *you'll* never find her again, and of course I was right. Five days later I get a telegram: "Married Logan Marriott. Meet us Carlton drinks at once." '

('Lila, I just got married to Logan Marriott.')

'Oh, Pony—Ernest could have stopped her.'

'Ernest couldn't stop a taxi.'

'They had so much in common.'

'Books.'

'Books were her life, Pony.'

209

'She was her own life and she didn't want it edited by Ernest. All he ever *did* was edit her.'

'He worshipped the ground she walked on.'

Pony giggled. 'Provided he picked it out first.'

Lila held a damp handkerchief to her face. In spite of the coolness of the day she was sweating profusely.

She said, 'I never knew—I always thought—they met at a dance.'

A formal dance, surely. Long white gloves and a waltz. Logan in tails. No wonder Ernest never forgave her. Running off barefoot into the night with a stranger and now, today, Pony still giggling about it.

She said, 'I don't think it's funny, Pony.'

'I do.'

'I *don't*. She could at least have said to Ernest, "Mr Marriott is going to see me home."'

This seemed to amuse Pony even more; her little high-pitched giggle rang out and was suddenly echoed by kookaburras in a tree. The picnic ground shook with bird laughter.

Against the noise, Lila said, 'It was a cruel thing to do.'

'Bosh and balls.'

'It was. And it was cruel what she did to Charlie Seay. To laugh at him behind his back.'

'She laughed at everything, Lila.'

'I don't understand her. I never did. I won't treat it as a joke.'

(No, I won't! I'm horrified by it. I've lived my life with jurisdiction because I believe rules are to be kept. You broke the rules, Sinden, and you suffered for it. Logan wasn't even there at the end. You tipped everything over to run off with a stranger who had a smile for you and it serves you right, my dear. I'm sorry but it does. I know you're dead and I'm not supposed to think ill of you but I can't help it. I'm very angry with you. . . . Or am I angry because Vanessa knew you better?)

She was amazed at her own feelings. Resentment surged through her.

She stood up, wheezing badly now. She would be ill by tonight. Poor George would certainly be up all night.

'PS. Come here.' Here voice was strangely high.

He was watching the dancers, ice cream on his shirt. He didn't move.

'Didn't you *hear* me?'

He turned, surprised. She rarely rapped out at him.

'Come here. Look at you. Ice cream all over your good shirt. Here, spit on my hanky and I'll wipe your face. We're going home.'

'Oh, you can't go yet, Lila. You have to wait for the boomerang.' Hands clutched at her. Someone tried to refill her glass. The woman in the leopard-skin dress was making for her with outstretched arms.

She pushed them away. What a dreadful raffish crew. They'd probably all been at that awful costume party and repeated the story, and laughed. Now they were laughing at her. Well, let them laugh. No wonder they were all failures, with their lack of any moral sense.

She wiped his face, wiping away the picnic, the past.

'Goodbye,' she said. Took PS by the hand and hurried him out of the summerhouse, Pony scuttling behind.

'What's up, love?'

'I think there's a boat at four o'clock.'

'Come over to the kiosk and I'll get you a cup of tea.'

'No, thank you, Pony.'

'Well, don't get your shirt off.'

Pony looking up at her like a hurt child.

'After all, we're Sin's friends. We knew her very well.'

Indeed you did!

The loudspeaker hummed and said, 'Now we come to the big event of the day—'

Pony grabbed at her.

'They're going to start now. Stick it out a bit longer.' The dancers had left the stage and a white-haired old man was standing at the microphone holding a sheaf of papers while a woman in a blue voile dress laid out gilt-painted boomerangs on a table.

Trapped now, Lila felt them being pushed along with the crowd towards the dais. Someone introduced the white-haired man as 'Mr Champion, our president.'

There was scattered applause and a voice called, 'Good on you, Champ.'

Mr Champion shuffled his papers, adjusted his broken glasses, thanked the committee, the ticket sellers, the pianist, the tea makers.

A man with beery breath behind Lila said, 'Get on with it, for Chrissake!'

Spots of rain fell. Mr Champion extolled the dead.

Canonised by clichés they had spent their lives avoiding, the defunct authors and poets became enshrined in the hall of fame, laid the foundations of a national heritage, handed down the torch and burned with a pure white flame at the mercy of Mr Champion's rococo prose. Relatives tripped up the steps to the platform and accepted gilt boomerangs with deprecating smiles. In the thickening gloom as rain fell, the crowd melted away, a ferry tooted dismally on the river and Mr Champion droned on, came at long-winded last to Sinden Scott, a brave little soul cut off in her prime just when she was about to reap the harvest, enjoy the fruits, find the pot of gold.

'Bear we our little sister to the Tomb . . .' intoned Mr Champion.

'She hath set down the half-filled cup of life.
From Sunlight she hath hastened to the gloom;
Mother an hour, and one quick year a wife.
Our Little Sister of the Pen! The brave,
Kind, sanguine spirit falters to the grave.'

PS tugged at her dress. 'Lila, I want to go to the—'

'Shh. In a minute. This is all about Dear One.'

'And now, a golden boomerang to keep her name returning.'

'Go and get the boomerang, pet.'

'No.'

'But it's for you.'

'*No.*'

'I'll come up with you.'

'No. *No.*' He pulled away angrily. 'I want to go to the—' Damp laughter from the few people left. Lila stumbled up the steps, shook Mr Champion's hand, accepted the sticky golden boomerang from the woman, turned and said:

'On behalf of her son—'

The rain poured down and the people scattered. She found herself alone on the platform. After all her fussing, not even Pony had waited.

It wasn't until much later that evening at home, atomised and berated by George, that Lila remembered they had left the boomerang on the ferry.

* * *

214

Everything in the Big House seemed very wound up, funny, spooky a bit, with no one around except Diana, who had opened the door when George brought him back. She had pulled him inside, saying, 'Oh, he's late,' and shut the front door in poor George's face. Her neck was red and splotchy. 'Your aunt's waiting for you upstairs, love,' she whispered. She prodded him towards the stairs with her great big hands.

'Don't worry, lovey,' she said, and winked at him.

He went up the stairs, holding on to the rail, and paused on the landing.

'Go on, don't keep her waiting, love. Please. Don't get us into trouble, there's a good boy.'

Diana was crying as she ran through the green baize door to the kitchen.

He knew what he was going to be asked.

No one was about upstairs and Vanessa's door was closed. He stood in front of it, wondering what to do next, when it opened suddenly and Vanessa nearly fell over him.

She said crossly, 'Doors are to be knocked on. Don't you know that?'

'Yes.'

'Let's hear you knock then.'

She closed the door. 'Now knock,' she said from inside.

It was one of those games she liked to play, so he obliged.

'May I come in?' Now she was telling him what to say.

'M'come in?'

She opened the door again. 'Certainly you may. Welcome home, PS. Did you have a nice weekend?'

'Yes.'

'Yes, thank you, Vanessa.'

'Kew, Vanessa.'

'Why are you late?'

'We missed the boat.'

'Who brought you home?'

'George.'

'Yes, you may sit down but I hadn't yet said so, had I?'

It was going to be worse than he thought. It was that picnic, of course. But he mustn't get Lila into trouble; she was sick.

'What did you do over the weekend?'

What a big moon through the window.

'I asked you a question, PS.'

'Er—nothing.'

'Where did you go?'

What if she didn't let him go home next Friday?

'Nowhere.'

'You didn't leave Neutral Bay?'

'No.'

It was going to be all right now. He'd saved Lila.

216

Vanessa took a bunch of keys from her dressing table and said, 'Come with me.'

They went across the hall and she unlocked the door of the spare room and snapped on the light.

The bed had been taken away and on the floor was a whole toy town and yards and yards of railway line with crossings and signals. At a little green-and-red station the train stood waiting with its perfect black engines marked BRITISH RAILWAYS and six beautiful carriages with windows and a red luggage van with sliding doors. Tiny milk cans stood on the platform, and tin people, a conductor blowing a whistle.

'Look,' said Vanessa.

She knelt and touched a switch. Lights sprang on in the little carriages and the train moved, sprang forward with a twitch and ran around the tracks, over a bridge on to a siding, shunted and raced forward again around and around the track.

'Oh,' he said.

'Like it?'

'Oh, yes. Yes.'

His head on the floor watching the little train rush towards him, thinking of a real bridge over a river with yellow jellyfish.

Then the train stopped, the lights in the little windows went out. He looked up at Vanessa.

She said, 'It took us all yesterday afternoon to put

217

this together as a surprise for you and now you come home and tell me a naughty lie.'

She didn't seem angry, but sad.

'A lie between you and me, who are friends,' she said.

Found out. He stared at the train. Was she going to send it back now?

'A lie between friends is the most hurtful thing in the world,' said Vanessa. 'Stand up, please.'

Stood up. Wondered, what next?

'Lila took you to that picnic, didn't she?'

'Yes.'

'Then why did you say you hadn't left home?'

'I don't know.'

'Was it because you knew I had said you were not to go?'

'Yes.'

'Did you think I would punish you if I found out?'

'I don't know.'

'How old are you?'

'You know.'

'What?'

'Six and a half.'

'Six and a half is old enough to know that I would never punish you for something that is not your fault, but Lila's. Don't you know that?'

He nodded.

'You were forced to go against your will, weren't you?'

He fingered the train engine.

'Don't touch that, PS. Did they say you had to go?'

'Yes.'

'Did they say why?'

'Because—um—the people knew Dear One.'

'Don't use that silly name. Say "my mother".'

He didn't want to, but he burst into tears, leaned against Vanessa helplessly, sobbing into her thigh, wondering what had made him cry.

Vanessa stroked his head. 'Was it awful?' she asked.

'Yes,' he gulped, hiccuping. 'Yes, yes,' he said, 'it was awful.' Anything to agree with her now, get it over. It wasn't really a picnic, he told her. There were no other children to play with, just a lot of grownups sitting around tables drinking stuff and he heard a little girl called Pony tell Lila that his mother never wore shoes and you know what, she ran off in the middle of the night with a strange man and there was a nasty old lady called Conchita, who called him Boy and knew a lot of poofters. She didn't like him because he'd stopped Dear One from finishing something. And it rained! And he wasn't going to write stories! Ever! Bosh and balls, he said as an afterthought.

'Whom did you hear say that?'

'Pony.'

'Promise never to say it again.'

'OK.'

'I promise, Vanessa.'

'Promise, Vanessa.'

'And don't talk about poofters either. A poofter is—well, an ugly name for something. Like calling someone a dago, see?'

She dried his eyes. 'Cheer up,' she said.

So he wasn't going to get into trouble after all. He needn't have worried all day. Because now, funnily enough, Vanessa was smiling and her voice was soft and pleased as though he'd just got top marks at Miss Pile's. Her eyes were very bright and sparkling and she patted him.

'Can I play with the train now?'

'Tomorrow. There's a jolly nice chicken for supper so go and wash your hands.'

She locked the spare room, led him to the bathroom. Handed him the new cake of Morny soap.

'Remember, PS, that you are never again to tell me a lie because I shall know.'

Nice smelly soap. Nicer than the plain yellow bath soap at home.

Vanessa crossed the hall, opened Ettie's door. Ettie put something quickly into the wardrobe, closed it, twinkled and glittered across the room, her little hands making knots in the air.

'Aha,' she said. 'Tum tum tum.'

'I knew,' said Vanessa, 'that if I made enough fuss, Lila would take him to that loathsome picnic.'

'Oh, my dear—' Ettie, very concerned, executed a small dance, made fawning gestures. Stopped, surprised, when Vanessa laughed.

'It seems to have had quite an effect on him,' said Vanessa.

'Ah,' said Ettie, understanding nothing but that Vanessa seemed not displeased. She stood still, obediently waiting for the next remark, while Vanessa studied her fingernails, found them apparently to her liking.

'Hysterical,' she said. 'Poor little thing.'

Ettie, directed now, said, 'Ah, ah—poor little lamb.'

'He turned to me, clung to me, Ettie.'

'Ah, yes, he would, Ness.'

Vanessa lit a cigarette, let the match burn down almost to her fingers, said:

'Well, we'll see. One can't hurry these things but—'

She seemed to see something beyond the room, behind the moon outside.

'I promised you it wouldn't be forever, Ettie. Our penal servitude in the colonies. We may all be back in London sooner than we think.'

'Ness, Ness, oh, you good thing.'

'Supper,' said Vanessa crisply. Then her back said, going through the door, 'There's no need to hide bottles in wardrobes, Ettie. No one is stopping you having a little sherry in moderation, but it must be out in the open.'

Lila slid the rabbit into the oven, slammed the door, burned her wrist slightly, sucked it.

'No letter,' she said to George. 'No letter, no telephone call the whole week. That's what worries me. When I got there today, the maid was waiting with him at the gate. I thought *she'd* come storming out of the house but the blinds were all pulled down as though they were out.'

'Good.'

'It's not good. Not when she's silent. Oh, I don't like it a bit when she's silent. Mater used to say, "Ness is quiet; watch *out*." He told me she's bought him a train, it fills the whole room and then—listen, listen, don't read the paper, I want you to hear this. She wouldn't let him play with it until he'd told her where he'd been. Blackmail, if you please. So of course he told her about the picnic. Had to. Now he's upset about telling on me. Hardly said a word coming home on the boat, wouldn't eat his jam sandwich. So meek and subdued all the time, saying, "May I?" the way she makes him. Every week he comes back more like a different boy. Listen, how long can it go on?'

George said, 'How long can we go on? I'm out.'

'What?'

'I got the sack today.'

Lila sat down heavily at the kitchen table and closed her eyes, thought, He didn't say that, waited for the illusion to pass, but in a moment the new, freshly painted black trouble clicked in her mind.

'My God.'

'Said it was temporary but—'

'No,' she said, 'I don't believe it. They don't sack people who work for the unions.'

'Even the unions are broke. They sacked Dave Petrie and he's worked at the Trades Hall for fifteen years.'

'George.'

'Two weeks' wages.'

'My *God*.'

'He'd better be.'

'I loaned Vere two pounds today,' she burst out. 'Some man she's been writing songs with got drunk and—'

'We can't keep the whole family, Lila.'

'We have to keep *him*.'

'I know.'

All she could think of now was that Vanessa mustn't find out. Not yet, anyway. Not until they could see light, see something ahead.

An old poster flashed into her mind. 'VOTE FOR GEORGE BAINES.'

'To think,' she said, 'that they could do this to a man who has all his life supported Labour. A man who was very nearly in Parliament.'

George said, 'You certainly picked a good time to remind me of that.'

They were floating paper boats in the discoloured tin bath in Mrs Grindel's laundry and Winnie said:

'Are you going to be on the dole like us?'

'What's the dole?' he asked.

'When your dad's out of work. Like Mr Baines.'

'He's not.'

'Yes he is. He got the sack. My mum says youse'll be going to live with your other aunty for good now.'

'I won't.'

'Yes you will.'

Angrily, he sank his boat with one fist.

'I'll never!' he said.

'You'll hafta.'

'I won't.' Will I? 'Why?'

'Because you're Another Mouth.'

His heart beating very fast, he looked at Winnie, at her gap-toothed grin, her stringy hair done up in cotton rag curlers, the ring of dried orange marmalade around her lips. Horrid Winnie. Always knowing about things before he did and scaring him. Wouldn't the Lawson children love to belt *her* with a big thorny stick.

'You're common!' he told Winnie. That was the Worst Thing you could call anyone at Miss Pile's school.

Winnie's face puckered up, turned puce colour and she began to cry, as she always did, in great silent gulps and gasps. She ran out of the laundry and into the kitchen.

'Mum. Mum. PS says I'm common.'

'What's *that*?' Mrs Grindel's voice very sharp, and when he came sheepishly into the kitchen, her face as red as Winnie's. Two red Grindel faces glaring at him.

'Did you call Winnie common?'

'She said—'

'Never you mind what she said; did you call her common?'

'Yes.'

'*I* see. Then Winnie doesn't want to play with you any more. Now you go home. Go on.'

'Sorry.'

'I'll give you sorry. Winnie's as good as you any day. Don't you come back here at weekends and put on airs just because you got servants waiting on you all week in that posh house. Maybe you'll be better orf living there and playing with those snobby Point Piper kids who think they're all the bloody Prince of Wales!'

No good telling her that the Point Piper kids didn't like him because he didn't have a father and was

225

a bastard. He went meekly out and climbed through the hole in the fence, saw Lila pegging the wash on the line, ran to her through a wall of wet sheets and long woollen underwear.

'What's up, pet?'

'Winnie said—'

'Mrs Baines!'

Mrs Grindel's red face over the fence. 'I'd like to speak to you for a minute, please.' Mrs Grindel as haughty and red as her own rooster. Lila went over to the fence and he heard mutterings of 'Needs a good smack if you want my opinion; what's she been teaching him? We was good enough for his real mother.' He hid behind the wall of flapping sheets until Lila came back and said:

'PS, you hurt Winnie very much.'

'She said I had to go and live with Vanessa for good.'

'I've told you over and over again—'

'She said George got the sack and I'd have to go.'

'Now listen, pet. George did get the sack—'

'I won't go. I won't live in that house. I won't.'

'Stop shouting and listen to me. George is out of work just for a little while—'

'Are we on the dole?'

Lila looked away a moment. Saw George digging a new vegetable bed on the wrong side of the yard where the plants would get no sun.

'No, we're not on the dole and we never will be.' But what *will* happen? I can't think about it now. Get *him* straightened out first.

'Now listen,' she said. 'Now listen, dear. You are *our* little boy and you belong to us just as much as if we were your real mother and father and it doesn't matter what happens, this is your home. The other place is where you stay during the week because it's near the school but—now pay attention, sweetheart, listen to Lila. We don't want Vanessa to know George is out of work.'

'Why not?'

'Because she might—well, I mean—it might upset her. So remember not to say anything about it. Try to remember.'

'What if she asks me?'

'Well—we'll just say George is working at home.'

'But that's a fib. *She* said if I ever told a fib she'd know.'

'But, goodness—' Oh, God, how to explain? 'Well—look; he's working in the *garden*, isn't he? So it's not really a fib. Just don't say he got the sack.'

'Well, but—if she asks—'

'You don't have to tell her *everything*! It isn't lying, it's—well—you have to learn not to tell *everything*.' I haven't explained it well at all. 'Just remember not to tell her that George is out of work.'

First the picnic and now this. The web of lies weaving

between two houses, she thought. She wondered again how many things Vanessa had forbidden him to carry back to her, as though each of them were selecting what part of her life must go back and forth in his suitcase. She seemed again to feel a crack widen under her feet, and with her instinct for knowing what must surely come, knew the crack would widen gradually until it reached across the harbour all the way to the other house; until it became a chasm, with Vanessa on one side and her on the other and then—and then what monstrous things would happen!

She sighed and said uselessly, 'Don't worry; it'll all come out in the wash. Now go and get your blocks and build me a lovely house and after tea you must take Winnie over a nice piece of cake and say that you're sorry.'

He trundled off to the house and she turned, saw George leaning on the spade, dreaming. Dreaming of what? Of jobs? Of money? Of Parliament and things that never came to them?

'Why *there*?' she called.

'What?' He turned.

'Why are you digging it there? Can't you see it'll never get any sun? *Any* fool can see that.'

He gaped at her, amazed. More amazed when she ran suddenly to him, put her arms around his neck.

'I'm sorry. I just want—' She paused a minute, then said into his neck, 'I just want something to go *right*.'

When the phone tinkled uncertainly, George put down the newspaper and picked up the receiver.

'Hello?'

A pause.

'Hello?'

'Is that—do I have Y2892?'

'Yes.'

'George?'

'Yes.'

'It's Vanessa.'

'Oh, hello. How are you?'

'I thought for a minute I must have the wrong number. I didn't expect *you* to answer. Is Lila there?'

'Yes, just a minute.' He called to Lila and she came quickly with floury hands and a questioning look.

'It's Vanessa,' he said.

'Oh, you picked it up,' Lila whispered. 'I said *not* to pick up the phone just in case—'

'Well, it's my phone. It's my house.'

'Shhhh. Shhhh. Hello, Ness.'

'Lila? How are you?'

'Oh, splendid, tiptop. Are you all well over there? Is Ettie well?'

'Lila, please don't launder the shirts.'

'What?'

'You laundered his shirts. It isn't necessary. I have an excellent laundress who comes in twice a week.'

'Ness, I don't like sending back the dirty—'

'There's a mother-of-pearl button missing from the blue stripe.'

'Oh, it may have come off when I was ironing. I'll—'

'Do you *mind* awfully leaving his laundry to me?'

'Well, really! I mean—ha ha—goodness, if I can't wash a shirt without being hauled over the coals. I've always looked after his laundry.'

'What you buy for him it's your right to wash any way you please, but I must ask you *not* to wash *my* shirts.'

'Well, if that's the way you want it.'

'Anything the matter with George?'

'No, why?'

'I just wondered why he's at home on Monday afternoon.'

'Oh. Well, he got a cold so he took the day off.'

'You seem upset.'

'I don't like to be bossed about and questioned, that's all. I don't boss or question you about everything you do.'

'No need to get upset about it; I was only curious.'

'Well, then, if that's all you phoned about—'

'Lila, I understand that picnic was a farce.'

Pause and breathing.

'I'm sorry if you're upset about it, Vanessa—'

'*He* was very upset about having to meet those terrible people. I'm hoping he will forget about it very soon. I certainly shan't.'

Click.

He heard the click of the phone being put down and then Vanessa's high heels hard on the hall floor, soft on the rug, then hard again outside the door of the study, where he was doing scales with Miss Colden.

Vanessa opened the door and Miss Colden jumped.

'Oh. We're not quite finished, Miss Scott.'

'I think that'll be enough for today, though.'

'Oh, certainly, certainly.' Miss Colden folding the music, darting up in her tartan skirt, ready to toss a caper. 'Practise, practise, PS,' said Miss Colden, but her eyes were eating up Vanessa. 'What a *pretty* dress! How turquoise flatters your eyes. Poor me. Can't wear turquoise. Sallow. Jolly nice of you to send tea in. None of the others do. Love my days here.'

Miss Colden was gone. Vanessa sat on the music stool beside him. She gave him the lightest suggestion of a hug.

'I want to ask you something, PS.'

He started a scale. She gently closed the piano.

'How are Lila and George?'

'All right.'

'Does George have a bad cold?'

'No. George is working in the garden.'

'Oh, that's nice. He can't be sick then.'

'No. He's working in the *garden*.'

'So you said. What's that frown for? I don't like frowns.'

He stared at the piano, wished that it wasn't Monday. Wished that it was Friday already. On Fridays at five o'clock you take your suitcase and you walk down the drive to the gate and then—

Vanessa said sharply, 'Ever since you came home last night you've been upset about something. What's the matter?'

'Nothing.'

'I don't like secrets between us, PS.'

He didn't like the way she said us. Always us, us, us. As though he belonged to *her*.

'I want to know what's the matter.'

He knew from past experience he'd better tell her something or she'd go on and on right up to bedtime.

'I made Winnie cry.'

'How did you do that?'

'I said she was common.'

'Well, actually you're absolutely right. She is. But one doesn't tell someone they're common, even if one thinks it.'

'But she said—'

'*What?*'

'I forget.'

'It must have been something very, very nasty.'

'Yes.'

'Oh, then you *do* remember.'

'No.'

'Well, that means you'd rather not tell me. I see. Did you tell Lila?'

'Yes.'

'Of course.'

He saw now that she had that sad look she got sometimes.

She said, 'I'm sure Lila was nice about it. Sided with you, didn't she?'

'Yes.'

Her arm went around him.

'I'm sure I'd side with you too if I knew what it was this stupid little girl said to upset you.'

'She said a fib.'

'What?'

'She said we were on the dole.'

'Oh? Do you know what the dole is?'

'Yes, it's like when they give you food and things when you don't have any money.'

'It's for very, very poor people who are out of work.'

'I know.'

'Then you had a right to be angry with Winnie because that isn't true. Only it would have been more tactful to have said like a little gentleman, "I'm sorry,

233

Winnie, but you're wrong. My uncle George has a good job." '

He thought now that he must be extremely careful because her eyes had that bright, excited look.

She said, 'Perhaps Winnie thought George had lost his job.'

'He *hasn't*!'

'Pianissimo, please. I'm not deaf.'

'He didn't get the sack. He *didn't*.'

'Is that what Lila told you to say?'

'*No*.'

All right, so she was stroking his head and being very nice but she wouldn't get it out of him.

'Remember what I said to you the other day about lies between friends?'

'Yes.'

'Look at me, PS. Has George lost his job?'

'No! George is working in the garden!'

She sighed, got up quickly then and walked into the hall, leaving the study door open, her heels clicking again to the telephone table. She looked up a number in the book and dialled, then said, 'Trades Hall? Mr Baines, please.' A pause and then she said, 'I see, thank you.' She hung up, beckoned him to her with a long finger.

'PS, you mustn't hide things from me. It's very wrong of Lila to make you, but it's wrong of you to obey her. It's time for you to learn that. Now I want you to go upstairs to your room and think about that until dinnertime. I know you're very fond of Lila but it is very wrong of her to make you tell lies to me because I am *also* your legal guardian and just as good to you as she is. I want you to think carefully about that and then if there are things you still don't understand, I will try to explain them to you. Up you go now.'

Blast! Blow! Thw*a*rt! Bastard! Navel! All the worst words he could think of. Bosh and balls. He'd given everything away again, just like the picnic.

He went slowly up the stairs and met Cousin Ettie coming down, leaning heavily on the banister.

'Ahhhh, what a long face! What's the matter, lamb?'

'Ettie,' said Vanessa, and then, as he reached the top, 'George has lost his job.'

'No! Oh, the poor, poor dear, and with hundreds and hundreds out of work. Oh, what rotten luck. Poor Lila. What should we do, Ness? Should I send them a cheque?'

He hung over the banister, trying to hear what Vanessa said, but heard only murmuring and then their footsteps going away towards the drawing room and a door shutting.

Vanessa shut the door and said to Ettie:

'Lila didn't want me to know. I can't imagine how long she thought it would be before I'd be bound to find out. What angers me is that she uses these things to make a gulf between the child and me.'

'Oh, Ness, I don't *think*—'

'Allow me to know better. She's adept at using misfortune to get her own way about something.'

Vanessa crossed the darkening room and went through an invisible door to the old house at Waverly, smelling of sickroom, death and flowers; saw Lila already in black, outside the door to Pater's quiet bedroom.

'I want to see Pater.'

'Not now, Ness.'

'Why?'

'Mater said not until after the undertaker has been.'

'You mean *you* said.'

'Ness, why do you always think I'm *against* you?'

'The other girls have been in. Agnes told me.'

'Oh, dear, I *told* Agnes—'

'Not to wake me up. Yes, you did, didn't you? I'd only lain down for five minutes—'

'Ness, there wasn't time.'

'To call out?'

'*Almost* no time.'

'What happened? Agnes says there's a bruise on his head.'

'Oh. Oh, isn't Agnes wicked! I told her *not* to tell you. He bumped his head against the bedpost. Oh,

Ness, it was a struggle at the end. It wasn't peaceful and that's why I thought—Mater thought it would be better—because you're so much more attached to him than the others—' For the thousandth time in memory she was pushing past Lila to Pater's door and finding it locked.

'May I have the key, please?'

'Ah, Ness, not now. Wait.'

'The key, please.'

'We're going to put on his blue shirt and comb his hair so it won't show where the little bruise is and I'm going to put Grandfather's prayer book in his hands. Oh, it'll be lovely when you see him, Ness. I want you to see him at peace.'

'You. You. Always what *you* want.'

'Ness, think of your nightmares!'

'Give me the *key*, Lila.'

'Shhhh. Shhhh. I've just got Mater to lie down. Oh, Ness, do be reasonable; don't make a scene, dear. It'll be so lovely when you see him, you'll be so happy you waited, dear. You'll be grateful all your life that—'

Now she was struggling with Lila, trying to force open Lila's strong housework hand.

'Vanessa, how can you? Outside his door like this—Stop it. Oh, it's terrible!'

'*You're* terrible.'

'I'm only trying to save you shock and hurt. Oh,

I don't understand you; I thought you'd be grateful to me.'

Lila, crying now, throwing down the key on the floor and walking away down the hall and up over a dry grass slope behind pallbearers with Mater leaning on her arm and the rest of them following behind; Agnes, Vere, Sinden and herself, but Lila in front because she was the eldest; and now standing around the open grave and noticing that her own yellow roses were not on the coffin; Lila's ugly phallic lilies, yes, of *course*, but not her yellow roses. Then gazing across the hollow earth to where Lila stood on the other side, catching Lila's eye, and Lila smiling back at her, the grave watery smile of the co-bereaved.

Fraud!

'Fraud!' she said aloud.

'Ah, Ness—they're in such trouble,' said Ettie.

Vanessa switched on the lamp, sent demons flying into the shadowing corners of the great drawing room.

'Indeed they are,' she said, and laughed. Now her brain felt fresh and clear and in it she began writing a letter.

Since then, everything had seemed to go faster, even the days hurrying through winter. It had felt to him as if he was being got ready for something. Coming home from Miss Pile's to lunch one day, he had come upon

Vanessa reading a letter to Cousin Ettie. She had put it away quickly and said to Ettie, 'Next month.'

New things had happened. At Vanessa's he had riding and dancing lessons added to his afternoons and people talked a lot in undertones. At Lila's, the silver spoons disappeared, George stopped smoking and people talked a lot in undertones.

'Where are the spoons?' he had asked.

'We lent them to a nice kind man,' said Lila.

'Will he give them back to us?'

'Yes, one day soon.'

Soon. Everything was soon. Vanessa was always saying, 'Soon', and 'We'll see.'

Diana said to him, 'Something's cooking, love.'

'On the stove?'

She went back to whispering with Ellen, the cook, and left him outside the baize door.

'What's cooking?' he asked Vanessa.

'Lamb,' she said, but he wasn't sure whether she meant him or what was for dinner.

Then one day Vanessa had taken him into the city and bought him a new grey flannel suit.

'Next *week*,' Vanessa had said to the man in the shop who was fitting him. What was going to happen next week? Coming out into the street and waiting for a taxi, they had spied his Aunt Agnes standing on a cold windy corner wearing her funny hat and handing out leaflets to the people hurrying by.

'Look,' he said. 'There's Agnes.'

'I know.'

'Aren't we going to speak to her?'

'Not now. There isn't time.'

'The day is at hand,' Agnes called to anyone who would listen.

Vanessa hailed a yellow cab and they got in. He waved to Agnes as they passed but she didn't notice him.

'The day is at hand,' she called again.

'What day is at hand?'

'Darling, you know Agnes is peculiar. That's why we don't see her much.'

'But what *day*?'

'Nothing, PS.'

'Is something going to happen?'

'Not the way she means.'

'Something nice?'

'We'll see.'

Only Vere seemed unchanged. Unexpectedly Vanessa let him go out with Vere for an afternoon when there were no extra lessons. She came for him after lunch wearing a bright purple dress a size too large for her and carrying a man's umbrella and almost at once he was bent double laughing because she did a funny thing and pretended not to be able to find the gate and started climbing over the fence. They went off gaily to town on the tram and to the pictures to see

Maurice Chevalier in *A Bedtime Story*; bought cream puffs and butterfly cakes; climbed the old stuffy staircase to Vere's room singing, 'In a park in Paree in the spring,' and there was Hester curled up on the untidy bed, the room crammed full of marvellous things to look at. She had added a gramophone which didn't play, an empty canary cage, a tortoiseshell clock with one hand missing and a big box full of men's ties. Painting ties was Vere's new job. While she made the tea, she showed him how she did it, dabbing the colours on with a little brush. She had painted a tie especially for him. It had a blurry koala bear on it and the letters PS. The *P* was a bit wobbly and the *S* had dribbled but he thought it was the loveliest tie he'd ever seen, admiring it in the cracked mirror as Vere knotted it around his neck, and he hoped that Vanessa would like it too and not lose it like she had carelessly lost his Mickey Mouse tie. Vanessa was always losing things that Vere and Lila bought for him. Vere squeezed him and said, 'There you are, dearest thing.' It was lovely, just lovely being with Vere again. She didn't ask him a lot of questions or say, 'Don't tell Lila, don't tell Vanessa.' The littlest thing sent them both off into fits of laughter and when she served them big cups of tea and the cakes, she put on an apron and a lace doily on her head and pretended to be a deaf waitress bringing all the wrong things, salt instead of sugar and soap on a dish instead of butter and he laughed so much that he got hiccups and Vere had to pat him on the back. Then in came beautiful Opal wearing a sea-green dress and a great black velvet hat. Opal had been down to Melbourne with a man called Archibald who was an absolute out-and-out thw*a*rt and King of the Bores and the whole thing had been folly, folly, and the worst thw*a*rt of the century, and Opal said she was so thirsty she could expire right on the spot and fell on the bed to prove it. She handed Vere a golden-coloured bottle and Vere poured them both drinks and their voices flew around the room like excited birds as they told wonderful dirt about Dodo and Widget and Steamboat, all of whom were absolutely undone, my dear, and mostly because men were terrible, were pigs, were bores and pimps and idiots into the bargain. They laughed about all this and he laughed with them and Opal put her sweet-smelling arm around him and said, 'How's Queen Vanessa?' and he said politely, 'Very well, thank you,' and Vere told Opal that Cousin Ettie wasn't very well again and that Vanessa was having the old problem with her and Opal seemed to understand perfectly though he didn't. He told Opal that he was going to Miss Pile's now and Opal almost went into hysterics and said that only Queen Vanessa could find a school with a name like that. It seemed to remind Opal of something because she said to Vere:

'Girl, guess who was on the train with me coming back from Melbourne?'

She spelled out a name and Vere put down her glass very suddenly.

'Are you sure?'

'*Almost* sure. When we changed trains at Albury he was standing on the platform. I'd *swear*.'

'You only met him once, didn't you?'

'Yes, but, girl, you don't forget *him*.'

'My God!'

'Suppose Lila and Vanessa know?'

Know what? Now he suddenly didn't want any more cake, because they had looked at him and then away. Did it have something to do with the day that Agnes said was coming? With what Diana said was cooking?

It must be.

'What?' he asked. 'What? Tell *me*.'

He thought for a minute that Vere had burst into laughter until he saw the tears and Opal holding on to her while she shook and shook and it was just like the way she laughed only the noise was different and he pulled at her dress.

'Tell *me*.'

Opal said, 'PS, the happiest day of your life will be when you're no longer a kid. Take it from one who knows.'

Vere blew her nose loudly, turned to him with one of her gay screams.

'Gorgeous thing. Oh, you gorgeous thing. I could eat you up, eatyouuup.'

243

With another scream, she noticed the time on Opal's fob watch, grabbed him, his overcoat, her hat and purse and in a moment they were running helter-skelter up the now dark street to the tram like two escaped convicts with the bloodhounds behind them.

On the tram he said, 'Vere, who was on the train? Who did Opal see on the train?'

'Oh, just a man she knew.'

'Does Lila know him? Does Vanessa?'

'No.'

An out-and-out fib. Even Vere!

The big house was staring at them angrily with all its lights on, as they went up the long driveway. You're *late*, it said.

'You're late,' said Vanessa. 'It's nearly seven o'clock. I've been frantic. I thought something had happened.'

'Sorry, Ness.'

'I made it very clear you were to have him home by six.'

Vere asked Vanessa something in an undertone, there were quick whispers, and then they went into the study and closed the door. From inside came angry voices. He waited, fearful now, knowing it was not about them being late. After a few minutes, Vanessa opened the door, saying:

'Kindly stay out of this. It's to do with Lila and me and you have no say whatever, for which I thank God!'

Vere said, 'Thank Ernest and thank Ettie's money.'

'That'll be enough, Vere.'

'Listen, I'll see him. I'll tell him what I think of both you and Lila.'

'Please leave my house.'

'*Your* house! Must be nice never having to worry your guts out about paying the rent. What a bloody parasite you are, bleeding Ettie dry all these years, forcing her back here where she's lonely and miserable—no wonder she's on the grog again.'

Vanessa took a step towards Vere and he ran forward and pushed in between them, yelling, 'Don't hurt Vere,' saw Vanessa look at him amazed and then at Ettie suddenly appearing in the drawing room door waving her little hands and saying, 'Shhhhh. Shhhhh, the maids. Think of the maids, lovely Vere, precious Vere,' and both he and Ettie were clinging to Vere and soothing her and Ettie was pressing something into Vere's hand, saying in a whisper, 'Buy yourself something nice, lovely Vere,' and Vere kissed both of them and waved and went, slamming the front door at Vanessa, who now stood apart watching them.

'Well, thank you,' said Vanessa. 'Thank you *both* very much.'

Over dinner a dreadful silence broken only by knives and forks and Diana slumping in and out with the dishes until at length Vanessa said, 'Where did you get that appalling tie? I've never *seen* anything so vulgar.' 'It's *not*,' he said. 'Vere *made* it for me.' Vanessa said sharply, 'You certainly seem to be very fond of *Vere*, PS,' and he looked down at his plate and Ettie said, 'Ah, poor Vere. Poor Vere,' and Vanessa threw down her napkin and said loudly, 'Logic is no part of this ménage,' and surprisingly left the table and went out of the room and he thought for one moment she was crying, but then Vanessa never cried except perhaps when there was a thunderstorm, and upstairs she was as businesslike as ever with tooth-brush, soap and pyjamas, hurrying him in and out of the bathroom and into bed.

'We saw Maurice Chevalier,' he offered her as a pipe of peace but she merely pulled down the window blind as though it had offended her by remaining up, snapped off the light as if to murder it and went huffily to the door, where she turned in the streak of light and said:

'Has Vere ever given you a train like mine?'

'No.'

'Has Vere ever given you books and clothes and riding lessons?'

'No, but—'

'Did Vere ever give up everything she liked and come thousands of miles to look after you?'

'Well, but—' 'But what? I don't see that there *can* be any "buts", PS. Goodnight.'

Not an angry voice but worse. That one that sounded swollen and sad. Much later she came softly back into the room, turned him from one side of sleep to the other, stirring his dreams for a moment. Or was he in the other house? Was it Lila turning him over and saying softly, 'Don't *worry*, PS. Don't worry.'

The Day came. It was the very next day, a black and raining day very suitable for whatever it was that had been cooking and bubbling and straining away at the Big House for weeks and making people speak in undertones. He knew at once when just after playtime Diana came for him at Miss Pile's wearing a mackintosh over her uniform and tiptoed into the classroom and whispered to Miss Pile who then looked at him over her glasses and said:

'Marriott, get your raincoat and galoshes; you're excused early today.'

He went down the line of desks as the other children looked up from their work at him. Cynthia Lawson smirked and made the club sign that meant 'Tell us later.'

Plunging up the hill in the rain, he decided not to ask any questions because whatever it was, it was going to happen now, in a few minutes. But he felt a little dizzy, as if he had just got off a merry-go-round.

They went through the back gate and through the kitchen garden into the house, passing through the

247

green baize door into the hall, where he saw the drawing room shut and heard voices behind it.

Diana said, 'Upstairs, lovey,' hurrying him up to his room, where his new grey flannel suit was laid out on the bed waiting for him to put on for whatever it was.

Vanessa had talked until her voice sounded dry and unusual, but she had talked well, she felt, carefully avoiding rancour and overstatement, presenting her case with clarity and logic; above all being scrupulously fair to Lila and George. Her speech rolled out, planned and assured and yet (here she couldn't help but congratulate herself) with clever little ad-lib touches that gave it an extemporaneous air and an objective tolerant humour so that she herself shone through her words at her best. She had expected interruptions but Logan merely nodded and occasionally laughed, a great belly laugh, throwing his head back and looking up at the ceiling and all the time turning over and over in his hands the Royal Doulton shepherd which he had picked off the table beside him. Her instinct was to say, 'Don't fiddle with that, please; it's fragile,' and ask him please to sit up straight and not lean his somewhat oily hair against the brocade of Ettie's wing chair. Instead, she continued her long oration, pausing only to light a cigarette from time to time, gaining confidence as she went along. After all her careful planning of the meeting on her terms, at the time to be chosen by her, he had, of course, in typical Logan fashion, thrown everything out of kilter by arriving without a prior telephone call. There he was, suddenly, at the front door, hatless and coatless in the rain, dripping over everything in the hall ('Hello, Ness, how's tricks?' as if they had parted only last week), unheralded in the middle of the morning after her three messages to the Hotel Waratah had been ignored. Thank God she had on a decent dress and by some cosmic miracle was in the drawing room arranging flowers so that she had been able to muffle some of her shock behind the tall Iceland poppies. Even her annoyance at being kept waiting for a whole day and night without word from him, the anxiety that he might have seen Lila first, was dissolved in the fierce surprise of seeing him actually standing there. It was ridiculous, but she was trembling and murmuring banalities about the rain, asking him had it been very cold in Bacchus Marsh, how was the train journey, how were Alice and his brothers? Bending, all thumbs, to put a match to the fire, thinking, How sad. He's changed. The looks are going, getting a little bloated in the face, lines around the eyes, the eyes smaller and deep gold; I'd thought they were blue. His mum was dead. No, really? She hadn't heard. She was *so* sorry. She would have sent flowers, a note of condolence to Alice. He had an ulcer and no longer smoked. Really? Really! Now he had disorganised her luncheon. Could

Ellen manage a quick soufflé? Should people with ulcers smell faintly of whisky? Should *anyone* smell of whisky at eleven in the morning? A quick shot to give him nerve? Poor Logan. Yes, yes, yes. She was readily agreeing with him over nothing. In her most Belgravia voice. '*Rather*. I should jolly well think so.' Until she caught him smiling at her impudently. Was he making fun of her? Thrusting her into the ridiculous role of a games mistress in a worthless comedy? He'd better not try, because she knew the lines; but careful, all the same—there was a lot at stake. Better get on with it. Drew herself a long breath, said:

'Logan, I asked you to come for many reasons . . .'

Plunged in. Her arrival. Lila's health. George's job. PS. Two houses. State school versus Miss Pile. Winnie Grindel versus Cynthia Lawson. Leftist labour unions versus Miss Colden and horseback riding. Vere. Agnes on street corners and in ruined temples. The writers' picnic, and finally, subtly so as not to shoo the bird away, Sinden. Sin's letter to her in London. Avoiding mention of Ernest Huxley but back to London. All the twists and turns of her tale led back to London.

Now she was tiring but exultant, positive, almost positive, that she had won, that he would agree, that it would all be signed and sealed that day and they would sail in a month. How wise she had been to be patient all these months and wait. To let Lila be the one to make mistakes, let time and the Trades Hall turn the tide from Neutral Bay to the grander shores of Point Piper. Already she saw PS in a school uniform. Cheam, perhaps, but they could go into all that later. Later, later, long after the P and O boat had sailed down the harbour and through the heads, leaving Australia behind and Lila and what was left of Sinden. What was left of Logan too. Bury him too, at last, this dead man walking around audaciously, coming into her room, year after year, stealing through storms, through the shaking of thunder, into her bed when she was afraid because her empty life shook and rattled like a train bearing her through nothingness to nothing.

Watching him, she took a toy gun, shot Logan through the head, screaming, 'You're dead, Logan. You're dead.'

Aloud, she said calmly:

'Well, what do you think?'

She was finished. There was nothing more to say so she folded her hands neatly and waited.

Waited. Sitting now, suddenly, on a hard wooden bench in the naked pink electricity that lighted the Bacchus Marsh town hall as the little band on the stage struck up with 'Three o'clock in the Morning' and the farm boys were coming across the floor with their pomaded slicked-down hair, hard cheap best blue suits, and holding out great red beefy hands to the giggling girls in their homemade evening dresses of violent-coloured net, sateen and Chinese silk, their faces smothered with white powder, their cheeks put on lopsidedly with dry rouge, gold bangles on their arms and into each bangle tucked their best lace hanky. She felt out of place in her blue voile dress and her towny red satin shoes. She clutched the little bead evening bag that Cousin Ettie had bought her last week in Melbourne and stared straight ahead with the stern casualness of the wallflower. She was a failure and she knew it. She had just been returned to her seat after the most humiliating attempt at the one-step with a sweating oaf who had left the giant imprint of his paw on her back. They had stumbled and bumped through the dance, loathing each other, with apologetic mumbles of 'Sorry . . . no, my fault,' until at last it was over and the oaf had escorted her back to the line of girls, muttered something about ginger ale and escaped. She had heard the giggles of the girls and whispers about 'Alice Marriott's towny friend'. She thought again desperately of joining Alice's mother, who was sitting with the older women across the other side of the room fanning themselves and waving to people, but she had tried this once and had been penalised for breaking the rules by having to drink a mug of scalding coffee with a disgusting skin of boiled milk in it, to force down a giant slab of marble cake, and accept their solicitude. 'Don't worry, lovey, you'll get a dance soon. Always more girls than boys. There's Alfie Watson. Hey, Alfie, come over here a minute, love. Come and meet Alice Marriott's friend from Sydney.' That was how she had got her oaf.

She turned to Alice now, because eyes were on her, pitying eyes, and she must appear vivacious and sparkling as the other wallflowers were now doing, admiring each others' dresses and crimped hair. But Alice was leaping up in her electric-blue lace dress and whirling off on to the floor with Jim Clark, leaving her destitute with nothing to do but again open her bag, again pretend to be searching in it for something. Where, oh, where was the good-looking brother? He had manoeuvred her once around the floor for the first foxtrot but shyness had overcome her so completely that after a few attempts at conversation he had given up and they had finished the dance in silence. Then he had gone off with a group of yokels, whom he obviously preferred, and she knew that they were having a forbidden beer outside on the veranda.

She gave up the pretence of looking in her bag, stared instead at the band on the stage, appeared to be raptly interested in the cracked canvas drop behind it, which represented a vista of rolling lawns, cyprus trees and fountains leading to an ornate biscuit-coloured mansion. A group of young bucks strutted in from the veranda and stood laughing and making coarse remarks about the girls. Logan was among them, standing out from the group with his superior looks and insulting smile. Now, suddenly, he had broken from the group and was coming towards her, weaving in and out of the dancers, lazy and unhurried, as though the waltz would go on forever and she would wait, certainly wait for him, certainly accept him.

He smiled down at her. 'Want to?'

'Thank you very much,' she said. Rescued at last, and breathless with relief and nervousness, she jumped up and they joined the dancers on the floor, got off to a bad start for she had become rigid, a ramrod.

He said, 'Relax and let *me* lead.'

Now, at last, she was getting the knack of it and suddenly everything was going right. They were circling and swaying to the music, backward and forward in the river of faces and arms, and now Logan had started to sing along with the band and to her own amazement she found that she was joining in.

'Three o'clock in the morn-ing—
We've danced the whole night through.'

Alice whirled by with Jim Clark and called to her, 'Having a good time, Vanessa?'

'Oh, yes, *yes*,' she cried exultantly, smiling back at Logan. She wanted the dance never to end. The boys were now reaching up and pulling down the balloons that hung from the ceiling. Logan had looped a big red balloon over her arm and they skimmed on and on.

When the waltz finished, she said, 'Thank you,' and turned, expecting him to walk her back to her seat, but Logan held on to her hand.

'"Jolly Miller",' announced the sweating MC.

Girls one way, boys the other. Walk until the music stops, face your partner, dance again. She hated to part from him, join the inner circle of the girls passing the outer wheel of boys, yet every time the music stopped, miraculously he was there facing her, once snatching her from the eager embrace of a stout fourteen-year-old boy who had rushed at her with a football tackle, and now the other girls had noticed and there were looks of female resentment and snubbed partners were lifting outraged eyebrows but she didn't care, it was fun to cheat and be selfish, it was delicious compensation for all the dances she had ever been to where, with her inability to unbend, to create the mystique of fun, she had sat mute and ridiculous through hours of torture. Now she was drunk and delirious on coffee and ginger beer. She had been shot out of a cannon and was sailing through the air to thunderous applause. She was dazzling and charming, the prettiest girl, the best dancer, her dress was lovely, so were her red shoes. Everything was perfect. She sang 'Look for the Silver Lining' and 'Moonlight and Roses', praying for someone to stop the clock, stop the earth from turning towards the morning. 'Oh, *no*,' she begged as the men stood to attention, the elderly watchers were helped to their feet and the band raced disloyally through 'God Save'.

Everyone streaming out now through the doors into the quiet street and cars were being cranked up, lorries full of yelling farm hands chugging away into the night, a few sulkies and buggies lurching off, their lamps bobbing in the warm darkness, goodnight kisses and laughter, the admonishments of tired mothers: 'Gracie, you come right home now; don't stop out with Alfie.' 'Good-oh, Mum.' 'Better say ta-ta; eight cows to milk in the morning.' 'See youse all at the flicks Satidy night.' 'Wait for Elsie; she forgot her purse.'

She was looking around in the glare of headlights. 'Where's Alice?'

'What do you want Alice for?' Logan said, and took her arm and they walked down the street towards the hotel. They hummed together, danced a few steps, walked again.

'Be here long?'

'Perhaps till Friday; whenever Alice is finished the sewing she's doing for my cousin.'

'I'll tell Alice to go slow.'

At the hotel door now, shaking hands formally. 'Goodnight, Logan.'

'Night, Vanessa.' Holding on to her hand. 'What do they call you for short?'

'Ness.'

'G'night, Ness.'

Creeping now across the hot dark bedroom so as not to awaken snoring Cousin Ettie, opening the lattice door on to the balcony, seeing, with half-expected delighted shock, him still standing under the yellow light at the hotel door, grinning up at her, then performing a deep bow, finally ambling off into the dark; listening to his hard echoing footsteps disappearing up the sleeping street.

Wakening next morning, she thought, What is it? What is so rich and new? Oh, yes. Put on her best skirt and blouse, spent a long time with hairpins and combs, could not touch the big country breakfast of steak and eggs, answered Ettie's fussing with monosyllables, almost spilled her tea when, glancing again hopefully at the door, she saw Logan standing there looking around the dining room. Breathlessly she performed introductions, upset the sugar bowl.

'That's *joy*,' said Ettie.

'Yes, joy,' she said.

'Then off we go,' said Logan.

'Ness, take my parasol, lamb. The *sun*, dearest.'

Into the bakery to meet his brothers, ghostly with floury faces and arms, Dave, Jock and Alan welcoming her in the heat of the ovens, poking fun at their lazy bugger of a brother, warning her not to believe a bloody word he said, informing her that Mum had spoiled him. Insisting that she eat a hot fresh roll. Everyone as warm and friendly as the smell; knowing that as long as she lived she would never again smell newly baked bread without thinking of this day. The first of many such days bumping along dust roads in his rattletrap Dodge, meandering through cool dairies past bored cows, walking through a sea of wheat.

Always, on looking up and seeing him beside her, she was renewed with the wonder of it. His physical presence was still miraculous to her, reacted upon her senses to such a degree that at times she felt intruded upon and stifled with unendurable joy. When these moments rushed upon her, she would blot him out, wishing to hold only the image of him, to be with him and yet not to be. For she had discovered that the deepest core of her happiness lay in the voids when they were apart, when alone she could examine the gifts of love from her own standpoint, lift them up and caress them uninterruptedly. Often at the end of a long afternoon she parted from him with relief, for now, grown into a miser, she could count her hoard alone and savour the hours until the evening, when she would receive more. When she was with him she felt nothing, she was capable only of stowing every look and word of his into an immense sack which she would later lug home to her secret cave. He seemed to be aware of her stealthy comings and goings, for he had developed a habit of stopping dead in the middle of something he had been saying and allowing her to be caught red-handed, wandering away into the corner

258

of her musing where her sack was hidden, and he would say:

'Well, how do you *do*? How are *you*?'

She would say, 'I heard you,' going red, and then he would laugh that disconcerting laugh of his which presumed that he knew exactly what she was up to and was vastly amused by it. Then bristling with delightful anger, she would ask what was so funny, please; and usually this produced another gift, for he then would put his hand on her shoulder and up along the back of her neck under the bun of hair, smiling now but seriously fond, so fond that again she would feel sick with elation, not wanting it to happen but to be remembered as happening.

Then Alice, bent horse-faced over Ettie's batiste blouse and pulling a needle through her exquisite scalloping, said quietly as Vanessa crossed the hotel room in a dream:

'We all think Logan's got a crush on you.'

Jarred, she wanted to say, 'Don't come in, don't come in here, it's private,' but she smiled and said, somewhat primly:

'Oh, he's just showing me around, Alice.'

'I s'pose you know he's the favourite. Mum and my sister Jean have spoiled him rotten.' Alice went on sewing and dropping trite remarks about bad pennies, black sheep and blood being thicker than water. All of them worried about Logan, wished for him to settle down, but he'd always been restless, never took things seriously, worried them to death. There was a girl, Alice said, biting off a thread, a real nice girl he had over at Parwan, a few miles away. They all hoped that one day soon—

Vanessa, hugging the sack to her, wished the girl dead immediately, struck by lightning. Yet she could not be sure of Alice's implication. Could not decide if this was a gentle warning or the vaguest sisterly hint that any nice girl would do, even Vanessa, if it would make dear old Loge settle down.

Now she was musing about this in the flickering dark and had completely lost track of the story on the screen, hearing only the tinny piano playing the 'Indian Love Lyrics' while Norma Talmadge, black-lipped and awash with glycerine, jerked across a tapestried room in a hobble skirt, fell on a mountain of pillows, warding off the carnal advances of Conway Tearle with a torrent of silent vilification that resulted in a subtitle reading, 'Not *that*, you beast!' And produced a thunder of catcalls, boos and stamping of farm boots on the wooden floor; cries of 'Do 'er over, yer flamin' jackass.'

She heard a voice in the dark say, 'Well, how do you *do*? How are *you*?'

'I'm *watching*,' she said.

'Come on,' he said. 'I'm sick of this mush.'

Stumbling over people and up the aisle, bending low so as not to get in the way of the projection, outside into the cooler night and into the old car.

'Where are we going?'

'Just for a ride.'

He cranked the car and they shuddered and jolted off in a series of explosions that shook the windows of the darkened shops, tore off down the main street and now past sleeping farmhouses on a rutted country road into a night ablaze with the eyes of rabbits, through a broken gate into a paddock where he stopped the car, turned off the lights, and darkness covered them.

'Cool here,' he said.

'Yes.' Hearing her own voice, tight and constricted.

'How about a cigarette?'

'Yes, please.' She would have her first cigarette and to hell with Mater, lace curtains and aspidistras. To hell with Lila too, and her Christian Temperance Lectures on Men Aflame with Demon Rum.

The cigarette seared her throat and burned her nose, destroyed what was left of her composure in a violent fit of coughing. He laughed, took the cigarette from her fingers and threw it out of the car, pulled her to him.

She felt no surprise. It had happened a thousand times before alone in her hotel bedroom, over dinner while Ettie rambled on, in the haberdashery store while she bought pink elastic; she and Logan had kissed and clung fiercely, promised to love forever, forever.

But now it wasn't true. Now, with the reality of him all around her, she felt alone. Felt arms, mouth, the beat of heart above her, but again she was outside of it, an observer of herself, watching herself cling and kiss, be kissed with care and technique, made love to and wanting to be made love to, and in her sudden yearning and desperation she cried to herself, 'Be here. Be part of it. Oh, God, oh, God, be part of it *now*.'

She closed her eyes, wanting only to be lost in the utter forgetfulness of herself, to sink and die with him forever. Willed it to happen. You, outside of me, die now this second. Die. You can. You can!

But it was nothing. She could not even remember his face now that she could not see it in the darkness. She saw only a ridiculous silent film of two people squashed uncomfortably in the front seat of an old car and a lonely paddock, saw her own legs entwined around the gears, her good linen skirt all twisted up, her garters showing, her hair coming down, hairpins in her neck, a faceless man with curly hair lumped heavily across her so that she could scarcely breathe.

'I can't,' she screamed, 'I can't.'

Pushed him violently away. Sat up, pulling frantically at her skirt, for Lila was watching, knocking on the windshield, Mater was hurrying across the paddock, furious, the other girls were laughing, everyone had seen her! She was disgraced and ruined, she was a slut, worse, she was common. Necking with the *baker's* boy in a paddock and her father a Cambridge scholar. Vanessa! Serve her right, said Mater. Mixing with tradespeople after all she'd been taught. How vulgar and common, common, *common*!

Fiercely she dug hairpins into her scalp, wounding herself savagely, hoping she had drawn blood.

After a long silence he said, 'What's the matter?'

'I can't.' Not *that*, you beast!

'What's wrong?'

'I just can't. I'm sorry.'

'Did I scare you?'

'Scare me? Why, I should *say* not. How silly. I'm twenty-three, for goodness' sake, I'm not some little schoolgirl!'

'Seems to me you're behaving like one.'

'Really? I just happen to believe there's such a thing as decency.'

'Oh, *come* on. You can do better than *that*.'

'I just think—well, one has to believe in right and wrong.'

'And you think this is wrong?'

'Don't you?'

'No, and neither do you or you wouldn't be out here parking with me in the first place.'

Parking! What a vulgar way of putting it.

'Well? What's the real reason?'

263

How could she explain about herself when she didn't understand her own untouchability? Quickly she grabbed for an alibi.

'What about your girl?'

'What girl?'

'Alice says—'

'*Alice* says!'

'Well, is there a girl or isn't there?'

'There's a girl I take to dances sometimes. Her name's May.'

'Alice says everyone hopes—'

'Oh, what do *you* care what Alice says?'

Not a rap, really. But . . .

'I wouldn't want to hurt her.'

'Oh, I see. This must have been bothering you quite a bit.'

'Well, yes, it has, as a matter of fact. I mean, I wouldn't like it done to me if *I* were in her shoes.'

'Of course, if there wasn't any girl, never had been any girl, it'd be all right to go the whole hog?'

'Yes.' If you must put it that way.

'I see. Nice to meet a girl nowadays with scruples.'

'I hope to keep them.'

'Oh, you'll *keep* them, all right. Don't you ever worry about that, Vanessa. That's one thing you'll always keep. Among others.'

'I hope so.'

'Dignity, pride, *honesty*? All those things? Better than behaving like savages, eh?'

'Oh, yes, yes, Logan.'

Now he was understanding, now it would be all right again. She put out her hand and caressed the back of his neck, wanting now the sweet safe embrace of the dream, the absolutely sanitary kiss, one she could carry home. The muttered words of contrition and love, plans to visit her in Sydney.

'Dear, dear Logan,' she said.

He guffawed.

'Honest to God, you take the cake. When it comes to frauds you take the bloody cake.'

He got out, cranked the car, and they roared off at such a speed that she had to hang on to the door to prevent being thrown out.

They sped back along the road, bumping furiously over ruts as rabbits scampered, a wallaby leaped in the headlights. Stunned with the suddenness of it, the pain and humiliation of being mocked by him, she could think only that now everything was ending in a shambles, that he had stripped her naked and laughed at her and that now the gifts she had hoarded would be worthless unless she could stop the car and put things to rights, stop the car before they reached the little bridge that led to the town. But what to say? It was like being caught with your hand in someone else's handbag. Explaining that you were looking for a handkerchief, a lipstick, *anything*! Then why was she sitting stiffly beside him saying nothing when every bump in the road led them nearer to town? Quickly, quickly, for now the white posts of the bridge were in sight.

Now she must speak, confess to any wild thing, promise anything to stop the wild rush to oblivion. But she was mute and he was singing. To her amazement, he was singing as if he was relishing the situation and mocking her at the same time because he was singing 'Three o'clock in the Morning'. And singing, he drove the car over the rattling wooden bridge and up the street towards the hotel as wretchedness and defeat enfolded her, lifted momentarily into hope when he drove into a dark side lane beside the hotel, returned redoubled when she saw that he was merely backing up to the hotel steps.

She wanted to scream and cry and stamp her feet, do all the obvious feminine things; cry out that he didn't understand her at all, no one did except Pater and Pater was dead; that she was all alone and terribly afraid and inexperienced; that she cared nothing for scruples and honesty, only for Logan; blubber like a child that she was wrong, wrong, wrong and that she would never pretend with him again if he would only love her and put things back where they had been.

But all she could say was her old prim reflex party thank you.

'Thank you, Logan,' she said. 'Goodnight.'

He leaned out of the car as she turned on the steps.

'Night, Vanessa.' He was gone in a roaring second, was now only a red tail light disappearing down the sleeping street.

All through the night, lying awake, she made up speeches for tomorrow. 'Last night was only—' 'You were right to be angry with me—' 'I'm glad it happened, Logan, because in a curious way it's brought us closer together—' All through the night she talked reasonably and Logan listened, pressed her hand, agreed.

She arose early, tired but calm now and confident. They were leaving today and so he must come to say goodbye. It was only polite. She dressed carefully, helped with the packing, grew uneasy as the morning drew towards noon, made frequent trips downstairs on feeble excuses about keys, timetables and taxis. Shamelessly, she telephoned the bakery to say goodbye to the brothers. The brothers said goodbye and they hoped that she had had a good time. She dared not ask if he was there. Speechless, she helped Ettie into the taxi. Well, they'd have no time alone but he would be at the train.

Eagerly she scanned the small crowd on the platform but there was only Alice with a giggling girl friend to see them into the first-class compartment, present them with bunches of wilting flannelflowers

267

and the prescribed remarks for departing strangers. A couple of times she caught Alice looking at her with the sympathetic eyes of a devoted but not very bright dog. A whistle blew. Alice and the girl friend waved handkerchiefs, diminished into blurred dots as the train chuffed off and Bacchus Marsh disappeared, dissolved into open paddocks of wheat and lucerne, cows and tin signs advertising Dr Morse's Indian Root Pills.

She sat bolt upright, turning the pages of the *Women's Weekly*, finding Sinden's new story and trying to concentrate on it, thankful that they had the compartment to themselves so that when Ettie at last wandered off to the ladies' room, she was able to give in completely to the misery that engulfed her. Pressing her face to the gritty windowpane she wept, and wished to die. Then standing aside, watching, saw suddenly that she was not weeping for Logan but for the irretrievable loss of herself, the missed chance to become wholly part of that mysterious area of her being where she had always been afraid to venture and on which a door had slammed. Grabbing at this spear of truth, she stabbed it again and again into the weeping girl until the weeping stopped and the eager, flirting Vanessa who had led her into all this was dead and bloody, propped lifelessly against the train window.

Then, over the noise of the rattling window, against sudden gusts of wind and rain, she became aware that someone was saying something. What?

'What?' she asked, resuming her present shape, turning her head back towards the room, towards the man sprawled in the wing chair.

'Hello,' said Logan. 'Well, how do you do? How are *you*?'

She sat up straight, brushing away the dead leaves of Bacchus Marsh that had settled in her lap. Stupid of her to let him catch her wandering away, laying flowers on her own grave. He knew where she'd been during this silence between them. She could tell by the amused look in his eyes, by the knowing grin, and by his childish delight in remembering his old 'How do you do?' joke with her. It was ridiculous. It was in bad taste. Pathetic, really. *He* was pathetic with his thinning hair and his ulcer; putting on that worn-out act, that passé charm. In a few years he would be a Dirty Old Man ogling girls on trams. Disgusting. She felt secretly pleased about his diminished power yet he seemed unaware of it, grinning at her and turning the china figurine over and over in his big hands.

She said, smiling back at him hard and bright, 'Would you mind awfully not fiddling with that. It's fragile.'

'You mean it's *Ettie's*.'

Still smiling, she rose, saying, 'How about a sherry before lunch?'

'If that's all you've got.'

'That's all.'

269

Handing him the glass of sherry, she sat again and waited, determined that she would speak no more until he had given some reply to her long peroration. But now it seemed as though he too was preoccupied with faint sounds of the past, for he was staring past her at the wet wisteria vines beyond the windows and whistling softly.

The clock whirred and struck.

He said, 'Where's the blue-sky gentleman?'

'Who? PS?'

'I s'pose you never heard of that. Family joke.'

He seemed to think he had scored a small point and so she made a big point of ignoring it.

'I've sent the maid to get him. If you'd phoned first—'

'Does he know I'm coming?'

'No.'

'Won't it be a shock?'

'I'm a believer in the *fait accompli*. Children worry far more in advance. Better to present them with the situation.'

'Yes, I s'pose with your vast experience with children you'd know better.'

'I *think*, in all fairness to *you*, Logan, that you should get an honest reaction and not something that has been carefully rehearsed. That's why I've had to keep Lila in the dark about our arrangement. She's so excitable and hysterical, she'd have been at him to

270

say this and that to you. God *knows* what! I've told you that she's made him conceal things from me and tell me untruths.'

He laughed and she said sternly, 'You don't think that's serious?'

'Oh, yes,' he said. 'Knowing what a stickler you always were for honesty.'

She had expected a barb or two, but suddenly the old wound hurt. She bent quickly to the fire and poked at a log long enough to excuse her burning face. Then she said, 'Actually, everything I've told you can be proven.'

'Oh, I'm dead sure of that, Ness, but of course I've got to get Lila's side of the story.'

'Naturally. I want you to.'

'I tried to ring her up this morning but their phone's out of order or something.'

'Cut off. They're in terrible trouble, Logan. Stony broke.'

'So's everyone.'

She was dying to say, 'Except me. Look around you at this room, my dear. Take note of the carpet, for instance. It's an Aubusson but that wouldn't mean anything to you, accustomed only to linoleum. And you couldn't know that those chairs are Queen Anne and that happens to be Amontillado you're swigging down as though it were cooking sherry. You're not impressed. You've made a big point of not being impressed. You haven't said a word about the house *or* about me. How do I look? Am I changed? Starting to look middle-aged? Spinsterish? Well, at *least* I'm not that confused girl who stared at you bug-eyed as though you'd hung the moon. I'd like to tell you how *you* look, my dear. But I can't because there's something I want from you.'

She said, 'There's a number where you can call and leave a message for Lila at a neighbour's house. But I'd rather you didn't phone until we've settled things.'

'Whatever you say.'

'I appreciate you not going out to see her before you talked to me.'

'Oh, I read my instructions very carefully!'

'Logan, I had to make *some* conditions.'

'Oh, that's all right, Ness. It wouldn't be you if there weren't conditions. You're footing the bill.'

'We could hardly talk about all this over a long-distance phone.'

'That's right, Ness.'

'I'd have brought PS to Bacchus Marsh but that would have meant disrupting school and all his other lessons. Besides being unfair to Lila.'

'Absolutely.'

'Besides, how was I to know you'd be *in* the Marsh?'

'Besides. Besides. Besides.'

'What?'

272

'Nothing.'

'Well, the obvious thing was to send for you.'

'Thanks. Before I forget my manners, thank you very much, Ness.'

'Well, I'm sure if Lila and George had had the money—'

'Thank you very, very, very much. Can I have some more sherry?'

'Think you should?'

'Think I won't behave?'

'You always behave, Logan.'

'*You* always say the right thing, don't you?'

'Don't try to spar with me, Logan.'

'Who's sparring? I'm not sparring with you, dear girl. I'm just asking for some more sherry and I'll be very frank with you, Ness. I had a couple of quick shots before coming.'

'Did you?'

'Now, you *know* I did.'

'Yes.'

'Yes, and you know why.'

'Here, Logan. But sip it.'

'*Sip* it, yes. You know why, don't you. What'll I say to him?'

'Just be yourself.'

'What's that? What am I? Or rather, what am I to him?'

'I don't honestly know, Logan.'

'Oh, come on, you can do better than that. You got me here. Got me this far. Least you can do is give me a clue. How do I explain myself to him?'

'I can't tell you what to say.'

'Come on, Ness. You know him and I don't. He doesn't know me from Cain. How do I explain myself?'

'I can't tell you that.'

'Well, *you* know me. Give me a hint, Ness. How should I behave with him?'

She was standing now beside the wing chair and he was looking up at her. It was PS's face, just washed, slightly troubled, asking where were they going? She thought, Yes, you're scared to death. In spite of all your protective jibes, you're really scared to death, and why wouldn't you be?

From her safe perch, she savoured his disadvantage, gloated a moment, decided to reward him with a compliment.

She let her hand rest lightly on his shoulder, feeling the strong back muscles, remembering a car in a dark field.

She said, 'Poor Logan. Just be nice to him.'

'But how?'

'You know how.' Her voice was low now. 'Like you were with me.'

Instantly she saw the glint of triumph, heard the impudent laugh.

'I *knew* you'd say that.'

She drew back her hand as if she had touched a scorpion. It was the same old trick to send her flying off her perch into the mud, squawking and fluttering in a loss of feathers, upside down in the dirt with his foot on her, their positions reversed, and hearing him say:

'But tell me, Ness. Why do you want him all to yourself? Why do you want to drag him off to London?'

It had all been carefully prearranged. The whole strategy designed to throw her off balance and then follow up the advantage like a prosecuting attorney who woos the witness with honeyed words and then whips out the damaging evidence. Now, flustered and confused, she must make her case badly, for that was what he had intended all along. He wanted her to plead on her knees for PS. Well, she wouldn't. A glacier would form in the garden before she would beg from him.

Baker's son!

Pat-a-cake, pat-a-cake, baker's man. Bake me a cake as fast as you can.

She lit a cigarette, taking her time, watching the match burn down. Then, when she had finally detached herself from him, controlled her desire to slap his face, she blew out the match, sat down and began again.

First, it surely must be clear that two homes were one too many for a child, confusing his loyalty and muddling him as to who was in charge. Secondly, Lila and George were incapable of providing for him any longer. They had done so, admirably, for six and a half years and the time had arrived when they should be relieved of the burden. Thirdly, the advantages of London were obvious. A good school, Continental travel, and later Cambridge, where her Pater went, but only if PS wanted it; this she would not enforce. Fourthly, Sinden would have approved.

'How do you know?'

'I have the letter she wrote just before she died.'

'She wrote a letter a day.'

'Not like this one.'

Exhibit A. Sinden's letter. He read it through with an expressionless face.

'You see what she says. "I'll *have* the children and Ness will *manage* them."'

'One of her six-o'clock-in-the-morning impulses.'

'Well, it *is* in black and white.'

'Your day probably. I bet she said the same to Lila. And to Vere. Even Agnes. Lucky for the boy your parents stopped when they did. He'd have had a hockey team of aunts all claiming him.'

'I believe she wanted *me*.'

'Oh, I see. Why you, Ness?'

'Two reasons. I have the wherewithal.'

'Yes, you do. What's the other?'

'I was closest to her.'

'Balls.'

'I beg your pardon?'

'Cut that out,' he said, rising suddenly six feet over her. 'Now cut that out, Vanessa. You didn't even know her.'

'What was that?'

'None of your family knew her. Vere, a little. Not much, but a little. I knew her absolutely.'

'Yes, of course.'

'Ab-so-lute-ly.'

He crossed to the cabinet and poured another sherry.

'I suppose,' she said, 'that that was why she called you her five-minute husband. But of course you wouldn't have heard of that. *Family* joke.'

'Well, it's nice. It's her. She could live more in five minutes than you could in five years.'

'Mmmmm. Unfortunately that's why she's in Woronora Cemetery. And you're right about me. I live my life sparingly and without waste. Especially emotional waste. I think that's why she says in her letter that she yearns for my profound sense of organisation.'

'Good description of you.'

'Yes. And I believe at the end—at the very end—she had great need of someone like me. I think she was finally sick to death of chaos and—and unpredictability. She said the child would be the postscript to her *ridiculous* life. Well, it *was* ridiculous. Always off course—always running off at some wild tangent; she had *no* discipline about anything she did. None!'

'Why so angry, Ness?'

'Not angry. Sorry. Why should I be *angry* about it?'

'Don't *you* know?'

'Good God, I'm not *angry*! I'm just very, very thankful that I'm not *like* that; that I know when to draw on the reins. That's all. And I'll tell you this, Logan, I'm jolly well sure she wished at the end that she'd had some of my caution.'

'How do you *jolly well know* what she wished at the end? You weren't with her. You were off being Lady Piss-Elegant in London!'

'Where were *you*?'

Got you, she thought. I've really got you this time, my dear. Try to wriggle out of that one!

He put down his sherry glass and she noticed with triumph that his hand shook.

She said quietly, 'Is it cold in here? You might put some more wood on the fire.'

He turned and obediently picked up a log, poked it into the fire and remained with his back to her, staring at sparks.

She said, 'Why did you give me PS?'

'Gave you half of him.' His voice sounded hoarse.

'Well, why? Why did you agree to let me take over Ernest Huxley's guardianship?'

278

'Alice and my mother thought . . .'

After a long pause, she prompted. 'What?'

'They always liked you. Mum liked you a lot. Mum always said—Oh, what the hell, I always stuck to what Mum said. It wasn't you. It was the money. That's the honest-to-God stinking fact of it. Alice and Mum said that with Cousin Ettie's loot he'd have the best of everything.'

'Do you think I've done the best I possibly can for him?'

'Stop talking, will you, Ness? God, I'm tired. I'm suddenly so damn tired.'

'Just this one question, Logan. Please. Do you think I've at least tried to do my very best?'

'How do I know? Yes, I suppose. Hell, I don't know. I don't s'pose you beat him and lock him in the cellar. What do I know about anything? Yes, I would think in your own way you've done bloody marvellously.'

'Then let me do the *most* I can. What I know and believe is the right and only way out of this impasse. Let me take him to London.'

There was a tap at the door and Diana's scared face.

'He's here, Misscot.'

Vanessa said:

'Oh, you're home, PS. Come here, darling.'

Logan, hearing the flip of sandals coming across

279

the hall, remained staring down at the fire, afraid to turn.

Vanessa was kissing him and her eyes had that very bright excited look. Who was the man? Who was the big man bending over the fireplace and kicking logs with his foot? Was this man the Thing? Was this a new teacher? Was he going to have even *more* lessons in the afternoons?

'PS, dear,' said Vanessa, 'this is your father.'

He kept on staring up at her, wondering if it was a joke. Out of the corner of his eye he saw the man turn and look at him and so he turned his head and looked at the man and they looked at each other for a very long while until the man said in a deep gruff voice rather like the one that George put on when he read a story (when he was a bear), 'Hello, PS,' and Vanessa said, 'Don't you think you might go and give Logan a nice kiss?' Logan! Oh, no, this couldn't be Logan at all. This man wasn't a bit the way Logan was meant to look; and *kiss* Logan? That would be awful, worse than anything. He took a step towards Vanessa and stared at her belt buckle until she turned him around and gave him a slight push and the man took a step towards him but didn't seem to know what to do either and was fumbling in his coat pocket and brought out something wrapped in brown paper and said, 'Here's a present for you.' 'What is it?' he asked, and the man said, 'Why don't you open it and see?' and so he unwrapped the parcel. It was a very disappointing present. It was just a stone. Just a plain old bit of stone with some glittery stuff in it and the man said, 'It's gold. I brought you some gold, PS.' Of course, it wasn't gold at all, anyone could see that, but Vanessa was pretending it was and saying, 'Oh, isn't that nice. Isn't that jolly nice. Logan dug that out of the earth for you. Now I *do* think you might give him a kiss for that,' and the man bent down and kissed him with very dry lips, scratching his face with his rough suit and smelling of something rather sweet the way Ettie did sometimes and then the man suddenly hugged him very hard and said, 'Jesus, God,' and kept holding on to him, not doing anything else or saying anything, just holding on until he pushed the man away, not rudely, but just so that he could breathe again because he suddenly felt a bit sick, knowing that this must really be Logan. Only Logan went out and found gold and Vanessa never told fibs and so the Thing was worse, much, much worse than he'd ever thought because Logan coming meant something terrible was going to happen just like Winnie had always said: 'They'll come and get you and take you away.' And now Logan was laughing and saying, 'Well well well,' and kept on saying it over and over again and Vanessa took the stone and put it on the table; wrapping up the paper neatly like she always did with parcels and said, 'I tell you what you *might* do. You might take Logan upstairs and show him your room while I see about luncheon. Logan, is a soufflé all right for you, oh, good, and, PS, I think Logan would like to see your train too, don't you?' and she went clip-clopping out on her high heels calling to Diana and to Ellen about lunch and he and Logan were left alone.

As soon as Vanessa had gone out of the room, Logan walked over to the cabinet and poured something out of a bottle and drank it very fast, and said, 'Where's the train, PS?' so he said in a whisper, 'Upstairs.' 'Will you show me?' Logan asked, so he nodded. There was no getting out of it, no use hiding, and nowhere to run because it was raining outside. He led the way and Logan followed as they went upstairs, not saying anything until they reached the top. Then he said to Logan, 'That's my room there,' and they went into his room and stood there, not knowing what to do next. 'That's my bed,' he said, and then he pointed out the wardrobe, the bookshelves and the little armchair, and opening a drawer, he showed all the gloves, socks and handkerchiefs, noticing that Logan looked at him all the time and not at the things, but he went on until there was nothing more to see in the bedroom. He said, 'The train's over here,' and they went across the hall to the spare room where the door was open and they both stood and stared down at the train. He knelt down and turned the switch and the little train darted off and ran around the track while they watched in silence until Logan squatted down on the carpet by him and said, 'By golly, that's a nice train, PS. I came on a big train all the way from Melbourne. I got on a train at Bacchus Marsh and went to Melbourne and there I got on another big train for a whole night and came to Sydney.' Logan seemed to think that this was great fun because he slapped him on the back and said, 'How'd you like to come on the big train with me someday and see all your uncles and aunts and cousins?' Was this what was cooking? Was Vanessa going to send him away with Logan? The very thought of it was so awfully frightening that he wondered if he should run out of the room and escape quickly that very minute, not even wait to find his raincoat, run through the rain and catch a tram and the boat home where Lila would hide him in some safe place. He edged away so that Logan would not be able to catch hold of him suddenly, edged as far as he could towards the open door, ready to run. Logan apparently noticed it because he stopped smiling and changed the subject quickly and said, 'Go to kindergarten, do you?' No, he explained almost in a whisper, not any more. Now he went to Miss Pile's and yes, thank you, he liked it. Yes, he had some nice 'chums', thank you. Yes, he liked his piano lessons, thank you. And riding school and dancing class. Thank you. How could he explain to a stranger like Logan that he hated Miss Pile's and those nasty kids, hated all the lessons in the afternoons, hated coming back to

Vanessa's every Sunday evening? If he said that, then Logan would be certain to take him away on that train. Fortunately, Logan seemed to have run out of questions and just sat there, clearing his throat every now and then as if he had swallowed a fly and staring at the toy train, and so he watched it too and now there was no noise except the train and the rain outside, and he wished that Vanessa would come and rescue them or better still that Logan would just go away and not come back.

Too much booze before lunch and then having to play follow the leader with Vanessa. Vanessa trying to pin you down, sticking a hatpin through your guts as if you were a dead butterfly she wanted for her collection. And now the boy. This white-faced little boy of yours, scared stiff of you, answering your idiotic questions with those sissy-polite manners she's taught him. 'Yes, thank you,' 'All right, thank you.' Anyway, you don't know what to ask him, you don't know what to say. Christ, what a situation. Why did you ever come? What can you do? What can you say to him? 'I'm Daddy. Your mum and me decided to have you'? He'd probably say, 'Thank you.' Not Sin's kid! She'd blow her bloody top if she could see what they're doing to him. What you've let them do.

'Logan, don't take up all the bed. Leave some for *us*.'

284

No, don't think about that now. And don't sit there clearing your throat. Say something to him.

'Logan, are you asleep?'

No, no. But turning now in bed, holding her. 'Well, how do you do. How are *you*?'

'Nicely, thank you. Have we met?'

'I don't think we were formally introduced but you're nice.'

'So are you.'

'But, listen, you couldn't be *us* yet.'

'Oh, yes I can. Am.'

'In four days?'

'I'm cosmic. Or is it clairvoyant?'

'Oh, you are. Well, if you're absolutely sure, my girl, then I s'pose that's all you want of *me*. I'll get up and go now. Where's my hat and spats?'

'Don't you dare move. In fact, don't you dare move further away from me for the next forty-six years.'

'I better make a note of that.'

'Just a brief note will do. "I promise to stay in bed with Sinden for forty-six years. Signed, L. Marriott."'

'Bit awkward for the hotel.'

'Oh, no. They'll advertise us as the longest-staying honeymoon couple in history. Occasionally we'll appear on the balcony and wave to the crowds.'

'OK. Later we'll go on tour.'

'With our enormous brood.'

'Your writing may suffer.'

'But it was for The Cause.'

'Right. And The Cause comes first. Where's the pillow? Oh, on the floor as usual. Here, lift your head a minute. That better?'

'Mmmmmm. Bliss. Everything's bliss.'

'Both of you more comfortable?'

'Yes, thanks. He's fine.'

'Oh, it's *him*, is it?'

'Has to be. I'm concentrating on fearfully masculine things like shaving brushes and football boots with spikes—ummmmm—brier pipes and dynamos, heavyweight champions and that statue of Laocoön.'

'Who was he when he was at home?'

'Don't know but it's a huge mass of great muscular men and serpents.'

'That ought to do the trick.'

'I think so, darling.'

'Well, keep working away at it.'

'I thought I would.'

'Have you decided what he's going to be like?'

'Absolutely. Fat. Noisy and rude. Not nasty rude—*cheeky*. Full of spit and fight, running through the house upsetting tables and yelling for bread and jam, driving us dotty putting goannas and toads in our bed, not scared of anything. Like all the Marriott boys, with a touch of Vere for fun. A bit serious sometimes and then, like you, bursting out laughing at the whole solemn world because it's so absurd. And turning up in some girl's life one day out of the blue because he's just like you, darling, a blue-sky gentleman like you. Oh, on the whole I think he won't be too bad. He won't be dull or pompous or dreary. I think he'll bring some light with him wherever he goes. As a matter of fact, thank you very much for him. I think maybe I'll kiss you for him . . .'

Oh, my God, Sin, he's here beside me and I don't know what the hell to say to him! Too much booze. I'm sorry, Sin. Sorry. Sorry. Sorry. So sorry I didn't come back. And after you went there wasn't any bloody point to anything. Oh, God, I'm going to blub in a minute. Jesus, don't let me blub in front of the kid!

Where was Vanessa? It seemed as if they were going to sit there all day, looking at his train. Then Logan started to make strange noises and he saw to his horror that Logan had begun to cry; felt his face go fiery red with the awful embarrassment of it; quickly turned off the train and got up and went over to the washstand where his boats stood in a neat orderly line and picked up his big yacht with the sails which had never yet been in the water and all the time the sound of crying went on behind him. Once a long time ago he had found George standing behind the loquat tree crying and he had run and put his arms around George's knees and in a minute George had stopped crying and patted him and called him 'Old Feller' and made a joke about onions getting in his eyes. But he couldn't run to Logan. He couldn't touch Logan because they didn't know each other and Logan might snatch him up and run out of the house with him. But Vanessa would know what to do. He started out of the room to call out to her but Logan said, 'Wait a minute,' blew his nose loudly and said, 'Sorry, chum. All over now. All over.' Then got stiffly up from the floor repeating. 'All over, all over.'

'Don't be frightened,' said Logan. 'I'm not,' he said, lying. 'No, don't you be,' said Logan. 'Don't you be frightened of anything. Your mother never was. She wouldn't want you to be. Don't you let them frighten you and don't let them just push you around, see? You do what you want to do, see?' That was a new idea, doing what you wanted to, but how? They always told you what to do, what to wear, where to live, every-thing. He wanted to say this out loud but no words came. Looked at his yacht.

'They look after you because I can't,' said Logan as if he had heard. 'But if they try to make you do something you hate, you bellyache and yell, see? You yell loud as you can and make a fuss. Understand?'

Imagine yelling at Vanessa and refusing to do some-thing! Logan certainly didn't understand *anything*. Just the same it was a rather thrilling thought and he looked at Logan admiringly. Maybe Logan wasn't *too* awful, after all.

288

'Now listen,' said Logan. 'I'll tell you a secret. She wants to take you away.'

So this was the Thing! Not Logan at all, but Vanessa.

Today? Where? He was feeling sick. 'Where?'

'England,' said Logan.

England! That was as far as the moon. He couldn't get home on Fridays from England! He'd never get home *again*!

'A long way away,' said Logan. 'Until you're grown up.'

Grown up! That would mean years and years. He couldn't take it in, even. He looked at Logan, speechless.

Again Logan seemed to understand because he leaned down and said quietly, 'Would you want to? Would you like to go?'

He shook his head, then again.

'I didn't think so,' said Logan. 'Well, don't worry, chum. I'll fix *her*!' He laughed, seemed pleased all of a sudden. 'I'll cook her little goose for her. You see, that's one thing I *can* do. One thing I can do for *you*! It's not much in seven years but it's something. You'll have to go on living with her here because I bloody well bungled that. But I won't let her take you away and turn you into a flaming Pommy. So don't you worry!' Logan winked.

So Logan was his friend after all. He wanted to say

something. Thank you or something. Ask him about gold and Dear One and why they were away in that hotel by the river with the jellyfish. What happened there?

Logan had saved him and it was like being let out of school, like seeing Lila come up the drive on Fridays, feeling safe. He was so relieved, he felt almost happy and now questions came to him quickly. Where was Bacchus Marsh? Why did Logan live there and not here? Did he still belong to Logan and if so was it all right now to tell everyone that he had a father? What really happened to Dear One? And was it *really* his fault? What to ask first? Quickly, before Vanessa came back, because now he didn't want her to come back. Now he wanted to stay here with Logan all day and maybe even sit on his knee and talk and talk and he would tell Logan all about everything and how he felt and how he loved Lila and George best but—

But then Logan picked him suddenly up and held him tightly, kissed him hard on the mouth, put him down and went quickly out of the room.

'Don't go,' he said, but it was too late for Logan was already halfway down the stairs, running now, escaping.

He ran to the stairs himself, started down, but then saw Vanessa come through the green baize door into the hall and before he could take a step angry words had begun. Very angry but not loud enough to hear everything they said. He stuck his head through the stairway railings and looked down. Logan was moving around a lot, waving his arms, and Vanessa was standing very straight and still the way she did when she gave strict orders. Muffled by the sound of the heavy rain on the glass skylight above him, their voices sounded like barking dogs. On and on it went, stopped, went on again, rising and falling until it seemed that the house was shaking, not with the wind outside but from the angry things they were saying to each other with words he couldn't understand even when they flew up to him. Below, he could see the top of Diana's white cap half hidden behind the green door where she was also listening. Then suddenly, Vanessa tried to pull Logan into the drawing room but he shook her off and laughed but in a jeering sort of way, and still laughing, he walked away from her to the front door and opened it and rain and leaves blew in, the pictures on the wall shook in fright and Vanessa too seemed frightened because she ran to Logan and took hold of him with both her hands and held on to him but he pushed her away and went off into the rain while she called after him and went on calling for as long as it must have taken Logan to go down the driveway and slam the gate. Then she closed the door and suddenly it was quiet in the house with only the drumming of the rain.

Vanessa stood looking down at the floor. He could not tell if she was crying because he could only see the top of her head and the sharp white parting in her red hair. Then she looked up and he saw that she was not crying and that she had noticed him. For a long time they looked up and down at each other but Vanessa's face was blank as if she had never seen him before in her life. Then she started up the stairs, moving very fast up to him, and her face as it came nearer was very white but there were big red splotches on her neck. She looked different.

'Were you listening, PS?' Even her voice was different, squeaky. 'Come on.' She prodded him towards his room where, forgetting her own rules, she sat on the bed.

'I'm sorry,' she said. 'It won't happen again. He's gone now, so don't be frightened. As far as I'm concerned, you'll never see him again. He is an awful man. Awful. A beastly man, PS. He has always tried to hurt me. Long before you were born he tried to hurt me. I'm glad you saw today how terrible he is. Because now you can be grateful that you escaped all that. That's what it would have been like all the time if your mother had lived because your father is a bad man.' Funnily enough, it sounded like a bedtime story: Once upon a time there was a bad father and a good mother and a little boy and they all lived—

'All the time,' she repeated, 'Isn't it a good thing she died? Aren't you glad you have me to protect you from him and take care of you? Mmmmm?'

She was talking as if he were a baby and this was unlike her. She lay down on his bed and closed her eyes.

'Come here,' she said. 'Put your arms round me and comfort me. Give me a nice kiss.'

When he didn't move, she reached out and took him to her, making room on the bed, placing his arms around her neck and squeezing him tightly.

'Don't worry,' she said, 'Logan can't get you because you belong to me. In fact, we belong to each other. Oh, listen, I have great plans and Logan is not going to stand in the way of them. So don't you worry, my dearest, my angel.' She kissed him all over his face. 'It's going to be simply splendid and think how nice it will be when you grow up and leave school—all the things we'll do together when you're a grown-up man. Just think how nice it will be for me too. I'll have a man to take me to the theatre and the opera and—'

Where? In England? Grown up and with *her*?

'No,' he said.

What did Logan say? Bellyache? Yell?

'No,' he shouted, pushing her away very hard, scrambling off the bed, away from her and those kisses. 'No, I won't go.'

Vanessa sat up, her hair untidily falling down and one of her eyelids twitching a little.

'What?'

'I won't go,' he shouted again.

'What did Logan tell you?'

'I won't go anywhere with you.'

'Did he tell you to say that?'

'No.'

'Did he tell you—'

'I won't go away on that boat. I'll—I'll get the police.'

'I don't awfully like that tone of voice.'

'I will, I will.'

'We're not going on a boat—yet. But if we were I rather think that you would do as you're told.'

'I won't.'

'Stop that, please.'

'I won't stop it.'

'You would prefer a smack?'

'I don't care.'

'Listen, I've been hurt enough this morning without this kind of behaviour from you.'

'I won't go away from Lila and George.'

For a moment she sat very still, her eyelid twitching.

'Did you tell Logan that?'

'No.'

'Yes you did. I know you did. You told Logan you'd rather live with Lila, didn't you?'

She took hold of him, shook him. 'Didn't you?'

'No, I didn't.'

'My God, you're just like him. As bad as he.'

'He's *not* bad. He's not.'

'Sit in that chair, please. We are going to have a talk.'

'No.'

'Sit in that chair!'

He felt the slap, saw her white face very close, her eyes like two green fires.

Then he ran out of the room, caught a glimpse of Diana crouching halfway up the stairs and holding her hands up as though she was praying. He hesitated just for a moment and then ran into the bathroom, slammed the door and turned the key. He heard Vanessa's footsteps, saw the doorknob turn and heard her sharp rapping.

'Go away,' he shouted.

He heard Vanessa's angry voice and Diana wailing, then Vanessa barking at her and Diana shouting something back. Then nothing but Vanessa's high heels going to and fro across the hall, going in and out of rooms. Once she came to the door and called out, 'Having a good time in there?'

'Go away,' he said, quieter this time. 'Shut up,' he said.

He heard her move away. Heard her lock the spare room. A little later she came to the door again and tapped lightly on it.

'I think I know who'll get tired of this first,' she called. Then he heard her footsteps moving away and going downstairs. There was silence now except for the rain and he felt wonderful. He could do anything. Anything he liked. He sat on the toilet and thought about what to do next. He put the plug in the bath and turned on the cold water tap, letting the big bathtub fill almost to the top. Then he floated the soap holder for a while. The most wonderful thing of all was being bad. Just like she had said he was. Well, he would show her just how bad he could be. He felt the excitement coming back again, thought how he would scream and yell at her, refuse to go to bed, refuse to eat, kick and scream. He would be all the things he'd always wanted to be. He would show her. Cook her goose for her. He wished now that he'd thought of doing it a long time ago. He would be so bad and wicked that she would no longer want him. She'd send him home for good because she couldn't stand him any more.

He was delighted with the thought. He looked around the bathroom to see what bad thing he could do next. There wasn't very much bad you could do in a bathroom. He climbed on the chair and opened the cabinet over the basin. There were a lot of Vanessa's things in there. Bottles and boxes of powder and something she put under her arms, sprays, orange sticks, her nail scissors, tweezers, bath salts, toothpaste, a bottle of pink gargle, a nail-brush, lots of things. He took them carefully out one by one and put them on the floor. Then he climbed on the toilet seat and managed to open the window. It took quite a long while to throw them all out the window and by the time he had finished he was wet through from the rain blowing in, and feeling a bit tired. Hungry too. He closed the window and sat down on the toilet again. He heard the hall clock whir and strike two. No one came. The house was silent as midnight. Even the rain had begun to stop. Could Vanessa have gone out? Escaped? Where was Cousin Ettie all this time? Didn't they even want to go to the toilet? But then he remembered the guest lavatory downstairs. What if they decided just to let him stay in the bathroom? How long could he stay? It was two days until Friday. Would a person starve to death? He began to feel a bit frightened. Suppose they had all gone away and left him alone in the house to punish him? Well, there was the phone. But then he remembered that Lila's phone was cut off and he didn't know the number of Miss Gulf's house, where they took the messages. He tiptoed to the door and listened. He felt his heart beating quickly now and knew that he really was frightened. Perhaps it wasn't a good thing to be all this bad at once, not all at once, but more spread out so that you at least got fed. After all, there were two whole days of this week left to be wicked in. Yes, perhaps that would be better. Tomorrow he would refuse to go to dancing class or better still go and be very rude when he got there, stick his tongue out at Miss McDonald, the teacher, and hit Cynthia Lawson quite hard in her belly. That's what he would do. But for now . . . He was about to turn the key when he heard footsteps coming up the stairs and then across the hall towards the door. Vanessa's feet. Something was put down on the floor outside and then she knocked and called out:

'If you're at all interested, there's a chicken sandwich and a glass of milk here.'

She clicked away across the hall and there was silence again. He waited for a while, counted twenty and then carefully unlocked the door, trying not to make any noise. He opened the door a crack and peeped out. A plate with a chicken sandwich and a glass of milk stood on the floor just outside the door. There was no one around.

He sidled out of the bathroom and picked up the plate and the glass, started to tiptoe towards his room when he caught sight of Vanessa in her room. She was sitting in the big yellow silk armchair and smoking a cigarette. She made no move and for a moment they stared at each other across the hallway.

'Hello,' she said. 'Listen, have you ever heard the story of the tortoise and the hare? They had a race, you see, which seemed pretty absurd because everyone knows that a hare can run very fast and a tortoise can't run at all. Well, what happened, *act*ually, was that the hare was so *sure* that he would win that he sat down under a tree and had a jolly nice nap, do you see? And so of course the tortoise caught up and passed the hare and won. Well, *I'm* a tortoise.' That seemed to be the end of the story so he went into his room and ate his sandwich and drank his milk. He felt suddenly very sleepy. He climbed on to the bed and heard, as he went to sleep, Vanessa singing softly in her room.

Lila laid Mater's best slightly darned damask cloth on the dining room table and got out the good dishes. There was no silver left and she hoped that Logan would not notice the kitchen knives and forks. The chicken was in the oven and she reminded herself for the eleventh time that she must not worry herself sick over the extravagance of it, nor of the few yards of cretonne hastily pinned together that morning to hide the cracks in the leather armchair. There was enough to be sick about. She had been sick ever since Vere's telephone call to Miss Gulf; had wandered deliriously up and down the street with threepences to pay for the calls to Vanessa (always busy, out, can't come to the phone, said the maid or cook), finally had got hold of Ettie, who said she thought that he was at the Hotel Waratah, and then at long last to Logan and the frightening garbled story.

She was afraid to ask too many obvious questions in front of the eavesdropping Gulf sisters and Logan's replies were so vague that she had wanted to rush to him then and there but Logan had said no, he would come over to the house so they could have a long chinwag. He would come late tomorrow for tea. He kept telling her not to worry because he was on *her* side. Good old Lila, he kept saying, over what seemed to be the noise of raucous laughter and the strumming of a ukulele in the background. She gathered that there had been a fight and that he had told Vanessa to go to hell, but this only served to increase Lila's premonition of doom. The rainbirds had been noisy all day.

When George came home, his creased face and hunched shoulders warned her that it had been another fruitless day of job hunting and she minimised the ominous facts. But that night, in breathless sleep, she had had troubled dreams in which she ran down endless white corridors on board a monstrous ship trying to find PS, and seeing Logan, tried to make him sign some adoption papers, but there was no pen, no ink and the papers were made of wool.

She had awakened wan and shaky, got busy in the dark winter morning with mops and pails. All morning she scoured and scrubbed, dropping wet tea leaves on the sitting room carpet to keep down the dust as she swept, fighting down the rising tides of asthma. Once, George, catching her kneeling, delving for fluff, said, 'Do you think he's going to look under the bed?' But she was touched when he went off and borrowed the Grindels' trowel, weeded the front lawn and painted the front steps with oven black.

Now, as she arranged the shillingsworth of daisies in Sinden's blue-sky vase and placed it in the centre of the table, she felt, in spite of everything, the quick anticipation of the hostess. It wasn't Cousin Ettie's posh house but it was home and it was the kind of home that Logan was accustomed to and that was on their credit side. She plumped the tired cushions on the sofa once more, inspected the chicken, looked at her rhubarb pie, felt better. Felt almost hopeful. Passing the bathroom, where George was shaving, she called:

'Don't use the guest towel; it's for Logan.'

'Think I was going to mop the floor with it?'

She hurried into her dark-blue morocain, put on her pink imitation pearls and Mater's brooch; put on dabs of dry rouge and lipstick, resented her long Scott face, regretted her mole. Back in the sitting room she arranged the snapshots of PS to show to Logan. The carefully selected happy pictures of PS on the beach, at the zoo, blowing out birthday candles and one sitting with George on a camel.

George came in wearing his blue suit and, watching his face absorbed in the paper she thought, I must handle this myself. Or as much of it as I can myself. 'You dear love,' she said silently to George.

At six o'clock she opened the front door and peered down the darkening street. A new twittering fear had begun in her.

'He must have missed the half past five boat,' she said.

'It wouldn't be Logan if he was on time,' said George.

By six thirty she had made four trips to the front gate and back.

'Look,' said George. 'The watched Pop never boils.'

'What?'

'He might have forgotten.'

'Forgotten!'

'You said he sounded blotto on the phone.'

'Yes, but—oh, no, he couldn't have forgotten. I said the half past five boat and he said yes and I said get off the tram at Ben Boyd Road and he was writing it down—'

'How do you know he was writing it down?'

'It sounded like it. He said how do you spell that? Oh, no, he's coming. It's just that the chicken is ruined, that's all.'

After a minute she added, 'He's coming because the child's whole future is at stake.'

'Yes, that would worry Logan,' said George.

Then the front gate slammed.

'I told you,' she cried triumphantly, and ran into the hall, arms outstretched in welcome, stopped when she saw Miss Gulf at the door.

'Telephone, Mrs Baines.'

'Oh, is it a gentleman? We're expecting—'

'A man. He didn't give the name.'

She hurried up the dark cold street with Miss Gulf, past the supper-lighted windows.

'We were right in the middle of our tea,' said Miss Gulf.

'I'm so sorry,' said Lila. 'But it must be important.'

'We don't *mind*,' said Miss Gulf. 'Only my sister isn't well, you know, and the telephone ringing frightens her. We don't like the phone ringing.'

'I know. I'm so sorry, dear.'

Into Miss Gulf's stuffy hallway, wheezing now, picking up the receiver.

'Hello?'

'Hello, who's that?'

'Lila. Logan?'

'Lila.' He sounded blurred. 'How are you? Well, how do you do, how are *you*?'

'Logan, what's happened? Where are you?'

'I'm at the Carlton with Vere. I rang up old Vere and we've been having a little spot of auld lang. She's a bloody marvel; doesn't look any diff'rent—'

'Logan, dinner's all ready and we're waiting—'

'Hello? Lila? Is it you?'

'Of course it's me, Logan. Listen—'

'Lila, I lost your number, see, and I had to get hold of Vere, so Vere's here with me and we're having a couple of spots—'

'You tell Vere that you have to—'

'Lile, I'm sorry about tonight. I have to catch the train.'

'The train! What do you mean? The *Melbourne* train? *Tonight?*'

'Ness's put a lawyer on me. Some chap she sent up with a paper about PS. Threatening me. Don't like to be threatened, Lila. Told him where to get off, no uncertain language. As I said to you, I'm on your side so don't worry—Just a minute, Vere's saying something.'

Lila heard Vere's loud voice in the background, then Logan put his hand over the mouthpiece.

'Oh, my God,' Lila said, and then, 'Logan—Logan, are you there? Hello?'

'What? Oh, hello, Lila. Yes, listen. Vere says to come on in now.'

'Where? Where?'

'To the train. We're going up to the station now. I'm on the—what's it, Vere? Vere says to tell you I'm on the second edition of the Limited but don't tell Ness, Lila. I don't want Ness around or that effing lawyer of hers. OK?'

'I'll come at once.' Oh, God, oh, God, what next?

'Something wrong, Mrs Baines?'

'No, Miss Gulf. Thanks so much. So sorry.'

She fled back down the street and into her own house, cannoning into George in the hall, blurted out the news, tore into the bedroom wardrobe to get her hat and coat, screaming, 'What time does the Melbourne express leave?'

(And even if we're on time, how to talk about adoption papers with Logan drunk and so little time?)

Leaving the ruined dinner, leaving all the lights burning, they slammed the front door and ran down the street to the tram stop.

On the ferry, chugging much too slowly to Circular Quay, she tried to assemble her thoughts, marvelling at George's calmness. He had struck up a conversation with the man next to them about the overcrowding of the harbour, too many overseas liners going too fast, not observing the speed limits. One day, George said, there'd be a bad collision. And pollution too on beaches. He was back making a political speech. She felt admiring, yet exasperated, then touched when at the Quay he hailed a taxi. The driver said he thought the Melbourne express left at eight o'clock. The big tower-clock hands pointed to a quarter to eight as they drove up the ramp to Central Station.

'Platform One,' yelled a porter in reply to Lila's screech.

They hurried into the cavernous smoky cathedral and threaded their way through the crowd, first to the wrong gate, then back to the right one, losing each other momentarily in the sea of people disgorging from the Lithgow train, got breathless and panting into the queue at Platform One.

At the gate, the guard snapped, 'Platform tickets.'

'What? What?'

'You havta have platform tickets, lady. Window Four. Go through that arch over there and turn left.'

George said, 'You wait here.'

'Run,' she cried needlessly for he was already running across the great hall towards the distant arch. Running, she thought, for someone else's mistakes, someone else's child.

She peered through the grille at the crowded platform beyond, trying to spot Logan or Vere in the dim brownish light. Trunks and bags of mail were being loaded into the luggage van and beyond it, people were leaning out of the train windows and talking to others on the platform. Some were already kissing goodbye, the last late stragglers were hurrying through the gate. The train moaned and lurched back a few feet as the engine was coupled on. The precious minutes flew by.

'Let me go through,' she begged the guard. 'I have to find someone.'

'You have to have a platform ticket, lady.'

'Jesus.' She had never said that irreverently in her life. Never felt so impotent, so angry. Frantically she turned her head towards the arch, saw George running back, almost knocking over a child, frantically waved him on. They ran through the gate and on to the smoky dim platform.

'Can you see them?' she said, scanning the lighted windows of the train.

'You look this side, I'll look that,' said George, and they hurried on, looking from right to left, searching the faces in the windows, the seated people in compartments opening baskets of fruit, the kissing forms, the weepers and consolers on the platform benches. The train seemed to stretch on endlessly. Now they were at the next to the last carriage, now the last, now the engine spurting fire; the shapes of hairy, shovelling men. They started back again. Doors were beginning to slam and lock all down the train. She saw a bright red dress and beads; gave a scream. 'There's Vere.'

Vere and Logan on the platform bench were calmly eating fried potato chips out of greasy paper. A bottle of Pilsener stood next to Logan's battered suitcase.

'Logan,' she cried, and he stood up uncertainly, gazing at her in a muddled way. Then he shouted, 'Lila!' staggered forward grinning, and she felt herself being picked up in the air, hugged and kissed. 'God bless you,' he said thickly. Put her down and embraced George. 'Dear old George,' he said. 'God bless you. Sit down, have a drink.'

'Where the hell were you?' said Vere, her face flushed and bright, laughing too loudly.

They all crowded on to the bench and Logan kissed Lila again.

'Logan, don't go—'

'Plenty of time,' he said, reaching for the bottle.

'Don't go tonight,' she begged. 'Come home with us. We've *got* to talk.'

'Plenty of time,' he said.

Vere took a teacup out of her bag and he filled it. 'Let's all have a loving cup,' he said. 'Good to see you, know that?' He slapped George's knee.

'Logan, stay with us. Come home with us now.'

'"Father, dear Father, come home with me now,"' sang Logan.

'He's got to escape the virgin queen,' said Vere, and Logan laughed and embraced Vere.

'Got to escape the virgin queen,' he said. 'Virgin queen's got papers. But it's all right. I fixed it all. I fixed it.'

'How did you fix it, Logan? What happened?'

'Good to see you, Lila.'

'Logan, for God's sake—'

'How've you been, Lila?'

'George, make him understand.'

'Look here, old chap, you better come along with us.'

George took Logan by the arm and they all stood up.

'"Come home, come home again, Kath-leen,"'
sang Logan. He emptied the cup, took hold of Vere
and they went into a travesty of a waltz. Two men
on the train leaned out of a window, bellowing and
applauding.

'All aboard,' yelled a voice.

A whistle blew.

'Got to go, love,' said Logan. He reached down
unsteadily for his suitcase and Lila clung to him.

'Logan, we want *PS*.'

'Right, dear.'

'You've got to let us adopt him.'

'Ab-solutely. Write to you about it, love.'

'No, you've got to stay and sign the papers.'

'No. No more papers. Won't sign papers, love.'

'*All aboard!*'

'Told Vanessa to go to hell. Told her she couldn't
take him out of the country. All fixed, love.'

'But that leaves everything just where it was. What
you've got to do is get him away from Vanessa. *We're*
his parents—'

The train jerked and moved slowly.

'Tell you what I'm going to do, Lila; I'm going to
write you a long, long letter about the whole bloody
thing. We'll get him away from the virgin queen. Don't
you worry, love.'

'But Logan—oh, my God—'

Vere screamed, 'Logan, you'll miss the train.'

309

He spun around, grabbed Vere to him, kissed her.

'Cheerio, kid,' he said.

'Cheerio, kid,' said Vere. 'Keep your chin up, kid.'

Logan kissed Lila again, made a stumbling movement towards George, saw George make a dart to catch him, side-stepped and stumbled towards the moving train, where a guard was holding open the last door.

Lila and George ran forward as the guard reached out, took Logan's arm and hoisted him into the train, slamming the door. Logan leaned out and Lila caught his hand, hurrying along beside the slowly moving train.

'We'll send the papers,' she cried. 'You've got to give him to us.'

He nodded, smiling, waving with his free hand. 'Going to be all right,' he yelled. 'Going up to the Northern Territory, up to the Roper River. Going to find *gold*, Lila. Send you all the money in the world. God bless you, Lila.'

Suddenly she was screaming, 'Do something, *do* something,' above the roar of steam and voices, but he kept nodding and smiling as the train gathered speed and their hands parted and he was being drawn away from her, his figure growing smaller, his arm waving to her over other waving arms, merging into them, vanishing.

'Do something,' she called. 'Do something.' She walked slowly after the quickly vanishing train. 'I'm sick of you,' she called. 'I'm sick of your dreams that come to nothing. You stayed away and let her die,' she said quietly now to the green and red lights of the lumbering luggage van disappearing down the track into the night. 'Let her die,' she repeated to dimming red and green lights and to a guard waving a lantern, felt her unmistakable gift come back to her and knew for certain that none of them would ever see Logan again.

She turned and walked slowly back down the platform, past Vere, still waving at the empty track, tears running down her face. She saw George waiting for her and took his arm and together they walked through the gate and found their way through the echoing arches to the Circular Quay tram.

'I'd like to know just who you think you are,' said Ellen, the cook, very hatchet-faced, one long hair growing out of her chin, putting the last of the broken bottles into the rubbish tin and slamming the lid down. They were standing in the kitchen garden under the bathroom window.

'I hope you know you got poor Diana the sack,' said Ellen, raising her voice so that Jocko the gardener could hear. 'Nice thing, I must say, when boys like you can do what they want and we have to suffer for it. I hope you're satisfied. I hope you're pleased with yourself. Losing a poor girl with a sick dad her job, to say nothing of giving me a lot of extra work. Hope you're proud of yourself.'

She went inside, slamming the wire door, and he heard her slapping dishes into the sink and muttering. A buzzer croaked and Ellen's face, like a hornet behind the wire, buzzed back to him.

'Hear that? That's old Mrs Bult ringing for her breakfast and that means I've got to take the tray up and down myself, thanks to you.'

Vanessa, cool as a cucumber, bundled him into his school overcoat.

'Look here,' she said. 'The next time you feel the urge to throw things out of the bathroom window, I'll give them to you and warn everyone to keep out of the kitchen garden until you're finished.' She buttoned him up rapidly. 'It so happens that most of those face lotions came from Paris and are unobtainable in this so-called country.'

She thumped his school cap on to his head as if she were corking a bottle, hurting his ears, tucking them in.

'However, that is only incidental to the fact that you might have seriously injured someone.'

Cynthia Lawson's mother took him to school, where the children peppered him with questions as to why he had had to leave early the day before.

'I had to go to the dentist,' he said.

'You're a liar,' said Cynthia.

'I'm not.'

'You are. And you know what we do to liars in our club? They have to be initiated all over again.'

'Shut up,' he said. But to be safe he stayed in the lavatory during playtime.

'Cowardy custard,' said Cynthia. 'We won't have cowardy custards in the club.'

He said he didn't care; who wanted to be in their silly club? When he got home he found that all his books were gone from the bedroom shelf including the brand-new Doctor Dolittle.

'No reading for two weeks,' announced Vanessa. 'And no train.' She was pulling on white gloves, going out. 'Actually I'm letting you off jolly lightly but I want you to think about it. I want you to think carefully about the tortoise and the hare. Learn something from this.'

He watched her crunch off down the gravel driveway like a queen to the car waiting outside the gate.

'Come here,' cried Cousin Ettie from her room, and he went to her gladly. She was sitting at the dressing table in a mauve dressing gown and putting eau de cologne on her face and around her old neck.

When she held him he could tell by the way her chest was going up and down quickly that she was crying.

She said, between gasps and silences, 'She's very hurt and upset, lambkin, but it's not entirely your fault.' She held him away and he saw that her face was all screwed up and red. 'It's not my fault either,' she said. She seemed to be angry. 'Even though I *let* her bring me here. I won't be blamed all my life for everything! I won't be blamed because I want to go *home*.'

He said, 'I want to go home too,' but Cousin Ettie wasn't listening.

'Damn,' said Cousin Ettie, and very unexpectedly she snatched up a silver hairbrush and threw it across the room. She was shaking now. 'I won't be blamed for everything just because I'm not wanted.'

She put her head down on the dressing table and wept loudly.

'Oh, lamb, what can we do?'

Then he had the great idea. It was better than being bad, and quicker.

'We could escape.'

The lunch gong rang, downstairs as if Ellen had overheard and was giving the alarm. ('Prisoners escaped. Call the guard.')

Ettie said, 'What?'

'We could escape,' he whispered.

The gong boomed through the house and died away, leaving the walls shivering with thrilling horror, and he saw Ettie and himself flitting over the lawn in black cloaks at dead of night; Lila waiting in the shadows with a coach, George masked and ready to whip up the horses and speed them all away to safety with Logan in Bacchus Marsh.

No. That was all storybook stuff. Go now, escape while Vanessa was out, as fast as they could. In a taxi.

He tugged at Ettie's hand. 'Come on,' he said.

'Ah, sweet thing.' Ettie reached for the cologne bottle. 'Nobody escapes. Well, we all belong to each other—that's the wretched curse of it, petkin. You'll find out one day.'

'Lunch is on the table, *please*,' screamed Ellen below.

Well, maybe Ettie couldn't escape, couldn't run fast enough. But he could.

He went downstairs, hearing Ettie close her door and lock it. He had lunch alone, taking no notice of Ellen's sour face, and when Mrs Lawson called to drive him to dancing class, he went meekly because now he had a plan.

At dinner that night, Vanessa said suddenly, 'In case you're interested, your father has gone home.'

So Logan had escaped. Logan had known what to do. Well, you just wait, he said silently to Vanessa, who was helping herself to peas and smiling at lemony Ellen; reminding her to take up Mrs Bult's tray.

On the windy, cold Friday afternoon, George came for him, and Vanessa, seeing George plod up the drive, said:

'Here comes George. You may tell them anything you please, PS. It's a matter of indifference to me what you blab to them about your father, but if you have a grain of sense, you won't tell them about locking yourself in the bathroom. I wouldn't. I wouldn't do that if I were you.'

The doorbell rang as if George was angry. Vanessa smiled and said, 'Now, when you come home on Sunday, let's turn over a new leaf, shall we?'

She went upstairs, saying to Ellen, 'I'm not in.'

'She's not in,' said Ellen to George.

'I'll wait,' said George, and sat down on the hard hall seat.

Ellen gave a big shrug as if she wanted to move the whole house and everyone in it off her shoulders; went off muttering to herself.

After about twenty minutes, George gave a big sigh and stood up.

He said, 'Come on, old chap; we'll talk about it at home.'

Lila, lying down on the sitting room couch, applying her atomiser, listened to PS's story. She had expelled so much emotion since the night at the train that she felt nothing but an extreme weariness and, when trying to concentrate, as though she were reading very small print in a bad light. She closed her eyes, seeing the action speeded up in a comic film of Logan and

Vanessa throwing custard pies at each other; Vanessa, dressed like a Mack Sennett cop, hitting PS with a rubber truncheon; PS locked in a bathroom throwing bottles; and comedy maids running in and out of doors, screaming.

She felt dulled and useless, as in her dreams, when seeing the house in flames, she found herself wading for help through treacle.

Wanting only to sleep, she thought that something must now be done.

'Something must be done,' she said to George, dazedly, over the washing up that night. 'I must speak to Sam Hamilton.'

George said something about lawyers and money, and laughed.

'The reason being—' she said, and thought of so many reasons that she simply stood there with her hands in the comforting, warm, soapy water and let all the reasons run down the drain. It wasn't only the matter of money (and that reminded her further that a decision must be made in a matter of days about taking in a lodger), but it was also a question of fighting. To fight anyone, let alone Vanessa, in her present state of mind seemed impossible. She wanted to forget the whole thing, go away to some quiet restful place in the mountains and be waited on hand and foot; above all not think about anything for a year. All the weekend she put off doing small things, moved in a trancelike state from room to room, misplacing scissors and leaving pots to boil over.

Sunday dragged by. At five o'clock she went and called over the fence to PS, engaged with Winnie in some mysterious game on the Grindels' veranda. Called the familiar, hated Sunday-afternoon cry of 'Time to get ready.'

He came into her bedroom, where she was sitting on the bed darning stockings, and at once she knew what was going to happen.

'I'm not going.'

He seemed to have grown half an inch taller very suddenly.

She put down her darning egg and automatically opened her arms, but PS took hold of the brass bedpost and hung on, ready to resist being picked up or moved anywhere again. She saw a giant implacability on the tight-fisted little face that made her feel suddenly the child, him the adult.

She said, 'Now listen, pet—'

'I'm not going.'

'Just for this week—'

'I'm not going back. I'm not going *back*!'

'Listen, listen—'

'I'm *not*.'

'Just let me tell you something. Do you know what adoption is? It means we go to a court and we ask a judge to give you to us. Now, first thing tomorrow

318

morning, George and I are going to Mr Hamilton, the lawyer, and ask him to take us to a judge—'

'No.'

'But, dearest, it's the only way. Then you won't ever have to go back.'

'No.'

'But, PS, if you don't go back tonight it will make Vanessa very cross and then the judge might say we were wrong. But if you wait just a week—or two—just until the school holidays—'

'I won't go back.'

'Just until we talk to Mr Hamilton.'

'No.'

(No, he won't. And I've run out of excuses. I can't feed him any more fairy stories about it being just a 'holiday', just for a little while, because Miss Pile has a nicer school. He's learned our tricks at last. He's not a baby any more. Well, fancy that. He's not a baby any more and I hadn't noticed.)

She stood up. Her weariness was gone, dissolved in the hard bright light of decision. Let the worst happen, she was grateful beyond words that he had made up her mind for her.

'All right,' she said.

Then she said in a voice suddenly altered to suit an older child:

'All right, but I think you should tell Vanessa yourself.'

'No,' he said, and then after a minute, 'Why?'

'Because she won't believe me but I know she'll believe you.'

'Why?'

'Because you decided yourself. All by yourself.'

'Then I won't have to go back?'

'No. But I want you to tell her yourself so she'll know it's not a fib I'm just making up, see?'

She pushed the hair out of his eyes and said, 'You must show her that you're not a little baby any more. That you made up your own mind about it, see?'

He nodded and Lila said, 'We'll go and ring up now.'

She went into the kitchen, found George asleep over the Sunday paper, hesitated a moment, then took three pennies out of the honey jar on the kitchen dresser.

Then up the street, being led rather than leading PS to Miss Gulf's door. Muttering the usual apologies but with her heart beating wildly now, Lila got the number and then asked Ellen to get Vanessa to come to the phone as the matter was urgent and finally there was a cool, 'Hello.'

She said, 'Something's happened. It's not of my making, Vanessa. No, no, he's all right, don't be alarmed. He wants to speak to you himself.'

She handed him the phone and PS said, 'I'm not coming back.' Then he said, 'I decided myself.'

The phone clucked. Clucked and clucked until Lila put out her hand to take it from him but again he seemed to decide what would be best and he hung up.

'I told her,' he said, and Lila, looking at him and seeing the frightening future crowded into that one moment, felt at the same time a remarkable joy.

PART THREE

THE LETTERS ON the dirty windows spelled ELTNEG
DNA and outside it people's legs and feet went by in the
rain and once a wet cat looked in the window through
DNA and down at them in the nasty-smelling office
where he and Lila had been sitting for hours. The
office was very cold even though there was a big fiery
radiator with a wire grille over its red eye. The room
smelled like school, smelled of ink and paper and old
cupboards and Mr Gentle's pipe. Mr Gentle was very
young, about fourteen, with very stiff yellow hair
cut short and flat like a nailbrush and a lot of yellow
hair on his hands. Even Lila had seemed to think that
Mr Gentle was very young because while they were
sitting in Mr Hamilton's office she had said, 'He's very
young, Sam. I wish we had someone more experienced,'
and Mr Hamilton said something about the legal aid
(or was it legal age?) and Lila had sighed and said,
'Oh, well, beggars can't be choosers but we'd feel so
safe with you, Sam,' and Mr Hamilton had said he had
three divorces and a contested will but Mr Gentle
would be just the ticket. Just the ticket, Mr Hamilton
kept saying, and patted him on the head and said,
'Well, PS, I knew your little mother and we'll get you
all fixed up, don't you worry,' and Mr Gentle had come
running up and hustled them into this room which was
so full of things it was almost like Vere's only no fun.

Then Mr Gentle had sat down behind a huge black desk covered with papers all tied up in pink string, and began smoking his pipe and asking hundreds of questions. They were all about the big house and 'Auntie Nessie,' as Mr Gentle kept calling Vanessa. She certainly wouldn't like being called that, and he could see her now, very tall and straight, giving strict orders to Mr Gentle not to call her by that 'appalling' name and very likely sending Mr Gentle upstairs to bed.

Whenever the questions got hard and Lila tried to help him answer, Mr Gentle rapped on the desk and said, 'Please, please! Let me hear it from the kiddie himself, Mrs Baines.' Mr Gentle said that he knew all about kiddies, he had a kiddie of his own whose name was Bruce.

When it was Lila's turn to answer questions, Mr Gentle gave him a glass ball to play with. Inside it was a little red house and when you shook the ball, a snowstorm whirled around the little house. Meanwhile, Mr Gentle wrote down everything Lila said, interrupting her a lot and sometimes cutting her short by saying, 'That's not relevant,' and Lila would say, 'Oh, I think it's very important,' and Mr Gentle would say, 'We'll see, we'll see,' or 'We have a good case without going into that.' The Case. It was all about the Case.

These days they talked about the Case all the time, and about going to the court. They were going to the court, Lila had told him, and there, if everything went all right, the judge would give him to Lila and George. He tried to picture the court and fancied that it might be like King Arthur's. With bright-red and gold banners, glittering armour, swords and a great throne. He had bragged about it to Winnie, who had laughed at him, showing her teeth all black with liquorice, and said that it wouldn't be like that at all and that probably he would go to jail, because that was what they did to people in courts. She *knew*! He would end up in Long Bay jail where they kept people chained up for years with only bread and water. Furious, he told her to go and boil her head. Whatever happened, whenever it was all over, then everything would be all right.

Just the same . . .

The Case!

He was thinking about the night Vanessa came in the car. The night after he refused to go back, just about tea time when the street lights were beginning to come on. He was in the front room when he saw the big car drive up and stop outside their gate. He ran to hide in the linen cupboard but Lila said, 'Don't be silly. She's not going to take you away.' He peeped while Lila opened the front door. There was a strange man standing there with very black hair and a very black suit who handed Lila a letter, which she read, leaning against the doorpost and puffing. Then she said, 'The answer is no. Tell my sister he is not going back.' The man then said that what Lila was doing was very serious and that Miss Scott was being very fair in giving her one last chance, but Lila kept saying no, no, and trying to close the front door and the man said sternly that Lila had forty-eight hours in which to return the said infant or then Miss Scott would appeal to the Supreme Court for full guardianship. After that, they whispered for a long while and then Lila untied her apron and went out to the car with the man. He waited alone in the quiet house listening to the kitchen clock ticking and wishing George would come home right now and send Vanessa away. After a long time Lila came back. Her face was very white and she was swallowing all the time. She said, 'Vanessa wants to speak to you for a minute,' and when he pulled away, catching hold of a leg on the kitchen table, ready to hang on, she said, 'Don't be scared; I'm coming too, pet. Just tell her in front of the lawyer that you don't want to go back.' So, feeling a bit sick, his knees wobbling, he went out to the car with Lila. There were two little pink lights on inside the car and he could see Vanessa wearing a big hat sitting in the back with the man in the black suit. When he came to the open door of the big car, Vanessa leaned forward and smiled.

'Hello,' she said, and he said, 'Hello.'

'This isn't like you, PS,' said Vanessa. 'This isn't like you at all. What's wrong?'

'I'm not coming back,' he said. 'I decided.'

The man in the black suit said something quickly and quietly and Vanessa nodded. With her long white-gloved arm, she patted the seat next to her and said:

'I tell you what, PS. Why don't you sit down here with me and we'll have a jolly nice talk about it.'

She seemed very pleasant, not angry at all. He felt suddenly a little sorry for having to be so cruel to her. She was smiling and the strange man was smiling. Even the chauffeur was smiling. They were all smiling at him. All he had to do was get in the car and explain nicely that this house was his home and it would all be over.

He put one foot up into the car but just as Vanessa reached out to help him, Lila screamed and pulled him back.

'I saw you,' Lila cried to the chauffeur, then to Vanessa, 'I saw what you were going to do. What a filthy dirty trick.'

The strange man said, 'Get hold of yourself, Mrs Baines.'

'I saw his hand on the door,' screamed Lila, and then suddenly it was like a cat fight and Lila was spitting words at Vanessa and Vanessa spat back, and their voices grew louder and angrier until people all up and down the street came out on their front verandas to listen to the terrible things they were calling each other, like 'kidnapper' and 'madwoman', and then Lila said to him, 'Get inside and stay there,' and he ran behind the gate and hung on, watching people strolling over towards the car and Mr Grindel called out, 'Let the kid alone!' and someone else called out, 'Leave him where he belongs,' and the street seemed to catch on fire with voices in the dark, lighting up and then dying away and lighting up again and Mr and Mrs Grindel started booing but the little circle of light around the car was the centre of the fire where Vanessa and Lila shouted and shouted things about hate and home. Shouted, 'I dare you—' and 'I defy you—' until at last the strange man leaned into the light and seemed to be reasoning with Vanessa and suddenly the light snapped off and the big car roared off down the street while a few people cheered and Mr and Mrs Grindel were helping Lila back into the house but it was a long time before anyone came to find him still hanging on to the front gate and being sick into the hydrangeas.

Since then all they had talked about was the Case and things began changing very suddenly all the time. A few nights later there was a lot of murmuring and spelling out of words over the tea table and the next day his Aunt Agnes came to live with them. She lived in the glassed-in back veranda room, where she hung up a picture of Jesus walking on the water at Balmoral Beach near the zoo. She sat at the kitchen table a lot of the time with her eyes closed and a smile on her face as if she was picturing something very nice happening. She told Lila that it didn't matter much who won the

Case as there was very little time left anyway, but Lila just sighed and said, 'Meanwhile, Agnes, your corned beef and cabbage is getting stone cold.' Agnes patted his head and said, 'Sweet thing, wait till you see the glory that is reserved for *thee*,' and Lila said, 'Let's hope the *judge* sees it.'

Lila hardly had time to talk to him these days. For one thing she had to get two meals every night because now George had his tea very early at five o'clock and then went off to work at night instead of in the morning. He had got a job, Lila said, as a night watchman to see that burglars didn't get into a factory. In the mornings and when you came home from school, you had to be very quiet so as not to wake up poor tired George who now went to bed after breakfast and got up at twilight. It was all back-to-front like the writing on the window above him. ELTNEG DNA.

Mr Gentle jumped up, washing his hands in the cold air, and said, 'Well, Mrs Baines, we'll see, we'll see.'

Lila said, 'But I have a lot more to tell you, Mr Gentle,' and Mr Gentle said, 'We'll put it all in your affidavit.'

Lila said anxiously, gathering her bag, her gloves and umbrella, 'Tell me truthfully, do you think we have a case?'

Mr Gentle looked at her fiercely and said, 'Well, I would venture to say there is no reason not to be optimistic in view of the fact that the presiding judge may very well be Mr Justice Hay-Piggott.'

'Why, what's he like?' Lila asked.

'Hard as steel, but fair, very fair, and he thinks highly of Sam Hamilton. They're both members of the Rose Bay Golf Club,' and as Lila's face immediately became pink with hope, Mr Gentle added, laughing, 'But that could also go against us. It could be the very worst thing for us. But we'll see, we'll see.'

Beaming, Mr Gentle jumped forward and opened the door, saying, 'We'll get going on those affidavits right away.'

In the outside office Diana was sitting, wearing a green mackintosh and trying to hide her big hands behind her small purse. She said, 'Hello, Master Marriott,' and he ran to her very surprised and Lila said, 'We're very grateful to you for—' but Mr Gentle rushed between them, laughing and muttering some-thing about a collision or a collusion. Shooing Diana into his office, he slammed the door.

As they went up the steps into the cold raining street, he said to Lila, 'Are we going to the court now?'

Lila said, 'Not yet, but when we do, Mr Gentle is going to speak to the judge and then everything is going to be all right.'

But when he looked up at her, her face seemed to be saying, 'Just the same . . .'

'Just the same . . .' Lila said to George, packing a thermos and a package of damp tomato sandwiches into his night bag, and then let her voice trail off. 'He said—well, he *practically* said that he thought the judge would be on our side because he's a great friend of Sam Hamilton's.'

'Just the same,' said George, 'it would have been better if Sam had handled the case himself. This bloke sounds very green to me.'

Just the same, Lila said to herself later, hearing PS and the new little friend Alan from across the street laughing in the sitting room. She tried to put an end to the nibbling doubts by once again adding up the positive factors but they dissipated under the ever-present ugly voice that murmured, 'Just the same . . .'

Agnes said, taking off her tricorn hat, 'I've had a very marvellous, joyous revelation.'

'Have you, Agnes?'

'Yes, and I want you to listen to me, please, and not fiddle at the stove like Nero.'

'I'm listening.'

'This afternoon Sinden spoke to me in the Temple—Lila, you're not listening to me.'

'I am, Agnes, but the potato pie has to be taken out of the oven.'

'If you're more interested in a pie than in hearing about a spiritual revelation—'

333

'All right, all right. There. Now I'm listening.'

'Thank you. This afternoon I was looking towards Jerusalem—'

'In all that rain?'

'Lila, if you're not going to allow me to tell—'

'I'm sorry; go on.'

'I was looking towards Jerusalem and suddenly Sinden spoke very clearly to me.'

'What did she say?'

'I'm about to tell you if you'll kindly stop interrupting me on every second word. Sinden spoke to me. She wishes you and George to win the court case. Well, haven't you anything to say to *that*?'

'You said not to interrupt.'

'I hope you realise the importance of all this. I'm not just making it up. The thing is that Sinden wishes PS to be with you and George on the Day.'

'On what day?'

'The Day. What day? Goodness gracious me— what *day*!'

'Oh, the Day, yes; I'm sorry I wasn't thinking.'

'Well, you had better think. Sinden is very much against PS being with Vanessa when the Day comes. So she has asked me to testify on your behalf in court.'

'Oh, I see.'

'I promised that I would. I gave Sin my promise.'

'I see. Well, the only thing is, Agnes—'

'So I'm prepared not only to sign an affidavit in your favour but also to appear in court with your other witnesses and defend your cause to the judge. There now!'

'It's very good of you Agnes but—'

'It's not good of me at all, Lila. Try to understand this from a less earthbound point of view. It is *Sinden's* wish. The judge must be made to understand this.'

'Uhuh. The only thing is that Mr Gentle thinks we have enough affidavits with George and Vere and the housemaid and Mrs Grindel and—'

'They are not in contact with someone on the Seventh Plane as I am.'

'I know but—well, Agnes, you know what judges and lawyers are like.'

'I know all about judges and lawyers. I'm not a fool, Lila. I've lectured to thousands of people here and in Seattle. And I'm not a *nobody*, thank you very much.'

'I didn't say you were, Agnes. *We* all know how sincere you are, dear, but other people may think—'

'May think what, please?'

'*Might* think it was a bit peculiar.'

'What's peculiar about it?'

'Well—'

'*I'm* peculiar. Is that what you mean, Lila? I'm a crank?'

'I didn't say that, Agnes.'

'That's what you think, all of you except Sinden, who knows better and who loved me more than any of you and sat and listened to me. She didn't agree then, but she listened. When have you ever paid me the courtesy to listen? So what do you know about me and about my work? You're worse than a sceptic, Lila, you're a hypocrite. You call me "dear" to my face and laugh at me behind my back—'

'Agnes, dear, I've never—'

'I've heard your little remarks to the others; I've seen your smirking to George when you thought I wasn't looking—'

'Gracious, I never—'

'Don't deny it, Lila, that's *more* insulting. But let me tell you something. I don't care about being laughed at. That's where you and I differ. I've never minded being a figure of fun for what I believed; far greater people than I have been scorned and laughed at. I wouldn't care if that whole courtroom rocked with laughter at me—'

'Oooo, watch out, your hat's in the butter. Here, let me put it on—'

'*Listen* to me, Lila. I wouldn't care because a long time ago, years and years ago, Mater laughed at me very cruelly and it made me cry. For the last time, for the very last time, Lila. Because then that was the very worst thing and when the very worst thing has happened to you you learn not to fear and I fear not.

Oh, I fear nothing. I fear not what man can do unto me. Whereas *you* fear everything.'

'Tommyrot!'

'You always have, even as a little girl, and I'm sorry for you.'

'Well, my goodness, everybody's afraid of *something*, Agnes.'

'Yes, but they don't all instil their fears into others.'

'Why, what do you mean?'

'You do. You've instilled your fears into George until—'

'I never—'

'Oh, yes you have. Worry, worry, worry about everything. Maybe he wouldn't win that election; well, he didn't!'

'That had nothing to do with—'

'Maybe he wouldn't get a job; then, what if he lost it?'

'Ha, ha. I s'pose it's *my* fault we're having a depression.'

'Don't go blaming outside circumstances, Lila; you were just as nervous in the boom, saving string and brown paper—'

'Heavens, if I can't—'

'Always worry, worry, negative, negative. Doubt is very catching and finally George started doubting himself. Oh, I saw it happen. I saw the change beginning in him. Why, he was a positive, self-confident man until you got at him with all your cries and omens; "Oh, you walked under the ladder, George," and "Oh, listen to the rainbirds." No wonder he goes to sleep all the time. And now you're doing the same thing to PS.'

'That's the most unfair thing I ever heard in my entire—'

'Exactly the same thing.'

'Would you mind telling me how?'

'You brought about this whole fight with Vanessa.'

'Oh, yes. Yes, of course. I wanted all this trouble.'

'You're afraid of Vanessa, Lila, and long before she came back you planted your little seed of fear in PS. Well, it's borne fruit.'

'My God, if you could only know how fair I've been. I've never ever said one word against Vanessa to PS.'

'You didn't have to.'

'Do you know what's been going on in that house? Do you know what the housemaid told us? He had to lock himself in a bathroom to get away from her! I suppose a child does that because of *my* fear!'

'Your *original* fear started the whole train of events.'

'Look, just whose side are you on?'

'The Lord's.'

'Really? You make it sound as if you're on Vanessa's.'

'No, but don't be so sure that you're absolutely right and she's absolutely wrong.'

'I can be sure of one thing, Agnes. We won't need your affidavit.'

'I take my orders from Sinden, not you. I shall go to the lawyer tomorrow and tell him that.'

'Yes, you do. You do. And Mr Gentle will tell you you're crazy. He will tell you you're a crazy woman!'

Lila, hearing her own ugly screech, instantly ashamed, turned from Agnes' crucified look, past PS's inquiring face around the door, and ran from the kitchen into the back yard.

Crazy! What a cruel thing to say to the poor wretch, with her pathetic clothes, worn shoes, cold hands and dignified believing heart. Believing nonsense but dignified because of its unswerving faith; craziness of the heart which can win an argument over logic in its very madness.

'Mad,' Lila said to the pepper tree. 'Mad as a hatter,' she said to the first cold winking star. It was ridiculous to get upset by anything Agnes said; absurd to be drawn into a debate with her.

And yet. And yet . . .

Suppose in a cracked way Agnes had hit upon some dreadful truth? But how? How could there be a pattern to all the years of failure and disgrace? Admittedly, even in childhood, her life had been a sea of qualms; a long-standing family joke regarding her distress over spilled

339

salt, broken mirrors, falling pictures, hats on beds and seeing three nuns. But what did all this have to do with George's disappointments? How could her prescience of doom have had anything to do with Sinden's dying? Sinden would have died anyway and George had been bound to lose the election because he had campaigned for prohibition and everyone knew that it had failed in America. All the worrying in the world had never changed Vanessa's personality so how could Agnes possibly say that those worries had brought about this battle over PS? No, there was only one unpleasant truth to face—that failure begets failure and after a while it is printed on the face, evident in the step, heard in the voice. Even the new dress will not cover it up or hide the shame of it from anyone, let alone a judge. But why was this her own fault? It wasn't fair. Nothing had ever been fair as far back as Lila could remember.

'Not fair,' she said aloud. 'Not fair.' And cupping her hands over her mouth, she cried like a child.

Vanessa came out of her room, dressed to go to town for her fifth visit with the lawyer. She crossed quickly to the stairs, deliberately not glancing at the closed and locked door of PS's bedroom. Since he had left, she had not entered the room. She had not even allowed the new maid, Elsie, to dust in there. Surprised by her own curious intuition that to prepare the room for his return might tempt unknown gods to overthrow the case against her, and annoyed at this singularly uncharacteristic behaviour, she had nevertheless succumbed to the superstition, locked the bedroom door and then dropped the thought of it neatly into the wastebin of her mind. From then on, whenever a doubt scuttled across her thoughts, she stepped firmly on it as she might on a cockroach. There was no cause for doubt; she had Mr Hood. Hadn't Mr Lawson, who was president of the English, Scottish and Australian Bank, himself recommended Mr Hood? She had been instantly impressed by Mr Hood's quiet luxurious offices and his funereal clothes—custom-tailored black flannel suits and black silk socks with clocks—his deep oratorical voice without a trace of that horrid Australian accent, and above all, his comforting redolence of guile. ('Tell me that again, Miss Scott. Aha! *Int*eresting!') In the shallow, sleepless dawns when her resistance to doubt was at bedrock, she turned her thoughts to Mr Hood and clung voluptuously to the echo of his rich red-burgundy voice and his massive assurance. She began to look forward to the visits to his office and subtly to prolong them. ('There was something else I wanted to bring up; now what was it?' 'Take your time, Miss Scott, I'm in no hurry.') She had begun to cart home small treasures—his glances and sudden dazzling smiles—would find herself stopped en route from room to room, gazing at the carpet, lost in the luxurious remembrances. Once, drawing on her gloves, her look fell upon a large silver-framed picture standing on his mahogany desk—a fish-faced woman in a dated dress—and she asked casually, 'Your wife?' Mr Hood answered curtly, 'Yes,' and then cast her a look of such gimlet-like intensity that her heart turned over, and speechless, she received with thrilling joy Mr Hood's message of silent anguish.

Blue today, she thought, taking out the soft, subtle Patou that she had not worn for a long time and putting on the lapis lazuli beads. She studied her face for a long time in the mirror, put on and took off earrings, fussed with perfume and avoided mascara; strayed dangerously into a brown study where vague figures moved and touched and from which Mr Hood emerged through smoke, annoyingly wearing Logan's face, so that she stood up suddenly, fracturing the absurd vision, and shook herself like a cat. But a moment later, the pleasant anticipation again flooded her being and an old vanity that she had not felt for years rushed over her. Mater, momentarily disinterred, said grudgingly, 'I'll say this much for Ness—she's the beauty of the family.'

Yes, and still pretty good, Mater dear, not too many lines and no grey hair and nice clothes help, so thank you for giving me away to Ettie, knowing that she really wanted Vere then. Your not wanting me has turned our pretty well on the whole, Mater dear, and while we're on the subject, I'd like you to know that I've done better than all the others put together so put that in your pipe and smoke it! How I wish you weren't dead, my dear; oh, how I'd love to sit you down and wipe that sanctimonious Church of England smile off your face, you and your malignant sweetness; you and your marvellous Lila—how you loved to rub her into me. 'Lila was so thoughtful today, Ness; look at the lovely scent she brought me.' 'Lila massaged my back, Ness.' 'Lila's got engaged to a lovely man, Ness; I *hope* you will one day.' And all because Pater turned away from you to me. Wasn't that it? Was that why, Mater? Kindly answer the question put to you by my lawyer, Mr Hood.

What?

Elsie at the door, a midget maid, apologetic for breaking into the sanctuary but the limousine was at the gate.

Vanessa put poor well-meaning Mater back in the grave, picked up the crocodile bag and passed through the hall, not glancing at the closed and locked door of PS's bedroom.

'Mrs Bult will lunch alone,' she said to Ellen's closed-up face, wondering at the same time if Mr Hood was altogether wise in calling Ellen as a witness; instantly forgetting this, forgetting everything, at the shock of Ettie flat on the carpet in the drawing room.

'My God,' she cried, dropping her purse and

343

running to kneel, feel the heart, but Ettie immediately stirred and laughed.

'Tripped.'

'Ettie, my God, did you hurt yourself—careful now, put your arm around me—here, lie down on the sofa. Oh, my God, Ettie, *really*. I could slap you. After all your promises and you've been so good too, for weeks. Oh, God Almighty, it's not even one o'clock yet.'

Vanessa quietly closed the door upon a curiously busy Elsie, dusting a table to death in the hall.

'Upset, Ness.'

'I should jolly well say you are. Suppose this had been the day you had to be in court? What would we have done then? Have you thought about that? Have you thought what you're doing to yourself anyway?'

'Oh, Ness—'

'It's no use just being sorry again.'

'I'm not.'

'What?'

'Not sorry.'

'Ettie.'

'That's what I *mean*.'

'*What* do you mean?'

'Shouldn't.'

'Shouldn't what? Drink? No, I should think not.'

'Go to court.'

'What?'

344

'Go to court.'

'Now what's this all about, Ettie?'

'Oh, Ness, Ness . . .' Tears watering the old face, little once-pretty mouth all puckered up, withered as if sucking alum.

'All right now, Ettie, let's have it out. What's happened?'

'Nothing's happened—just I think we're wrong.'

'*I'm* wrong, you mean.'

Nods, just like PS. Nods and gasping. Wet ball of handkerchief going up and down, strong smell of sweet sherry.

'I'm wrong and Lila's right, is that it?'

'How do you know he wants to come back?'

'Because he does.'

'He said—'

'Naturally she's using every influence over him to—'

'Let's escape.'

'All right, Ettie; I wish we could too but—'

'No, that's what he said to me, Ness.'

'When?'

'The last time he was here. I was upset, homesick, and you'd been very cool, very cool to me and I was hurt—'

'What did PS say?'

'He came into my room and he said, "Oh, Ettie, let's *escape*." '

Escape! Ettie's little stone word hit Vanessa between the eyes; momentarily she saw the judge hand down a decision in favour of Lila. It took several seconds before Mr Hood, with a gigantic effort, was able to restore her to her unalterable conviction.

'Nonsense!'

'He said it!'

'Children will say anything when they're upset.'

'He wasn't upset; I was.'

'Well, you could have misinterpreted it. He certainly didn't mean he wanted to escape from *us*.'

Just the same, suppose in some roundabout way Lila got hold of this muddled tale? Suppose her lawyer—'Ettie, put this out of your mind and don't refer to it again. To anybody.'

Ettie gave an unexpected laugh. 'Don't tell,' she said, baring her little yellow teeth in a ludicrous imitation of Vanessa's smile. 'Don't tell, Ettie. Don't tell Mr Hood.'

'Tell Mr *Hood* anything you like.'

'P'raps I will.'

'All right.'

Vanessa, suddenly tall with annoyance, got up and went to the door. A sudden outbreak of mumbling followed her.

'What, Ettie?'

'Said how dare you treat me like this.'

Ettie looked like an old rag doll, its wig in wisps, its kapok stuffing gone into lumps, but the blue glass eyes blazed as brightly as the little swinging diamond heart.

The doll stood up, swaying just a little, took uncertain steps towards Vanessa, who caught hold of the absurd rubber hands, and they stood, holding hands, until Vanessa in her astonishment said, 'How am I treating you?'

'Had enough,' Ettie said.

'Of what, exactly?'

Ettie, pulling away her hands, raising an imperious untidy head, gave the look of an angry duchess. Attaining a tipsy dignity and with slow articulation, she said:

'I have had enough of second place.'

'Ettie!'

'PS, PS, PS, PS, PS—' Ettie curtseyed to an invisible PS, slipping sideways until Vanessa grabbed at an arm and manoeuvred the swaying figure safely into a chair.

'Ettie, *darling*, that's not fair. You have never taken second place to PS.'

Thinking, clumsy of me. How clumsy of me not to take all the little hints. Jealous children. The very young and the very old. And so she's made up this story about him wanting to escape. Even the word is artificial and just like her. Just like she was in Paris that time, when I met that rather nice Englishman. The hysterical scenes.

All right *then*; nothing lost but a mild flirtation and dinner at Lapérouse but *now* . . . Dear God, what would happen if she turned against me now?

'Ettie, PS is my *ward*. That doesn't alter *our* relationship. *You've* always come first.'

'Not lately.'

'I'm sorry if you've thought that.'

'All my friends have noticed it.'

(What have you told the bridge ladies? The lace-tatting group?)

'Ettie, darling, I want you to have your lunch and then lie down for a while—'

'I don't want lunch. I won't lie down. Lie down! I'm not ill. Think I'm ill or something? I'm not a *child*!'

'Ettie—'

'Order PS around. Don't order me.'

'If you'll let me finish . . . I was going to say I'd put off going to the lawyer today and we'd spend the afternoon together—perhaps go for a nice drive and have tea at Watson's Bay—'

'I don't want to, thank you very much.'

'What *do* you want then?'

Sulky silence and Ettie's mouth as forbidding as a rat trap.

Vanessa reached out to take one of the doll hands but instantly Ettie snatched her hand away and gave Vanessa a blue glassy stare.

'Just tell me what you want, Ettie.'

(Exactly like PS. That awful weapon of silence.)

'Shall we take a little trip up to the Blue Mountains for a few days? I'd rather like the change myself, darling. Do you remember the Ritz in Leura? The walks we took, years ago, and the motoring trips down into Megalong Valley to have scones and Devonshire cream? Lovely big log fires and that heavenly sharp air? Frankly, it sounds like paradise.'

'You go.'

'I don't want to go alone, dearest.'

'Then take Mr Hood.'

(So, it's Mr Hood too! Well, well! So Mr Hood's your latest rival, is he? I could wish that were true, my dear, because if I have to put up with many more years of this childish nonsense, I could be very easily persuaded to go off and leave you to flounder alone.)

'I'm afraid you *are* being childish, Ettie.'

'All you ever talk about day and night.'

'I'm sorry; I apologise.'

'Sick of hearing about Mr damn Hood day and night, night and day. PS and Mr Hood. I say to hell with them.'

With frightening suddenness, Ettie picked up and flung the Doulton figurine at the fireplace; the head lopped off, rolled across the tiles.

For a second, Vanessa could not believe that it had happened. Then, hearing her heart beat loudly, confirming it, she stooped to pick up the fragments, heard behind her Ettie's thickened voice say:

'My housemaid will attend to that.'

Vanessa said quietly, 'Very well.' She picked up her bag and gloves, and opening the door, went out and stood in the silent hall. She waited, counting the moments, assessing the time that it usually took for contrition to begin; smiled when she heard on schedule the sounds of smothered weeping. Then, after counting slowly to ten, she re-entered the room as the figure in the chair arose, teetered towards her, flung itself on to her, embracing her tightly; a woolly white mop of hair that smelled faintly of old bureau drawers was in her face, muttered gaspings at the breast. The diamond heart scratched her.

'What is it?'

The contorted face peered up at her.

'Oh, Ness, forgive me.'

'It's all right, Ettie.'

'Hold me, Ness. Oh, how awful of me.'

'I said it's all right.'

'Kiss. Please, Ness. Kiss, kiss.'

(Oh, God, this part is always worse than the rows themselves.)

'Ah, dearest. So ungrateful of me, wicked. How you must hate me.'

'Nonsense, Ettie.'

'Wish I were dead.'

'Rubbish. You belong to me. You're my own little mother.'

(Sick-making, the utterly sick-making formula for peace; and yet it's true. I do love you, old woman of the sea around my neck, my other child.)

Ettie, giggling and wiping her eyes, said, 'Oh, aren't we fools?'

Vanessa, reaching at last for the urgently needed cigarette, said, 'Yes, and it has to stop. You know what I mean.'

'Yes, Ness.'

'No more drinking, Ettie.'

'Never, never. On my solemn word of honour.'

'Promise me.'

'On the Bible.'

'Otherwise it means a hospital.'

'I swear to you—'

'I mean it, Ettie. I could lose the case over it.'

'I know, I know.'

'I could lose PS.'

'I know.'

Ettie's remorseful face promised anything. Large cheques, jewellery, life insurance, lavish bequeathments. So Vanessa said, 'PS never wanted to leave me.'

'No, Ness.'

'Remember that, if it should come up in court.'

'Yes, Ness.'

Vanessa picked up the headless figurine and said

as punishment, 'After I leave Mr Hood I'll take this to Hardy Brothers and have them rivet it.'

'Thank you, Ness.'

Vanessa put the figurine into her handbag and with a loud snap closed both the bag and the conversation.

Later, watching Vanessa go down the driveway, holding her hat against the blustering August day, Ettie pressed her face to the cold window, breathing mist on to it, and said dutifully:

'He didn't want to leave you.'

'The court will rise.'

They stood up, shuffling and coughing, in the vaulted, dingy yellow-walled courtroom that smelled of carbolic and old dismay as the tipstaff opened the door and stood aside, and in a quick black swirl of gown, the Honourable Mr Justice Hay-Piggott entered.

The Hanging Judge, Lila thought, squinting at the six-foot-four figure gazing crossly down at them with the face of an aristocratic fish, thin steel spectacles jutting out between the absurd grey curls of his wig, long thin blades of hands shooting cuffs, moving papers impatiently, anxious to dispose of this trivial fight between two guardians and get back to the Spanish Inquisition. The granite cliff of face bobbed up and down as though irritated already at the clerk mumbling through the preliminaries of 'Supreme

Court of New South Wales in Equity, mutter mutter in the matter of mumble mumble Marriott, an infant under the age of twenty-one years and in the matter of the Testator's Family Maintenance and Guardianship of Infants Act of nineteen sixteen.'

At the same time, an already halfhearted shaft of winter sunshine through the high, dirt-encrusted windows died. Greyness filtered suddenly into the court, absorbed faces turned to grit, shadows formed in ugly pools around the lawyers' desks, hid the spectators' gallery in deep gloom so that Lila felt her heart twitch at this sudden ill omen and heard rainbirds mock and screech. She turned her head to look across the court at Vanessa, impervious to rainbirds and loss of sunlight, assured in black, assured with pearls, and listening raptly, happily, it seemed to Lila, as though she were in a cathedral and being married to Mr Hood, who was turning now and glancing back at Vanessa with the same assured secret look.

Lila glanced away, needing suddenly the same calm reassurance from Mr Gentle, who appeared not to be listening to the preliminaries and was fastening paper clips into a chain.

Lila, as they sat, squeezed George's arm and whispered, 'Never mind, right is on our side.'

George said, 'What?' loud enough for heads to turn and make Mr Gentle glare at them and put a stubby baby finger to his lips.

Lila, wheezing slightly, corrected already, touched her new white straw hat from Mark Foy's end-of-winter sale, felt again that it was ill chosen, saw that by daylight her wool suit was not mauve but puce, and realised that she had been wrong in not going to the ladies' room once more on the ferry.

Now Mr Hood was on his feet.

'Your honour, if it please the court . . .'

The voice was deep and rich as greengage plums. It presented the affidavit of the Deponent, Vanessa Scott, spinster, now residing at 36 Wolsley Road, Point Piper, appointed guardian of said infant by deed of disposal of guardianship . . . All about Ernest Huxley, all about Sinden and Logan and Lila herself, hereinafter referred to as the Respondent. Every time Mr Hood pronounced the word 'Respondent', he hung on to it a moment in a pitying, deprecatory tone and the information, though correct legally, was subtly weighed in Vanessa's favour ('I then undertook, at severe personal sacrifice to myself and to Mrs Ethelreda Bult, to return to Australia and to take up my duties on behalf of my late sister . . .') and against Lila ('The Respondent was then and is now the wife of George Mason Baines, who I understand is at present employed as a night watchman at the Uneeda Packing and Boxing Company, Limited . . .'). The Respondent, it seemed, had resented the Deponent's legal rights as Guardian under Deed of Disposal (respectfully offered as

Exhibit A), and had placed every obstacle in the way of a harmonious working arrangement, even going so far as to encourage the said infant in evasions and deceptions and also to influence said infant's loyalties and affections.

And so on.

Vanessa, in Mr Hood's rococo voice, now described her house in the terms of Valhalla and her income from Mrs Bull in round golden figures. Lila's house was maintained to be clean and modest but inadequate, especially since the recent addition of a lodger in the person of another sister and 'member of a religious sect that predicts the end of the world'. Mr Hood paused here and carefully allowed a spectral Agnes to caper insanely through Lila's house and a slight riffle of amusement to run through the court. Lila cast a quick glance at Mr Gentle, expecting to find him making furious notes of rebuttal about everything, but he was lost in contemplation of a long-disused gas chandelier.

Mr Hood gravitated to Miss Pile's élite academy and the joys of piano and riding lessons, of which said infant had now been deprived due to the unpardonable action of the Respondent, and came to the fatal Sunday when, contrary to the terms of the arrangement, the infant had not been returned home to Wolsley Road and, prompted by the Respondent, had been obliged to break this news to the heartbroken Deponent; presented then as Exhibit B, a letter to the Respondent drawn up by Mr Hood at request of the Deponent, requiring the immediate return of said infant; described the Respondent's hysterical refusal to do so, and in closing respectfully asked his honour to award full custody of the said infant to the much-wronged Deponent.

In the slight pause that followed, George yawned loudly and Lila nudged him, frowned at him fiercely and craned her neck to see if Mr Gentle would now leap up with thunder and lightning to destroy Mr Hood.

But Mr Hood was now requesting the court's permission to elucidate the affidavit further by questioning his client, who was in court and Vanessa rising, slim and svelte, about to receive a citation, crossed to the witness box and agreed to tell the whole truth and nothing but the truth, so help her God.

Mr Hood smiled at her encouragingly, and began to read in apocalyptic tones a letter from Sinden, garlanding her impulsive phrases until they became cries for help. 'I *yearn* sometimes for your profound sense of organisation. . . . I've always said, "I'll have the children and Ness will *manage* them." ' Lila pursed her lips, thinking of Sinden's way of putting things in the superlative; of how she would have ridiculed this mealy-mouthed lawyer and Vanessa too, sitting there with that pious attitude and playing the role of a bereft mother, her head a little to one side and her face tinged with just the right amount of wounded dignity. It was dreadful, simply dreadful, what they were doing to Sinden's memory with this vast hypocrisy.

('Lila, I never meant Vanessa to take me *literally*!' 'Well, I know you didn't, darling. But it's that dreadful lawyer of hers.' 'Lila, stand up and tell them I was only joking.' 'Sweet angel, I can't do that because we're in court, but don't you worry, darling; don't fret, Sin, dear. Wait until Mr Gentle reads your last letter to *me*.')

Drifting off, over a grave banked with blue irises, Lila came back reluctantly to hear Mr Hood reading a letter from Ernest Huxley assuring Vanessa that she was the only right and proper person to take over his share of the guardianship.

Having established Vanessa as Mother Machree, Mr Hood abruptly changed his tactics and leaped upon her ferociously.

'Now, Miss Scott, were you on close terms with your late sister?'

'Yes.'

'Why, then, didn't Mrs Marriott express a wish for you to be a guardian in her will?'

Shaken by surprise, Lila thought, But that is *our* point. He's taken *our* point.

Vanessa answered calmly, 'Because I was then living in England.'

'I see. And were you content with the arrangement of the child being left entirely with Mrs Baines?'

'At the time, yes.'

'Then you had no personal wish to become a guardian?'

'None. I felt that my first duty was to my employer, Mrs Bult.'

'Naturally. During this time did you correspond with Mrs Baines?'

'Yes, occasionally. Her letters to me were usually just short notes of thanks for gifts I sent to the child.'

'What did these gifts usually consist of?'

'Oh, clothing and books.'

'Nothing financial?'

'Oh, no. Never.'

'You never sent money to Mrs Baines?'

'Never. That would have been insulting.'

'Why?'

'Well, because they were in financial difficulties.'

'You were aware of their circumstances?'

'Well, yes.' A slight laugh. 'Yes.'

'Did this disturb you? I mean, did it disturb you in regard to your nephew?'

'Well, of course.'

'Why did you do nothing about it?'

'There wasn't anything I *could* do. Mr Huxley had been named guardian, not I.

'Where was Mr Huxley?'

'In the United States.'

'Wasn't this a very impractical arrangement?'

'Very. But my late sister was somewhat impractical.'

'She was a *writer*?'

'Yes.'

Mr Hood paused and a little shiver of laughs ran through the room. Lila was shocked to notice that Mr Gentle laughed too.

'Why do you suppose that your late sister would have appointed Mr Huxley as guardian if he was in the United States?'

'I haven't the earthliest idea.'

Mr Hood shook his handsome head in bewilderment and gave a loud sigh.

'Did Mr Ernest Huxley approach you in regard to changing this very impractical arrangement?'

'Yes.'

'Mr Huxley approached *you*.'

'Yes. He was in London on business and asked to see me.'

'What took place at this meeting?'

'Ernest—Mr Huxley said he was very unhappy about everything and that he was especially worried about PS.'

The judge leaned forward and spoke for the first time in a morocco-leather-bound voice.

'About whom?'

Mr Hood whirled, gown flying, towards the bench and bowed.

'PS, your honour. It's the child's nickname, I believe.'

Mr Justice Hay-Piggott picked up a steel pen.

'BS?'

'*PS*, your honour. It stands, I believe, for "postscript".'

Vanessa said to the bench, 'It was my late sister's name for him.'

'The mother's nickname for him?' The judge raised Santa Claus eyebrows and wrote PS, as one might sign away Austria.

Mr Hood turned back to Vanessa. 'Did Mr Huxley then suggest—'

'PS!' said the judge, and looked doleful. 'Proceed, Mr Hood.'

'Did Mr Huxley then propose that you take over his half of the guardianship, Miss Scott?'

'Yes. He had no desire to return to Australia and he felt that Mrs Baines should now be relieved of part of the financial burden and I agreed. She had received no financial aid whatever from the child's father.'

'The father, Henry Logan Marriott, was then living in the state of Victoria?'

'Yes.'

'But he was located and executed the Deed of Disposal of Guardianship.'

'Yes.'

'Where is he now?'

'I have no idea.'

'He has no fixed employment?'

'None that I know of.'

'Is he addicted to alcoholism?'

'Yes.'

'Now, Miss Scott, on your return to Australia, did you immediately take up your duties as guardian?'

'Not right away. We had to look for a suitable house and engage servants.'

'Naturally. So for a short time, no change was made in the *status quo*.'

'None. My nephew remained with Mrs Baines.'

'Now what was the attitude of the Respondent?'

'Very resentful.'

'Very—?'

'Resentful.'

'In what way?'

'She telephoned me to come to the house, which I did. She then proceeded to tell me that she was very much against my action and very disapproving of Mr Huxley.'

'Why?'

'As I remember, she said that Mr Huxley had no right to delegate authority to me and that he had a *duty* to my late sister.'

'But he wasn't exactly doing anything about that duty, had not, in fact, for six years; isn't that correct?'

'I would say so, yes.'

'Nevertheless, the Respondent showed instant resentment of you?'

'Instant. She said that her home was quite adequate for the child.'

'And what was your opinion?'

'That it was not.'

'For what reasons?'

'Well—for one thing, the child's bedroom was just a tiny box of a room without carpeting of any kind. Furthermore, the only toilet facilities are outside the house.'

Mr Gentle, finally present in court, rose and waved a baby hand.

'Objection, your honour. Counsel is merely involving the witness in a series of opinions prejudicial to the Respondent.'

The judge peered down, found Mr Gentle, coughed and said, 'Counsel for the Respondent will have opportunity later to disprove that there was no carpeting in the room in question and that the toilet facilities are outside the house.'

Mr Hood flashed a dazzling smile at the bench.

'Your honour, the condition of a slum dwelling is of less importance to my—'

'Objection,' shrilled Mr Gentle.

'I withdraw the word "slum",' capitulated Mr Hood, and Mr Gentle nodded petulantly and sat down, rubbing one eye.

'In fact,' said Mr Hood, 'we are less concerned at the moment with the condition of the er—house than we are with what took place. Now, Miss Scott, what tentative arrangement did you make with your sister?'

'We agreed that the boy was to come to me every second weekend.'

'Why only at weekends?'

'Well, I didn't think it was fair either to my sister or to the boy to make any drastic changes so soon.'

'I see. How long did this arrangement stand?'

'Oh, let me see. About two months.'

'What brought about the change?'

'I paid a visit to the child's school.'

'What school was the child attending?'

'A state school.'

The judge looked down at Vanessa. 'A *state* school, you say?'

'Yes, your honour. A state school.'

'A state school,' said Mr Hood, and smiled. 'Did you think it too was inadequate?'

'Yes.' Vanessa smoothed her skirt, seemed to admire her shoes a moment, and Lila pursed her mouth, thinking, They make it sound like something out of *Oliver Twist*.

Vanessa said, 'Well, the kindergarten class appeared to be very overcrowded. There were thirty-two other children in the class and lessons were held outside. The headmistress told me they had no space inside.'

'Even in winter?'

'I have no idea what arrangement they made in

winter. I made a tour of inspection with the head-mistress and I found it in an unspeakably run-down condition. The toilets were in a filthy—'

'I'm sorry, but we cannot discuss toilets, Miss Scott, without fear of prejudice.' Mr Hood turned and smiled at Mr Gentle, who smiled back. 'So then you had the child enrolled at an academy—a private school operated by Miss Charlotte Pile?'

'Yes, it was very highly recommended to me.'

'Did the Respondent protest at this change?'

'Yes, she did.'

'But you overrode her objections?'

'I felt I had to. Finally she agreed to reverse the arrangement and let my nephew come to me during the week to attend school and go to her on weekends.'

'And this arrangement was held to until the weekend of July the fourteenth of this year?'

'Yes.'

'What happened on that weekend?'

'I held to my part of the agreement and the child went to Mrs Baines for the weekend. About six o'clock on the Sunday evening I received a telephone call from my sister, who simply said, "PS has something to say to you." '

'PS,' said the judge.

'What did your nephew say to you, Miss Scott?'

'The child said, "I'm not coming back. I decided myself."'

'That was all?'

'That was all. He then hung up.'

'Do you know of any reason that might have prompted him to say this?'

'None.'

'Were you shocked? Surprised?'

'I was horribly shocked. And afraid.'

'Do you think that the child might have been prompted by someone to say this?'

'Yes. Indeed I do.'

'Do you believe that he wanted to return to you as usual?'

'Yes.'

'Why? Did your little nephew appear to be upset, distraught?'

'Frightfully distraught.'

Mr Hood fiddled with a watch chain.

'Did you then retain me as counsel to write a letter ordering the Respondent to return your nephew within ten days of the date of this letter?' Mr Hood waved the letter like a flag.

'Yes.'

'Did you further instruct me to deliver this letter to the Respondent in person?'

'Yes, I did.'

'Will you state what happened on the evening of July the seventeenth of this year?'

'Yes. I went to the house of the Respondent and

waited in the car while you delivered the letter to her. After a few minutes, my sister came out to the car. She appeared to be very hysterical and she said, "PS is never coming back to you and I don't care what Mr Hood says, you will have to get a court order." I then asked very calmly if I might see my nephew.'

'Did the Respondent agree?'

'After some hesitation she went into the house and came back with the child. I said to him, "What's the matter, PS? This isn't like you at all." '

'And what did the child say?'

'He repeated what he had said on the telephone. "I'm not coming back to you. I've decided." '

'"*I've* decided."'

'Yes. So then I said, "Why don't you sit down here with me and we'll have a talk about it."'

'Meaning for him to get into the car?'

'Yes.'

'It was a cold night.'

'Yes, very cold actually.'

'And you didn't want the little boy to have to stand in the cold street while you talked to him.'

'Exactly.'

'Exactly. Proceed.'

'Well, I put my hand out to help him into the car and—'

'Just a minute. Did he seem reluctant about getting into the car?'

'Oh, absolutely not. Eager, in fact. He put his hand out—'

'The child put his hand out *first*?'

'Yes.'

'You're sure of that?'

'Positive. He reached out for me and just as I put my hand out to help him into the car, my sister caught hold of him and pulled him back.'

'The Respondent pulled him back forcibly?'

'Yes, and held on to him.'

'Did she say anything?'

'Oh, yes. She was extremely overwrought and hysterical and started screaming at me and calling me a kidnapper and attracted the attention of neighbours. She then encouraged the neighbours to boo at me.'

'Was the child upset?'

'Of course. He was struggling to get free of her and crying.'

'Struggling and crying.'

'Crying piteously.'

Mr Hood threw up his arms in a gesture of heart-rending pity for all the homeless, bereft children of the sad world.

'The little boy was struggling and crying to get to you. So what did you do, Miss Scott?'

'Well, finally I told the chauffeur to drive off. I didn't wish to prolong the child's agony. I knew that it was impossible to reason with my sister any longer and that I should have to resort—to *apply* to the court for restitution.'

Mr Hood took a cambric handkerchief from his sleeve, blew his nose loudly.

'The *twists*!' said Lila to George. 'The wicked twisting. I'm thankful Mater is not alive to hear her.'

'What?'

'Mater. Glad she's dead.'

'Why?'

'Tell you later.'

'Now, Miss Scott, there's one thing I would like to make clear to his honour. You have said that the Respondent often defied your wishes in regard to your ward and also encouraged him to deceive you.'

'Yes.'

'Can you give us an explicit example?'

'Yes. Last May, I believe it was, she overrode my objections and took him to a writers' picnic.'

The judge looked down. 'What kind of picnic?'

'A collection of writers were giving a charity picnic. I believe it's called the Pen and Ink Club.'

'Why would you object to that?'

'I do not consider these people fit company for a child of six and a half.'

'You knew these people?'

'I know some of them. They were friends of my sister Sinden. I consider them Bohemian.'

Mr Justice Hay-Piggott frowned at Vanessa. 'Bohemian? Is that a classification of some sort?'

Mr Hood said, 'Do you mean shiftless, erratic, bizarre?'

'Yes,' said Vanessa.

'When the boy came home, did he tell you about this picnic?'

'Not at first. He had been told to say nothing about it.'

'How did you ascertain this?'

'He was so very disturbed and tense that I sensed what had happened. I said, "PS, you mustn't worry about anything but you must tell me the truth. Did Lila—"'

'Meaning the Respondent?'

'Yes. "Did Lila make you go to the picnic?" and he said, "Yes." '

'Did he then describe this—this *picnic*?'

'Vividly. He was very confused about the people there. He said they were very strange and there had been a lot of drinking.'

'Some of these writers were drunk?'

'Apparently, from the way he described it. And also there was a lot of talk about his mother in front of him.'

'What kind of talk?'

'He had got it into his head that his mother never wore shoes.'

'How?'

'I believe someone there told a story of how my late sister met Logan Marriott at some fancy-dress dance party and ran off with him without her shoes.'

'Objection, your honour,' shrilled Mr Gentle. 'This is merely assumption and there is no direct evidence that any story—'

Mr Hood smiled. 'Your honour, we are not trying to establish whether the late Mrs Marriott ran off into the night without her shoes. We are merely stating what the child told.'

'Objection overruled,' said Mr Hay-Piggott, and looked for a long time at Mr Gentle.

'The child was upset at this story?'

'Naturally.'

'And were you upset by it?'

'Frankly,' said Vanessa, and became queenlike for a moment, 'I have no idea *how* my sister met Logan— met Mr Marriott, but I consider it wrong for a child to hear a coarse story about his mother.'

'Continue.'

'Well, he then maintained that it was implied in front of him that he had been responsible for his mother's death.'

Several women near Lila said, 'Ooooossssh,' and the judge tapped lightly on the bench with his gavel, looked like a hooded eagle about to fly.

Lila hid her face for a moment, feeling waves of asthma rising, heard Mr Hood say:

'Is it possible, Miss Scott, that the child was making this up?'

'I do not believe so. He said he was told by one of these writers that he must finish a novel my sister was writing at the time of her death. He then said that he would never become a writer, never, and he used a vulgar expression that he had picked up from these people.'

'What was the expression?'

A slight pause.

Vanessa, eyeing her shoes again, said, 'Bosh and balls.'

The judge leaned down. 'Bosh and what?'

'Balls, your honour,' said Mr Hood, and bit his lower lip.

Mr Justice Hay-Piggott wrote a word.

After the sniggers died down, Mr Hood said, 'Anything else?'

'Yes.' Vanessa, satisfied with her shoes, gazed directly into Mr Hood's eyes. 'The child then asked me what a homosexual is.'

The intake of breath was like a rip tide that carried Lila with it and flung her on a beach.

'Did he use the word?'

'No.'

'What word did he use?'

'An ugly word.'

'What?'

'Is it necessary to—? Poofter. He said, "What is a poofter?"'

Before the judge could ask the same question Mr Hood flashed the answer in a loud, richly appalled voice. 'Poofter is a slang word, your honour, used to describe a male homosexual.' Eyebrows sky high, the judge asked how it was spelled and Mr Hood obliged. Then, weighted with shame, he gazed at the floor and asked:

'Did the child explain his reason for asking?'

Vanessa said, 'Well, it seems that one of his mother's friends had been described as a—well, by this word.'

'Did you attempt to explain the word to him?'

'I simply said it was a horrible ugly word that he must never use, like dago.'

Lila, sensing eyes on her, feeling publicly stoned, thrashed around in her mind for answers, remembering uneasily that Conchita Ewers had rambled on about something of the sort. Something about some young friend of Sinden's who had committed suicide. All this fuss over some chance remark that Lila could not even remember. Was that really what the word meant? She ought to have asked George at the time but too late now, the damage had been done.

'Did you protest to your sister over the incident of this *unfortunate* picnic?'

'No, I felt that much stronger action was necessary. I felt my nephew should be taken away from Mrs Baines' influence altogether.'

'Did you then get in touch with the boy's father?'

'Yes.'

'And did Mr Logan Marriott come to Sydney at your request?'

'Yes.'

'And at your expense?'

'Yes.'

'What did you propose to Mr Marriott?'

'I asked permission to take the child to England, away from this dangerous friction—at least during his formative years.'

'What was Mr Marriott's reaction?'

'Well, unfortunately he was intoxicated. He was incapable of understanding the situation and I could get nowhere with him.'

'He was too drunk to give a decision?'

'Yes.'

'But was there only *one* meeting? Didn't you try again?'

'He then refused to answer any of my telephone calls and suddenly left for Melbourne the following night.'

'Did he communicate with the Respondent?'

'I understand that my sister saw him off on the train.'

'Mrs Baines saw him *off*?' Mr Hood looked stunned. 'Went with him to the station and *saw him off on a train*?'

'Yes.'

'The following *night*?'

'Yes.'

'And was it the following weekend, the very *next* weekend, that the boy was not returned to your house as usual?'

'Yes, it was.'

'Thank you, Miss Scott.'

The point seemed to hang in the air and glitter, the false image of Lila with gun in hand forcing Logan on to a train.

Silent applause followed Mr Hood's leisurely walk back to his seat and died away as Mr Gentle got to his feet. His robe and cocky walk did nothing to disguise his youth and when he spoke, his voice was high and nasal. Vanessa regarded him with the gentle disdain of an archduchess being asked impertinent questions by the plumber.

'You say Mr Marlowe was drunk?'

'Who is Mr Marlowe?' asked Vanessa.

'Er—er—' Mr Gentle was shuffling papers, grinning, as Mr Hood scraped a chair back and said, 'Your honour—'

The judge said witheringly, 'Is counsel referring to—'

'*Marriott*. Mr Marriott. Sorry.' Mr Gentle laughed. Mr Hood laughed. Vanessa smiled wryly.

Lila thought, If he can't even get the *names* right!

'Good-oh; sorry,' said Mr Gentle. 'Was Mr Marriott too drunk to discuss your taking the child away from his original foster parents or did he disagree?'

'He was drunk.'

'I see. In other words, you didn't even have a discussion.'

'We had a discussion.'

'Was it a long discussion?'

'Fairly long.'

'How long's that?'

'Well, I don't remember—an hour or so.'

'An *hour* or so.'

'Perhaps not quite as long as that.' Vanessa twisted a little.

'Even so, Mr Marriott couldn't have been very drunk or you wouldn't have spent that much time arguing.'

'I was putting my case to him.'

'Then he must have listened. He must have known what you were saying.'

Silence.

'He must have understood you, known what you wanted. Did he understand what you wanted?'

Vanessa said sullenly, 'Yes.'

'*Yes.*' Mr Gentle pounced on the word, ran gaily around with it, tossing it up in the air like a spaniel with a ball. 'Yes! He knew what you wanted and yet you still didn't get anywhere with him.'

'He was emotional and intoxicated—'

'But he never gave his permission for you to take the boy away from Mrs Baines, did he?'

After a second, Vanessa admitted defeat on this point. 'No.'

'*No.* Because he wanted his son to be with the aunt who had taken the little boy from his dead mother's arms!'

Mr Hood sprang up. 'Objection, your honour. That is assumption!'

'Objection sustained.'

'Just the same, he got it out,' whispered Lila to George.

'Miss Scott, you've implied that your nephew wished to return to you. Do you believe then that he was happy in your home?'

'Most certainly.'

'I see. Can you explain why on one occasion he locked himself in a bathroom for several hours?'

Vanessa smiled. 'Oh, yes.'

'You admit he fled into a bathroom and locked the door?'

'Yes, and I blame myself entirely. I shouldn't have let him see his father. The child somehow got the wrong impression that his father had come to take him away from *me*.'

'Are you sure it wasn't because you had threatened the boy and struck him?'

Mr Hood was objecting loudly and the judge, sustaining the objection, reminded Mr Gentle that he must have supportable evidence before trying to bully witnesses into confessions and that the witness was in court in the role of applicant. She was not on trial.

Mr Justice Hay-Piggott then wagged a long finger at Mr Gentle.

'This is your first appearance before me in this court and while admiring your zeal on behalf of your client, I must remind you that this is a Supreme Court in Equity and I will allow of no police-court pyrotechnics here. If you're in doubt as to the proper procedure, I suggest you approach me first.'

'Yes, your honour,' said Mr Gentle, smiling, admonished.

'Have you any further questions to ask the witness?'

'No, your honour.'

Vanessa stepped down from the witness stand and the judge recessed the court until two fifteen.

Lila, forcing down some half-cold mincemeat in the Kosy Korner, said, 'I'm afraid the judge doesn't like Mr Gentle.'

George said, 'Oh, you can't tell with these legal blokes. They all sing out to each other in court and get together in the evening for a drink at Tattersall's Club.'

'How would *you* know that?'

Her snide rebuke made Lila instantly ashamed. She felt further humiliated when, guiding her through the traffic, George took her hand and led her back to the court like a child.

In the dirty corridor, busy with bobbing grey wigs and black gowns, they came face to face with Vanessa, talking in undertones to Mr Hood, and for a moment the sisters glanced at each other like strangers in a bus. Then separately they made their way into the assembling courtroom.

Cousin Ettie Bult's affidavit added nothing of importance except to laud Vanessa's unselfishness, loving kindness, self-sacrifice and good taste. While Mr Hood was reading it, Lila looked over at Ettie and the old lady's returning smile said, 'Well, she *is* all that and you also are a dear lamb so couldn't you and Vanessa make up and let me take you all for a charming expensive dinner somewhere.'

Mr Hood (wisely, thought Lila) made no attempt to question Mrs Bult but hurried on to the affidavit of Miss Charlotte Pile, who described the select advantages of her private school and under direct examination went on to say that Miss Scott's little nephew was showing great advancement. When he had first come to her, she said in plum-coloured tones, the boy had been unable to spell the simplest words but had, during the week before he had been unfortunately taken out of her school, completed a short composition entitled 'What I Saw in the Gar-den.' (Offered as exhibit, one child's exercise book.)

In closing, Miss Pile noted that the boy's Australian accent was at first so bad that the other children had had difficulty understanding him but that this had been corrected.

Mr Gentle bobbed up to ask Miss Pile what, in her opinion, was wrong with an Australian accent? In his own richly mutated vowels, Mr Gentle asked:

'Wouldn't you say that our Prime Minister speaks with an Australian accent?'

Miss Pile gave a tinkling laugh. 'Aim' afreed he does.'

The judge smiled at this and did nothing to admonish the laugh that rippled through the courtroom.

Miss Claire Colden, of the London College of Music, said under examination that her pupil had been showing advancement, had quickly accomplished a piece entitled 'The Emu's Tea Party'. Miss Colden then waxed so enthusiastic over Vanessa that even Mr Hood looked embarrassed. After an unsatisfactory exchange with Mr Gentle over the advisability of beginning music lessons at six and a half, Miss Colden, on being dismissed, turned to the judge and said in ringing tones, 'Your honour, may I just say that Miss Scott is the finest, most charming, most loving, marvellous woman who has ever employed me and I'm proud to speak in her behalf.'

Ellen Glossop, cook and domestic, stated that she had been employed by the applicant for the last seven months and that the house was luxurious and 'run beautiful'. Yes, the little boy often had come and chatted with her in the kitchen; he was bright and happy. In fact, in Ellen's opinion, if anything, he was spoiled. Too many expensive toys and fussed over too much, waited on hand and foot, if you asked *her* opinion. Mr Hood, pleased as punch, reminded Ellen that opinions stood for nothing, only facts counted. Ellen, lemon-mouthed, nodded and took a handkerchief from a handbag that Lila, squinting to see, felt sure had once belonged to Vanessa.

Mr Gentle jumped up.

'Miss Glossop, why was the housemaid Diana Huggens recently discharged?'

'Search me.'

'You must have some idea.'

'No, I don't. They said she was no good.'

'Was that the only reason?'

'Far as I know.'

'Think carefully now. Are you sure it wasn't because the maid, Diana, had witnessed ill treatment of the child?'

Ellen fumbled with her bag. 'Not that I know of.' Then, looking Mr Gentle in the eye, she added, 'I stick to my job in the kitchen and I don't gossip about what goes on in the house.'

'Have you ever seen Mrs Bult the worse for wear for drink?'

Ellen replied that *sometimes* both Mrs Bult and Miss Scott had a sherry before dinner.

'I asked you if you'd ever seen Mrs Bult intoxicated?'

'Not me.'

'Are you telling the truth?'

'Yes, I *am*. I know what the oath means.'

'I *hope* you do,' said Mr Gentle.

Mr Hood objected to the line of questioning and its implication.

The judge coughed and said, 'Well, if the implication is that a sherry before dinner constitutes excessive drinking, we may all be found guilty indeed' and the courtroom laughed obediently at the judge's first real joke; the judge appeared pleased, wiped dry lips, asking Mr Hood if there were any further affidavits. On being told there were none, Mr Justice Hay-Piggott adjourned the proceedings until the following morning at ten thirty.

Mr Gentle, rushing off to catch a beer before the six-o'clock-closing-time crowd, said, 'Now, Mrs Baines, tomorrow's our turn and they're going to get it where the chicken got the axe.'

PS, running into the front hall, hurling himself on Lila's stomach, said, 'Did we win?'

'It's not over yet, pet. Gracious, what a dirty face.'

'Why?'

'Well, they have to ask a lot more questions yet.'

'Will it be over tomorrow?'

'I don't think tomorrow, precious. Pet, don't hold on to me; I have to get George's tea or he'll be late for work.'

She heard George's cry of anguish from the kitchen, hurried in; saw his album of newspaper clippings on the linoleum floor, the mess of crayons, the sprawling paintbox and the cup of multi-coloured water; the little boy Alan stretched on his stomach looking up surprised at George's angry face.

'Lila, look what they've been doing.'

'Oh, my God. PS, where did you get—'

PS, trailing behind her, said, 'We didn't have anything to colour.'

Lila bent and picked up the album, saw the yellowing newspaper headline: 'G. M. BAINES WINS ELECTORAL NOMINATION FOR LABOUR. CANDIDATE WILL CAMPAIGN FOR STATE ELECTION,' and George's face crayoned out of recognition.

'He's defaced every picture in the book.'

'PS!'

'We couldn't find anything to colour.'

'This is George's precious book. You've been told never to touch—'

'We didn't have—'

'That's *enough*.' George's explosion shook the room. 'Don't do any *more* to me. That's enough.'

'George!'

'Enough is *enough*!'

The air quivered and lay still. In the silence they heard Agnes from her glassed-in porch singing:

'I am going, I am going to the Land,
I am going with His lantern in my hand.'

George's head turned in the direction of the little crooked voice and his mouth hardened further. Lila touched the stone man. Is it all my fault? Yes, said the stranger, looking back at her. Your family, said the stranger, and Lila recognised him as George Baines, standing on that turn in the road of days before he met her, baffled a little at himself and by the extraordinary possibility of what might lie ahead, alone as yet and untouched by her. But she had waved her hand to him and he had turned and come down the road towards her. Love, she had said, will accomplish everything for us, and believing, he had followed down her road in search of the ever vanishing miracle until now they stood in the kitchen at the decimal point of twenty-nine minutes past five on Tuesday, the fourteenth of

August, nineteen hundred and thirty-four and looked at the mutilated book of his life.

'PS is sorry,' said Lila, meaning I am sorry. I am truly sorry. I meant for us at this moment to be on our way to London where you were to receive your knighthood and consult with the Prime Minister. But instead we had to give Mater a home, then Sinden, then PS and Agnes, who chose this ill-begotten moment to remind you of where you turned off the road. But is it so far gone? Does it take only crayons and a hymn to end the journey now? What can I say to you? What will you say to me?

'Cup of tea,' said George at last, and Lila went gratefully to the safety of the gas stove as he turned and went outside.

Why?

'Come here, you good thing.'

George felt the hot sun; put down something. A spade? Came, spitting on his hands to stop the blisters, up through the shaking paspalum grass to where she was sitting under the pepper tree at a little card table. She was wearing bright blue sailor-cloth pants and an old pink shirt of Logan's. She put a stone on the pile of typescript and as George came up, covered the page in her typewriter.

'Don't look.'

'How's it going, Sin?'

'Bloody. I've just found out the girl in this is like me. She realises everything too late.'

Sinden thumbed her nose at the typewriter. 'Bugger you, Myra; why couldn't you have found that out a hundred pages back and saved me all this revision? Has the postman come?'

'Yes, but he comes again this arvo.'

'Bearing a letter from my five-minute husband and then I'll *be off*!'

'Off where?'

'Over the rainbow to find the pot of gold. To wherever this ridiculous place is. I'll be living in a tent and boiling billies of hot tea for great, sweating, hairy prospectors washing out their gold by the river, and at night, sitting round the campfire making damper and singing all the old songs to the moon and the night insects, so damn far away from Sydney where there's always a need to do something that should be needless like making money.'

A rainbird flew out of the pepper tree and squawked a mocking 'Weee—awwk' at her.

'Damn you, I don't want rain!' She screwed her face up at the sun, and looking for something lost in the sky, her hand guarding her eyes, she asked, 'George, does anyone *find* gold?'

'I s'pose they still do—occasionally. But not like Ballarat in eighteen fifty-one. He might find tin, though.'

'No, it's got to be gold. That's all he believes in. I don't mean like some rotten old moneybags, but to fulfil himself. A little gold would be enough. Then we'd buy a bakery in Bacchus Marsh. I'd love that—writing and baking bread—and I think it would satisfy him, to have done it himself. I'd be more easily satisfied. I just want two things apart from him. I want a book published in the United States and a son. Neither of them need be very successful. Just mine. But for Logan it's *got* to be gold.'

She looked down suddenly and a drop of water fell from the cloudless sky on to her page of untidy typing.

George put his hand down on the pink shirt and she turned without a word, burying her face into his chest, her arms tight around him.

George said, 'I love you, Sin,' and taking her chin, lifted her protesting face and kissed her.

'I know.'

'But I love you,' he said, feeling the truth explode in his throat, feeling sharp pain between his eyes and no longer hearing the fat locusts croak in the tree but only cries of something in himself.

'I know you do,' she said, and suddenly twisting away, she stood up, small and with her face disarranged, looking at him. 'Well, I know you do, dearest George. And I love you.'

Like a stopped film, they froze into absurd attitudes for a moment; then resumed the projection of their lives at normal speed; he to slap at a fly on his bare arm, she to brush a leaf out of her hair.

'George, don't tell Lila yet. I haven't even told Vere, but I'm getting one of my wishes. I'm going to have a baby.'

A window flew up urgently, a blind rattled and light streamed into the dark, cold garden.

Lila called, 'George? Are you in the WC? Come and have your tea. You'll be late for work. George, do you hear me?'

Do you hear me, Sin? I love you.

That's why everything. And Sin, I'm easily satisfied too. All I want is—What? Sleep.

Vanessa studied her nails, listening to Mr Gentle reading Lila's affidavit. Really! That distressing accent. Not only that but the embarrassing, really *embarrassing* sentimentality of it all. The boy's 'little' mother wanted this and that. The boy's 'little' mother wrote her last letter from the hospital where she was dying, begging the good kind Baineses to take her child. Why not 'short but wiry', just for a change. The 'short but wiry' mother wrote a letter. The Baineses' house was 'modest but full of love'. Does that excuse an outside toilet? Near to a 'convenient public school which his playmates attended and good enough for the son of a shire councillor'. To obtain votes, no doubt. 'A boy needs a father's guidance.' Poor old George, half asleep over there. Couldn't guide a horse. Time for the mud to fly. Into this life of suburban bliss came the Deponent.

'Autocratic, aggressive, sly, demanding and living on the endowments of a well-to-do elderly relative.' Inference: coercion and blackmail. ('Ettie, I'm going to have that child by hook or by crook and you'd better finance the undertaking or else!') Right from the start 'Deponent had gradually encroached' on Lila's time and influence and had been impossible to deal with, even giving orders that Lila was not to launder the child's shirts. As time went by this monster had regulated the boy's every waking hour, adding needless lessons in the afternoons, allowing no time for recreation and play, locking up toys and so regimenting him that it was no wonder the poor little boy became more and more reluctant to return to the Deponent on Sunday nights and more and more persuasion was necessary by good, kind, motherly Mrs Baines to induce him to go back. He had often become hysterical; he—

Vanessa, to soothe herself, turned to look at the back of Mr Hood's thick, muscular neck and drifted peacefully into a recurring fantasy.

'Vanessa, for a long time since the case, I've wanted to say something to you.'

'I know, Jonathan.'

'What an intuitive woman you are.'

'Jonathan, don't—'

'But, my dear, my dear—'

'We're both so hopelessly tied. You to your wife and I to PS.'

388

'Ness, are you saying we can't even meet again?'

What?

Damn. She'd missed something because the court was buzzing softly and Lila was getting up and going into the witness box.

Vanessa watched her. Oh, that mincing walk and that sheepish devoted smile, crossing the courtroom as though she were taking a cup of tea to Mater. Years of butter not melting in her mouth. Poor old George. Married to that fake.

Mr Gentle said, 'Mrs Baines, have you ever tried to influence your ward in any way against the applicant, Miss Scott?'

'Never.'

'Did you advise him not to return to her?'

'No. It was his decision. I tried to get him to go back at least for that week until we could get some legal advice.'

'You tried to reason with him?'

'Oh, yes. But he kept saying, "I won't go back, I won't go back," and every time I tried to take hold of him, he hung on to the bedpost and screamed. So I finally told him that it was all right but that he must tell Vanessa himself.'

'On the subsequent night when your sister came to your house with her lawyer, did you forcibly prevent the boy from getting into the car?'

'Yes, because I saw the chauffeur had his hand on the door, ready to slam it.'

'Did the child cry and struggle to get in?'

'Absolutely not. He clung to *me*.'

'Did you scream out to the neighbours?'

Absolutely not, said Lila. Vanessa had behaved like a crazy thing. Her abuse of Lila had been so terrible, so loud, that naturally the neighbours had been attracted by the noise. It had brought on one of Lila's rare asthmatic attacks. A doctor's certificate verified that Mrs Baines' attacks were induced by emotional stress.

Guided and steered by Mr Gentle, Lila basked in a spotlight of flatulent goodwill-towards-men. Pursued by arrogant writs and threats, poor Logan Marriott had been forced to flee Sydney on a train to escape Vanessa. Her sister Agnes, a temporary lodger, did belong to a religious sect (here Lila paused uneasily) but she did not try to impress her beliefs on the child, knowing that Mr and Mrs Baines did not adhere to them.

Here Mr Hood stood up and asked, with the judge's permission, was Miss Agnes Scott in court?

No, said Mr Gentle.

'Not *here*?' Mr Hood looked astounded.

'Owing to the fact that Miss Agnes Scott has only been living in Respondent's home for the last month or so and was not present during any of the incidents applicable to the case, her affidavit has not been requested.'

'*Not* requested? I see.'

Mr Hood sat down, eyebrows sky high, and Agnes's absence in court was duly noted.

Skipping lightly over the unfortunate picnic, aware of traps, Mr Gentle averred that Mrs Baines had been within her rights to take the 'little' boy to meet some of his 'little' mother's friends. And hadn't the mother herself been a writer?

A 'little' writer, thought Vanessa. A short but wiry novelist.

'I believe his mother would have wished him to go,' said Lila on cue, and touched her eyes with a handkerchief.

'Is it true, Mrs Baines, that during this picnic, it was implied in front of the boy that he'd been in some way responsible for his mother's death?'

'No.'

'Not at any time?'

'Never.'

'Where did he get this idea?'

'From his other guardian.'

'From the *Deponent*!' Mr Gentle's turn to put on a look of horror. 'How do you know?'

'He told me that Vanessa had said he was late coming and so his mother had died.'

'When was this?'

'A long while before the writers' picnic.'

'Before?'

'Yes. Vanessa had taken him up to see Dear One's Little Garden—'

The judge looked down crossly. 'Dear who's what?'

Mr Gentle elucidated.

The judge, writing, asked Lila, 'This is what you call the grave?'

'Yes, your honour,' said Lila. 'We think it's nicer.'

Mr Hay-Piggott regarded Lila fiercely. 'What have you told the boy about his mother?'

'Well—' Lila seemed flustered. 'That she's with the angels.'

'With the *Rangers*?' The judge looked affronted.

'*Angels*, your honour.' Mr Gentle spluttered. 'Now, Mrs Baines—'

'Wait a minute.' The judge waved a pen at Mr Gentle. 'I don't understand. If the boy thinks his mother is with the angels, how can he also believe that she is in some little garden?'

'He didn't,' said Lila and Mr Gentle in chorus.

'I'm asking the witness,' said the Judge irritably.

Lila said shakily, 'He thought of the little garden as a sweet sort of—memorial where we leave flowers and things—'

'What things?'

'I mean, just flowers, your honour. We've always made it seem nice for him. Then my sister went and told him that Sinden was down there in a *box*.'

'We can presume that that is the truth,' said the judge. 'I don't understand the point of all this.'

Mr Gentle said, 'But, your honour, the point is that the Deponent wilfully undermined all the careful training—'

'Careful poppycock,' said the judge. 'I must remind counsel we are not in session to hear a lot of emotional balderdash about gardens and angels. The point *is* that the boy learned that his mother died in childbirth.'

'Yes, your honour.'

'And that he learned this from the Deponent?'

'Yes, your honour.'

'That's all we need to know. Good gracious, we don't need to write a book about it. We've already taken up far too much time on unimportant points. Now, do you have any further questions?'

Mr Gentle said quickly, 'No, your honour,' and sat down as Mr Hood approached Lila with a gleaming smile.

'Did you go to the train to see Mr Marriott off to Melbourne?'

'Yes.'

'Because he wouldn't come to your home?'

'Oh, *no*.' Lila was indignant. 'He was coming. I had dinner all ready and at the last minute he rang up—'

'He didn't come to your home?'

'No, but he'd been—'

'So you had to go to him.'

'He was leaving that very night.'

'Well, then, naturally he wouldn't have been able to come to your home.'

'Yes, but—'

'What did you discuss with him?'

'Nothing. There wasn't any time.'

'What would you have discussed with him?'

'Well—about PS.'

'*What* about your nephew?'

'My husband and I wanted Logan's approval to adopt PS.'

'Ah, I see. But you weren't able to bring this up?'

'Only briefly.'

'Oh, then you *were* able to discuss it. I thought you said *nothing* was discussed.'

'Just as the train was leaving,' Lila had begun wheezing.

'And what did Mr Marriott say?'

'He said he wanted *us* to have PS.'

'Was anyone else present when he said this?'

'My husband and my sister Vere.'

'Oh, your *husband*. Naturally. Was Mr Marriott sober when he said this?'

Lila swallowed several times, seemed to be fighting for breath.

'No. But he understood and he said to write to him.'

'I'm sorry; I didn't hear that.'

'To write to him.'

'Write to him where?'

'We don't know where he is. We—'

'Aren't you feeling well? Do you want a glass of water?'

Lila shook her head, regained her voice with an effort. 'We then wrote to him care of his sister.'

'Was there any reply?'

'No.'

'No. Knowing Mr Marriott's talent for evasiveness you could hardly have expected a reply. Once he was safely on that train and off into the blue, did you honestly hope that Mr Marriott would give a decision in your favour?'

'We thought that perhaps—since he was so angry with Vanessa—'

'I know you are not feeling well but I must ask you to speak up.'

'I'm sorry I—'

'Did you *expect* an immediate reply in your favour?'

'Well, no—'

'No, of course not.' Mr Hood's tone was kindly and conciliatory. 'Why should you? You had not seen him for over six years, so why should you *not* assume you would not hear from him for another six. Were you angry when the train left?'

'Somewhat.'

Mr Hood cupped an ear in pantomime.

'*Somewhat.*' Lila gasped.

'*Somewhat angry*. Yes, I should think so. I should think you went home very angry indeed. Was it the next Sunday that the boy refused to go back to Miss Scott?'

'Yes.'

'It was the very next Sunday, a few days, in fact, after you had been frustrated in your attempts to get the father to agree to your taking the boy away from Miss Scott, that the boy refused to go back?'

'Yes.'

'And you still maintain it was solely the *boy's* decision?'

'Yes. Yes.'

'You are asking the court to believe that, out of the blue, a six-year-old child suddenly made up his own mind not to return to his other guardian? You maintain that this extraordinary timing was merely coincidence?'

'Yes.'

Mr Hood remained silent while Lila exploded into a fit of wheezes and gasps, struggled for breath, flopped and wriggled in his fishing net. More than enough time to present a lying witness caught in her own asthmatic floundering. Then he bestowed on her a pitying smile and said, 'Perhaps you had better stand down,' putting out a hand to help Lila step from the witness box into the grave he had dug for her.

Mr Gentle was up, waving little black wings and squawking that it was being implied the witness was in bad health; the witness had never been in bad health, was perfectly capable and willing to stand there all day and answer questions, provided they were put to her in a reasonable manner.

The judge maintained that the questions had been put in a reasonable manner and asked Mr Hood if he wanted to ask anything more.

Mr Hood said agreeably that there was no point in further questioning Mrs Baines. Mr Hay-Piggott cast a look of malignant dislike on both lawyers; warned them in his most leather-bound voice that it was to be hoped that proceedings would be wound up that day, and adjourned for lunch.

Mr Hood hooked an arm around Vanessa coming through the swinging doors into the corridor, and said, 'So far, so good, but we may have a difficult time with that housemaid. Might have to recall you to the stand if she gets tough.'

At the same time Mr Gentle was reassuring Lila that once he got Diana on the stand things would really swing their way. Not that they needed it. If ever there was an open-and-shut case, Mr Gentle added, this was it. And by the way, the judge had asked to interview PS in chambers tomorrow afternoon. Ettie, blundering out of the seedy ladies' room, came face to face with Lila going in and in a reflex action they clutched each other.

'Lila! Ah, you poor, poor lamb. How are you?'

'Ettie. Oh, my dear, your hands are icy cold. Haven't you got your gloves?'

'Ah, dear thing—so kind of you—got my muff but it's freezing in the—er—courtroom.'

'Yes, isn't it? Someone ought to complain. Not even a radiator in the middle of August.'

'How's the little—'

'He's fine, Ettie. Oh, Ettie, who would ever have thought that this—We didn't want this.'

'Ah, I know you didn't, you poor dears. Neither did Ness.'

'Well—'

'Poor you. Poor Ness.'

Vanessa, spiralling like smoke around a corner, caught them red-handed. 'Ettie!'

Ettie's little diamond hands moved uselessly in the air, made feeble protests at being drawn away, signalling that they were all lovely people at heart. Blood, said her fluttering hands, was thicker than water. Couldn't everyone kiss and make up now, before more damage was done to the soul?

'After all,' she said to Vanessa's knotted face, 'her mother was my first cousin.'

'Of course *that* excuses everything.'

'Ah, Ness—'

'Please. I'm very nervous today.'

Vanessa felt her nervousness grow during the waning afternoon. George Mason Baines, with no issue of his own, loved the boy and a boy needs a father. Mr Baines had provided an adequate home through thick and thin for more than six years. Mr Baines had had vicissitudes but they were not overwhelming. In fact, the prospects for improvement, for quick reinstatement in the Trades Hall, were so blinding that it seemed an inopportune moment to turn on the dusty green-glass courtroom lamps. Mr Hood asked in a respectful tone for what party had Mr Baines been a candidate in the 1926 election? Ah, the *Labour* Party. Yes, of course. Then, had the *Socialists*—beg pardon, Labourites—been instrumental in obtaining his employment for the trade *unions*? Yes. And Mr Baines was now working as a night watchman? Only temporarily, owing to a cut-back; I see. Were politics discussed much in the house? Not much? That's surprising considering your interest in the Labour Party and unions and *strikes*. Objection? I beg your pardon, no inference meant at all.

Housewife and neighbour Mrs Florence Grindel had witnessed cleanliness, good wholesome food and happiness next door. House good enough for little mother to live in for some months prior to her confinement. Everything milk and honey until arrival

399

of Deponent from England. Remarked then on change in child. Nervous, fearful. Witnessed threats and wild behaviour of Deponent towards poor Mrs Baines. Considered calling police. Child sick in hydrangeas. Wonder to her he hadn't refused to return to Deponent long before.

Now, at last, the housemaid, and the courtroom sat up and straightened its back. Vanessa smiled to hear herself described as a 'martinet' and 'strict disciplinarian'. How silly of this young lawyer to put such words into the mouth of an inarticulate slavey who probably thought a martinet was some kind of cocktail. Dumb Dora. Poor thing in her terrible beret with a rhinestone koala bear pinned to it, her bile-green dress with all that awful ruching, stumbling now towards the witness box, puce-faced, numb with the shock of being of importance. Almost immediately, the judge became impatient and rapped at Diana to 'speak up, for goodness' sake. If *I* can't hear you, I'm sure nobody else can.'

But, to Vanessa's relief, Diana made a wretched witness. Glazed with stage fright, her butter fingers muffed every ball that Mr Gentle tossed hopefully at her. She grew vague about times and events and frequently had to have portions of her affidavit read again to her. Every damaging admission was drawn out of her with red-hot pincers and sighs of pain. 'Y-e-e-s, well, the old lady sometimes took a few.' Well, not drunk exactly, more *tipsy*, like. Always nice to *her*, though. No, she couldn't say Miss Scott was cruel exactly, more 'stern'. You had to watch your *p*'s and *q*'s with her. The kid had too many lessons and not enough time to play with other kiddies after school. The kiddie was often so 'knocked up' (translation for the judge: 'Tired, your honour') he had to go to bed before it was even dark.

Had she ever seen Miss Scott strike the child?

After a long pause: well, yes, once.

Well, it was the day the father came and there had been a big bust-up. Even they could hear it in the kitchen and the father told Miss Scott to go to hell and left. Right after that, Miss Scott had run upstairs and pushed the kiddie into his bedroom and slapped him for no reason. Then the kiddie had come running out and locked himself in the bathroom. Oh, for hours. None of them could get him to come out. It got her goat to see a poor kiddie suffer and so she'd spoke up to Miss Scott and got the sack then and there.

Thank you.

Mr Hood said, 'Are you used to hard work?'

Oh, yes, she was indeed. Came from a farm, where she milked ten cows before daylight, cooked for twenty farm hands, worked eighteen hours a day, even when she was a kid.

'Eighteen hours a day,' said Mr Hood, 'and you consider an hour's piano lesson or a ride in the park overtiring for a boy of six?'

'Well—'

'When you were employed by Miss Scott did she ever correct you? Complain about your work?'

'Oh, yes, she—'

'Was she ever harsh with you?'

'Yes. Oh, she could give you the rounds of the kitchen if somethink was out of place, like if you forgot the serviettes.'

'Made you feel bad sometimes?'

'Well, I don't like bein' roared up. I did my best.'

'Must have made you feel very hurt when you were discharged.'

'Too right. With my dad sick and all.'

'Are you employed at the moment?'

'Part time in a bottling works.'

'Do you like this as much as your previous job?'

'No, but I don't get my head blown off.'

Mr Hood turned away, then wheeled suddenly back. 'Oh, just one other thing. Where exactly was the child standing when you saw Miss Scott hit him?'

'In his bedroom.'

'Where in the bedroom?'

'Oh, I can't say for sure.'

'Why not?'

'Well, see, I was coming up the stairs—'

'Oh! You were on the *stairs*! Could you see into the bedroom?'

'Well, not right in but—'

402

'Then you didn't see the boy slapped at all.'

'Well—'

'*Did* you see the boy slapped?'

Diana clenched and unclenched her mammoth hands. 'Well, no, but I heard it.'

'You heard what *sounded* like a slap?'

'Yes.'

'Thank you.'

Moments later, the rattle of machine-gun fire as Miss Gwenevere Scott's borrowed amber-glass beads broke and rolled in every direction as she mounted to the witness box.

'Oh, my God, my beads! Sorry, terribly sorry.'

Laughter. Ushers scurrying around on the floor, bending and retrieving the noisy beads and handing them to Miss Scott, who meanwhile had dropped her bag.

The judge, patience worn thin, rapped and reproved everybody.

Now what on earth could Vere have to say?

Dressed like something out of a musical comedy, thought Vanessa, locking at Vere's scavenged finery, a purple wool suit, large black velvet hat with a brass arrow which had apparently pierced her skull and emerged beside her left ear, and, to set off the ensemble, somebody's stone martens.

Ettie murmuring, 'Vere-de-Vere looks very nice,' and giving Vere a little secret wave of encouragement.

No need to tell Vere to speak up; she was on the stage and her high, excited soprano voice rang through the court and echoed from the high dirty ceiling.

Logan Marriott had told her that he wanted Lila and George to have the child. He was worried to death because Vanessa was breaking the boy's spirit. He wasn't so very drunk when he said it either. No, they'd just had a couple of beers together at the Carlton and the reason he was scooting out of town on the train was because he was so thwarted by Vanessa.

So what?

Thworted, then. Logan knew what Vanessa was up to and he'd only come because he wanted a peep at his own son. Vanessa wanted the child all to herself. That was obvious. Why? Because Lila often let the boy visit her, Vere, for an afternoon at the pictures or the botanical gardens and Vanessa had only let her have him once and even then had created a most 'undoing' scene because they were five minutes late coming home and had attacked her so savagely that the child himself and Mrs Bult had tried to intercede. She had been told not to visit the house again.

Mr Hood stood up and waved a long finger at Vere.

'Just one question. Don't you think a guardian has every right to exert some discipline over a child?'

'It depends on the child.'

'Is this child different from others?'

'No, but he's a good child. I don't think he needs to be disciplined.'

'What *do* you think he needs?'

'One less mother.'

The courtroom rocked. Even the judge smiled and Vanessa and Lila said 'Absolutely' to Ettie and to George. Mr Justice Hay-Piggott reminded Mr Gentle that he wished to interview the boy in chambers the next afternoon at two o'clock and set a date two weeks in advance for handing down his decision. It was over at last.

'Did we win?'

'We don't know yet, pet.'

'Oh.' Annoyed with the idiocy of grownups who run courts. 'When? When?'

'Oh, very soon now. In about two weeks.'

'Two *weeks*!' Years! Just like grownups! 'Wait and see.' '*Maybe*.'

'Guess what? Tomorrow we're going into town and you're going to talk to the judge, all by yourself. Scrumptious?'

Scrumptious! Did Lila really think that *that* was a treat?

'Can Alan come?'

Mr Gentle was waiting for them by a big iron gate outside a very dirty old building which had iron bars on the windows. For a moment, he hung back and held on to Lila's hand. Was this really a jail, like Winnie had said, and had Lila and George just been telling a lot of fibs about him having to see the judge? They went through the gate and up some steps to a big door on which there was an emu and a kangaroo holding up a shield. Mr Gentle rang a bell and after a little wait the door was opened by a fussy young man who seemed in a hurry and said everything twice very quickly—come in-come in, sit down-sit down—and sat them down in a dark office full of books and papers. While Lila took off his overcoat and gloves and combed his hair, the young man spoke into a box on the desk and said, 'Your honour, the Marriott boy is here,' and there were some rumblings and sputterings from the box and a click and Mr Gentle told him not to be nervous and to be sure to tell the truth about everything; no matter what the judge asked him, and Lila was saying, yes, darling, tell the truth, it's very important, and kissed him. Then there was a long wait and so they all stared at the walls and from time to time Lila asked Mr Gentle a question and Mr Gentle sucked at his pipe and said maybe, perhaps, we'll see, and that he hoped that it wouldn't take too long because he had someone waiting at his office for him right now. Finally there was a loud buzz on the box and the fussy young man listened to some rumbles and said, 'Yes, your honour,' and told them the judge was ready now and Lila said again don't be nervous now, pet, and tell the truth, and the fussy young man tapped on a door and opened it and beckoned him to go in. Even Vanessa would have thought the room was very grand, like something in the Hollywood pictures. The walls were of shiny, polished wood and there were bookshelves right up to the high ceiling. The carpet was soft and deep like long grass and everything was very big—very big leather chairs and a desk as big as a tennis court and a fireplace twice as high as he was, in which a big fire crackled and popped. But the biggest thing of all was the judge, standing by the fireplace and looking down at him, and he suddenly thought of God. The judge was exactly like God to look at, with his white hair and white eyebrows, only wearing a suit. So like God, in fact, that he almost got down on his knees but instead held out his hand politely and the judge gave him a huge, cold, white hand and said, 'How do you do? Are you PS?' and he said, 'Yes, thank you,' and the judge smiled and now all at once he didn't feel nervous at all, only impressed, the way he'd be if it really was God.

The judge said, 'Sit down, PS,' and helped him up into one of the leather chairs, which was so big that his feet just stuck out in the air.

The judge said, 'Do you like chocolate?'

Yes, he said, thank you, and the judge handed him a big shiny red-and-gold package of Nestle's, the giant size which must have cost at least two shillings, and he said, overwhelmed, 'Thank you very much.'

'Don't eat it all at once,' said the judge. 'If you got sick, your aunt would blame me.'

Which aunt? Vanessa, of course. She didn't believe in chocolate for children because of their teeth and so very likely she'd given the judge strict orders about it and perhaps the judge didn't like that, was a teeny bit annoyed with Vanessa. The way he'd said 'your aunt' sounded as though he might be, and that was good. That meant everything was going to be all right and the judge was going to tell him in a minute that he was going to give him back to Lila.

'Now then,' said the judge, sitting down near him and folding his big, white, marble-looking hands. 'Now then, PS, I'm going to ask you one or two questions and I want you to remember that this is all just between you and me, so don't be afraid to tell me the truth, understand?'

He nodded.

'Do you have a puppy?' asked the judge.

'No.' Was the judge going to give him a puppy too?

'If you had a puppy, would you care for it and look after it?'

'Oh, yes.'

He was thinking how Vanessa hated puppies, would never let him have one. She always shooed stray dogs out of the garden. 'Go away, you nasty thing.' Once when they had been walking down the road, a little brown puppy had come running up to him and Vanessa had snatched his hand away from beginning to pat it and said, 'No, don't touch it, PS, it might have ticks. Shooo—go away, go on,' and the poor little pleading thing had cringed and shivered all over with fright. Lila had given him a little mongrel puppy when he was four, but the stupid baker's boy had left the gate open and the puppy had got out, been run over. Lila had cried over it much more than he had and when he had asked for another, had said, 'Oh no, oh no, pet; I couldn't stand any other dog to have poor little Winky's collar.'

The judge was saying, 'Now a puppy has to be taught, doesn't it? Not to do certain things in the house? Has to be spanked when it's naughty? Eh? So it will grow up to be a nicely behaved dog?'

Yes, he agreed, wondering what this was all about anyway.

Well, in some ways he was like a puppy, the judge explained. He wasn't old enough yet to know everything that was right and wrong and so he must be cared for and looked after until he was able to decide things for himself. Did he understand this?

Oh, yes.

'Now then, if you had a puppy and you had to give it away, to whom would you give it?'

That was a hard one. Who? Winnie? Alan? Cynthia Lawson?

The judge helped him out. 'Wouldn't you give it to the person who you knew would look after it the best?'

'Yes,' he said gratefully, knowing for sure now that the judge meant Lila because she loved puppies and was always stopping in the street to pat them: 'Oh, you dear little thing. Oh, wazza sweet ittle baby ting oo is!'

The judge seemed to know, like God, what he was thinking because he said, 'Your Aunty Lila has been very kind to you, hasn't she?'

Oh, yes, he told God; oh, yes, he loved Lila and George.

'And your Aunty Vanessa? Hasn't she been very kind to you also?'

Yes, oh, yes. He supposed it was better to be polite about Vanessa. 'Specially now that he was sure the judge was going to give him to Lila.

'Why didn't you want to go back to her?'

Funny. It was hard to say why. He'd never thought so before, but it was. He'd never been asked why straight out before and he began thinking of all the things, the sadness he felt away from Lila in the big house, Vanessa and her strict orders, Miss Pile and Miss Colden, the fright about going away to England and Vanessa hugging him on the bed with her and—it

410

was like being asked a hard question in class with everyone looking at you and being nervous that if you came out with the wrong answer, then everyone would laugh at you, and now he saw that the judge was frowning and tapping his fingers together as if he was in a hurry.

'I don't know,' he said to the judge.

'Why did you *tell* her you didn't want to go back?'

On the phone that night? Was that wrong? Of course he'd had to tell Vanessa himself. Lila had explained that to him but perhaps she hadn't explained it to the judge.

'Lila said I had to tell Vanessa that I decided myself.'

The judge seemed to understand completely because he nodded, and turning around, picked up a gold pencil and wrote something down on a pad on the big desk.

Just as he was going to explain to the judge, in case Lila hadn't, how it had all started that Sunday and about his plan to escape from Vanessa, the phone buzzed and the judge picked it up and said, 'Yes, who? All right, put him on. Hel*lo*, Sir Frank . . .' and went on talking for a long time, so he read as much as he was able to of the label on the chocolate wrapper and then looked around at the pictures on the wall, which weren't very interesting; mostly old old men wearing long grey wigs who stared back at him crossly. There

411

was also a very large photograph of the King. He was thinking how sad the King looked (and no wonder, with all the troubles he had) when the judge put down the phone, and catching him looking at the King, said, 'Do you know who that is?' 'The King,' he said and noticing that the judge looked pleased that he knew, and feeling certain that the judge of all people must have inside information, asked, 'Is he sad because they're going to shoot him?'

'Nobody,' said the judge sternly, 'wants to shoot the King of England, son. Who told you that?'

'Winnie,' he said, explaining who Winnie was. Then the judge said that Winnie was wrong and that everybody in the British Empire was loyal to the King. Occasionally, the judge explained, there were bad kings who had got themselves shot. But they were in *foreign* countries and they were not like King George, who is good and kind to everybody, even the blacks. The judge gave him quite a lecture about it, blowing his nose every now and then very fiercely, making scratching noises on his bristly white moustache, which was neatly waxed into two little points. Finally the judge took a big gold watch out of his waistcoat pocket, gazed at it for a minute, wound it, put it back and said, 'Well, PS, thank you for coming and having this little talk.'

So it was over and it hadn't been bad at all, a treat almost, because the judge had been so nice. So nice, in fact, that it seemed perfectly all right to ask straight out:

'Can I go *home* now?'

'Yes,' said the judge, 'you may.'

If the judge had wanted, he would have given him a big kiss on his white old cheek, but he shook hands politely again and then, feeling the need to do something more to show his gratitude, he made his dancing-class bow.

'Goodbye,' he said.

'Goodbye,' said the judge.

All the way home on the ferry, sitting inside because it was cold, he burbled to Lila about the interview and she nodded and laughed a little about the puppies, said, 'Fancy, pet,' and '*Aha*,' until he got to the bit about the King, when she said almost crossly, 'You shouldn't have said that. *We* don't believe that.

'Yes, but—'

'Why do you always have to *tell* everything? Always telling Vanessa *everything*. And now the judge. Don't you know the judge is hired by the government, which *is* the King? And fancy bothering the judge with what Winnie said. Goodness. What a funny boy you are; you're just like your mother—never tell *me* anything but prattle about everything to a stranger.'

'Well,' he said, cross with Lila for not giving him credit, 'anyway, we won. The judge said I could go home.'

413

But Lila didn't seem to be listening; she was staring out of the cabin window at the grey harbour and the screeching seagulls following the ferry.

Agnes, when he told her, bursting with importance on to her little glass porch, seemed to agree with him. She said in a faraway voice:

'In America, where I have lived and lectured, they don't need a king. They have President Roosevelt.'

But why?

Why, he protested, did they have to go back to the court? It was all over, wasn't it? The judge had said so, had said that he could go home.

Lila, washing his face (quickly, because she knew they would miss the nine-thirty ferry, knew they would be late, that things would have to go wrong this morning, like the clock), said, 'Not quite.' The judge hadn't quite meant that. Why? Had the judge fibbed to him then? No, pet, of course not. It was something to do with red tape. The judge had to hand down something called the minutes of the court and they had to be there and so did Vanessa. No, George was not going. Poor George was too worn out.

'Quickly now, PS. I'm waiting to know which tie you want to wear. Don't stand there wasting time.' Then, wasting time herself, hugged him.

Agnes, putting on her funny hat, said, 'Even though my affidavit was refused, Lila, I will pray for you for

414

Sinden's sake.' Kissing him, she said, 'PS, in thy father's house are many mansions,' and Lila said, 'Let's hope after today there'll only be one.'

George, getting ready for bed, ruffled his hair and said, 'Well, old chap, tonight we'll kill the fatted calf, eh?'

There wasn't time to ask what this meant for Lila was already hurrying him through the front gate and down the road to the tram stop. When a scraggly black cat darted in front of them and squeezed through some palings, Lila said, 'Oosssff,' as though she had stepped on something sharp. 'Pretend we didn't see it,' she said, and later, hoisting him up the step on to the tram, 'On the other hand, it could be lucky.'

They went, hand in hand, up the dirty steps into the wide, cold hallway of the court, where men in black gowns and grey wigs were hurrying up and down and people were sitting on benches, waiting, with long, sad, worried faces. One lady was crying and the other people looked at her and then looked away and went on reading their papers or just staring ahead of them. There was a smell of ink and coal and damp stone walls and the bare wooden floors were worn very smooth with all the hundreds and thousands of people who had walked in and out. It was dirtier than the Neutral Bay School, he told Lila as they sat down on a hard bench, and Lila said she hoped he hadn't told *that* to the judge, but yes, it was a very old building, over a hundred years old and it had been built by the convicts. Fancy that.

'Fancy that now,' said Lila in her put-on cheerful voice and with the laugh she used when she pretended everything was all right though it really wasn't. How about a nice little marmite sandwich, she asked him as if they were at the zoo having a treat. No, he said, shaking his head at the little damp package of sandwiches she took out of her bag. No, not now. Why did they have to wait? Where was the judge? In the court, Lila told him. There were other cases ahead of theirs and Mr Gentle would come and get them when it was time. He must be very quiet and still when they went into court, she told him, putting the sandwiches into his pocket in case they had to wait a long time before lunch. Oh, it would be so interesting for him to see the judge up on his high bench in his robes and he must try to remember every bit of it to tell Winnie and Alan when he got home tonight. And Lila, as she said this, caught her breath suddenly as though she had swallowed a fishbone and he saw that Vanessa had come through a door with a tall, very black-haired man, the same man who had come with her in the car that night there had been all the screaming. It was the first time he had seen Vanessa since that night and it seemed now so long ago that he had almost forgotten what she looked like. It was as if Vanessa had never been real, only make-believe in a game, and yet here

416

she was, swinging through the door in her dark-blue dress and her fur coat, her black hat with a gold ball on it, Vanessa, very real, very tall and straight, ready to give strict orders. When she caught sight of them she drew herself up sharply, and for one frightened moment he thought that she was coming straight for them, coming to shout at them, perhaps to hit him for being so wicked to her. But Vanessa simply stood very still, staring at Lila, and looking up at Lila, he saw that she was staring back at Vanessa and it was as though they had never seen each other before and yet at the same time as if they had been told awful secrets about each other.

Then Vanessa turned her back on them and her back was very straight and angry, and next to him he heard Lila begin to make purring sounds which meant her asthma was coming on again, meant something was wrong. But what? What could go wrong now? Everything had been settled with the judge, hadn't it? He turned quickly to Lila with the questions on his face but she only smiled and he saw that her lips were trembling, and now there was no time left for questions because Mr Gentle had come flapping up in a black gown with a little grey wig perched crookedly on his yellow hair and he was speaking in undertones to the tall black-haired man, who nodded and then, taking Vanessa's arm, led her away through a big arched door. Then Mr Gentle came up and whispered to Lila, who said, 'Oh, no—why? Can't he be with me?' Then there was more whispering and finally Mr Gentle said, 'Now, sonny, come along with me and I'll show you where to wait.' He drew back quickly towards Lila but she said, 'Go with Mr Gentle, PS,' and Mr Gentle took him by the hand and they started off down the long hallway. Lila called out, 'Wait. Wait a minute; I forgot his gloves,' and came running after them, purring very loudly now and pressing his woollen gloves into his hand, leaning down and kissing him wetly and saying, 'Don't worry, pet. We won't be very long.' Looking back as Mr Gentle tugged him along the corridor, he saw Lila wave to him, blowing kisses, and saw her turn away and walk towards the big door where Vanessa had disappeared.

Mr Gentle whisked him around a corner, down some steps to a door, knocked on it, and a voice said, 'Come in.'

It was the room where he had waited with Lila to see the judge and the same fussy young man was sitting behind the desk.

'He's to wait here,' said Mr Gentle, and the young man nodded and Mr Gentle flapped out, closing the door.

What? Why? Was he going to see the judge again?

'Sit down, sit down,' said the fussy young man. 'Over here by the radiator where you'll be warm.'

What were they doing? Lila had promised he'd see the judge in court with her; be with her all the time.

He sat down on a hard chair and the man turned back to the desk, reading a long paper. It was very quiet in the room. Every now and then the radiator gave a little *sping* sound and a clock ticked slowly like water dripping. There was a cold feeling in him now, spreading all through him, and he wanted to go to the bathroom but didn't like to ask the man.

Nothing to do but wait and look at the dull pictures on the grey walls. Whatever they were doing, it couldn't take too long. But would Lila know where to come and get him? He tried to think of it being safely over and of how they would go home on the ferry-boat and sing all the way and then have the fatted calf, whatever that was, but the cold feeling went on spreading through him and it was like the night he'd wakened and found Lila and George had left him alone in the house.

What could they be doing that would take all this time? Was it an hour? Two hours? He looked up at the big clock but the numbers were strange to him, all funny X's and V's. Wasn't it lunchtime? Or even after? But then wouldn't the judge sooner or later have to go home for his tea? Everybody went home when it was night. Everybody except George, who went to work. By now he was sure it was long after lunchtime and something awful had happened, so awful they couldn't tell him yet. Lila had been locked up or had fainted,

419

like she had one day on the back steps, suddenly falling down flat like a rag doll and frightening him terribly because he thought she was dead. Perhaps they had taken her away somewhere to a hospital and in the excitement had forgotten all about him. Now he was icy cold all over with fright. He thought of opening the door and running before the man could stop him. But where? There were so many doors outside. Suppose he couldn't find her in this big building?

Just as he was making up his mind that he must risk it all the same, must get up and go, run quickly before another minute ticked away, a buzzer rang on the desk and the young man put down his papers and said into a box, 'Yes, your honour.' Quacking noises came from the box and the young man said again, 'Yes, your honour.' At the same moment there was a tap on the door and to his relief, Mr Gentle came into the room with the tall black-haired man who had been with Vanessa. The young man said, 'Go right in, gentlemen,' and they crossed the room without even looking at him and opened the door to the judge's room. He caught a glimpse of the judge taking off his black robe as they closed the door behind them.

Where was Lila? If it was over, why hadn't she come to get him? As if in answer to his question, the young man said, 'Won't be long now,' and sat down again to read. Lila must be waiting outside then and any minute now . . .

420

But it seemed an awfully long minute. He could hear voices from behind the door and the judge's dry cough. Once, straining to listen, he thought he heard the judge say, 'Mrs Baines.' Perhaps Lila was in there with them, had gone in through another door with the judge, and he hung on to this hope until at last the door opened and he saw that the judge was alone with Mr Gentle and the black-haired man; heard the judge say, 'Oh, I think to avoid any scenes . . .' and dropped his voice to a low mumble while Mr Gentle and the other man nodded, looking very serious, said, 'Yes, your honour. Thank you, your honour,' and started to come out when the judge said to Mr Gentle, 'Oh, wait. There's one other point in regard to Mrs Baines,' and drew Mr Gentle back into the room.

'Well, now,' said the black-haired man, smiling and showing a lot of very white teeth. 'Well, now, PS, I'm Mr Hood. How do y' do? Goodness me, you've had quite a long wait, haven't you? Now let's see, got your coat?'

What? What was all this?

'Where's Lila?' he said. 'I have to wait for Lila.'

'Ah, I see,' said Mr Hood as though he didn't see at all, and opened the other door, and they went out into the hall but not back the way he had come with Mr Gentle.

'Where?' he asked, cold all over hanging back until Mr Hood took his hand, opening another door as sunlight hit them and he saw the little gritty courtyard where he and Lila had met Mr Gentle that other day.

Millions of little bright specks swarmed in the air, in his eyes, like beetles; yet he knew they were not really there. Nor was Lila. Beyond the iron fence there was a big black car and a chauffeur was holding open the door.

He said, 'No,' but could hardly hear his own voice. 'No,' he said, but went on down the steps towards the car, feeling cold and wet down his legs, walking stupidly like a baby as if any minute he would tumble over. 'Can I see the judge?' he asked, and Mr Hood laughed and said, 'Oh, not now. The judge is very busy,' and hoisted him into the big empty car, got in beside him.

Off they went, as he turned to look out of the back window but could see hardly anything because of the swarms of bright beetles everywhere blotting out the people in the street walking calmly about their business as though nothing was going on. Perhaps this wasn't going on and he would wake in a minute in his own safe room.

'Do you know who that is?' Mr Hood was pointing to a statue. 'That's Queen Victoria.'

Past St Mary's Cathedral now and flying under the great Morton Bay fig trees and up William Street to King's Cross, down past Rushcutter's Bay, the stadium one side and the harbour blue and shining on the other, towards Edgecliffe, towards Double Bay and beyond

422

that—another hill, then one more. He closed his eyes to shut out the beetles.

There wasn't any doubt where they were going!

'Look,' said Vanessa, opening the door to his bedroom. A big shiny blue car stood by the bed; blue leather seats, real rubber tyres, black fenders, steering wheel, a horn, pedals. A big Meccano set in a red box, a model ocean liner with three funnels, a big grey stuffed donkey on wheels, a little theatre with a curtain that went up and down and a set of little cardboard people whose legs and arms moved on strings, to act on the little stage; two new Doctor Dolittles, *The House at Pooh Corner*, *The Tale of Pigling Bland* and boxes of games—Lotto, Snakes and Ladders, and Horseracing.

He couldn't feel anything about these presents. He couldn't think about it now, couldn't think about anything yet. There were still beetles buzzing about in his eyes and ears.

Vanessa was talking all the time, forgetting her own rules and sitting on the bed, still wearing her black hat with the gold ball on it. She seemed to be explaining something to him but he couldn't take it in, couldn't hear properly because the room was so noisy and bright and he knew that he mustn't cry in front of her because he didn't want her trying to comfort him, trying to put her arms around him. He looked just past her all the time, looked through the window at the distant chimney pots of the Lawson house. By keeping his eyes very wide open and swallowing a lot, he was able to stop himself from crying but the effort made his head ache and his throat sore. The important thing was to keep looking out at the chimneys and to pretend that none of this was happening; occasionally to nod so that Vanessa would think he was listening.

'Darling,' Vanessa was saying, 'are you listening to me? Do you understand?'

Yes, yes, he understood. Of course. How do you get a chimney to stay up?

Really, Vanessa was saying, really, darling, everyone should be very happy, even Lila. He must see that the judge had taken endless trouble thinking it all out so that there could never be any arguments or trouble again. Yes, everyone was going to live happily ever after. But he only half listened. Something about the long school holidays and Lila which Vanessa thought was jolly fair considering everything that had happened. Lila was to have half of something or other but a long way off, after Christmas. Easter too. And when a public holiday fell on a Monday—did he understand? One must bow to a court decision and Vanessa would bow to it, even though she was disappointed that they had not got everything they wanted. However, that was Logan's fault. They would have got to England if Logan had not been such a stupid, vindictive fool eager to hurt her for reasons she would not go into until he was older. Never mind, everything would be one long treat from now on. There was to be no school, no piano or riding lessons for the rest of that week. It was to be a ripping holiday until next Monday with only the two of them. Would he like to go to a matinée at the theatre next Saturday? A picnic at the zoo? Ian Lawson's birthday party?

He just kept on looking at the chimney pots while she went on and on. Next year there was to be Edgecliffe Preparatory School, then, when he was ten, Cranbrook Boarding School. Listening to her mapping out his life reminded him of a dream he sometimes had of standing on a railway line with a great enormous express train bearing down on him and being unable to move a foot. Thank goodness the little new maid came bustling in at last to say that Vanessa was wanted on the telephone.

Vanessa said he could never guess in a million years what was for lunch, took a quick look at herself in the wardrobe mirror, seemed very pleased with her reflection, pleased with everything, and went clicking off downstairs.

One day, he thought, he would be grown up and then he would find the judge. You wait, he said to the judge, you just wait, seeing the judge cower, beg for mercy on his knees while the rope was put around his neck and PS (who now looked like Richard Arlen) gave quick orders to the other cowboys to get on with the lynching.

But that was only pretend and this was real. The bed was real and the wallpaper and the smell of the big house and the sound of the grandfather clock chiming downstairs. The very, very worst had happened and who could count the years it would go on. It was what Vere called 'the bloody end'. There would be no use in trying to escape because the judge would only have him brought back again. The judge was law, under the King, and that was stronger than anything in the world except God. Stuck. Absolutely stuck. Forever. Even if he were allowed to go home for—what was it?—public holiday on a Monday, no good saying he wouldn't come back because Mr Hood would come for him in a car. No use now, anything. He felt in his pocket for a handkerchief and found Lila's crushed package of marmite sandwiches. It was surprising to find himself crying like a baby over some silly sandwiches but he gave in to it, diving on to the bed and holding the pillow over his mouth so that nobody would come running. He cried until it became hiccuping; then as even the hiccuping finally stopped, he lay still, looking up at the ceiling with its white plaster ornaments. The beetles had stopped buzzing around now and he felt heavy and sleepy, wanting to nestle down into sleep and hide there from the feeling of loss. He knew that something was lost and gone and that it wasn't only

Lila. Whatever it was, he would never find it again and like the moment now of falling asleep, like the moment of being born, he would not remember.

Coming unexpectedly with warm rains and bursts of hot sunlight, steaming the lawns, the spring made Vanessa more than usually burdened with the sense of sadness and loss which comes to most people with autumn.

Spring with its vulgar, bursting, vernal greening had always filled her with a sense of mortality. She felt herself to be in direct contrast to it, full of musings on age and uselessness. In London, she had briskly dispensed with it under new cretonne slip covers and firmly shut it out behind dry-cleaned drapes.

But here, the spring was not English and gentle— hinting apologetically at summer, with bluebells and lambing. Here it was harsh and abrupt, assaulting one with sudden sharp, salt, seaweed smells, aromatic eucalyptus and the sickly sweetness of wattle. It rang with the laughter of kookaburras and the squawks of galahs.

She wakened too early in the mornings, aware of the new white-hard sun and the old remembered smells that turned her mind constantly back to Waverly. Sometimes, emerging suddenly from sleep, the persistence of girlhood was so intense that she seemed to hear Pater call to her and Sinden laugh softly.

'Go away,' she said to them, and pushing these ghosts away and kicking off the sheets angrily, would rise and brush her hair. But the ghosts lingered, nourishing their pale ectoplasm on the warm fecund air, hovering on the stairs, constantly reminding her of their presence in the smell of beeswax floor polish, linseed oil, camphor and cedarwood. Outside, the briny harbour smell mingled with arum lilies and the air was full of thunder. It made her feel that someone was walking silently close behind her and when the trees dropped tiny nuts and berries on her head and shoulders she jumped with fright.

As the days lengthened and warmed, her nervousness increased. She became quickly irritable, finicky over the folding of napkins and the necessity of scouring toilet bowls. She peered into kitchen sinks and investigated the laundry minutely; went through the house scattering orders and criticism until Ellen twice gave notice, twice took it back for a small increase in wages. In her methodical way, Vanessa tried to find a reason for her sense of disquiet. It was merely the weather, she told herself. It was the horrid Australian spring added to the natural after-effects of the court case. She had heard, or read somewhere, that victory brings with it a sense of defeat; the longed-for thing, when it comes, is not as sweet to the taste as the anticipation. Tomorrow she would feel better, get hold of herself. But more and more she strayed and the hot sky pushed down on her, full of thunder and the warnings of rainbirds. Heavens, she thought, I'm getting to be just like Lila. Then caught herself gazing across the harbour as she often did these days, wondering what Lila was doing at that exact moment, surprised to find herself wondering.

Did Lila hate her? An icy silence lay between the two houses. Lila might as well be on the moon, so why wonder about her? What was this curious new weakness that allowed Lila to intrude suddenly on her thoughts? Angry with herself, she slammed drawers, shutting Lila inside them. To hell with her.

Perhaps it had something to do with Ettie. There was an odd secrecy about Ettie these days and it was not concerned with drinking. Vanessa searched through the known caches and could find no bottle; yet Ettie tittered about, laughing easily as though she had some secret information that amused her. Was Ettie getting senile? On the contrary, she seemed more than usually alert, more socially active. Unexpected elderly ladies arrived in the afternoon for bridge and tea. ('Really, Ettie, you might have warned me. I don't think we have any cake in the house; I'll have to send Elsie out.' 'Tee-hee—I've already sent her, Ness.') It began to give Vanessa the feeling that she was the dependent one. Perhaps again, it was just this deadly spring, bringing inertia to her but filling Ettie with a new boldness. It could only be the spring of Capricorn that made Ettie suddenly take to gardening and sent her out in a large straw hat to trowel and weed among herbaceous borders. But this detracted from Vanessa's power. She was no longer able to question Jocko the gardener. He was now in cahoots with Ettie, and without any advice from Vanessa, they planted and potted, transplanted and limed relentlessly in the hot sun.

Sometimes, too, the maids would interrupt her with, 'Oh, but Mrs Bult said . . . An order had been countermanded. Vanessa, feeling a slight slap in the face, would hurry on to some other aspect of the housekeeping. When she complained that this was undermining her prestige, Ettie merely laughed at her and waxed even bolder, even going one night to the Double Bay cinema with Elsie. Vanessa was shocked but held her tongue, and hating the spring and what it did to people, excused Ettie's behaviour because there was nothing else to do.

Everything was the same, she told herself without conviction. Everything was just the same, only—only what? Why could she not shake off this ominous feeling? The ghosts hung in the air, pushed out of closets at her, whispered among the vines, and in order to exorcise them she must find the real reason.

She searched around in her mind, half-seeing it in periphery, afraid to look it in the face, putting off, excusing, delaying the showdown with herself, until, sapped by exhaustion and anxiety, she was unable to pretend to herself any longer.

It was PS.

It was something elusive that she couldn't nail down. She had anticipated remonstrance and questions and had prepared careful answers to both. He asked nothing and instead of storms there was a deadly calm. He was the model child. At first she was relieved and pleased with the success of her training. But as the weeks went by, she came to suspect something deliberate about his politeness. It occurred to her that, perhaps without even being fully aware of it, he was using her own weapons against her. She tried to prod him into arguments but to no avail—black was white if she said so. She longed for a good healthy bad-tempered screaming match that would break the ice but he maintained an obdurate submissiveness. So damned solemn and obedient that sometimes she wanted to shake him. He went about the house like a little shadow. He had developed a habit (was it planned?) of being suddenly in her path, so that hastening downstairs she would find him sitting on the landing ('Honestly, darling, stairs are not for sitting on. What are you doing?' 'Nothing.') Nothing; it was always nothing that he was doing, nowhere that he was going, nobody that he had seen today. Coming into a room, she would almost fall over him, standing just inside the door; or turning from her dressing table, discover him behind her, dreamily absorbed in the bedspread, making her jump. ('Heavens! I didn't hear you come in. It's polite to

431

knock, you know. Is there something you want, dear?'
'No, thank you.' 'Well, then can't you find something
to *do*?') She began to dread the late after-school hours
when she must invent joys, create distractions. He
would sit lumplike on her lap while she read Doctor
Dolittle until her throat was hoarse, or they would
sit silently playing ludo until, convinced that he was
only playing to amuse and distract *her*—had purposely
robbed her of her position—she would rise, defeated,
and rush out of the room on some pretended errand to
the kitchen. She told herself that it would all pass, that
he could not keep this up. But more and more she felt
he was playing some secret game with her and unless
she could learn the rules (and who can learn the rules
of children?) she would be beaten.

The toys were part of it. Filling the bathtub for
him and floating his ocean liner, she would return to
find the boat abandoned while he lay on his back in
the middle of the upstairs hall, playing with a piece
of string. Tripping over his fallen donkey, she bent
to stand it neatly upright when, appearing suddenly
behind her, he said, 'He can't stand up.' 'Why not?'
she asked. 'Because he's dead.' 'Oh, oh, poor Burro.
Why is he dead?' 'Because.' Then, shutting a window
against a sudden rain, she had seen that his new car
was standing in the downpour with its lovely leather
seats being ruined; had darted into the garden and was
wheeling it on to the side veranda when she saw him

432

watching her from behind the vines. 'PS, you mustn't leave your car out in the rain. Do you want it to rust? Do try to remember.' 'I'm sorry,' he said, bouncing a dirty rubber ball, and she knew instantly that he had wheeled the car out into the rain so that she would find it there. The impudence of it took her breath away; the hurt made her want to hurt him—hit him hard. He lifted an angelic face to her but the glint of amused triumph in his eyes had given him away and was so exactly like Logan that she turned away, shaking. 'Go and ask Elsie for a rag,' she said.

Once, waking early in the morning, her throat parched, she got up for a glass of water and found his door open, the bedroom empty. Pulsating with fright, she tore downstairs full of unreasoning thoughts of Lila, abduction and flight; ran from room to room until she found him, still in his pyjamas, squatting on the floor of the silent drawing room.

'What are you doing up? It's only six o'clock.'

Something he was hiding in his hand.

'What's that you've got?'

Obediently he held out his hand. He was holding the little piece of rock with the fool's gold that Logan had given him.

'What are you doing with that?'

'Nothing.'

Again he simply gave her that look of calculated innocence.

'Please, PS,' she said. 'Please . . .' Petering out because she wasn't sure what she really wanted of him.

She took the piece of rock and put it in the drawer of the sewing table.

Turning away from his upward gaze—it was too early in the morning to have to look at Logan—she opened a window as though she had come downstairs on purpose to do that and said, 'Do you have to creep around the house at dawn? If you wake up too early can't you stay quietly in your room and read or play with your toys? Is there something the matter with them?' Found that she was talking to an empty room.

Meaningless things, of course, and it was absurd to attach significance to them. Mrs Lawson, to whom she dropped a casual hint about it, offered her a Benson and Hedges cigarette and a morsel of assurance. Children were often like that, especially at that age. She had had similar trouble with Cynthia, who had been denied a pony and had fought her passively for six months. Vanessa, a computer at heart, vowed that she would stop adding two and two to everything he did. Yet, that very evening, when told he might now leave the table, passing Ettie's chair he flung his arms around her neck, and kissing her all over the face, said in a high-pitched imitation of someone, 'Oh, I could eat you up. Eatyouuup.'

434

'Oh, oh,' squealed Ettie. 'What lovely kisses and I didn't even ask for them.'

Vanessa, adding this to her list, said, 'Aren't *you* the favoured one!' She thought that Ettie shot her a look that said, 'Serve you right,' before returning to her seed catalogue. Vanessa ate her blancmange like crow.

She watched and waited, adding and subtracting, nursing her grievances, regarding them alone in her room as though she were looking for mothholes in the fabric of her existence.

Punished. She was being punished for doing the logical thing. The right thing. In PS's case it was the unreasonable punishment of a child who cannot understand what is best for him. But in Ettie's case it seemed to Vanessa that the punishment was malicious and even more childish. Ettie, always jealous and possessive, was punishing her for winning the case; had in an inverted way sided with PS against her.

When Ettie mentioned that one of her bridge companions was shortly going to England, Vanessa grasped at a straw. Why shouldn't Ettie go with her? They could manage perfectly well, if Ettie would like the trip. PS and she would take a smaller house, a flat, even.

But Ettie merely turned an astonished baby face to her and said, 'Why, Ness! I could never leave you. Besides, I don't want to go. I don't want to leave the garden.' Armed with gladiolus bulbs, Ettie marched out, leaving Vanessa and the situation just where they had been.

A mistake to bring it up. Like the mistake she had made with Miss Colden. It had been a monstrous slip to confide in Miss Colden. But she had always seemed so reliable, so flat-heeled and sensible, and after all, she worked so much with children that Vanessa had yielded to the temptation. The music teacher had listened attentively, patting Vanessa on the arm sympathetically, until the word 'ingratitude' touched a spring deep in Miss Colden's tartan heart.

Ingratitude was something she knew all about.

Miss Colden had come back from London, left her dear little flat in Chelsea ('Just like you, dear Miss Scott') to care for a girl named Lloydie, her friend since school days. Lloydie had got a tiny spot on the lung and Miss Colden had nursed her through a tricky operation, taken her to the mountains, cared for her, given up her musical career for her. In return, Lloydie had betrayed Miss Colden. The first intimation she had had of Lloydie's treachery was a receipt she had found ('I was just looking in her drawer for a comb, Miss Scott') for a pearl necklace that Lloydie had purchased for a girl named Mickey. ('Not that I was expecting anything for myself, Miss Scott.') Well, then, by Jove, Lloydie, without paying back one penny of all the money she owed Miss Colden, had gone into business with Mickey. They had opened a little coffee shop together and furthermore . . .

Vanessa, only half listening, had thought, Oh, God, why did I open my mouth? Why is it that if you confide a problem to people like her you have to take one of theirs in exchange? Finally, she had got up from the piano stool, hoping to put an end to it, but to her horror, Miss Colden had suddenly flung herself on to Vanessa's bosom, bawling horribly that she was so lonely. So lonely now without Lloydie that no one, except you, dear Miss Scott, could understand.

Vanessa, detaching herself from Miss Colden's embrace, had said that she did not understand and that furthermore she had no wish to.

Well, really! Miss Colden said, buckling the straps of her music case, well now, really. She had seen no reason why she could not be frank, especially as Vanessa had confided in her. She had considered Vanessa a *friend*. Dear, dear, one could certainly be wrong.

Yes, agreed Vanessa, one certainly could. And incidentally, she had been thinking for some time of enrolling PS in the Conservatorium of Music. She would not require Miss Colden's services any longer; would mail her a cheque that night.

Miss Colden had said bitterly, 'You're a fine one to talk about ingratitude, I *must* say.'

Vanessa had felt a pang of guilt watching poor Miss Colden trudge down the drive. There was something so defeated about the small kilted figure. Nevertheless Miss Colden had had no right to assume that she would be sympathetic to this tasteless little story; certainly had had no right to embrace her, touch her in that common, emotional way.

'We just didn't see eye to eye,' she told Ettie.

'Oh, what a shame. The poor dear.'

'Why is she the poor dear?'

'I'm sure she needs the money, Ness. It seems cruel, after she came to court and helped you get PS.'

Impossible to explain to Ettie.

However, the music lessons had given her a limp excuse to telephone Mr Hood. Well, now, Mr Hood had said patiently, decisions of that nature could be left entirely up to her.

But she needed advice, she had added quickly. Oh, no, it wasn't the kind of thing she would want to discuss with the judge. The judge might even think that she was not managing well. Yes, four o'clock would be fine.

What she needed was Mr Hood's firm masculine reassurance. She was surrounded by foolish women who were prey to the emotional mutations of spring. Mr Hood was a man, and a lawyer to boot, who would have no truck with fancies. He would give her that look of deep secret approval and she would be her own strong self again.

438

But Mr Hood greeted her with a surprising lack of enthusiasm and once in his office, she found it hard to explain why she had come. It was impossible to put her disquiet into words. Everything she said sounded false and out of character. She could not logically explain why toys left out in the rain frightened her.

Twice Mr Hood glanced at his watch. Finally he said, 'I'm a lawyer, not a psychologist, but aren't you making too much of this? The boy's going through a natural reaction and if I were you I'd ignore it. Let things ride for a bit.'

She wanted to say, 'But it's me. I'm running down like a clock and it isn't my imagination. I'm frightened.'

Instead she said, 'Thank you.'

Got up and shook hands, thinking, Oh, yes, you were all charm when you had a big fat fee coming to you but now I'm a nuisance. Her annoyance gave her a measure of calm. She walked out, resolved that she would confide no more in anyone.

This tug of war was between her and PS alone.

And he was waiting for her. Turning the corner into her quiet green street, she could see him looking through the grille of the front gate towards her. She waved. He did not. Yet he continued to stare right at her, vanished into thin air as she approached the gate; coming into the garden she saw him scuttling through the grape arbour towards the vegetable patch.

'Hello,' she called brightly. 'Wait a second.' But he was gone.

Please stop this game. Please!

Summer pushed spring out of the way with aching-hot blue skies, drying up the garden and browning the lawns so that the early evenings were full of the sound of gushing water from hoses and sprinklers, lawn mowers and the chatter of birds and people equally gasping for air, betting on whether or not there would be a cool, sweet, southerly buster. Everyone said it was unusually hot for October, yes, terribly hot for this time of the year and if it keeps up, imagine what it will be like by Christmas, heaven help us.

Vanessa kept the house as dark as a tomb. Sitting in the marine light of the drawing room and touching her wrists and temples with eau de cologne, she went joylessly about her preparations for the birthday party.

Lemonade, ginger beer, ice cream, paper hats, games, get the name of the hired magician, hire a slippery slide, paper streamers and gifts for the treasure hunt.

Pretty invitations.

'Whom do you want to invite?'

'I don't know.'

'Well, here's the list I got from Miss Pile. Kevin Beresford—shall we ask him?'

'I don't mind.'

'Jill Boynton-Jones? Is she one of your friends?'

'No.'

'Rather not have her? Say yes or no. It's your party.'

'I don't mind.'

'We can't have the whole class so I just want to know who your special little friends are, see?'

'I don't have any special friends.'

'Course you do. The Lawsons are your friends. You go to their house. And Jacky Green. Hilary. Aren't they your friends?'

'Some.'

'Well, tell me which ones, PS. The invitations have to go out tomorrow. What's going on in the garden?'

'Nothing.'

'Oh, I thought there must be something fascinating, the way you're staring out at it. Might I have your attention for five minutes, please? Please?'

As always, she felt pride in her work, surveying the dining room with its canopy of bright streamers and paper lanterns. Pale-blue paper plates and cups, the bonbons in glistening scarlet and green tin foil, the gifts at each place setting all wrapped in gold and silver paper bunched with ribbon. At each place a white paper rabbit held out a card requesting Jill or Kevin (in Vanessa's neat writing) to sit here. The slippery slide stood in the garden; the clues for the treasure hunt (racking her brains for clever humorous rhymes) had been hidden in the salvia bushes, the letter box, the hole in the fig tree and seventeen other carefully-thought-out, not-too-hard-to-find places. The drawing room had been cleared of breakables and the chairs stood in rows now, ready for the magician. Ellen had sweated over the cake and it sat miraculously in the pantry, two tiers of icy white ringed with blue and pink whirls, sugar roses holding up seven blue candles and 'PS' in delicious sugary silver balls.

She had lingered long in toy departments, choosing her own gift, finally had decided on a butcher's shop (the little windows read J. GRUBB & SONS) with counters, scales and minute cleavers. The little roasts of beef and loins of lamb were marzipan.

She bore it into his room, clearing the early-morning catarrh from her voice as she sang 'Happy birthday to you,' and caught a flash of appreciation on his face, quickly concealed. When Lila's brown-paper parcel arrived with the postman, he unwrapped it solemnly and held it for a long time. It was a tin sailor which, upon being wound up, jittered into a dance that was distressingly remindful of locomotor ataxia.

(Shall I explain that Lila can't come? Blame the judge? But all I will get is that closed-up look.)

He asked no questions. It was as though nothing special were going on.

'Look,' she cried eagerly, holding up paper stars. 'See?' she said, holding out little baskets of peppermint creams.

'Yes,' he said.

Please, oh please.

Stop the game.

The rainbirds called their prediction while she was dressing, and opening her bedroom window, she looked out at the sky and saw thunderheads piling up at sea. The air was sticky and hot.

Damnation. Don't let it rain after all my trouble. Except for the magician there's nothing for them to do inside. What does one do with fourteen children inside a house? The success of the party was of immense importance to her; it could, she felt, even be the turning point in this curious battle which was not of her choosing.

Promptly at three o'clock the children started to arrive in twos and threes accompanied by a swiftly departing mother or chauffeur.

She stood with PS in the garden, pleased with him in his blue blazer with the brass buttons, proud of his prim, dignified manners.

'So glad you could come,' she cried gaily to the little girls in their party dresses with the big pink and blue sashes.

'Hello, there,' she said to the boys in their best suits.

443

'Oh, how lovely,' she gushed, as PS opened each proffered gift.

The children automatically segregated themselves from their opposite sex, stood mute in little languid groups, remote as elderly people.

A dreadful lull.

'Lemonade,' called Vanessa hopefully as Elsie appeared, wheeling the mahogany cart on to the lawn. Lemonade and exquisite little *petits fours* and tiny sandwiches of bread and butter and 'hundreds and thousands'.

They lined up. Sullenly, it seemed to her.

'There's going to be a big tea later,' she warned them, laughing.

The sun came and went. Went for good. Dirty yellow clouds cast a verdigris light over the garden and the air grew hotter. Dullness ballooned over them.

'All right, everybody'—clapping her hands like teacher. 'We're going to have a game now. Who wants to put the tail on the donkey?' Waving the blindfold. 'Who wants to go first?' They stared at her resentfully. Then Cynthia Lawson said, with a sigh, 'Oh, all right; I will.'

Very little laughter, even when little Jill somebody-orother put the tail in a very ridiculous and somewhat suggestive place. Vanessa caught two defectors wandering away, ran after them ('Now, boys, everybody must play *together*. This is PS's *party*.'), returned them to

444

the game; laughed and called, 'Bravo', fought the ludicrous feeling that she was the only one behaving like a child.

The game petered out and like sheep they began straying over the lawn.

'Treasure hunt,' she announced firmly, herding them into one pack, feeling the perspiration running down her back. She had not planned to have the treasure hunt until much later, but aware of the gathering clouds, made a quick decision.

Pairing them into twos, boy-and-girl teams, took forever. Turning from a little girl to select a partner, she would return with a reluctant boy to find the girl gone. One nasty little boy whose name she had forgotten fought her off with no-nos and threats of tears.

'But, *dear*, if you don't play some little girl won't have a partner.'

'No, I don't want to.'

'Oh, well, all right then. You just watch. Now, Hilary dear, whom do you want to hunt with?'

'I'm not Hilary, I'm Margaret. *She's* Hilary.'

'So sorry, dear. Ian dear, do you want to hunt with Margaret?'

Oh, what fun, what fun, she said to them, and bitterly to herself, Oh, for God's sake, do try. For my sake, try.

Finally they were paired up. Gaily, she handed out the first clue, watched as they pored over it, asking what her handwriting meant. Again and again, tirelessly, she went through the simple rules while they stared at her dully.

'Got it? Off you go and jolly good luck to the winner.' They went off, already breaking up into threes and fours. A shambles, but for the moment they were occupied, and wishing them all in hell, Vanessa lit a cigarette and went inside.

She found Ettie talking to the magician, a waxlike man with dyed black hair and gravestone teeth.

'Didn't know it was going to be this bunch,' he said.

'What do you mean?'

'Same bunch I had a month ago. At Mrs Rutherford's party. They've seen pretty well everything I do.'

Vanessa said irritably, 'Mrs Lawson should have thought of that. Can't you find something new they haven't seen?'

The magician said it was going to be pretty hard to fool this bunch. This bunch went to a party once a week. Too many damn parties if you wanted his opinion, with a depression on and some kiddies starving.

Vanessa said crisply, 'I'm not interested in your opinions. Just pull a rabbit out of a hat!'

'Whatever you say, *miss*.'

What a hateful man. Well, she'd cook his goose with Mrs Lawson and the other mothers.

'Miss Scott?'

446

There was Cynthia, hair ribbon coming down, hot and resentful at the front door.

'Miss Scott, Molly Barker found the *treasure*!'

'*Already*?'

'Yes, but *she* was with PS!'

'Oh, but Cynthia, PS didn't know where the treasure was hidden.'

'Well, how did they go right *to* it?'

She went out with Cynthia into a sea of argument. A wraithlike little girl in a blue organdy dress was holding the prize tenaciously.

'Now, children, I'm sure that Molly and PS didn't cheat. PS, you didn't know where the treasure was hidden, did you?'

That innocent look.

'No,' he said. 'The clues were too easy.'

Thank you very much! You're a great help, I must say.

Forcing a smile, she said, 'Never mind; there are consolation prizes for everyone.'

But not for her.

The party was turning out to be a failure, as torpid as the air.

By tea time, it had become so dark that they had to turn on the lights in the dining room and while, mechanically, they sang 'Happy Birthday', thunder rumbled in the distance. She could already feel the spookiness which always swept over her when lightning was in the air; the old dreaded childhood fear that still made her want to hide in closets with a pillowcase over her head. She prayed that the storm would hold off long enough for the party to be over, so that she might then shut herself in her room, pull down the blinds and stuff her ears with cotton wool. But the thunder rolled nearer and when pale sheet lightning flickered outside the windows she said in an undertone to Elsie, 'Put the knives away.'

('Don't be such a silly-billy, Ness.' 'I can't help it, Mater'. 'It's only combustion; it can't hurt you.' 'It can. I saw a picture of a little girl all burned up.' 'She was standing under a tree. It's only dangerous if you're standing under a tree.')

'Oho,' she laughed, as the thunder cracked now almost overhead. Remembering an old childhood joke, she said, 'They're moving furniture in heaven,' but the practical children of today looked up from their ice cream, unamused.

'What about a nice quiet game in the drawing room as soon as you've all had birthday cake? PS, when you're finished, would you take your guests into the drawing room?'

She ran upstairs, closing windows against the sudden fat raindrops, shuddering as the rocking claps sounded directly overhead and shook the house deeply below her.

448

Nerving herself, she started downstairs again, pausing once on the landing when a boom of thunder overhead startled her so that she wanted to scream. Ridiculous. Neurotic, at her age, still to be unable to throw off this silly phobia, but there she stood, shaking all over.

Old maid. Cringing on the stairs, afraid of a little thunder. Terrible if one of the children caught her. Humiliating. Holding herself rigid, she went on downstairs, and hearing laughter, thought, Well, at last they're enjoying themselves; perhaps the storm has livened them up. Putting on a bright smile, she went towards the drawing room door, then stopped dead, her hand gripping the glass knob, hearing PS say in a clear light voice:

'Oh. Oh, I say, what jolly awful thundah.'

Unable to understand for a moment, she waited.

'Ugh, what fraightful lightning and thundah; we'll all be killed.'

For a boy of seven it wasn't a bad imitation. He had even caught the nuances of her voice, the slightly Mayfair accent. She pushed the door open. He was mincing up and down in an approximation of her walk; in one hand he held an unlit cigarette while with the other he prodded a sofa cushion. 'Oh, PS, PS,' he said, 'you must get up, do you heah me?' Then, spinning around at the sound of thunder (which Vanessa no longer heard), said:

'Oh, hold me, Logan. Hold me.'

The children laughed and Cynthia said, 'Who's Logan?'

'My father.'

'Does he live with you now?'

'No, but that's what she says sometimes when she's frightened.'

He hugged the cushion, wriggling all over, shaking with pretended terror. 'Oh, oh, Logan. Hold me!'

The children laughed and some clapped their hands at his performance. Then, when thunder again rocked the house, they began imitating him, running around, jumping up and down, calling in high, excited voices, 'Oh, hold me, hold me. Oooo, Logan!' It had suddenly turned into a nightmare game, a madhouse of children capering in time to the thunder in an obscene travesty of her.

Then PS saw her. When he smiled, an electric shock went through her. She sprang across the room, knocking over a gyrating child, feeling the roots of her hair tingling, her face on fire, and grabbing him, she shook him.

Shook him and shook him, speechlessly, hearing nothing but explosions in her ears, hearing the roaring of water, of boiling surf, while blinding lights burst in front of her eyes and the curious faces of the still children watched, drawing in a ring around them. Shook him, seeing his face gradually going purple, his arms dangling, not resisting her, while all the time he continued to smile at her. Smiled and smiled while she shook and shook, hearing now the ugly panting sounds coming from her as her strength drained, and beaten, she pushed him and he fell away from her, fell heavily on the floor and looking up with an intensity of hate, smiled once more.

Then, turning away from him, she saw through scalding water the blur of fascinated angelic faces.

'Go away,' she said in a husk of a voice. 'Go home.'

Blundered through an earthquake, past the falling walls of the room, past Ettie and the maids, turned to stone, towards the hall, towards a staircase that was tumbling towards her, fell up it.

Cried out. She had not cried like that for as long as she could remember. Not even when Pater died.

Lying now in the muggy darkness, she could hear nothing but the steady drip of water on tin, an occasional toot of a ferry.

Twice Ettie knocked on the door, murmuring about aspirin or a tray. Did she want dinner on a tray?

'Go away,' she said.

Go away!

Much later, she heard the bubbling of his voice, mingled with Ettie's cooing, and heard him going into his room, probably to bed without brushing his teeth

451

in order to punish her, and she laughed, thinking, What could possibly punish or hurt me now? She felt as remote from him and Ettie as the Pleiades. Let them go their childish ways for now. This time was hers and now that the first shock of unbelievable hurt had passed, she could think clearly, stand outside of herself and watch with a certain amount of pride the return of her own inner strength. The shock, the final exposure of PS's hatred, had destroyed the last remaining wall of pretence between them and given her an extraordinary release. Now that the explosion was over, she was no longer afraid; a conclusion had been reached and to her orderly mind it must now have a purpose. She must and would survive this, she must rise up strong and renewed, belonging to herself. She must reach beyond the deceiving explanations which in the past she had always clung resolutely to, bandaging her wounds before setting out blindly to be wounded again.

No longer.

It will hurt a little, she said, being the doctor. But you are being born tonight and so for a little time you must endure the pain.

Start.

Start at the beginning and remember them all. The dearly loved faithless and cruel ones. Go back into the classroom and look at pale, lovely Miss Mortimer. How you loved her. Took her custard apples and green maidenhair fern and put them on her desk in front of the giggling girls; composed, agonisingly, a lyrical ode to her in poetry class. What a slap in the face when she said, I do not care for mush, Vanessa, even when it scans, which meant, I do not love you—you are only one of twenty-six meaningless pupils, and you saw, suddenly, that really she had a face like a haddock and a soul made of dried walnuts. The boy at Waverly with the classic shoulders and the face of a Bellini cherub. When he kissed you and held you a moment, you were filled with such unbelievable joy that you wanted to give him everything you possessed, which, at fourteen, was one shilling and tenpence in small change; you pressed it into his hand and he threw it down on the grass and said, look I don't take money for it; went and told his friends that the little Scott girl wanted to pay for it and they roared! So you ran to Pater and blurted it all out in a fit of sobs and Pater said, but my dearest, those boys are just very ordinary, just trades-people, and they wouldn't understand that you were just being sweet my angel and anyway I love you more than all the boys in the world. But when you confided in Sinden, she said, oh but Ness you hurt his pride— I would have just let him kiss me. But Sin, you said, I was only trying to show him I loved him back, the way I do when I give Pater little things, and Sinden said, well Ness they can't all be like Pater.

Maybe one can, you said, seeing him run ahead of you, pure of heart like yourself. Tender and admiring.

Not wanting to defile you, only love you, love you so that the sex would only be part of the divine relationship.

But why must you legislate people Ness? asked Vere, all bosom at nineteen and with a parade of lovers. You can't legislate people. Rot, Vere. I'm not trying to legislate, just sift a little and find what I'm looking for. But do you know what it is? Certainly. And you went on hammering the shapes and souls of men until they resembled nothing but strangers and you could not love them. Tom, Dick and Harry all refused to be made over in your mould. But one came close, seemed to fit. Beautiful Logan in Bacchus Marsh with that tenderness and respect that made you certain—almost certain—that he understood.

Wrong again. Logan was sly and treacherous; the baker's boy fumbling for you in a dark paddock and even though you wept for him you knew he could not be changed.

Oh, but when you heard! They thought you were hysterical that day, sitting on the terrace at somebody's dull luncheon at Henley on Thames when the cable came in typical Sindenese saying, darling I have married beautiful teeth Bacchus Marsh guess who isn't life incredible letter follows. And everyone said good heavens Vanessa what can be so terribly amusing? Do you remember him? Does he have a wooden leg? You said you were laughing because honestly it was very funny but a family joke, impossible to explain. Impossible to tell them that suddenly you were choking with fury. Not over Logan—oh to hell with him, you got over that hurt years ago—but because Sinden had been able to do something you couldn't. Because Sinden always had been able to love without trying to change anything. Sinden was really the pure in heart, unquestioning, unafraid to run out in the storm and find what she wanted while you quaked in closets with pillowcases over your head.

What a fraud you are, Logan had said.

If only you had understood him then. Because it all came to nothing and there was no love.

Even the man in Paris, when you said I can't leave Ettie but knew it was because you couldn't change him.

None of them.

Ah, but if you could mould the child!

Not Logan, but PS. If PS loved you, it would (in Pater's words) restore the years that the locusts have eaten.

But PS detests you and you are beaten. From now on there will be no one. You are quite alone.

You don't know how to love.

All right, now you've said it. At least you know who and what you are.

Now you have been born.

* * *

Someone, Jocko probably, was mowing the lawn and she turned, opening her eyes, to gaze stupidly at the clock and was astonished to find that it was long after ten.

For the first time in her life she had gone to sleep in her clothes and it amused her slightly to find that she had already begun her new life (remembering instantly and clearly) by doing something out of the ordinary.

She undressed and took a shower, grateful that PS had gone to school and that Ettie was not yet up and about. She wanted a little more time to prepare herself for them.

She felt a curious sense of suspension, of being neither happy nor unhappy, and at the same time released. The ominous feeling of the last few weeks had vanished—and this morning the summer sounds and smells brought no ghosts with them. She was no longer wavering. She knew exactly what she must do and the anticipation of it had begun to please her; it itched a little, like a healing cut.

Wanting change, she dressed her hair differently, moving the parting further to the side and folding the soft bun a little lower. She looked, she thought, rested and well, considering everything. She put on a new shantung dress which she had been saving. (For what? Where do I ever go? Who ever really looks at me?) She put on her tan-and-white shoes, and admiring herself in the mirror, lingered, fully aware of the acceptance of her own vanity and the new freedom of not caring tuppence if anyone caught her or what anyone thought because there was now only herself to please.

She went downstairs and through the green baize door into the kitchen and asked could she have some breakfast. Anywhere will do, she said pleasantly to Ellen and Elsie's startled faces expecting a woe-begone creature or an avenging angel. But eggs, please, if it isn't too much trouble, and some bacon too, as she was starving. Absolutely starving.

'I somehow missed dinner,' she told them needlessly.

She sat in the warm sun in the dining room. Someone had thoughtfully removed the paper streamers and all the reminders of the party. She read in the *Sydney Morning Herald* that tonight the world would end. That was, according to a Dr Pollack and the disciples of the Temple of Everlasting Love, where they would gather at sundown to await the arrival of the Saviour. Poor Agnes. Who is going to have ever such a red face? Feeling the need now to talk of inconsequential things, she delayed Elsie, bringing the eggs at a run, with chat about the weather, summer uniforms and the scandalous price of fish. When Ettie came wavering in, kissed her inquiringly, she said, 'Dear, I'm all right, really. Really. I don't want to talk about it.'

Wait.

She walked around the garden, admiring everything, smelling roses and hibiscus, and feeling that this morning the salt-harbour breeze and tang of damp eucalyptus leaf were not distressing reminders of lost youth but merely pleasant assurances that she was very much alive. She chatted for a time with Jocko, asking questions about soil and espaliers, granting him quick, easy smiles and small compliments. At noon, watching the gate, she remembered suddenly that this was swimming-lesson day and that PS would not be home until after three.

Three long hours yet.

Ettie observed her curiously, following at short distances, humming nervously; and finally, getting no clue, she disappeared upstairs with a pretended headache.

At three thirty, Vanessa stood in the drawing room, impatiently watching the road for Miss Pile's car. It was close to four before it appeared. She saw him climb out and wave, delaying until the car had driven off before he turned in at the gate and came up the driveway very slowly, holding his wet bathing suit and gazing up at the house reluctantly. When she heard him coming in the front door she called out:

'PS, would you come in here a minute, please.'

Funny. She hadn't even told him to first go and hang up his wet bathing suit. So he held on to it, not knowing

458

what to do or what was coming. She looked different too. Not just her hair, which looked pretty, very pretty, today, but her face. Almost as if she were someone else. Someone he didn't know.

He had expected that right off she would deliver punishment for the naughty thing he'd done; one of those longwinded speeches of hers, all about friends and hurt and gratitude, finally telling him that there would be no going to the circus, no reading in bed for a long time, and he had been ready with his sorrys. Ready to tell her that he didn't really know why he had done it, it just seemed a funny thing to do at the time.

Instead of that, she asked him about swimming. Was he doing breast stroke or overarm? Which did he like best? It was as though nothing had happened at the party, maybe ever. Like having to talk to someone's dull mother while your playmate has gone out of the room. This certainly wasn't like Vanessa at all, and frightened, he felt that something terrible must be coming—it was always terrible when she was very still and polite.

But suddenly she looked directly at him and said in a very quiet, distant voice:

'Since this concerns you first and foremost, I'm telling you before anyone else. I'm giving you up.'

He didn't understand. Giving him up? To what? Who? Alarmed, he thought of the police. The judge.

'For good,' said Vanessa calmly. 'Do you understand? Tomorrow I am going to the judge and shall explain to him that I wish to withdraw from my guardianship and that nothing will change my mind. It will be up to the judge then to decide what will be best for you under the circumstances, but I would think that he will have no other recourse but to give you to Lila.'

He couldn't move or speak so he just sat there, feeling his wet bathing suit against his bare knees. He knew now that what he'd done had been so bad that it had changed everything.

Then Vanessa said, looking out of the window, 'I'm going to talk to Lila about it this evening. I'm going over to see her. In the meantime I'd rather you didn't mention it to anyone, even to Cousin Ettie.'

All this time. Over and over he had dreamed of this and knew it would never happen. But she had said it. Said that he was going home for good. Why couldn't he jump up and down and scream with joy?

Vanessa didn't want him any more, because of what he'd done. Yet she didn't seem to be upset, not even angry. She was gazing out at the late-afternoon shadows on the lawn with her head a little to one side as though she were listening to music far away.

After a while she said in the sort of polite voice she always used to a stranger who rather bored her:

'I hope you'll grow up to be something.'

It seemed to be over because she got up suddenly and he thought she was going to walk quickly out of the room but instead she crossed to the fireplace and for a moment she looked up at the picture of his mother and said:

'Everybody's going to get exactly what they want and that now includes me.'

She took a cigarette out of the box on the mantelpiece and looking for a match, pulled open the little drawer of the sewing table. The stone Logan had given him rolled out and fell on to the carpet, glittering in the red sunlight.

Vanessa picked it up.

She said, 'This isn't really gold, you know.'

'I know,' he whispered.

'You'd better hang on to it,' she said, handing him the stone. 'When you're older, it may remind you not to go scrambling around all your life for the wrong thing. There are certain things that one just can't have and hankering after them can make you miss the right ones.'

She found a matchbox and lit her cigarette, watched the flame burn down.

Then she said, 'Everybody looks for something that we call love. An awful lot of people never find it and they end up with something that isn't any more real than the gold in that stone. Nobody can tell you which is real or fake—it's a different thing to

461

everybody. It isn't what Lila thinks or what I think. It isn't just being kissed and cuddled and tucked warm into bed either. One day you'll be hurt and there won't be anyone to say, "Oh, come here, pet, and I'll kiss it and make it better." There'll only be yourself.'

She stopped again by the window and glanced out at Jocko hosing the rose beds.

'Poor thing,' she said, and for a minute he didn't know whether she meant him or Jocko. 'You haven't had much of a chance up to now, being pushed and pulled around by all of us. Remember that grownups can be jolly well wrong about a lot of things. Remember that I told you that. Listen, PS, after I'm gone don't let them try to turn you into something you don't want to be. And don't just be a PS to your mother. Find you. If you can find out who you are and what you are, my dear, then you'll know how to love someone else. That's all I have to say.'

That is the last thing I will ever say to you, she seemed to be saying. He looked up at her face and saw that she was neither angry nor sad but gone away from him. In the room but no longer there, in a funny way. Something had been taken away from him and it frightened him. He didn't understand all this stuff she had told him but he knew it was a goodbye.

Now he wanted her to slap him and scream at him that he was wicked, the wickedest boy in the world, so that he could tell her that he was really sorry—so

462

sorry now for what he did. Sorry for both of them in a way.

He wasn't happy with the wonderful news. Perhaps later on he'd be happy but not now, not until he'd been able to say something sweet to Vanessa.

But he couldn't think of anything and knew that this was his last chance because Vanessa had put out her cigarette, picked up a scarf and her bag and was going towards the front door.

He ran after her, and hearing him, she stopped for a moment with her back towards him. He came up beside her and when she didn't move he put out his hand and touched her gently on the arm, and finding nothing to say, waited there beside her until she gave a funny little laugh and said:

'Well, well, PS. It seems that I have finally done something to please you.'

Then she went out, banging the front door, leaving him alone in the suddenly dark hall.

Vanessa took the tram to Circular Quay, sitting outside and not caring if the wind blew her hair about. She had come out hatless and had forgotten her gloves but it added to her feeling of informality. When the nice young tram conductor took her fare, she smiled at him like a young girl going to town for a pleasant outing. She looked forward to the twenty-minute boat trip to Neutral Bay. She had never before taken the ferry to Lila's house, had always gone by cab or hired car over the Harbour Bridge, but for one thing it was not yet five o'clock and she wanted George to have left for his nightly job so that she and Lila could be alone, and for another it seemed part of her expiation. There must be no showing off to the neighbours, no driving up in a big black limousine. She wanted to arrive unannounced, ring the doorbell and say to the dumbfounded Lila, might she come in? Could she come in, as she had something important to say that could not be said over Miss Gulf's, telephone. So might they just sit in the kitchen and have a cup of tea quietly together as in the old days at Waverly?

My dear, Lila would say excitedly to George later, you could have knocked me over with a feather. There was Ness at the front door, come all the way by boat and tram, and just as nice as she could be, asking might she come in. Well, my dear, I don't know what has happened but she's a *new* person! Now, you know that even as girls we were never close and then when she said, when she told me—

No, stop, she cried elatedly to herself, laughing at her old trick of playing the scene ahead of time. It wouldn't be like that. Lila wouldn't have changed— would still be bitter about the court case, instantly suspicious of motives and very much on her guard over Vanessa's sudden about-face. But in the end, Lila would understand. Perhaps even see that in giving up PS there was a healing up of the years.

Giving up. That was it. Oh, what blessed relief there is in giving up something. The absolution of resignation. Oh, why fear? In resignation there is honesty and purity of the soul. At bedrock there is a peculiar peace.

She looked around at the gradually crowding tram and at the tightly knotted worried faces around her reading the bad news in the evening papers, and she wanted to cry out, 'Look at me, everybody. I've got the answer, kids.'

The sun lowered. They swung towards town into the evening bustle. She climbed off and on to another tram, where she had to strap-hang all the way to Circular Quay. She walked on air through a turnstile and through the faintly silver light down the little wooden gangplank on to the ferry. Nothing bothered her. Not even the rude, shoving businessmen, leaping for the best seats outside so that there was no room for her.

'Terrible,' said someone behind her. 'Terrible,' agreed a weary woman shopper, 'the way everyone pushes and barges. No respect any more. No manners today.'

She laughed, not caring a hoot about being pushed and jostled with the evening crowd or that some oaf had trodden on her tan-and-white shoes, leaving a big black smudge.

She found a seat inside the ladies' cabin, which

smelled of old wet rope, tar and detergent. She had bought an evening paper but did not open it. She was too alive with thoughts.

A toot, and they were off, pushing away from the wharf, and she watched the retreating city beginning to flicker with night signs against the dying sun. A huge bottle lit up, poured red lights into a white-light champagne glass, commanded that you drink 'PENFOLD'S WINE', erased itself, lit again and poured, erased and lit, vanishing as they chugged out over the darkening harbour.

Soon there would be another boat, which would carry her down the harbour and out of the Heads towards Ceylon, Aden, Naples and so to London, never to come back.

Breathes there a girl with soul so dead (asked Miss Mortimer in poetry class) who never to herself has said this is my own, my native land? Yes, ma'am, and it's I!

She closed her eyes and saw Harrods, saw Portobello Road. But not quite yet. There was an obligation to Ettie. If Ettie wished to remain transplanted in her new garden, spreading her roots, all right. On the other hand, if she wished to go 'home', they would return together and then, once safely back in London, gradually the bonds could be cut. There would be scenes, of course.

You are deserting me!

No, I am taking myself back. Mater gave me to you but I am now taking myself back. It has been long enough.

If Ettie decided to stay, well and good; she would be able to sail sooner. Without a salary, second class or tourist might be all she could afford but it didn't matter. It would be the *Argo*, sailing to new worlds where something waited for her. Something vast and incalculable that had waited for her through the years she had wasted, fussing and fuming about the importance of being nothing.

There would be time to think of all this on the ship. There would be time after that, when she had a nice little cosy flat to herself. There was endless time. All the time in the world was hers, for she had just been born.

But were they stopping? Were they already at the wharf? Bells and whistles sounded. The engines reversed. Were they going back? People were running to the windows, standing on the seats, all looking out.

'What is it?' she asked.

'They're jumping over,' someone screamed.

'Who?' she cried. 'What is it?'

She stood up and was pushed by the crowd. Astonished, she saw they were climbing through the windows.

'The other side,' a man yelled at her.

'Is it a fire?' But he had already pushed past her.

They were all pushing past her out of the cabin; had gone suddenly mad. She rushed with them into the bottleneck at the door, heard the deafening blast of the huge whistle right above them and saw, in an instant, the immense shadow looming over them, scooping them up with the frightful noise of steam and steel, lifting her up with the others, then letting her fall with the others, sprawling into arms and legs so quickly that she felt no shock, only one flash of thought:

Dear sweet Jesus, Agnes was right. It's the end.

But being hurled down as water struck her into blackness, then into dazzling, blinding light.

No. The beginning.

Lila said, 'Who is it? We seem to have a bad connection.'

The worried voice from Mars seemed to be screaming now 'Ettie.'

'Ettie! What is it? What's—'

Something about Ness.

'Can you speak up?'

'Is Ness with you?'

'Ness? No. No; why? Is PS ill, is—'

The gargling voice said something about PS. 'What?'

'PS says she went over to see you.'

'To see me? What about? Is something wrong?'

Something about four o'clock and being worried to death.

'What about four o'clock? What happened?' Lila screamed back into the phone, and Miss Gulf said from the bedroom, 'Mrs Baines, my sister's trying to sleep.'

Lila said, 'Speak slowly, Ettie.'

'. . . and PS says she . . . to see you . . . hasn't come home.'

'No, she didn't come here. I've been home all day.'

Ettie said something about the accident. What? Hadn't Lila heard about the terrible ferry accident? It had been on the wireless all evening. A P and O liner and a ferry collided. . . . Yes, yes, terrible but—

'Ettie, she wouldn't have come without phoning first. Anyway, Ness would *never* come all the way by tram and boat—and why on earth would she come here? This is the last place—'

Poor souls. Some of them trapped inside. Went down in seconds.

'Not Ness, Ettie. Never on a ferry. Probably with friends and hasn't noticed the time. But is PS all right? Is he up so late? Can I speak to him, please?'

Hello? But Ettie had hung up.

A bright full moon hung over the back yard and one of Mater's old wives' tales stirred in Lila's mind. If you slept with the full moon shining on your face you would go insane. That was the genesis of the word

469

lunacy. People became disturbed during the full-moon cycle and Ettie had responded to it and had probably taken a little too much wine with dinner.

She leaned over the damp veranda rail and stared down into the motionless garden. The black moon shadow of the pepper tree reached across the straggly uncut grass towards George's dead vegetable patch. Nothing stirred. Even the night crickets were still. Everything lay in a dead bleached light. Her washing on the line dangled with spectral arms and legs.

But why would Vanessa be coming to see *me*?

She looked across the harbour and saw a distant Manly ferry twinkling serenely towards the Heads, carrying home late sleepy theatregoers.

It's lunatic to think that anything might have happened. Ness is home by now and probably furious with Ettie for phoning me.

The thought of Vanessa, tall and angry, soothed her for a moment. She could see her very clearly. She was standing now in the pink-lit safe drawing room at Point Piper, watching a match burn down, her eyes half closed and saying something very cutting.

But away in the distance where the dark headland jutted out between Neutral Bay and Cremorne, a little circlet of lights bobbed on the dark water.

Would that be the place? A fairy ring of little lanterns on buoys to safeguard the harbour traffic from—How deep would it be there?

She shivered.

Ugh. A goose walked over my grave.

She went quickly inside to the silent kitchen. The thought that had struck her was so shocking that she felt her face go hot with shame.

If Vanessa were dead . . .

'God forgive me,' she said aloud, and pulled down the blind to shut out the oppressive moonlight.

God forgive me, she said to herself again, feeling the beginning of a terrible prescience.

'He is nigh unto us,' bellowed Dr Pollack, sweating with disappointment. 'He comes. Glory in the highest.'

'"Praise Him all ye lands",' sang Agnes, leading the reluctant few disciples who still remained. '"He is come",' she sang as the moon sank and darkness swept over the Temple.

They sat again in murmuring silence and Dr Pollack said, 'Friends, He comes to us in many ways. Don't forget that we can't always see Him with our blinded eyes but I tell you He is here among us. We have not come in vain.'

'Not in vain,' repeated Agnes, seeing several others leaving.

'"I am going, I am going to the Land. I am going with His lantern in my hand. Amen".' They sang again as a slight wind stirred the lantana bushes.

'He is in the wind,' Dr Pollack assured them. 'He is in the stars. He is all around us. He comes.'

They sat again and waited, coat collars turned up against the chilly wind, bottoms numb on the hard concrete. Below them the surf slapped and sucked at the beach, retreated beaten to try again tomorrow. Lights bobbed on the distant harbour, the last tram from Balmoral whined its way up the hill and a nocturnal animal in the zoo gave a despairing cry for Africa.

No one came.

The telephone awakened the sleeping big house very early in the morning and he heard Elsie answer it. After that there was a lot of coming and going up and down the stairs. Boards creaked everywhere. Doors opened and shut and once he heard Cousin Ettie say angrily, 'This is my house and I will do as I wish.'

He dressed himself quickly, finding last night's clothes surprisingly not put away but lying untidily on the floor where he had sleepily left them for Vanessa to tidy up.

Vanessa's bedroom door was shut so she must still be asleep, having come home so late last night; goodness, it must have been late. He had never been up after eleven before in his life. But what had happened? All Cousin Ettie had said, after the telephone call, was that he was a good precious lamb to stay up so late but Ness was all right, perfectly all right, and goodness, she could see the sandman right now so off to bed, petkin. He went downstairs, where Elsie gave him a frightened look. Her face was as red as a prawn and so was Ellen's.

Did Vanessa come home? he asked, and yes, yes, they said, she was OK, love. How about some nice porridge with them in the kitchen to save laying the table in the dining room? He sat and had his porridge and treacle while they whispered and spelled things and twice the telephone rang and they got in the way of each other trying to get to the telephone first. Then a doctor came in a car and hurried upstairs, and frightened now, he asked is Vanessa sick? No, love. Your cousin Ettie's feeling a bit crook this morning. Just a bit crook, that's all. How about some nice scrambled eggs, eh? What a treat. But his appetite was suddenly all gone. He knew something was very wrong because Ellen said he was not going to school that morning, he was going to have a real nice holiday-what-a-treat! Nobody seemed to know what to do with him. Go and play, they said. What a crime to be inside on a lovely morning like this, they said, wheeling his blue car into the garden, and when he lingered half in and half out of the doorway, trying to listen, trying to spell, they shooed him with, aprons and red hands and gaping big smiles to run and play, find something to do, and finally Ellen said quite sharply to for God's sake get out from under their feet. Jocko was talking over the fence to the gardener next door and when they saw him coming they stopped talking very suddenly and made some very poor jokes about Santa coming pretty soon now, eh, almost November now so almost time to hang up your stocking. Poo, he said to them, Santa is George. I saw his boots once.

It was a funny lost feeling not going to school and he wondered what was going on at Miss Pile's and if they were all whispering about him in class. He looked up a lot at the house towards Vanessa's window but the blind stayed pulled down and so did the one at Ettie's window.

Finally Ellen opened the kitchen door and called him.

'Your aunty's coming,' she said.

'Which one?'

'The other one.'

'Lila?'

'Yes. She's just phoned up to say she's coming right after lunch for you.'

'Am I going home?'

'Yes, love. Now I'm going to pack your little bag so be a good boy and don't go upstairs, see, there's a love. Because Mrs Bult's quite crook and the doctor's given her a nice pill to make her sleep so we don't want to wake her up now, do we?'

Ellen went off on tiptoe.

So it was true. Vanessa meant it. She had given him up and Lila was coming after lunch to take him home.

474

But—

Was Vanessa still cross with him? So cross that she wouldn't come down just to shake hands and say goodbye? So he could say his piece now. He had it all ready and it was very nice really, the nicest thing he'd ever thought to say to anyone, even Vere. She hadn't been a bit cross yesterday, only different, so why wouldn't she open her door and come clicking downstairs the way she always did, asking, Where was this? What was that doing there? Had the post come? Or something. Well, she would come down for luncheon, as she called it.

But she didn't.

While Ellen's back was turned he slipped out of the kitchen and went upstairs, trying to avoid the places that creaked. He knocked on Vanessa's door and waited for her to say who was it? When she didn't, he turned the glass handle very softly and opened the door a crack. The room was very dim but he could see the bed neatly made up with the eiderdown quilt folded at the bottom and Vanessa's satin slippers standing by it. On the dressing table were her silver hairbrushes and combs and the picture of Grandfather Scott all waiting for her. The only sound was the faint ticking of her little gold clock on the table by the bed.

Vanessa had escaped.

He was certain now. She had run off and left them all, without a goodbye or anything and that was what all the whispering was about and why Cousin Ettie had to have the doctor. There was something spooky and sad about all these things waiting for Vanessa, all these things that she had left behind without a word. Not even goodbye.

He closed the door and went downstairs as fast as he could away from them. Away from that silent, spooky room and into the sunlight, and seeing Lila coming in the gate, he tore down the driveway to her and cannoned into her, nearly knocking her down, asking anxiously:

'Where is Vanessa? Where is Vanessa?'

Lila looked very old and tired and her face was a funny grey colour.

She said, 'Darling, Vanessa's gone away.'

'Where?'

'Well—'

It was a long while since he had seen Lila and perhaps she had grown old in that time. How very grey her hair was, under her prune-coloured hat.

'Where?' he asked again.

Lila didn't seem to want to say. She took his hand and they started walking up the driveway towards the house in silence.

Finally Lila said in a choked up voice:

'She's gone to a nice place for a rest—sort of like a place in the country.'

'But she didn't take any of her things,' he said. 'Did she just escape?'

'Yes,' said Lila. 'She escaped.'

'Oh,' he said. 'Well, she wanted to. She was going to give me back, you know.'

But Lila didn't seem to hear. She was just standing there holding a handkerchief up to her face.

It wasn't until much later at home, in his own bedroom, and after there had been a lot of arguing in the kitchen, that George came in and sat down on the bed, stroked his head and said:

'PS, we're not going to tell you fibs any more. Vanessa has died, PS.'

Funny that he couldn't feel anything, not even very surprised. Only as if something had stopped and it was very, very quiet everywhere in the world.

'Oh,' he said. And then as the quietness grew and grew, 'I see.'

Lila thought that her flowers looked very nice. Yellow roses in a sheaf. Pondering dazedly at the florists, still unable to believe what had happened, the reason she was buying flowers, she had asked vaguely for something simple, not lilies—her sister had disliked lilies. While the young assistant had flustered around trying to sell her some vulgar wax everlastings under glass (a nice permanent reminder, madam) which would have outraged Vanessa, she had seen the roses and remembered something long forgotten, some mix-up at Pater's funeral and poor Ness's yellow roses quite accidentally left behind at the parlour. They were the most expensive things in the shop and Lila had had a shameful moment of indecision before saying she wished two dozen and just a simple ribbon, please. She had written on the card: 'With love from PS.'

The coffin was banked with flowers. Most of them were extravagant wreaths with non-committal calling cards reading 'Mrs Alexander G. Lawson' and 'Mrs John Boynton-Jones'. Vanessa might have thought them too obvious. Even Ettie's enormous wreath of white carnations and pale-blue cornflowers seemed an overstatement of grief. Ettie, too ill to be present, was crying out for attention, for Ness please to look, please to understand that *her* grief was deeper than all the others'.

Certainly the yellow roses were the nicest and someone at the parlours must have thought so because only the roses lay on top of the mahogany casket.

So hot, thought Lila. And her black dress smelled so terribly *new*! Seven and ninepence for a black straw hat at Way's and wouldn't you know that right away something would go wrong with it. The brim would not stay down, kept flipping up, giving her a silly schoolgirlish appearance. She was fiddling with it now, worrying about her hat, the heat, and who should go to the cemetery with them in the limousine.

The young minister was saying that God in His infinite wisdom had seen fit to gather up the soul of their beloved sister Vanessa. Vanessa, a dutiful servant of the Lord, had been taken to glory because her life, though short, had been full of generosity and kindness to others.

How Vanessa would have hated this psalm-singing young hypocrite mouthing clichés, hurrying them through because very likely there was another service to follow.

I am the Resurrection and the Life; if any man come unto me . . .

And what hypocrites we are, thought Lila, looking across at Vere dabbing at her eyes, at the cook and house maid blowing red noses.

She wished that she could weep for Vanessa. Weep for her honestly and not out of a feeling of guilt and horror because she had died violently in a second when a ferryboat captain had misjudged his speed.

Let us pray.

But only one of them here in this pitifully small attendance knew nothing of the way she died. Vanessa's heart just stopped, Lila had told him, and he had accepted it in the same curiously detached way he had accepted the whole thing. In years to come she would tell him what had happened, leaving out the things they had told George when he had had to go down to the wharf because, well, *someone* had to go.

She had repaid George's kindness by getting angry with him, by yelling at him not to tell her things that would give her nightmares for years to come. Oh, God, poor Ness, poor Ness, she had cried out, and then excoriated her anguish by fiercely overriding George's objections to PS's attending the funeral. Vere and George had both said he should not go and she had screamed at them to mind their own business.

'He will pay Vanessa some respect!'

But why didn't he cry?

She looked down at him, sitting between her and George.

If there was anything at all that lingered on, could see them all sitting there, it might be comforting to know that one person cried honestly for it, even a child.

But PS was counting the brass studs on the seat.

They stood under the brazen sky while kookaburras laughed in the gum trees and a hot dry wind blew bits of old newspaper and dead leaves over their feet.

The minister rattled on while Lila held on to the brim of her hat, shielding her eyes from the blazing sun, feeling her new black dress sticking to her back, remembering the same heat, the same noise of flashing insects, the same sad smell of freesias when seven years ago they had stood here for Sinden. How strange it was. Seven years and a few days' difference. Everything was the same, and yet so different. Then she had been so racked with grief that George had had to hold her up.

480

Now she felt only wretchedly hot and tired and was longing for it to be over. Well, it was nearing the end. They were slipping ropes around the coffin, ready to lower it into the opened earth.

'"Yea, though I walk through the valley of the shadow of death . . ."' intoned the minister in the dry voice of one announcing yet another departure of a suburban train, and PS took a step forward. Lila glanced down at him, hoping that in this final moment of parting he might burst into a flood of reasonable tears, thus absolving them all and giving some meaning to the worn-out ritual. But she saw on his face only the brightness of curiosity.

He edged forward another step but this time she caught hold of him by the shoulder and said in an undertone, 'Stay here.'

'I want to see.'

'There's nothing to see,' she whispered almost angrily.

'But is it in there?'

'What?'

'The *other* box.'

Appalled, she wanted to slap his face. She wanted to shake him and to cry out that he was morbid and unnatural and how dare he ask such a question? But that would simply prove to George and Vere that they had been right. It was her own fault. She had wanted to make a gesture of atonement to Vanessa and had made

481

the wrong one. Even at the very end she had made one of her usual mistakes and she heard Vanessa say, 'You *know* I would have given strict orders that he was not to be here, Lila.'

I'm sorry, Ness.

'Amen,' she said aloud in response to the minister, closing his prayer book.

'No, dear,' she said to him quietly, turning him away. 'There's nothing else there.'

'Vanessa said there was.'

Yes, fancy telling the child a thing like that! Nevertheless, no worse, perhaps, than bringing him today. Pots and kettles.

Forgive me, Ness.

They walked slowly back to the waiting limousine. Vere was already lighting a cigarette before the car had even reached the cemetery gates.

After Vere had left to catch the ten o'clock ferry, taking with her what was left of the cold salmon and a chipped teacup, Lila put on her felt slippers and sat down at the kitchen table to write the letter to Logan in care of Alice Clark, wondering whether he was in Bacchus Marsh or off on his everlasting restless search; wondering if her letter would ever reach him in some remote mining camp, whether he would even care.

It was difficult to write to Logan about Vanessa, to write to one stranger about another. For surely Logan and Vanessa had never really known each other well, had they? It had been in a moment of drunken aberration that Logan had signed PS away to Vanessa, and thinking of this, Lila wanted to scratch out her polite, stilted phrases and write, 'If you had never consented, none of this would have happened and she wouldn't be . . .' Instead she wrote, 'In spite of our misunderstandings, I know that her heart was in the right place, Logan, and that in her own way she tried to do the best for PS . . .'

Absorbed in composing her eulogy, she was only half aware of the beginning of rain on the tin roof of the laundry but when lightning flashed outside the window, brightening for an instant the whole yard, she rose and pulled down the blind, grateful that the suffocating night was being broken up and that they would sleep cool and restfully.

It was then that she heard the scream.

'Lila!'

In the dimness of the light from the hall she saw that he was sitting bolt upright in bed.

'What is it, pet?'

A nightmare? He'd never been scared of thunder and lightning.

'*She's out there!*'

The ghost outside the window?

'No, pet, no one is—'

Thunder interrupted her directly overhead and she

reached out her arms to him. He pushed at her with his fists.

'She's out there all alone.'

'No, no, sweetheart. She's in heaven with the angels and Dear One.'

'No. No. No,' he screamed. 'She's out there in the dark in that *place*.'

She struggled with him as he threw himself away from her down on to the bed, holding the pillow between them, frantically turned and tossed, screaming out again and again that Vanessa was out there all alone where they had left her; cried out that there was no one to hold her.

'PS, listen, listen. She's not frightened of the thunder any more. She can't even hear it.'

But nothing she could think of to say or do would stop the screaming. He was like an animal run over. He fought off her caresses, hurling himself from one side of the bed to the other, as she tried to hold him still, tried over and over again to make him understand that dead people did not fear storms, did not fear anything, that they were safe from all harm and all unhappiness, but he grew wilder and more hysterical, beating his fists on the bed until, frantic, she ran to the bathroom for a glass of water and tried with impotent soothing words and sounds to get him to take a sip but he twisted aside, holding the pillow over his face and murmuring into it nothing that she could make into the slightest sense.

She sat helplessly beside him like an intruder while the thunder rattled and complained outside the windows, rumbled at longer intervals until it became only a distant sound in the heavy downpour of rain, and he finally lay still, seemingly spent, on his back and let her take the pillow from him; let her rearrange him in the tossed bed, smoothing and tucking sheets and making gentle *shh*ing sounds.

When he said something that she could not hear, she leaned urgently down, asking:

'What, precious?'

'I made her cross.'

'No, pet,' she said, shaking up the pillow and lifting his head on to it. 'Oh, goodness me no, dearest. You made her happy.'

He gave a whimper, and turning away from her, began to cry with long, deep, gasping sobs of inconsolable grief.

Thank God, thought Lila, feeling her breath coming more easily now, feeling that this crying was natural and good. But how strange children are. He had loved her after all.

Then, as she felt the sudden prick at her eyes and throat and the gush of her own warm, releasing tears:

Do you see, Ness? Somebody minds.

The grass was brown and had not been cut for a long time and the roses were dead. Those were the first things he noticed as he walked up the driveway with Lila and George. He hadn't wanted to see the big house again but Lila had said he must come and help her pick out the things he wanted. Vanessa had given him so many lovely things. Far too many to take them all home, Lila had said, so the things he didn't want would go to the orphans. They had brought suitcases with them and the big heavy things would come later in a van.

Cousin Ettie was going home to England to live with her cousin Esmé, that was why. The big house was being given up and Cousin Ettie was selling all the furniture. Why? Well, Lila had said, because the furniture makes her sad.

The garden certainly looked very sad. No one had hosed it and the brown dog from next door had got in and was scratching in the salvia bushes.

'Shoooo,' he said to the dog. 'Go away.'

'What a funny boy you are,' said Lila. 'I always thought you liked dogs. Oh, poor doggie. He's only looking for a bone.'

The front door stood open and in the hallway there were big wooden boxes and trunks with labels on them. His blue car was there and somebody had packed a lot of his books in the seat, tied up with string. It was very wrong of them because Vanessa never allowed his car to be in the front hall. It belonged on the side porch. And why was Ellen standing there talking to Lila and George in a blue dress that wasn't her uniform? And why had all the pictures been taken down from the walls, leaving big white squares where they had hung?

It wasn't right what they'd done to the house and they ought to know that Vanessa would be terribly cross if she could see the dining room table piled with cardboard boxes full of dishes and glasses; with the silver jugs, the butter dishes, gravy boats, cups and saucers that had been set before him so many times. He wandered from room to room, wondering why the house seemed so small and finding things in the wrong places—the umbrella stand in the pantry and Vanessa's yellow silk chair in the den where the piano used to be.

In the kitchen a strange man was standing on the table and doing something to the light in the ceiling.

'Hello,' said the man.

'Where's Elsie?' he asked.

'Dunno,' said the man, drinking out of a beer bottle.

Vanessa would have said, 'Tables are not for standing on. Get down from that table. Standing on a table in your dirty boots!'

'What are you doin' here, eh?' asked the man. 'Come with the visitors?'

'I live here,' he said, and went through the green door into the hall where Ettie was standing with her arms around Lila and George.

When she saw him she gave a little choked-up

sound and he ran to her and said, 'Ettie, everything's in the wrong place.'

Ettie hung on to him like a little girl and he felt the scratch of her diamond heart on his cheek. She smelled of lavender and the other thing and she had got smaller. She was only a little bigger than he.

'Gone,' said Ettie, moving her little hands in the air, as though she were waving an invisible wand and in a second the house and all of them would vanish in a puff of pink smoke. 'Going home, petkin,' and then, falling sideways against Lila, she said in a pouty little-girl voice, 'But I don't *want* to now.'

Lila said, like she always did to him, 'Of *course* you do,' and George gave him a wink and said, 'Go upstairs and see Vere.'

What was Vere doing here?

He ran upstairs eagerly and stopped when he saw that Vanessa's door was open and that Vere was standing in front of the mirror wearing Vanessa's black hat with the gold ball on it.

Seeing him, Vere turned and let out a screech.

'Oh! Oh! What a fright you gave me. Is that my child? Oh, is that my child or is it a *wolf* come to eat me up?'

But Vere's joke seemed silly and babyish today. Perhaps it was because she was wearing that hat and she'd already got it out of shape. Vanessa never wore it pulled down on the side like that.

When he walked into the room he saw that Vere had made it as untidy as her own. Things were all over the place. On the bed was an old battered suitcase packed to the top with Vanessa's things; her night-dresses, her pink satin quilted dressing gown, a green dress he remembered, shoes and bottles of scent. Her hats sat on the rolled-up mattress and her dresses, looking empty as air, were strewn around everywhere. More of her shoes stood on the dressing table, where Vere had spilled a box of powder.

He sidestepped Vere's clutch and said:

'These are *her* things.'

'PS, somebody has to have them. Don't be a thw*a*rt, pet. When somebody dies you have to do something with their things.' Vere was looking at him through blue cigarette smoke, dropping ash on Vanessa's pink carpet.

'Listen,' she said. 'Did you know she left you a lot of pennies to have when you're twenty-one?'

'Did she say?'

'Mr Hood said, darling.'

Mr Hood? What would *he* know? Vanessa kept her pennies in a little leather purse and besides, she was cross with him and had given him up.

'She gave me *up*,' he said, but Vere was already trying on a yellow straw hat, banging the brim around.

'Don't,' he said. 'Don't put it on like that.'

489

'Oh, you funny child; don't you think she'd rather I had it than the bloody Salvation Army?'

Would she? He was thinking about the night Vanessa said mind your business, Vere, leave my house!

Well, perhaps Vanessa wouldn't mind now. But it was still *her* room and he took the shoes off the dressing table and lined them up neatly on the floor where *she* would have put them. Vere had stubbed out a cigarette in Vanessa's little blue hairpin dish. He emptied it into the wastebasket and wiped the dish with his sleeve.

'My God'—Vere laughed—'what a little tidy-er upper you've become.'

He was thinking about the day he threw everything out of the bathroom window and Vanessa had told him that she was a tortoise. His eyes filled up for a minute and he stamped his foot to stop it from happening and went out of her room, remembering that there *was* something she told him to keep.

He went into his own room, where he found Lila bent, red-faced and puffing, over a big cardboard carton. Packing his things into it and saying she didn't know where on earth they would be able to put his train at home. While her back was turned he opened his shirt drawer quietly and felt in the back of it and the stone was still there where he had left it, but Lila, seeing him in the mirror, said, of course, 'What's that, PS?'

'Just something.'

'Let me see, darling.'

Why did they always have to *see* everything?

'Oh, where did you get *that*?' But he knew she knew. 'Oh, you must take good care of that, pet. That's *gold*.'

Poor Lila. 'No,' he said. 'It's not real, it's just pretend.'

He went out and downstairs, meeting Agnes halfway down, and she had Vanessa's umbrella in her hand.

'Hello, Aunt Agnes,' he said 'Are you going to keep that?' and then felt sorry because they had said he must be nice to poor Agnes because the world didn't come to an end after all and she had lost her temple. They had gone past it the other day on the way to the beach and George had said, 'Look, PS, we can go to the pictures there now. Do you want to see *King Kong*?'

Agnes closed her eyes a minute and said, 'Don't be sad, PS,' and he went on downstairs wondering why she was the only one who knew that he was.

They were tying Vanessa up in brown paper parcels and he could hear their voices from all over the house calling, Do you want this? Shall we throw this out? Is this your size?

He went and sat alone in the greenish-lighted drawing room, all pulled to bits, and listened to them going up and downstairs and from room to room and knew that there was something he had to remember.

491

But what was it?

He looked at the painting of his mother, which was propped up against a chair. She stared back at him, cross with him for being late, but it didn't seem to matter any more because they didn't know each other. Only Vanessa knew him, knew all about him, and he knew that he must remember what she said. He must remember it quickly now before they had wrapped her up in parcels and suitcases and carried her away in different directions and in so many little pieces that none of her was left and even he would forget her.

Already he couldn't remember her face and he shut his eyes, trying to see her that last day when they sat here in the late afternoon, when she was no longer cross, only already far away, beginning her journey.

Keep the gold, she said, so you'll know what's real and what's fake.

But that wasn't the important thing.

Over there by the window she said, I hope you'll grow up to be something.

Leaning out of the window and hearing Jocko mowing the lawn: Don't be a PS.

That was it. You'd better find out who you are, my dear, she said again now, quite clearly, and there was no more, he could remember no more, but it didn't matter if he could remember this much and do something to please her.

PS.

'PS,' they called from the kitchen. 'PS, come and have tea. Come, pet. Where are you?'

So he slipped the piece of stone into his pocket to keep forever and walked into the kitchen and said to all their backs fussing with teapots, with scones and jam, 'Who am I?'

They all laughed, even Ettie laughed. He was playing a game, they thought, and Vere said, 'Let me guess! Are you Captain Hook?'

'No,' he said. 'Who am I?'

They guessed and guessed again, like kids. Was he Don Bradman the cricketer? Kingsford Smith the airman? Ronald Colman?

Finally, tired of it, they said, 'You're PS.'

'No,' he said. 'I'm not any more.'

Lila put down her cup in the little silence.

'What do you mean, pet?'

'What's my *name*?' he said.

'Goodness me. You know what your name is, darling. You can even write it. Why do I have to tell you?'

George said, 'That's *his* business, Lila.'

Lila wiped crumbs from her mouth and said in her once-upon-a-time voice:

'Well, you're William after your grandfather and Scott for your mother. You're William Scott Marriott.'

'Yes,' he said, 'that's who I am.'

Vere, reaching for him, laughed and said, 'But you'll always be PS to us.'

493

'No,' he said. 'I'm Bill.'

They all laughed and he could see that they didn't like the idea of his being Bill at all and would go on calling him PS until he was very old, maybe thirty.

'I'm Bill,' he said again.

Lila said, 'Oh, but PS, Dear One called you that because you're all we have left of her.'

To be parcelled up and handed around like Vanessa's things?

'No,' he said, and meant it so much that suddenly they were all very still, all looking at him as if he were some strange thing from the North Pole. He looked back at Lila until she finally shifted her glance to the window, looking sad and troubled as she did when she heard rainbirds long before anyone else.

Then George said, 'Have a piece of cake, Bill.'

'No, thank you,' he said politely, and went out through the hall and down the front steps into the deserted garden, walking backward down the drive, step behind step, and scuffing the gravel the way he liked to do. He felt important and mysterious because now, like Vanessa had said, there was really only him. Bill.

'I'm Bill,' he shouted back to the big sad house, to the next-door dog, who looked at him, surprised.

He climbed on the front fence to be taller and shouted it again.

'*I'm Bill!*'

494

Shouted it again and again as loud as he could so that wherever she was she might hear him and say something back and then he listened, staring up at the house, where the sun, going down, had caught at the windows and set them all on fire, especially Vanessa's, which was blazing with real gold.

He heard their distant voices coming from the house. Nothing but their voices and the tooting of ferries—the dry movement of the trees answering him. Yet, listening very carefully now, he thought that he might have heard something else, just for a moment and a long way off, much farther than the garden, farther than where, by craning his neck, he could just see the Watson's Bay Lighthouse beginning to wink at the harbour going out to sea.

He couldn't hear what Vanessa said now but he would hear it some day in some other place.

Text Classics

For reading group notes visit textclassics.com.au

The Commandant
Jessica Anderson
Introduced by Carmen Callil

Homesickness
Murray Bail
Introduced by Peter Conrad

Sydney Bridge Upside Down
David Ballantyne
Introduced by Kate De Goldi

A Difficult Young Man
Martin Boyd
Introduced by Sonya Hartnett

The Australian Ugliness
Robin Boyd
Introduced by Christos Tsiolkas

**The Even More Complete
Book of Australian Verse**
John Clarke
Introduced by John Clarke

Diary of a Bad Year
JM Coetzee
Introduced by Peter Goldsworthy

Wake in Fright
Kenneth Cook
Introduced by Peter Temple

The Dying Trade
Peter Corris
Introduced by Charles Waterstreet

They're a Weird Mob
Nino Culotta
Introduced by Jacinta Tynan

Careful, He Might Hear You
Sumner Locke Elliott
Introduced by Robyn Nevin

Terra Australis
Matthew Flinders
Introduced by Tim Flannery

My Brilliant Career
Miles Franklin
Introduced by Jennifer Byrne

Cosmo Cosmolino
Helen Garner
Introduced by Ramona Koval

Dark Places
Kate Grenville
Introduced by Louise Adler

The Watch Tower
Elizabeth Harrower
Introduced by Joan London

**The Mystery of
a Hansom Cab**
Fergus Hume
Introduced by Simon Caterson

The Glass Canoe
David Ireland
Introduced by Nicolas Rothwell

The Jerilderie Letter
Ned Kelly
Introduced by Alex McDermott

Bring Larks and Heroes
Thomas Keneally
Introduced by Geordie Williamson